Artifact

Artifact

A Novel

Arlene Heyman

BLOOMSBURY PUBLISHING

NEW YORK • LONDON • OXFORD • NEW DELHI • SYDNEY

BLOOMSBURY PUBLISHING
Bloomsbury Publishing Inc.
1385 Broadway, New York, NY 10018, USA

BLOOMSBURY, BLOOMSBURY PUBLISHING, and the Diana logo are trademarks
of Bloomsbury Publishing Plc

First published in the United States 2020

ISBN: HB: 978-1-63557-471-5; eBook: 978-1-63557-472-2

LIBRARY OF CONGRESS CATALOGING-IN-PUBLICATION DATA IS AVAILABLE

2 4 6 8 10 9 7 5 3 1

Typeset by Westchester Publishing Services
Printed and bound in the U.S.A. by Berryville Graphics Inc., Berryville, Virginia

To find out more about our authors and books visit www.bloomsbury.com and sign up
for our newsletters.

Bloomsbury books may be purchased for business or promotional use. For information on
bulk purchases please contact Macmillan Corporate and Premium Sales Department at
specialmarkets@macmillan.com.

For Jacob and Yonit, and for Reuben and Michelle

Honesty, which stands mostly for intellectual integrity, courage, and kindness, [is] still the virtue I admire, though with advancing years the emphasis has been slightly shifted and kindness now seems more important to me than in my youth. The love for and dedication to one's work seems to me to be the basis for happiness. For a research worker, the unforgotten moments of his [or her] life are those rare ones, which come after years of plodding work, when the veil over nature's secrets seems suddenly to lift and when what was dark and chaotic appears in a clear and beautiful light and pattern.

—Gerty Radnitz Cori, biochemist and winner of the Nobel Prize in Physiology or Medicine for 1947, as quoted by Sharon Bertsch McGrayne, in Nobel Prize Women in Science: Their Lives, Struggles, and Momentous Discoveries

CONTENTS

Part One   1

Part Two   25

Part Three   57

Part Four   77

Part Five   139

Part Six   185

Part Seven   245

Acknowledgments   263

A Loose Part   267

Artifact

Part One

1984*

S he did not want to disturb the rats. Breathing "Lullaby and Good Night," trying to keep the wire cage in her arms steady, she walked down the dimly lit hall. The lab equipment was turned off for the weekend and there was no sound except for the soft, slapping noise of her slippers and her low song. Occasionally a rat lifted its head and sniffed the air.

Lottie worked in a pair of cutoff dungarees and a T-shirt her Gross Anatomy class had given her, which showed the muscles of the chest and back labeled in Latin. Her dark blonde hair was twisted and piled up on top of her head with a test-tube clamp.

The radio said it was the hottest August night since 1945. On the highways to Long Island and the Jersey shore the traffic had been bumper-to-bumper all day, the cars bulging with sun umbrellas, baby carriages, bicycles tied to roofs. After dinner when she had walked toward Central Park in search of a breeze, the close streets seemed to her vacant and forlorn. The charged life of the city dimmed in August. Most of her colleagues were on

---

* This is a novel that takes place, for the most part, in the 1950s, '60s, '70s, and '80s, transitional periods in the lives of women. Of course, we are still in a transitional period in the lives of women, and so, also, in the lives of men.

vacation; during the day a few technicians came in, the department secretary, occasionally a worried graduate student.

She liked being alone in her lab in the hushed city, undisturbed by the rhythms of others, a pleasure she didn't experience often now that she had small children again. Davy was two and Simon was five and they were wild, bucking things. Her eighteen-year-old, Evelyn, usually had friends over who sat in Lottie's study working on her home computer or making clothes for college on her sewing machine. Her husband, Jake, had private music students weekday afternoons and on Saturdays. And in August his fourteen-year-old daughter, Ruth, blew in from L.A. like a small low-pressure front that brings a storm. She danced for and cooked with her dad, pointedly ignored the boys, and took pokes and jabs at her stepmother. Lottie tried not to poke or jab back, and she certainly never said what she often thought: *Fly away, little girl. Go home. Disappear.* She tried to schedule a major experiment every August.

On the counter the caged rats shifted restlessly in the moonlight.

She switched on the tensor lamp at the dissecting table and the light above the sink, tied herself into a faded green surgical gown, drew on a workman's glove, and ran the cold water. She slid open the lid of the cage, gripped the nearest quivering animal, and lifted it out. She raised the paper cutter blade and positioned the animal's head on the platform, his squirming body just off the edge. His pink feet kicked the air. He began defecating black pellets, urinating in spasms on her glove. She brought the blade down crunching through the bottom of his neck. The head lay on the platform. Lottie held tight to the body, which continued to struggle, spraying blood through the open neck. Her cheek was suddenly wet. Thrusting the body under the cold water, she held on until it quieted and stopped. Then she dumped it into a plastic bag, and laid the head on the dissecting table. She shook the glove off and, taking up the scalpel and forceps, dissected out the sublingual and submandibular salivary glands, easing them into a beaker of fixative. She washed her face, barely seeing its wavy dim features in the tarnished paper-towel dispenser, and reached into the cage for the next rat.

She liked to set a rhythm, do what had to be done steadily and speedily.

The smell of blood was in the room now and the rats knew. They squawked in their cage even before she touched them and no matter how firmly she held on they wouldn't lie still. In the air-conditioned room she was sweating.

Lottie had been intermittently irritable the last few months, ever since a microscopy journal that had solicited a paper from her had sent it back for extensive revisions. She had developed new techniques for spotlighting each organelle of a particular cell in the salivary gland, the function of which no one understood, although it was implicated in several diseases, one of them fatal.

The journal's referees had savaged her paper, from the typing to the heart of the work: she was not describing the actual cell at all, nor the real components of the mucus, but only the distortions created by the very techniques she was advocating. One critic finished up:

> This paper is not acceptable for publication since it is replete with accidental and random findings. It is no more than a collection of artifacts.

She had read the lines twice, then crushed the critiques into a ball and stuffed it into the bottom drawer of her desk.

A month later a small grant proposal of hers was rejected; she'd heard from a colleague in Washington that if only she'd cited a few papers by committee members or invited one of them to give a seminar at her place . . .

The following week her chairman phoned. He had heard about the grant and thought it was unjust. She was one of the most productive people in the department with a bibliography second in length and quality only to his own. The graduate students stood on line for her seminars. She was innovative, she was creative. Unfortunately, he had bad news for her himself.

"No promotion," Lottie said.

He was terribly sorry. She must be aware she was on a frozen budget line. Actually they were all small animals caught in a glacier, if he could speak for a moment from the paleontological point of view. The state was cutting back funding, NIH was tightening its belt, there was nothing he could do. Next year it would be a different ball game; she could rest assured he'd go to bat for her then.

It was the third year he'd handed her that wilted bunch of metaphors and her husband told her to sue. "It's discrimination against women and you're just sitting back and taking it." He cited a microbiologist, a woman well known in her field, who'd said in a recent *New York Times* article: "Women scientists have two choices: bitterness or foolishness."

Lottie said she wasn't famous enough to make resounding judgments, and if she let herself get involved with lawyers, she wouldn't get her work done.

Jake said, "At least go to the grievance committee. There must be a grievance committee. What do they call it—human resources. We need the money."

"I'm not licking ass."

"Who asked you to lick ass? Go in and *yell*. You're not *yelling*. You only yell at me."

Her paper was never far from her mind. The editor had heard her deliver it at the cell biology meetings in Cincinnati six months before. The referees were independent of him; still there shouldn't be such a disparity in their opinions. Could her oral presentation have been so much better than her written one?

Her papers were almost always published, but they were invariably sent back for rewriting. Meticulous in conceptualizing problems and running experiments, she was impatient when it came to presenting results, as if to linger over the final draft made her a cosmetician or an interior decorator. In her diagrams she rarely labeled everything that needed labeling; she expected her typists to correct her misspellings and not add any of their own; and she wrote up her conclusions in a matter-of-fact way. Colleagues would take some obvious point and polish it up, surround it with five or six true but tried ideas, in the public domain, then pass off this rearrangement as dazzling new stuff. She came with the real thing in a crumpled brown wrapper. And she did it emphatically, as if there were virtue in such a presentation.

There are quite a number of typing errors, etc., which I have marked in pencil.

. . . A significant problem with this paper is that the description of the author's methodologies is far too skimpy. We are not told the source of the glutaraldehyde; the osmolality of the individual fixatives; the length of time these were applied . . .

Many of the objections to her paper were of this order, but there was also at least one major substantive disagreement. Her point had been that different fixatives and buffers preserved different aspects of the cell, just as various epochs in history brought out various aspects of human beings. One should choose a fixative and buffer according to those aspects one hoped to illuminate. The referee wanted her to use other fixatives and buffers, claiming that hers damaged the cell contents while the ones he suggested would preserve them "correctly." She knew they would just do different damage.

Another referee objected to her manner of sacrificing rats. She had killed them first and then dissected out the salivary glands and placed them in fixative. This referee thought that in the few minutes between death and the fixative, the glands underwent permanent distorting changes and hence what she had reported was "mere artifact." He wanted her to inject the fixative into the living animals. Early on, before deciding on her current method, she had in fact killed a few rats by fixing them alive. The results were no more "natural," and the technique took more time and was more unpleasant.

To get the paper published, at least in this journal, she would have to run the whole experiment through again, probably several times, killing rats in a variety of ways, using a number of unnecessary fixatives. It would be tedious. She was working on another project. Rats didn't grow on trees, nor technician time. Her chest tightened as she thought of going to the department business manager, that cheery bureaucrat, justifying the cost of each rat to him, putting her crumpled referees' reports in his hands. She felt like punching someone.

In the end she phoned her chair and cajoled and shamed him into giving her the money out of the department slush fund.

Then she typed each of the referees' objections on a separate sheet of paper and taped them to her lab walls. As the results came in, she posted them on the sheets, in black ballpoint if the referees were right, in red magic marker if she was right. Her handwriting was large and flowery, full of bold swirls and curlicues, and she often had to add several pages to the original one in order to fit everything in. By the end of that hot July the walls were festooned with poinsettias and bright clusters of holly berries; the place looked like Christmas. She had two colleagues check her work, although she intended to run it through once more in August. Lottie cheered up.

Running a bath for her sons (she was wearing shorts, had her foot in the tub water, testing it), she imagined bits of letters to that editor who had twice urged her to revise and resubmit.

> I regret not answering earlier but I have been immersed in an important experiment.

The boys, covered with washable finger paints and standing by with gunboats and water pistols, jumped in and sent the water level over the top.

> I have not answered sooner because I have been flooded with requests for this particular paper and am considering sending it to the *International Journal of Cell Research* instead.

As she bathed her boisterous blue and yellow sons, she refuted each objection the anonymous referees had made. She scrubbed and rubbed and rinsed them back to flesh color. She toweled them dry, handed them off to Jake, then sat down at the computer and typed out a letter to that editor:

> Beyond all the verification and justification of my techniques are two issues that are fundamental. The first is the whole point of the paper, which the reviewers seem to have missed: namely, that there is no "correct" morphology of the granules in this gland, but rather that the fixative, buffer, and additive combination will determine which constituents will be preserved, which destroyed.

The other issue is philosophical and has to do with the concept of artifact. It should be clear to anyone with experience in this business that all one ever deals with is artifact, and that one's skills in creating and interpreting artifact are largely the measure of one's abilities as a morphologist/scientist. From my perspective the issue is not, is a given structure artifact? But rather, can the conditions under which a given artifact is produced provide information about the actual nature of a particular organelle that cannot be analyzed in its natural form? We are dealing with a biological equivalent of the uncertainty principle, and all fine-structural morphologists and cytochemists should be aware of that.

Jake brought her a cold glass of seltzer with a piece of lime.

"Everyone asleep?" she said.

"You kidding?" He kissed his wife's damp forehead. "Tell me when you're done," he said. "All the stars are out."

The night watchman had come and gone. Lottie took off her gown and put it in a shopping bag along with a dirty lab coat and a pair of thick socks she'd had around since the winter; she would run them through the washing machine at home. She usually did the lab wash late at night or early in the morning when the kids were asleep; she didn't like them getting a look or a whiff. Although she'd sponged down the countertops twice, the room smelled of blood and urine and fixative. She washed them again. Not cautious by nature, in the lab she was painstaking, and unforgiving of those who were not. A graduate student had once left a highly corrosive solution in an open beaker and the janitor had knocked it over and then mopped it up with paper towels; he needed skin grafting on his fingers. Lottie wouldn't work with the student anymore and he had to get a new thesis topic and adviser. Someone had written on the wall near where the accident occurred: ONLY STARFISH REGENERATE LOST LIMBS. Lottie let it stand.

She carried the plastic garbage bag of rat parts into the cold room. Except for a few cats and a rare monkey, most of the black bags here contained rat corpses—rats who'd had tumors implanted in their heads, who'd breathed in cigarette smoke every hour of their short lives, who'd eaten their weight in saccharin and sodium nitrates, who'd had their fetuses androgenized and estrogenized in utero. She thought what unimaginable, un-ratlike destinies these animals had had. We should build a monument to them in every city.

Strands of hair escaped from her makeshift upsweep. She tried to blow them away, not wanting to touch her face. She locked her lab and showered.

The clean hot water pounding away at her, she looked at her body with some curiosity and no great sense of familiarity, as if she were a cadaver for the medical students—which she one day, far in the future, planned to be. They'd be luckier if they got her now: a forty-two-year-old woman only a few pounds overweight, five at most—Jake said a woman ought to have some hills and valleys (but fat was the enemy of the anatomist, making the field slippery, infiltrating the organs). Yes, now was the best time to dissect her, the muscles of her long Bjornstad legs well delineated (her mother's were still strong and shapely at seventy), with all the main structures in place, nothing worse than a few burns and discolorations on her hands, some gleaming stretch marks on her still fairly taut breasts and belly, one long white caesarean scar from her last-born, Davy, who had gone into fetal distress and had to be scooped out in a hurry. The trouble had been a tangled, knotted umbilical cord.

Had Davy been doing somersaults or some intrauterine exploration? Two years later, she still worried about him. He was a lively child, lean and rangy, always in motion. Around the house he acted like a born investigator. Lottie had to screw plastic boxes over the electric outlets and tie the refrigerator door shut. She had installed a wooden gate around the TV set after the VCR repair shop called to say someone had inserted coins deep into the slot for tapes.

Her daughter, Evelyn, who sometimes babysat Davy at the town playground, called him a jumping bean; one afternoon he fell off the monkey bars and broke an arm. At the Whitney Museum with Jake and Simon, he ran into an exhibition of mesh houses; wires sliced through his cheek as if it were a peeled hard-boiled egg. Jake had had the wits to take him immediately to a plastic surgeon.

She worried less about Simon, her heavyset, muscular, more sedentary five-year-old. He was inquisitive and disputatious and exasperating, but he was on a longer tether than Davy; Simon roamed in his imagination.

On afternoons when Jake stayed late at school to conduct orchestra rehearsals or give private music lessons, Simon watched for him at the living room window. Before Jake could cut the ignition, Simon was beside the driver's door waiting for his father to hand over his flute or piccolo or violin. Slowly and erectly and carefully, as if he were balancing the instrument on his head, Simon carried it in its case around the front of the car across the lawn and up the steps. If Jake had several instruments, Simon would make several trips, and Jake would let him have that pleasure.

Afterward, Simon would bring a bottle of celery tonic with two straws to the living room, and a peanut butter and marshmallow sandwich that he had made and cut in half.

What would happen to these children of hers? Evelyn was nearly grown up, but these little ones . . . When you had children in your twenties, it could cross your mind that you might not stay with your husband, but you took for granted that you'd both be on earth for all time. Lottie was forty-two. Jake was forty-one. His father had died of cancer at forty-one.

Outside the night was hot and airless, as if someone had sucked the atmosphere out of the city with a pump. She carried her laundry bag past the sleeping attendant, Abe Bazile, a Haitian man in his fifties whose child had died of leukemia a few months before. He sat slack in a folding chair on the sidewalk, all bones and dark hollows, like a reamed-out, abandoned mine. As she tried to ease the old station wagon out of the lot without disturbing him, it backfired sharply—an ominous sound in the city night; and she cursed Jake, who'd promised to get it fixed, then cursed their finances. Abe sprang to embarrassed attention and called out, "Night, Doc," after her disappearing car.

She drove up Amsterdam Avenue, past the hulking buildings of Columbia University, then crossed west on 125th Street. It was two thirty in the morning and the stores were lit but gated. A thin fellow in a red iridescent shirt weaved down the sidewalk alone, a huge radio propped on his shoulder blaring out the news: "Polls show Reagan over the top!" The man disappeared into a doorway as a police car moved slowly beside the curb.

She passed the A-OK Pawn Shop, yellow-lit and locked, three liquor stores, a Colonel Sanders franchise, a night spot called This Bitter Earth. Hot, sad sounds of a saxophone wailed out the open door. A statuesque hooker in a silver-sequined dress and Lucite high heels stood negotiating with a john a head shorter than she. Her thickly powdered skin gleamed with sweat. Lottie wondered if the woman was ill. Lottie wondered if the woman was a man.

In the lit city where even the dark rivers sometimes seemed ruddy or pale or gray, thinned with the shadows of artificial light, she never felt easy after nightfall. It was not the crime rate that unsettled her most, not even the pitiful stretches of poverty, nor the sudden explosions of sound: it was the intrusive unfamiliarity of massive buildings, hard edges, a vertical landscape.

Lottie waited at the light, then turned with relief onto the West Side Highway. She increased her speed, the dense city receding and thinning out, the Hudson River interposing itself between her and the Palisades, giving her a sudden sense of space and view. In the approaching distance the bridge was two blue-studded mountain peaks that sloped to form a valley between them. Wet warm air was forced in through the open windows as she continued to accelerate, an automobile-made breeze; her air conditioner had died a month earlier. Few cars passed. In the steamy night, alone on the empty highway, she drove a car cluttered with wrappers from M&M's, a tube of Ev's candy-pink lipstick, crumpled sheets of music, crumbs of animal crackers, and two pacifiers—one with the soft plastic bitten through and hardened—on the backseat.

Besides her own sizeable family, she was accountable for technicians and doctoral candidates who were writing theses under her. A colleague had died a few months earlier and she had inherited his doctoral candidate, a student from Sri Lanka, that tormented country. He had been eight years in the department without bringing his thesis and defense of it to a satisfactory conclusion. Once Lottie had had dinner at his dingy flat in East Harlem. All evening his pregnant wife and six children had tried desperately to please her. Lottie attempted to engage one boy in a game of pick-up sticks but his hands trembled so that they had to quit.

Less troubling but equally binding were her obligations to teach the medical students, to sit on various committees, and to publish. In hopes of making some extra money (at least Lottie had hopes of making some money), she and her friend Olivia had begun planning a high school biology text aimed not only at young men but also at young women, which they hoped might get adopted in a few forward-looking parts of the country. New York City? Chicago? California? It would be their second book together.

When all of this had come upon her she didn't know—slowly, imperceptibly, like a pound or two gained every year but overlooked, until one day in passing an interior mirror she saw with surprise a very substantial figure, responsible, solid, a matron. Who, me, Lottie?

It wasn't all ballast, was it? Or the weights they drowned kittens with?

No, she told herself, she was full and anchored to the wharf of the world.

And her work fit her, almost as if it had been genetically determined. She was right from the beginning an observant, passionately curious child who lay for hours in summer fields watching the doings of lizards and bugs and worms. Staring through binoculars for a glimpse of a sparrow's eggs hatching, she stayed all day in a tree one time when she was twelve, straining her eyes.

Yet she'd also ended up where she was because of a series of random events. She'd married days after she got her undergraduate diploma, and then during the long hiatus between college and graduate school she'd had Evelyn, worked as a lab technician, and separated from her husband, falling out of synchrony with the academic calendar. Lottie'd started graduate school in January, an awkward month; and the internationally renowned professor, an expert on the new technique of electron microscopy, already had a full complement of graduate students. In February a coup occurred in a small central African country she had never heard of before, and one of the professor's graduate students on a government grant packed up and left despite the university's attempts to dissuade him. She still remembered the photo of him in the campus newspaper: smiling and waving, a bulky figure bundled up in a thick black parka against the Wisconsin winter.

She'd gone uneasily to see the professor again, but he said he was holding the man's place until his return. When weeks later the African was hanged, she went again. The professor sullenly accepted her on the condition she finish the student's project: he was working on rat salivary glands.

Ignace Sezibera had been his name. Many students mourned him and she felt vaguely guilty and also grateful to him—odd feelings, both of them. And she never completely forgot him. But his project became her project and she finished it, then found a way to go further, her own way, the work exciting to her.

It took her too long to realize that what excited her bored most people; they were impressed she was a scientist but no one wanted to hear the lyrics.

"I'm *very* interested," a dean's wife told her at a cocktail party in Charleston, where Lottie'd given a lecture, "I don't meet that many women scientists."

"You do us all proud," declared a middle-aged woman in a red sweater dress, who identified herself as a former president of a D.C. chapter of NOW.

"So what do you actually *do*?" urged a broad-chested man who wore a large ruby ring. Another guest had told her the man was a solo tenor.

"Well," Lottie said uneasily. "This may sound odd to you but I study rat salivary glands. They're more important than people think."

"Ah," the dean's wife said.

"You're sure you want to hear about this?"

Everyone nodded emphatically.

"Well, the work I'm starting now is intriguing. You see, the male has a cell that secretes some enzymes that aren't present in females. Now, if male glands are different from female glands, then maybe the difference has something to do with reproduction. And in fact one of my hypotheses is that it's related to copulation." Lottie looked at her listeners intently: "You wonder why it's in the mouth, huh?"

"Mmmmm," the tenor practically hummed.

"You may or may not know that one of the things that go on rather extensively in animals before they copulate is *licking*. The male specifically licks—"

"Ah, *licking*," said the tenor.

"Licking," Lottie said.

"At first I thought you said *looking*," said the former NOW president.

"She said 'licking,'" said the tenor. "*Licking*. I get it."

"Yes, well, the male licks the vaginal area, actually the perineum, of the female. And one of the enzymes that's present in the male salivary glands is an enzyme called kallikrein that makes kinins—When you get a wound or an infection, you know how it gets all red and swollen? Kinins are generated, which cause blood vessels to leak and swelling to occur. I've just written a grant application about this: my hypothesis is that the kallikrein from the male generates kinins from the female secretions in and around the perineum. And these would stimulate swelling and a transient irritation that would make the female rat more receptive. So this would be like a naturally occurring Spanish fly, if you will . . ."

The tenor ran his tongue slowly, clockwise, over his lips. Lottie widened her eyes in momentary annoyance, then realized he wasn't directing the gesture at her, probably he wasn't even conscious of making it, so lost in reverie did he seem. She continued more buoyantly:

"Now, one of the ways we're going to test this is to excise the salivary glands in males and then put the males with cycling females and see if the females will actually *present* to them. That's something the females do when they're receptive—they go into lordosis—that's where the back humps and they stick their rear end into the air." Lottie figured what the hell, it was a party, she had a soft spot for singers; so she leaned over and raised her backside. "Up goes the female's rump and then the male mounts. Are you with me so far?" She leaned over farther.

The former president of NOW nodded vigorously, her reading glasses, which hung from a dark elastic strap around her neck, bouncing back and forth against her sweatered breasts.

The dean's wife smiled. "I especially like the part about the kinins and the kallikrein. They sound like cloth." She fingered the cotton of her skirt.

"That's a lovely suit you're wearing," the former president of NOW said. It was white, with a pattern of large red roses on trellises.

"I made it myself." The dean's wife blushed.

The tenor was still gazing off into the distance, as if contemplating the ramifications of Lottie's experiment. On an inspiration Lottie straightened up and turned around. Ten feet behind her, beside the makeshift bar, a young man with long, black kinky hair and silver bracelets up his shaved, bare arms stood blowing him kisses.

* * *

Now she drove off the highway onto a two-lane nearly unlit road that she knew by heart. It was bordered by large shade trees that overarched to form a leafy roof in places—Simon called it a "tree tunnel." The air coming in the windows turned cooler, sweeter; she opened her mouth and breathed it in with her whole body. Although the fields were dark, the trees black shapes faintly outlined in the moonlight, and all she could see was an occasional night-light on the porch of a distant farmhouse or in the front room of a gas station, she knew where things were, could take her sights almost through her pores: it was a soft familiar darkness. The road she was driving on now in her forties was the kind she'd been on as a child with her family in Michigan, returning home from visiting relatives: her father driving; her mother next to him, her head sometimes on his shoulder; one of her father's young sisters, usually Alma, next to her mother, leaning against the car door, a faint sweet scent emanating from her skin and her coat (Lily of the Valley and Shy Violet were two of the names on the labels of the colored glass perfume bottles on her aunt's dresser). In the back of the car Lottie sat next to her beloved grandmother, who would be wearing a bright hat, her dark hair rolled and twisted and turned into a high crown, a few wisps loose now; and on the other side of her grandmother were Lottie's brother and two sisters, half-sitting, half-lying against each other like litter mates: she could remember the warmth and smell of their bodies, the sounds of their breathing in the dark, an occasional small burp or fart. Back then she'd lived in the big house, been the oldest daughter of Mr. Kristin the mayor, and Jeanie Bjornstad Kristin the teacher, and Evelyn Kristin's favorite grandchild: everyone said she was the smartest child of the first family. (*Too smart for a girl. Just get herself into trouble in the end.*) Would she get into trouble in the end?

Where she lived now was a town very much like the one she'd grown up in—rural, supported by farming, Presbyterian, bright with fresh, harsh white paint and yellow forsythia and gaudy tiger lilies, plants that made it through hard winters and burst out when it was time in pride and self-reliance, a kind of fierceness. In the spring the air was suffused with the odor of apple blossoms, a scent that always saddened her, and in early summer with the sweet smell of lilacs. Nowadays she was the lady scientist, the one who had kids from two different marriages, and another kid, a dark-haired one, who showed up for half the summer, and a Jew for a husband (although you had to hand it to him, he started the high school's crackerjack orchestra—it had a statewide, really a countrywide, standing—and he accompanied the choir every Sunday at the Unitarian church *for free*), and two ratty cars and a place that needed a paint job and a mow job, bad.

As she pulled into their gravel driveway the dogs yapped briefly and then quieted, recognizing whatever modern-day dogs recognize: The rhythm of the mistress's motor? The scent of her buffers and fixatives? She got out of the car and stretched for a moment in the moonlight. The night was dense with tiny intermeshing sounds—insects and frogs, a whip-poor-will crying monotonously far away, the dogs moving restlessly behind the house. She did a few slow painful knee bends, recalling ruefully her days as a cheerleader. Then she took her pocketbook and laundry bag and briefcase, and, patting the dogs briefly, went in through the back.

The night-light was on in the kitchen. A few coloring books lay open on the floor, crayons nearby, marbles scattered here and there, a couple of them glowing brilliantly in the dim light. An Oreo cookie had been stepped on and smashed. No one had cleared the remains of dinner off the kitchen table. She looked at the chart on the refrigerator to see who was in charge of dishes. *She* was. She didn't mind the disarray so much as she felt annoyed at the food left out. She put the margarine and milk in the refrigerator, noting the DO NOT TOUCH signs in the handwriting of her stepdaughter, Ruth, on two covered casseroles—probably dishes for the fancy dinner she made with her father on Saturday nights.

The door to the bedroom off the kitchen was open and she could hear the girls' soft breathing. *Girls. Two of them. Still here, that dark one. Ruth hadn't flown away anywhere.* (These thoughts about her stepdaughter came to her in swarms like mosquitoes. She wanted to be rid of them, they irritated her, made her feel unworthy; she also wanted to be rid of Ruth, swat her away, *smash*.) It was hard on Evelyn to have to share her room every August when Ruth came; but Ruth, at fourteen, couldn't be put in with the boys and she couldn't be asked to sleep on the living room couch like an overnight guest. It wasn't easy for Ruth either, especially since she was orderly by nature and disdained Evvie's cluttered ways, so much like Lottie's.

The only neat part of the house was Ruth's half of the room, as if a magic circle had been drawn around it. Lying on her stomach, her arms at her sides, Ruth slept almost stiffly, on guard, the sheet smooth up to her neck, her black hair in two long tight braids like sentinels, her pink ballet slippers aligned beside the bed. She was thin and dark and angular, on her way to being tall.

At eighteen, Evelyn was taller than everyone in the family but Jake. She was built on a grand, monumental scale, like a Viking queen—people told her she resembled Liv Ullmann, which delighted her. Across the room she turned in her twisted sheets, mumbling. Lottie closed the door quietly.

Upstairs, Jake was asleep in his undershirt and boxer shorts, one arm off the side of the bed, the other around two-year-old Davy. Jake snored softly. Davy lay on his side, hips and knees flexed, as if sleep had caught him running. Above their heads through the bedroom skylight Lottie counted five stars. She eased the child out from under Jake, felt Davy's diaper—it was dry—and carried him to his crib. Simon was in bed with the new baseball glove Jake had given him, and his recorder. These were her brown-haired children, a cross between the two of them, everything burnished, those eyes she could almost see her blue genes behind, that berry-bright skin. In the bathroom she brushed her teeth and patted some after-bath splash on herself. Then she ran a piece of toilet paper over the toilet seat—Simon often forgot to raise it—and peed quietly into the toilet bowl full of their pee (at night they didn't flush so as not to disturb anyone, and also to save water) and closed the lid.

She got out of her nightgown and eased herself into bed beside Jake—he smelled faintly of sweat and Davy's baby powder—and snuggled her alcohol-cooled breasts against his warm back. She licked two of her fingers and massaged her clitoris with them. She put her other hand under the elastic waistband of his shorts. He was moist and soft. Lightly she stroked the hairy skin of his thighs, the corrugated scrotum, the delicate fine skin of his penis. She felt him bloom slowly, like a night flower.

"Lottie," he said, turning toward her half-asleep. "Sweetheart."

She kissed his eyelids.

She helped him take off his shorts, and dropped them on the floor next to her side of the bed. Sleepily he kissed her throat and her breasts and her belly. Then he lifted himself over her and came into her slowly. She lay on her back running her hands through his thick wavy hair—Davy's already had something of the same texture—and looked up through the skylight at the bright stars.

Lottie woke at eleven in the morning to a sudden flood of rock music as if the pipes had burst. She ran to the window. Doing her exercises, Ruth was out front in her black leotard with a massive transistor radio blaring. What the Warnicks, the gentle old couple across the street, must be thinking seeing this black-haired child-woman on the front lawn, her legs in the air, sensual music saturating the area as if they were hosting a block party! "Do it in the back!" Lottie yelled, her head out the window. Ruth acted as if she hadn't heard her.

After a moment, Lottie thrust her arms out the window as well and waved them around to catch Ruth's attention. The girl seemed not to see her although she was facing Lottie's way. Lottie picked up the morning newspaper that Jake must have been reading earlier and rolled it into a truncheon, then unrolled it. She ripped some pages into pieces and let them drop out the window. They wafted here and there in the warm summer morning, a few coming down a couple of feet from Ruth without seeming to attract her notice. Lottie hollered the girl's name twice and then in a fury took a bottle of hand lotion off the dresser and threw it at the radio. She missed them both.

Ruth turned the radio down a little. She looked up at Lottie.

"What's the matter with you?" Lottie said. "Don't you hear me? Don't you see me?"

Ruth shook her head no.

"Turn that off!" Lottie yelled.

Ruth turned it down a little more.

"You didn't see me? I can't believe you didn't see me. I'm right in front of you! I'm dropping newspaper out the window! What did you think it was, snow?"

The girl began doing pliés.

"I'm *talking* to you!"

"I'm *listening* to you. What do I have to do, salute?"

"Show some respect," Lottie said.

"Look, what do you want anyway? I'm doing my exercises."

Lottie took a deep breath. "Just do them in the back. I want you to keep that radio down and do your exercises in the back."

"I'm not going in the back. There's dog shit all over the back."

"Well, use the exercise mat."

"I don't want to. It *smells* back there. And I like the radio loud. Why can't I have it on loud? It's after eleven. What are you going to do, sleep all day?"

Lottie, her head and arms out the window, remembered reading about a French woman who committed suicide by jumping from the roof of Nôtre-Dame cathedral; she hit an American tourist who was standing on the ground and both women died.

Lottie took a deep breath and after a moment said in a softer voice, "What's wrong, Ruth? What's wrong? Turn the radio off, please, and come into the house. I want to talk to you."

"I don't want to talk to you!" Ruth yelled. "I'm not going into the house! Anyway, it's not a house, it's a shit house!" She turned the music up full blast.

Lottie, in a rage, saw Jake's van pull into the driveway. Jake waved to her and to Ruth, then walked around to help Davy out of the child seat. The dogs leapt out of the open car and Simon, wearing his baseball glove, went with Evelyn to the trunk. Davy toddled after Simon and tried to take his baseball glove away from him and fell down. Jake threw Ev the keys and she opened the trunk and began lifting out the bags of groceries while Jake picked up Davy, who looked to be crying. With his free hand, Jake made a hand gesture to Ruth to turn the volume down. She continued doing jumping jacks, ignoring him. Slowly, as in a pantomime or a silent movie, the musical score now punk rock, a snare drum doubling on an electric guitar in thudding, monotonous four-quarter rhythm, all of them—Jake holding Davy and with his free hand imitating turning a doorknob; Evelyn lugging two bags of groceries; Simon dragging a mesh bag of oranges—walked to the middle of the lawn. Ruth began doing *battements tendus*.

Jake gestured to Ruth to come help with the groceries. She shook her head and pointed up at Lottie. Jake smiled up at Lottie, then turned back to Ruth. He beckoned to her again but she turned away from him and stamped her foot. Lottie could see her face was contorted. Jake walked over and turned the radio off. And all at once, as if a silent film had metamorphosed into a talkie or Lottie had lost her senses and now in a single instant regained them fully, Ruth was standing in the middle of the lawn in her pink ballet slippers screaming in a harsh cracked voice, "I hate her! I hate her! I hope she drops dead!"

"I only wanted her to turn it down," Lottie said to Jake. He was sifting flour for waffle batter. Evelyn, wearing an oversize white T-shirt over her halter and shorts, was squeezing oranges with the electric juicer. It made a buzzing sound as she pressed them against the reamer with the heel of her hand.

Lottie said, "It was on so loud I'm surprised all the cows in the area didn't abort."

Grinning, he tapped the sifter against the bowl a few times to knock the flour loose. "Just let her be. She'll come around."

"I can't stand it when she wishes me dead."

"She doesn't mean it."

"She means it."

"Well, everybody wishes everybody dead now and then."

"Oh, Jake, she won't talk to me. She won't look at me."

"That's how she is. She sulks. She does the same with me."

"Well, I can't stand it."

"Well, she knows you can't."

Lottie cracked eggs into a bowl and beat them with a wire whisk. "I'll bet she still holds it against me that you're not with her mother. And she knows it's not my fault."

"She knows and she doesn't know."

"Maybe I ought to have a talk with her."

Evelyn cut four more oranges in half. "She doesn't look in the talking mood, if you want my opinion."

"I don't want your opinion."

"What am I supposed to be, a statue?" Evelyn took the wire whisk from her mother and held it aloft in her right hand. It trembled there, egg dripping. "Who do I look like?"

Lottie yelled, "You're getting egg on the floor! For God's sakes, Evelyn, don't start up now!"

Ruth burst in with the pink bottle of hand lotion. "She was throwing things at me." She stood next to her father. "Do you think it's right of her to throw things at me?"

"I didn't throw anything at you! I threw it at the radio! I couldn't get your attention! You wouldn't pay any attention to me!"

"What do you mean, I *wouldn't*? I couldn't hear you! I couldn't see you, I had the sun in my eyes!"

"That's bullshit!" Lottie yelled. "You have a million reasons for everything, but they're all hoked up. Why don't you say there was an eclipse going on so you couldn't see me?"

"Are you calling me a liar? Is that what you're calling me?"

"Yes!" Lottie cried. "That's what I'm calling you!"

"Look, honey, please," Jake began. They both looked at him. "My dears, cut it out, both of you. You have to cut it out. Ruth, don't exercise on the front lawn. Do it in the back or go out in the fields. And cut the volume in half. All the cows will miscarry from that stuff."

"We don't have any cows! She's a cow! You always take her side."

"Don't call her a cow!" Jake let out an exasperated sigh. Then he laid a hand on his daughter's shoulder. "I don't always take her side. She shouldn't throw things at you."

"I didn't throw things *at* her! If I wanted to throw things *at* her, I would have *hit* her."

"Lottie." Jake had a pleading look in his eye. "I wish you wouldn't throw things at her. And if you didn't throw it at her, then I wish you wouldn't throw things *near* her. If you want Ruth's attention, go down and get it."

"Yeah," Ruth said grinning.

"Don't 'yeah' her." Jake withdrew his hand. "Do you hear me?"

Evelyn cut two more oranges and pushed the halves, one after another, down against the reamer. They all listened to the buzz.

"You're cutting too many oranges," Lottie said. "That's enough."

Ev shrugged but stopped. They stood in the quiet kitchen.

After a moment Lottie put the sponge back in the sink and dried her hands on her apron. She held out her right hand to Ruth. "Come here, little calf."

Ruth looked at Lottie.

Lottie continued to hold out her hand.

Ruth looked down at her feet in their grass-stained ballet slippers. She pointed a foot, then relaxed it. Without looking at Lottie, she turned away from her and walked out the back door.

During breakfast Lottie tried to act as if bygones were bygones while Ruth answered her in monosyllables. Afterward, Jake got out his flute and Evelyn her violin and they began playing Telemann's *First Canonic Sonata in G Major* in the living room. Jake played in his dungarees, barefooted and barechested in the heat, swaying with his platinum flute, eyes half-closed, sweat dripping. Ev, in voluptuous halter and flowery shorts, her hair a bright cloud, her finger- and toenails newly painted a soft rose color, stood concentrating on the score. She moved the bow lightly, brightly, as if it were a wand. After a while Ruth noiselessly pushed aside some story books and a can of talcum powder to clear an eight-foot-square space in front of the players. She found a green ribbon that had been on a box of chocolates one of Jake's pupils had brought him, and tied it around her neck. She did a half dozen pirouettes, then took off in a sweet summery improvisation, as if she were picking flowers and following the flights of bees or birds. As she danced, the pinched quality left her face and the thinness of her body softened. She seemed easier, hardly more than a child dancing to music, given up to it, lost and at peace. Simon, masterly and joyous, stood on his chair and waved his arms vigorously, conducting as he'd seen his father do innumerable times, as he'd seen the maestro do at Carnegie Hall where Jake had taken him for his first professional concert. Davy watched Simon and then bounded out of Lottie's lap and waved his arms in imitation. Simon shot him a dirty look. Slowly, Lottie leaned back in her old chair, got her feet up on the hassock, and let the morning's misery recede a bit, return and recede again; but she could not send it out to sea.

Part Two

L ottie's father had been an engineer and was retired now, with an explo-
sive temper that hadn't been damped down by age. That he had been
town mayor for two terms and later became third vice president of a major
American automobile company indicated that his public behavior might
have been different, but she rarely saw that side of him—except when he'd
explained things to her, from the Mixmaster to the atom; then, he drew
diagrams carefully and spoke gently and patiently. Growing up, she'd
received monthly science kits he'd ordered for her in the mail: erector sets
and volcano eruption kits and gyroscopes and flywheels and gravity goo.
Once when he'd had a daylong engineering conference in Detroit, he gave
her a ten-dollar bill and showed her where the science museums were and
let her attend by herself; twelve years old, she'd felt grown up; and she was
fascinated. Her dad had wanted her to be a nurse, maybe even a doctor; *he*
had wanted to be a doctor, but there had been no money early on.

Only as an adult did she understand: her mother had become pregnant
with her, and in order to marry, her father had had to drop out of college six
months short of his degree. And he didn't finish: he had no money. He had
never wanted children. What he had was a rigid sense of responsibility. For
the first few years they'd lived in an old farmhouse he'd bought cheap. Rain
would come through the roof onto two-year-old Lottie. There was no elec-
tricity. A single outhouse. She'd hated the freezing, scratchy wood toilet seat
in the dark night, the rough newspapers to wipe herself. Why had she let
herself be toilet trained? At the time, she'd been so proud. But then her

parents would be sleeping with the new baby, Adele, in their warm bed; Lottie, the "big girl," slept alone. When she needed to pee, there was a chamber pot. But sometimes, angrily, she peed in the bed, warm sweet pee; it got cold, and then she'd cried for her mother. Her father would yell his head off.

She had an early memory she found no one to confirm, not ever, nor would anyone disconfirm it and so she never dismissed it. Dad had driven the car, Mom in the front passenger seat holding the new baby, a boy; Lottie, age three, in the back with Adele. Dad parked in a church lot and her parents got out, Mom carrying the baby. Adele began to cry and Lottie remembered making funny faces at her in the back of the car, trying to cheer her up. She cried and cried. It got dark. Her parents came back without the baby, although her mother's body sagged from the missing weight.

After that, she never peed in bed again.

As a child, she'd asked Adele if she remembered: no.

Lottie'd asked her mother, who turned and walked away, shoulders drooping. But then her mother often turned and walked away; she never yelled and only once had Lottie seen her cry.

Very soon after the visit to the church, they moved far away, out of the Upper Peninsula into the Mitten, into a spacious house with internal plumbing in the small town of Sleeping Bay, although there was no bay there; and they never returned to the old town; no one even mentioned the name of the town, as if they hadn't lived there. Lottie didn't remember the name, as if it were the last name of one of the husbands Adele would go on to marry—four so far, and she was again beginning divorce proceedings.

Their mother must have been very fertile because she had a third daughter, Bridget, whom they called Bridge, and another son (if that first one had been real), Gerry. Gerry stayed and became an easygoing, talkative, chubby boy who loved flashy clothes and rarely combed his hair. Gerry's relaxed ways nettled their father, who tried diligently to improve him; his indifferent athletic abilities and poor scholastic performance caused their father real anguish. On hot weekend afternoons her father stood out in the backyard in an old baseball uniform and hit and pitched to Gerry for a couple of hours at a stretch, yelling "Get your glove down" or "Get your glove up," or "Get your body in front of the ball." *Get, get, get.* In the flashing sun Gerry seemed mostly to fumble or bobble, and then their father would yell, "Stop daydreaming!" "Hustle!" "Get the lead out!" and often the session would end with Gerry hit by a pitch.

His mediocre grades did not improve either despite the mayor's tutoring: "Show me all your work, show me every step." "Do what I tell you! Do exactly what I tell you!" These sessions would usually crescendo into a spanking, Gerry's pleas and screams resounding throughout the house until their grandmother, who started living with them when they moved to the big house, could be found to intercede.

Despite several feints their father never laid a hand on the girls, perhaps because he thought they fell under their mother's (or his mother's) jurisdiction; but he would give them the silent treatment for days. Once when Lottie was "getting the glacier," Gerry sneaked into her room to cheer her up with a joke or two, cackling so loud at his own punchlines that their father came upstairs and yanked him out by his hair.

For really serious offenses their father would mete out banishment: when Gerry was caught cheating on an English exam, he was sent off to Aunt Paola's, one of their father's six sisters. Adele, who turned into a knockout, was sent to Aunt Gilda's when droves of boys took to howling under her window on spring evenings and their father intercepted a package of French ticklers. And Bridge, three years younger than Adele, was exiled to Aunt Letitia's for getting drunk and painting an original musical composition on the pale blue body of the family car.

These banishments, albeit temporary, frightened Lottie. As a child, she had rebelled against her father's increasingly gloomy expectations by doing well in school but had never heard a word of praise out of him. Had he been afraid of spoiling her? Unlikely, although she liked to think so.

He was equally severe with himself, prone to overwork and depression: when in middle age he suffered a heart attack, he couldn't be persuaded by his doctor to pursue a graduated exercise program. (And besides, he knew more than the doctors.) Instead, her father began a rigorous Olympic-athlete-style plan they used for recruits in the army. Two weeks after his first heart attack, while setting the table for supper Lottie had heard the thud-thud-thud of him jumping rope upstairs, like a metronome keeping time with Bridge, who was practicing scales on the living room piano. After a few scales, Lottie didn't hear thuds any more. She ran upstairs to find him sitting on the bedroom floor, his hands pressed against his chest—he had ripped his undershirt open—the rope tangled around his feet. Although in the midst of his second heart attack and white with pain, he insisted on driving himself to the hospital.

Their mother, Jeanie Kristin née Bjornstad, six years older than their father, was not interested in imposing standards on anyone. Even her children called her Jeanie. A cool lean blonde, she was considered the town beauty, although she was probably thirty when they moved. And she was deemed an intellectual as well because when she was young, she had earned a master's degree from the state college and she'd taught English at a high school somewhere before she married. In the big house, as Mrs. Kristin, she spent her time reading novels and chain-smoking. Pleasant, even-tempered—whatever her children did was all right with her—she never scolded them nor especially comforted them. Usually if Lottie was upset, her mother patted her knee and told her it would pass. "Que será, será," she said and went back to her book.

A clear, almost chiseled memory: at age eleven or twelve, Lottie was in the backyard near their screened-in porch where her mother sat reading in warm weather, the angora cat, Moondust, licking its tail on the cool, gray stone floor—the cat would die and be replaced by another, and another, all of them white angora cats named Moondust—the white sweet smell of apple blossoms from the backyard trees mingling with the ever-present cigarette smoke. Lottie became aware of a low sobbing. It was soft and muffled, but intense.

"Jeanie?" Incredulous, Lottie stood outside watching her mother. Lottie pressed her nose against the screen.

Passionate tears ran down Jeanie's engrossed face—she read and wiped her eyes.

Jeanie looked up for a moment and waved her hand a few times, to wave away a fly or maybe she was fanning away the smoke and heat. Or was it

Lottie she wanted to wave away? Lottie worried about that. Jeanie continued to read and weep.

Breathing in that sweet acrid air, Lottie stood a long time on the steps outside the porch pressing her face against the screen, unnoticed.

What had made her mother cry? Was it only the book, Lottie wondered. Alone, invisible, she returned to the house. In the hall mirror she saw the harsh red imprint of the screen on her nose and cheek.

Her mother had named her after Charlotte Brontë, whose novels were full of weeping tormented governesses and the married men they longed for and virtuously renounced. She was grateful to her grandmother, who had rescued "Lottie" from Charlotte. Lottie thought it a spunky name—it had a fullness to it.

Her grandmother, her father's mother, who opened a small hat shop for ladies, became respected in town, even a little feared. An observant woman with a sharp tongue, she had reported a workman whom she noticed installing rusted water pipes on public property; the plumbing company lost its contract. One summer while her grandchildren played on the Potowatami River bank, she spotted cracks in the pilasters of the town bridge, which had passed inspection handily that spring; the inspector and the president of the contracting company were charged with bribery. When the vet and the pediatrician were uninterested in the toxicity of the rat poison the exterminator was spreading in the park, she bombarded the newspapers with letters that prompted an investigation of pest control throughout the state, and fines.

Lottie remembered her grandmother inspecting the outdoor bird feeders on winter mornings. Evelyn Kristin was Lottie's height, five feet nine inches, with a trim erect figure despite generous breasts whose outlines were visible even in the long dark stylish shearling coat she wore. Carrying a tray of suet balls and sunflower seeds, she strode through the deep snow in high rubber boots, her rich hair twisted into a low braided bun, on her head a stylish hat of her own design, some black or maroon or red cloche or beret or pillbox. After morning rounds she packed lunches for her grandchildren and sometimes walked with them to school before taking the bus downtown to her shop.

Lottie admired her grandmother's financial independence. Although she had contributed part of the down payment for the house, she insisted on paying Lottie's mother a monthly sum for her room—she would give Jeanie the money behind her son's back—and she could afford to spoil her grandchildren with spectacular store-bought presents. After Lottie had spent a day in a tree watching a purple finch lay her eggs, her grandmother had bought Lottie a telescope and a treehouse.

The grandmother did most of the cooking at home and made many of the children's clothes. She had a real genius for what she called "sightsewing": if Lottie saw an outfit she liked in a shop window, Grandma would buy the material and make a near replica.

One or two of her father's unmarried sisters were also always living in the house. She remembered them trying out new dance steps, getting into water fights and cookie dough fights. They smelled fresh to Lottie, accustomed as she was to the odor of cigarette ashes and cat hair. On Sunday mornings Lottie rubbed her father's relatives' backs with perfume from colored glass bottles and massaged their hands and feet with lotions. Alma, the youngest of the aunts, had splendid strawberry blonde hair and when she felt beneficent, she let her niece brush it. Lottie also washed and set and combed out her grandmother's hair, which retained its reddish mahogany color into old age.

As an adult it had occurred to Lottie that her mother, an only child, her parents dead in a car accident since she was a teenager, might have felt like a boarder herself in their big house teeming with her father's vibrant kin, and perhaps she found solace and good company in her books. Or perhaps she felt protected by her books, barricaded in, numbed, Lottie didn't know. (How had her mother let that boy be given away, if she'd let that boy be given away?) Her mother had never had a hard word with any of her husband's relatives; she let them do what they wanted and she read.

When Lottie was thirteen, the family was at a local water hole except for Gerry, who had been sent to Aunt Lisa's as a punishment for she couldn't remember what. Lottie had bought herself a hot dog with her spending money and gone into the water eating it. Her father was taking a walk with her two sisters, and her mother lay on a lawn chair reading and smoking.

Lottie dog-paddled with one hand, held the half-eaten hot dog in the other, and began to choke. Trying to get her mother's attention, she waved her arms and kicked up water. She thought to throw the remains of the hot dog and bun at her mother but didn't have the strength. Coughing and sputtering, she felt herself grow light-headed and start to go down, without anyone seeing her. She struggled to stay up, to keep before her the image of her mother, which grew two-dimensional and far away, like an old photograph of a slender woman lying in a chair, the sun glinting on her blonde hair, the same color as Lottie's, and on her pale oiled body. The picture was hazy, from the cigarette smoke and the sun; it had been overexposed, the figure whitening into the bright sky. Lottie became unconscious with this image in her mind's eye.

She was told afterward that a man who was standing near her in the water—a stranger (and strangers were rare in that small town)—had grabbed her and pulled her out and embraced her in his arms, and pushed sharply upward on her rib cage to dislodge the bit of hot dog. Her father was frantic, her mother dazed, and the stranger got away with nothing more than a thank-you and a pack of Lucky Strikes her mother had managed to put into his hand.

After her father had finished admonishing her (which he did in an uncharacteristically sweet, relieved, even hushed way) and after Lottie's fright was past, she thought about the incident for months. Only a doctor would have known a maneuver so sophisticated and there *had* been a medical convention in Detroit at the time; but it seemed too providential that a lone doctor, hot and bored with the meetings, would have driven a hundred miles to their old water hole. For a while she had a special feeling about herself as if she'd been saved for an extraordinary destiny, a mission like Joan of Arc's or Madame Curie's, and she supposed if she'd been a different child she would have prayed to God to tell her what it was, if it was. But her family weren't believers; Lottie grew up thinking no adult believed in God, that He was like Santa Claus, a story adults made up to get their children to behave, and that every adult was in on it. Her family didn't pray; they thought deeply about things for a long time, they read, they discussed Topics at dinner. After a while the aura faded and she thought less about it, wished just for the usual things—to be loved by Charlie Hart, who lived a block away, to make cheerleader in ninth grade. As an adult when she thought of the incident, she saw herself go down, invisible, and she was unable to dispel a certain feeling of uncanniness and loneliness that suffused the memory.

Charlie's family, Norwegians and Danes and Germans (almost the whole town came from the same genetic stock), were a soft-spoken, physically large clan, blond polar bears who were restrained and clumsy except for Charlie—who seemed to have received the family's entire ration of grace and much of its shy warmth. True, Charlie could be reserved, as if speech were not manly, even when he was eight and nine and ten, but he was physically exuberant: he would often walk to school with Lottie and her brother and sisters, shadowboxing along the way, or dribbling imaginary basketballs. Sometimes Charlie encircled Lottie, holding her wrists so that, batless, ball-less, bases loaded, she was able to slam one out of the park; Gerry and Adele and Bridge ran around, touching trees. On one occasion he did cartwheels and handstands from Lottie's door practically to the schoolhouse door, the others somersaulting and flip-flopping as best they could. In someone else, these performances would have seemed braggadocio, but in Charlie, they were outbursts of bodily energy and radiance, the trumpet of the swan. Everyone, even older kids, honked along after him. And although he was handsome, he wasn't the least bit aloof or conceited: he had a goofy side, a kind of whimsical humor that she could never see coming and that delighted her.

Charlie Hart, Charlie Hart, Her life's a fart without Charlie Hart. Despite some teasing in high school, Lottie, suspect for her grades and scientific interests, was validated by Charlie's affection for her—Charlie: team captain, star.

She admired him with her future anatomist's eye.

When they were in their early teens, she had heard from one of the girls that if you rubbed a boy's neck while you were dancing with him, that gave him a hard-on, but she couldn't find any evidence in the library of a neurological hookup between the neck and the penis. They danced in the Kristin basement—*Hold me close, hold me tight / Make me thrill with delight*—and Charlie said it was the dancing that did it. Charlie said practically anything did it. Then he said it was the closeness to her, it was looking at her, it was thinking about her that did it.

From the age of fourteen they would go to a hilly part of her father's land, where they were secluded by pines and white birches and a few large blueberry bushes. She liked to go in daytime. Once she took her copy of *Gray's Anatomy* with her and said, "Come out of me, Charlie. I want to see you."

He pumped.

"Please! I mean it!"

"Later."

"*Now*, while you're still all *there!*" She began raising herself on her elbows.

He slowed his pumping; his breathing grew less hoarse; he groaned. Then he laughed and came out of her. He got to his feet, his penis engorged and glistening. It was the beginning of fall and in the distance she could see cornfields that had been harvested, the dried stalks, not yet cut down for fodder, shining pale in the sun. As she sat on the ground looking at him, he bent over, erection v'd toward the sun, and stood up on his hands, penis now v'd toward the earth. He circled her once slowly on his hands, his face and organ red.

"You show-off," she laughed. She lay down and kissed him hard on the mouth. She got on her knees and took his penis in her mouth but he lost his balance and fell on her. They laughed and rolled together in the grass and she got his head in her lap and kissed him again, kissed the soft blond fluff that had begun growing on his upper lip, kissed the sparse hairs on his cheeks, avoided three whiteheads he had on his chin. She gently laid his head on the ground and got on her knees and sucked at his nipples for a long time, ran her tongue around his belly button, slowly licked her way down to his groin. She kept her eyes on his face, his bright beloved face. His eyes were squinched closed as if he were in pain, his lips opened spasmodically, and train sounds came out of him, also a few tears, as slowly, slowly she sucked him off.

She liked to get Charlie to cry during lovemaking. If the coach benched him, he was expressionless. Once when his hands were on the ground during practice, a teammate wearing cleats stepped on Charlie's pinkie, and he screamed—his finger was broken in three places and had to be set; Lottie had gone with him to the emergency room—but he didn't cry. Yet she could get tears out of him by flicking her tongue below the glans of his erect penis, the "frenulum"—she learned all the words—by being so light with her tongue, and then stopping, stopping, so that tears of torment filled his eyes, she was his sweet torturer, and then she sucked, sucked, and brought him off wailing.

"You're so—so—wide open," Charlie said to her. "I hear guys talk in the locker room about getting to first base, second base . . . It all seems so stupid and far away. I don't say a word about you and me. I feel like I own the golden goose. How'd you become so, so—the way you are?"

She knew she was sexually forward, that it was unusual that she didn't feel self-consciousness or shame with Charlie. Why was she so different? Was there something wrong with her? She didn't tell him that she worried she was more like a boy than a girl, or more like a man than a boy. Maybe there weren't even that many men like her. Maybe she was a freak.

She didn't say any of this but said instead, and it was true, too, "I want to know everything about my body, about your body, I want to try everything there is in the world, I want to try it all with you."

He shook his head as if to clear it out. "You're out of this world. You come from a wild planet." Then he said, "I love that planet."

Still, it took them a long time to know how to get her to orgasm; his thrusting and thrusting didn't do it. She found a small part of herself above her vagina that made her warm and wet if she rubbed it. Sitting, she pulled her labia open and thought she saw between another set of tiny labia a diminutive protruding pink pea. It hid from her. Next day she brought a magnifying mirror and after they kissed for a while, and he had his finger in her vagina, she got out the mirror and they saw the little beast together, a small sea creature hiding in the clear warm liquid. Shyly it disappeared. She got her finger on where it had been and rubbed gently and smoothly. The whole surrounding landscape began to throb. Charlie leaned in close and watched. As a painful pleasure tore over her, she suddenly gushed a clear liquid that got into his nose and eyes. "Hiya!" he cried in greeting, and triumphantly. Had she peed? Couldn't be. She licked his face. It tasted like some very dilute pee. Should she be embarrassed? But he seemed elated. And after that, Charlie did not consider it an afternoon well spent unless they found her "sly one, silly shy one" as Charlie called it—he could come up with a phrase or two—and she rubbed it or he licked it into showing its small self and then when her vagina would start going into spasms, she would thrillingly come up with a great fanfare of fluid. Lottie's geyser! Sometimes she worried it meant she was a man, that she came that way, spurting. But mostly, she was delighted.

At the dead end of a hot, still July the year she was sixteen (and it looked like Alaska was really about to become the forty-ninth state and she and Charlie were dancing to "Volare"—all in Italian!) her father, wearing a straw hat to protect his fair, balding head, rowed her and Bridge and their mother out to the small island in the middle of the river. (Adele was at Aunt Virginia's and Gerry had been sent to an Outward Bound camp to "build character.") Lottie wore dungarees and a large sweater. The others wore loose short-sleeved shirts over bathing suits. Thick suntan lotion glued down the light hairs of their arms and legs.

"How can you bear being swaddled on a day like this?" Her father asked, his long, lean arms gleaming, sweat beading his eyelashes. He paused to swab his face impatiently with a large moist handkerchief.

"It's cotton, the sweater," Lottie said uneasily.

"Well, you can't swim in it. I haven't seen you swim this summer. Have you seen her swim, Jeanie? Has she swum?"

Their mother looked up from the novel she was reading and took her cigarette out of her mouth. "What is it?"

"Has Lottie swum this summer? Have you seen her swim?"

"Lottie, have you been swimming this summer?" Jeanie looked confused. "Hank, why am I asking her that? Why don't *you* ask her?"

"Of course I've swum. Haven't I gone swimming?" Lottie looked at Bridge.

Bridge nodded. Lottie imagined Adele and Gerry nodding, too.

She began singing "Row, Row, Row Your Boat," her voice sounding high and thin and childish to her. The only sounds in the quiet day were the lapping of their father's oars, his soft grunting, and her high voice. She was relieved when Bridge joined in singing and "playing" the piece with the fingers of her right hand against her thigh; they kept a two-person round going until her father tied the boat to the pier. Bridge jumped out. Lottie hoisted herself up carefully, perspiring.

Jeanie spread a large pink sheet on the ground. As they sat eating, their father, who seemed preoccupied, said to Lottie: "Your shoe's untied."

She wore black and white oxfords.

"Jeanie, doesn't she have sandals? Doesn't this girl own any summer shoes?"

"What do you mean?" Jeanie asked.

"No summer shoes? No summer clothes? Don't you take her shopping?"

"I give you money, don't I?" Jeanie said to Lottie. "You've bought things, haven't you, dear?"

Lottie said, "Of course. I went twice with Grandma."

Their father bit into a pickle. "All right. All right. Anyway, tie your shoe."

Lottie was sitting on the pink sheet, her legs in their dungarees straight out open in a V in front of her. In her baggy sweater she bent over to tie her right shoe. Only her mother, who was looking out over the water, failed to see that Lottie couldn't reach her foot. After a moment Lottie awkwardly folded up her left leg and moved her foot with the untied shoe onto the hill of her left knee. Quickly, she tied the laces.

Her father's sun-reddened face flushed darkly. He got to his feet and stood for a moment with his hands on his lean hips, then gestured to Lottie to follow him. She rose with difficulty. He left her standing and went back and tapped Jeanie a few times on the shoulder. The three of them walked a distance away from Bridge, who lay back and closed her eyes. Her father glowered down at them; her mother smoked; Lottie stood with her hands on her belly.

Finally her father yelled, "You're supposed to be so goddamn smart. Don't you have the brains to use protection?"

"We use protection."

"What kind of protection? Toothpaste? Do you plug his dick with toothpaste?"

"Rubbers," Lottie said. "We use rubbers."

"Rain rubbers?" He laughed bitterly. "Galoshes? What kind of nincompoops are the two of you?"

Jeanie said to her husband, "Accidents happen, dear." She added, "You know that. At least they're fertile."

Her father bellowed to them to get back in the boat, they were going home.

After a silent dinner they convened in the evening in her father's large wood-paneled study (Bridge played piano in the living room and then went to bed), the door and windows locked, dark green shades pulled down to the sills, the cream-colored translucent curtains drawn together. Her father paced across two large Kurdistan rugs and swiped at his face and neck with a fresh white handkerchief with his initials, HSK, monogrammed in a corner in navy thread.

Her grandmother stood erect on the other side of his broad desk watching her son, her forehead and nose glistening, her hair braided and pinned up in front like a tiara. Her beige linen suit—she seemed dressed for a business meeting—was wrinkling in the heat. A green-glass-shaded desk lamp illuminated the square gold earrings that hugged her grandmother's ears and the orderly piles of documents and pamphlets and folders on the leather desktop.

Behind her grandmother, Lottie sat barefoot on the cool wood floor, her back against the paneled wall. Under her armpits and on her belly, dark wet blotches stained her yellow housecoat.

Across the room on a wooden banquette, her mother sat alone in light slacks and a loose-fitting white blouse. In the stifling heat only Jeanie, wrapped in smoke, seemed not to sweat.

"Why didn't you tell your mother?" Her father shouted at Lottie in a whisper. "Why didn't you tell your precious grandmother?"

He walked to the far side of the desk and punched his index finger several times at Lottie's grandmother: "If a feather falls from the wing of a sparrow in this town, it doesn't reach the ground without your knowing.

"The girl's mother's got her hands full keeping track of Madame Bovary and Anna Karenina. Who's the one who gets pregnant in Thomas Hardy?" He turned to his wife.

"They all do," Jeanie snapped.

"You've had five—you've had four pregnancies!" He yelled at Jeanie, then turned back to his mother: "And *you've* had seven!"

"Leave them alone," Lottie managed to whisper.

"Keep quiet, or you're going to your room! We'll decide things without you, miss!" He clapped his hands together. A few papers quivered on the tops of the piles on the desk. He walked over to Lottie and squatted down facing her; he gripped her chin hard in his hand. Lottie held herself still and tried to keep her eyes on his eyes; her throat had dried out and she kept swallowing.

"No shame? No guilt?" he whispered, his breath sour, his fingers pressing into her jaw.

She wanted to back away but she was already against the wall. She could see the small pools of fluid in the inner corners of his pale blue eyes, the frizzy rose-colored blood vessels, the tiny dark cross-hatchings on the skin under his eyes. Her voice startled her even though she barely breathed out, "Anything I do with Charlie is all right."

"What? What?" Her mother called anxiously from across the room.

Her father shook his head disgustedly but loosened his grip a little as he said, "Miss Big Brain here says anything that goes on between her and Charlie is hunky-dory."

Jeanie touched the space between her collarbones as if feeling for some tiny gold crucifix or medal that wasn't there.

"Don't take away the child's dignity," her grandmother said.

"She's taken away her own dignity. She's stripped away the whole family's dignity." For a moment her father's eyes were full of woe. Then they narrowed and Lottie saw only his pale eyelashes dotted with a few hard, grainy flecks of sand. "Here comes the bride." He wetted her with his spit as he chanted. "All dressed in white. Here comes the mayor and his daughter the whore."

Lottie flinched.

"How dare you call her—*that*!" Her grandmother cried out as she rocked up on the toes of her shoes. "You apologize— The girl's due an apology—"

Her mother mustered up, "Hank, please. Please. You know, after all, you know very well, after all—what happened with us . . ."

"What happened with you?" Lottie asked.

"Shut up, everybody shut up!" Her father was now really shouting. "Did Charlie talk you into it? Did he hand you some kind of horseshit?"

"Charlie talk me into something?" Lottie exclaimed in a soft amazed voice, trying to move her face out of his hand. In his temple a thin, hard-looking blood vessel seemed to pulse dangerously. Lottie feared he might have a stroke or another heart attack and die.

"Her due! Her due! Her due's a good strapping! I won't be made a fool of—"

"We were three blind mice, dear," Jeanie called out anxiously.

"What do you mean, three? You're telling me I should have been attending to the size of my daughter's breasts? To the protuberance of her belly button?" As he yelled at his wife, he took his hand away from Lottie's face and stood up. Lottie shot a grateful look at her mother, and at her grandmother, and refrained from rubbing her sore chin.

"What do we do now," her grandmother said. "That's the question."

"Lower your voice," her father said, although he was the only one shouting. "What do you mean, 'What do we do?'"

"There are options." Her grandmother's voice was firm.

"Options?" he hissed.

Lottie got up from the floor with difficulty and walked clumsily across the room to the banquette where Jeanie was sitting beside a pitcher of ice water and four glasses on a tray.

"Is she getting rid of it? Is she going to give it up for adoption? Are we going to bring up the child?" Her grandmother's tight-hair tiara seemed to jump on her head as she spoke.

"I'm not getting rid of the baby. I'm not giving the baby away." Lottie stood holding the pitcher.

Jeanie took the pitcher out of her daughter's hands and poured a glass of water for her. "Nobody's giving the child up for adoption," Jeanie said.

"Does Charlie know about this?" Lottie's father asked.

The cold water revived her and she nodded. "Of course."

"And his family?"

"No."

"Does he say you have *options*?"

Lottie shook her head.

"What does he say?"

"I don't see what bearing that has," her grandmother said.

"He's just the father," her father said.

"He's a boy," her grandmother said.

"Well, I'd like to know what good ole Charlie has to say. I mean that 'boy' doesn't talk much. But he has for sure gotten us into deep doo-doo."

"Don't make fun of him," Lottie said.

"I should make raw meat of him. Isn't that what fathers do in books?" He looked to his wife. "Where is Charlie anyway?" he asked Lottie. "Why isn't he here?"

"Why should he be here?" her grandmother said.

"He's with his family," Lottie said.

Her father pointed at her belly. "His family's here. He's got a responsibility."

Lottie said stiffly, "He wanted to come, but I told him no. I called him as soon as we got home from the lake."

"Why no? Why suddenly now no?"

"I thought I'd have enough—fighting with you all."

"So what's your fight with him?"

"He wants to get married and work at the Esso station."

Her father nodded a few times. "You don't want to marry him?"

"I do. I don't want him to quit school. Football's everything to him. He's got colleges calling him and he's not even a senior."

Her father said, "He doesn't think his family would help him out either?"

"What do you mean 'either'?" her grandmother said.

"He won't let anybody help him out," Lottie said.

"Why not?"

In spite of herself, Lottie began to smile. "He says it's his puff-pie."

"His puff-pie? Charlie said that?" Jeanie shook her head, but she was smiling, too.

"I don't care if he calls it his porkpie or his cow pie," her father said.

Her grandmother said, "Lottie's not leaving school. I know a doctor in Cincinnati . . ."

"She's around seven months, maybe more." Jeanie's smile was gone. She took her last cigarette from the pack and crumpled the paper and cellophane.

"Well, maybe they can still do— Anyway, he also knows about— placement."

Lottie put her arms across her belly.

Her grandmother walked over to her and touched her hair. "You'll have other children. I had my last child at forty-six." She stroked Lottie's brow and her cheeks.

Lottie would not look at her now.

After a while, her grandmother said, "Any mare can colt! What about high school? What about college? Who knows what you might become? Jeanie, tell her. You got an advanced degree!"

Jeanie tapped the cigarette against the wood banquette. "I can't," Jeanie said. "I can't advise her what to do."

The first week in August Bridge was dispatched to a music camp in upstate Vermont, and the house fell silent.

Lottie's father had not spoken to her since the evening they had all gathered in his office. Her mother left cigarettes burning in different parts of the house and her grandmother sewed woolen winter dresses for Lottie "for after." Lottie knew only that she had a living, breathing, turning presence inside her, whom she must shield. She missed Charlie; he had a summer job teaching little kids tennis, and when she saw him in the evenings they were often arguing about his insistence he quit school and marry her. Lottie wasn't sure what they should do when the baby came. She knew she'd have to drop out of school herself but she figured in time she'd get a GED and meanwhile stay in her family's home and do some kind of work. She hoped once the baby came her father would love her/him and let Charlie move in. Charlie said she was for sure smarter than he and so she had to stay in school. Her grandmother wouldn't hear of her dropping out and didn't think Charlie should drop out either. Her grandmother sometimes felt she should give the child up, other times that her mother and grandmother could bring up the child together. For the first time in her life, Lottie avoided her grandmother. Her father seemed thoroughly miserable and always angry.

After his tennis camp workday was over, Charlie would come by for dinner and later they'd go out for a walk in the dark. When they weren't arguing about what to do, they'd end up quiet at the same place on her father's land where they used to make love; they'd see the silver birches ghostly in the night and she'd remember what they'd done there. And she didn't regret it. Even though she read that lovemaking wouldn't hurt the baby, when they sat down it was so they could be silent together, and she would often pull down her pants and Charlie would place his hands carefully on her belly or he'd put his cheek up against it or his ear. Her belly was very warm and his cool face and hands soothed her.

Although they couldn't agree, Lottie wasn't unhappy and she wasn't lonely. She felt accompanied. If she played music in the house—and sometimes she lay in bed, door closed, with the radio on low, "*To be loved! To be loved! Oh, what a feeling to be loved.*"—the baby squirmed or rolled around. Was she a hula-hoop dancer? Was he a gymnast? Sometimes she thought she saw a foot or a tiny fist on the surface of her belly. And in the middle of the night when she'd be awakened by his movements, she would sing him a lullaby. During the day she taught her how the blood flowed through the chambers of the human heart, how fish breathed under water, why it rained. Charlie called him their football and their home plate and, once, she didn't know why, their loaf of pumpernickel.

Two nights before Lottie was to take the train to her Aunt Paola's in Whitefish, Montana, where she would stay until she gave birth, as she walked up the stairs to her bedroom, she felt a gush of fluid between her legs. Her dress grew wet, her bare feet were wet. There were dark jelly-like clots on the stairs.

Was this the normal breaking of waters, four weeks early? But why the blood clots? And she had a sudden tight, cramping pain that made her clutch at her belly. In a fright she took off her dress and underpants and washed her thighs and legs and feet with soap and water in the second-floor bathroom. Should she wash between her legs? Fearing she might damage the baby, she left some blood between her legs and put on a sanitary belt and pad and fresh underpants and a light blue seersucker bathrobe her grandmother had made for her. She put her dirty clothes in a paper bag and took a pail and some rags from the cabinet under the bathroom sink and got on her knees and began cleaning the stairs. The hard pains kept coming and she bit the inside of her cheek to keep from crying.

Her mother and her grandmother came out of her father's study.

"What are you doing?" Her grandmother called from the foot of the stairs. "Get up! Do you hear me?"

As Lottie, holding on to the banister, began to rise from her knees, a second rush of darker fluid washed down her legs.

The town obstetrician was vacationing in Vancouver. The family doctor listened with his stethoscope but couldn't hear the baby's heart.

"It doesn't mean much," he tried to reassure them in his office. "In the big hospitals they have equipment . . ."

They drove to Detroit with all the windows open, her father, mother, and grandmother in the front, Lottie lying on the backseat, a rubber sheet and an absorbent cotton pad over a pillow beneath her buttocks. To keep the weight of the baby off her cervix, her bare feet were up and out the window. Jeanie poured Lottie small paper cups of Tanqueray and handed them over the front seat down to her. She lifted her head and drank to stop the contractions.

They didn't stop.

Lottie looked out the window between her feet. The sky was a hazy reddish gray from the lights of Detroit and the smog left by the smokestacks.

She shifted her weight back and forth from one buttock to the other, hoping the baby would kick.

A month before, she and Charlie had seen a performance of *The Pirates of Penzance* in the town park: when the drums boomed, the baby banged. She had held Charlie's hands against her jumping belly.

Now she asked her father to turn on the radio. Loud.

Down at the end of Lonely Street at Heartbreak Hotel.
Oh, I'll be so lonely, baby.
I'll be so lonely, I could die.

Nothing moved but the passing headlights.

They arrived at the crowded emergency room at two in the morning. Gin-woozy, Lottie stepped around three small children who were sitting on the floor in the waiting area eating fried bananas and spare ribs.

She eased herself down next to Jeanie on a bench near the entrance and waited while her father and grandmother made their way to the front desk. Between titanic contractions she slept.

In the large examining area people sat or lay on gurneys. A sunburned, freckle-faced medical resident wheeled Lottie to an examining table behind a curtain: "You're sure it wasn't urine? What color was it? Any clumps of tissue?" He closed his eyes as he felt over her belly. Then he put on a metal helmet, a stethoscope emerging from it like an eye upon a stalk, and leaned over, pressed the cold eye to her belly. He listened for a long time, moved his head to another part of her belly, listened, moved. In the noisy room he walked around the gurney and listened from the other side. After a while he called in a slender resident with a crew cut and dark-framed glasses and handed him the helmet.

"Is the baby all right?" Lottie asked, as the second man bent over her.

"Shhh," the freckled fellow said, not unkindly, a finger to his lips.

When the slender resident had finished, they called over a small, white-haired nurse who wore a similar helmet. She listened to Lottie's belly, then shook her head.

"Get a flat plate," the first resident said.

An attendant wheeled her down to Radiology.

"Will the X-rays hurt the baby?"

"Can't answer," the attendant said. "Don't know."

Meanwhile, more blood gushed out between Lottie's legs.

A white-coated man who didn't know either helped her get up on the Formica table and moved the X-ray machine back and forth over her belly, then went away and stood behind a barrier. "Hold it! Hold it! Okay, move. You can move now."

But she couldn't. She felt the weight of the baby constricting her chest, lying on her heart so that it was afraid to pump. Nothing in her moved; even her mind seemed to have stopped working so as not to damage the baby. She had turned to stone.

They started a Pitocin drip. The cramps began to come more often now: she could not lie still. Someone told her to relax.

"Is the baby okay?"

"Breathe through your mouth."

Between the close contractions she imagined quails in the brush, terns in the Arctic ice, flamingos in Florida, a finch in a big oak tree on her family's property—all bearing down to expel huge eggs. She raised herself and pushed.

Feces came out.

A nurse brought a bedpan and got it under her. The odor began to diffuse throughout the small room. Would she push her baby out into the bedpan?

A nurse wiped her with iodine. Someone changed the sheet.

A chunky doctor entered the room followed by three medical students in short white jackets. His hair was covered with a cloth cap; he wore a green mask over his nose and mouth, so she never really saw his face. He held out his hands and a nurse gloved him. He felt for the baby. It hurt and Lottie pushed frantically against his hand.

"Try to wait," he said in a heavy French accent, squeezing two of her bare toes in a friendly but imperative way.

A nurse handed him a long metal instrument.

"What's that?" Lottie beseeched him.

She felt something cold inside her. In the quiet room everyone heard the terrible cracking sound of bone breaking.

"What did you do?" Lottie cried out. "What did you do?"

"Push," the doctor said gently.

Lottie rose and, holding onto someone—Where was her grandmother? Where was her mother? Where was Charlie?—pushed the baby out.

As the residents and students and nurses gathered around in the absolutely still room, Lottie caught a glimpse of a small open hand, a bloody foot. She thought they put the baby in a black plastic bag.

The attendants wheeled Lottie into the room she was to share with a middle-aged woman wearing an auburn wig who was sitting up in bed listening to *The Right to Happiness* on the radio. A small fan whirred on the woman's night table without flustering the hairs of the wig.

The two attendants set the gurney next to the bed and eased Lottie onto it. Her grandmother kissed her forehead. Jeanie thanked the attendants and the nurse who was writing on a clipboard. Her father stood, a tall frozen figure inside the doorway.

"Excuse me, sir." Charlie hurried past him, his wide face blanched except for his blue eyes and a few pimples on his forehead. He carried a bouquet of three red roses in green tissue paper. His father, a muscular gray man in a denim shirt and work pants, stood outside looking down at the floor, his hat in his hand.

"Sons of bitches," Lottie's father spat out.

As if acknowledging the truth of the remark, although no one knew whom it was directed at, Charlie's father nodded a few times in the hallway. Charlie hunkered down his head at Jeanie and shrank even further into himself as he passed Lottie's grandmother. He wore a navy blazer that Lottie and he had shopped for together a few months before and that was already too small for him, the material pulling across his still broadening shoulders, the sleeves riding several inches above the thick bones of his wrists.

Charlie laid the roses alongside Lottie's pillow, then stood pushing his fists at the skin of his cheekbones, kneading it as if he would pull the skin up and cover his eyes with it. Was he trying to keep from crying, Lottie wondered and thought how extraordinary, for every drop of fluid had gushed out of her on the stairs, had bled out with the baby, and her eyes were full of sand.

Her grandmother put the roses in a water glass on the bedside table and left the room; the roses stood there, too long for the glass, straggly. Jeanie drifted away and closed the door. The fathers left. Finally they were alone together except for Lottie's roommate.

Charlie closed the curtains around the bed so the roommate couldn't see them. Then he knelt down beside Lottie's bed.

She was shivering. Charlie took her hands and kissed them, then rubbed them for a while. She continued to shiver. He went into the bathroom and came back with two clean towels, which he laid over her on top of the blanket.

Her teeth chattered.

He took off his blazer and put it on her, and when she didn't stop shaking, he took the blazer off her and then removed his sweaty shirt and undershirt and helped Lottie into them. He put the blazer back on her and buttoned it. Kneeling bare-chested, he rubbed her feet and calves under the blanket. He took off his socks and put them on her.

She began shuddering, almost rocking.

Charlie unbuttoned the blazer again and his shirt and hoisted his T-shirt up around her neck and untied her hospital gown and kissed her swollen goose-fleshed breasts.

Then he got up on the bed and straddled her and, keeping his weight on his hands and knees, lowered himself slowly as if he were starting a push-up and laid his bare sweaty chest gently like a hot moist compress across Lottie's breasts and loose belly.

She closed her eyes. She wrapped her arms around his back and neck. She lay trembling listening to her neighbor's radio and the dry whirring of the small fan and held on to Charlie.

Ten days after she "delivered," school began. Lottie walked from class to class carrying a book bag that contained breast pads, two extra pairs of underpants, and mastodon-size sanitary napkins to catch the thin pale yellow fluid she exuded now that the flow of blood had dried up. Walking and sitting were still painful and so was defecation despite the sitz baths and ladles of milk of magnesia.

Had the doctor sewn her front to her rear? She answered the usual questions in the halls—yes it was hot enough for her, her vacation had been a bore, she couldn't wait to graduate—but spoke little to anyone, except to Charlie, and not much to him.

Did people know? How could they know?

Her fellow cheerleaders must have had the idea she'd torn a ligament, because one of them told her to keep an Ace bandage on and another touted

the town chiropractor. Toward the end of the month the girls chipped in
and bought her an orchid on a plastic wristlet to wear as a spectator to the
first game of the season. "Hope you'll be shaking things up again real soon!"
The card showed a plump baby holding an orange rattle.

The baby card had to be a fluke; her sister cheerleaders were neither cruel
nor subtle.

Lottie's English class spent September and part of October reading the
Romantic poets, too self-dramatizing for Lottie's taste: she feared she would
never be able to see a crowd of daffodils again without thinking of getting and
spending. One morning she was at her desk reviewing her notes on "Hyperion"
when someone dropped a folded paper down the front of her scoop-neck
blouse. She turned quickly. There was a press of people behind her, boys and
girls, hurrying to get to their seats before the bell rang. She fished out a small
stiff square of heavy bond paper that had been folded many times.

Before the next class she stopped at the bathroom to read it. Girls were
jammed up in front of the small mirror, chatting. Anna-Rose Jorgmann,
one of the cheerleaders, whispered to Lottie, "Oh God! I'm sure I bled
through!"

Lottie sat down on a toilet and opened her pocketbook. Four verses were
typed and centered on the page, followed by a paragraph of commentary:

I

Ah, what can ail thee, wretched Lot?
So haggard and so woe-begone?
Is Charlie's dick all red and hot
Up your ass again?

II

Does he set you on his pacing steed,   5
And nothing else do all day long;
But suck your tits and bang your cunt
With his great big dong?

III

I see a lily on thy brow,
With anguish moist and fever dew;   10

Has he come full in your face again?
And bit your little clit too?
                    IV
I saw his starv'd lips in the gloam
With horrid warning gaped wide,
Is he eating you out too much, dear Lot?   *15*
On the mayor's hill side.

When she got to the last line of the poem, she let out a hard cry.

"What's the matter?" Anna-Rose called through the wall separating the two booths.

"Nothing."

"Period? No period?"

"There's a daddy longlegs in here."

"Madame Curie afraid of a spider?"

"I wasn't expecting company."

On the mayor's hill side.

She read the line three times.

She saw the hilly land with the birch trees where they used to make love. Had someone hidden behind the trees and watched?

She read the paragraph at the bottom of the page:

Notes to Variorum Edition: This poem survives in several stages of composition and in different versions. All copies were written about the same time, presumably in late September 1819. The copy reproduced above is as near a fair copy as any, although having finished the stanzas, the Poet added the following alterations in pencil, which he later crossed out:

Stanza 1: line 3. all] so   line 3. red] *thick/full*

Stanza 2: line 4. dong] shlong   line 4. With his great big dong] And make sweet moan.

Stanza 3: line 4. And bit your little clit, too?] And filled your sweet ears, too?] And pulled your dear tits, too?

What was a "Variorum Edition"? There was only one guy in the senior class, Nathaniel Burden, and maybe one girl, Katie Gann, who were high-tone literary types—oh, maybe there were a couple of others—but none of them was in her English section. How many people were involved in this? Had the whole class been hiding among the birch trees? Did they all get together over a few beers and potato chips and dictate the thing? *Remember when he fucked her up the ass? Yuk-yuk. Put that in. Remember when he rode her so long that Alicia-Mae peed in her pants?*

Maybe one of the girls combing her hair in the bathroom had had a hand in this. Maybe Anna-Rose Jorgmann. If Lottie stayed on the toilet until everyone left, she'd be late for calculus. Was anyone in her calculus class in on this? She wanted to go home and get into bed.

That evening Lottie waited for Charlie after practice; because she couldn't bear to look at any of her fellow students, she stood a few blocks away from the school inside the wire mesh fence of a public park. It was cold and semi-dark. She stood by a tree that had lost most of its leaves. Oh, she could have met Charlie at her house—her parents and grandmother and Adele were at a piano recital where Bridge was playing. Her father had forbidden her to be alone with Charlie, but she didn't give a damn what her father forbade. Truth was, except that her father's prohibition made a child of her, she didn't much mind not being alone in the house with Charlie; she hadn't felt any sexual interest in a long while, and it had hurt the one time they'd tried it and they'd stopped.

Charlie walked by alone whistling merrily and she felt like smashing him, but she called his name quietly.

"What's up?" Charlie went inside the park, put an arm around her, kissed her cheek.

Lottie took the poem out of her book bag, then resumed guard duty at the fence.

"Did you write this?" he whispered.

"Are you crazy?" She got the class's mimeographed copy of "La Belle Dame sans Merci" out of her bag and held it up next to the typed version. "Some goon wrote it," she whispered.

Charlie read them both slowly, squinting in the twilight.

"Do you think somebody saw us?" Lottie mouthed when he'd finished.

Charlie shook his head.

Lottie said, "I think somebody saw us"—she dropped her voice—"do stuff."

He shook his head vehemently. "Do *what*? You think somebody saw me come in your face? You think somebody saw me bite your—whatever he called it?"

"It's hilly where we made love." He couldn't hear her because of the wind and she had to repeat herself.

"It's no hillside."

"It's my father's land."

"That's a safe bet." He reached for the mimeographed sheet. "Look, Lot, it's a line right out of the poem:

> *And there we slumber'd on the moss,*
> *And there I dream'd, ah woe betide,*
> *The latest dream I ever dream'd*
> *On the cold hill side.*

And it comes up again two stanzas later—"

"Why are you grinning?" she said. "It's not Milton Berle."

"I don't know."

She looked down the street through the iron-mesh fence, then hissed: "You like that part about your big red dick."

Charlie didn't answer. She put her hands on his hot face; he was blushing. She moved away from him.

He followed her.

"Do you think if I hadn't walked up the stairs? Maybe it wouldn't have happened if I'd slept downstairs in the guest room?" She ran the fingers of one hand over the moist cotton waistband of his sweatpants. She could feel the tucks in the material and his warm flesh. "When I had the flu in December, I took a couple of aspirin. Could that have had anything to do with it? Twice I used glycerin suppositories." She had a momentary feeling of embarrassment talking about suppositories.

He took her hand away from his pants and held it in both of his. There were dead brown leaves everywhere, some with frost lines on them. Walking,

Charlie and Lottie made crunching noises as if they were stepping on small bones.

"Do you think if you're not born, you feel any pain when you die?" Lottie began to cry.

"What?"

"Do you think it was a boy or a girl?" She reached for his pants again and tugged at them as though she were a child pulling at her mother's skirt. "I saw a foot. I saw a hand. Sometimes I wake in the middle of the night with the feeling they left something in there."

"Lottie . . ."

"A finger could have snapped off without anyone noticing."

She pulled him urgently behind a shed that held sports equipment and squatted down and awkwardly took off her underpants and spread her legs apart.

He looked around wildly.

"Down there—is there—a smell—something rotting—down there?" As she moved his head down between her legs, she fell backward onto the frozen ground, the leaves crackling under her.

Charlie got down on his knees and unzipped his jacket and laid it so it covered her from the waist down and he stuck his head under the tent and looked between her dark legs and breathed in deeply through his nose a few times. He kissed the insides of her thighs.

She moved his head slowly back away from her. "There isn't anything, is there."

He shook his head.

She sat up, leaves and frozen bits of dirt in her hair and on her buttocks and thighs, and pulled up her underpants and cried.

During the next days she combed Keats but could put together only a single line in rejoinder:

> *May you fall*
> *Silent, upon your prick in Darien.*

Charlie wrote carefully:

Swig your own skeez, cocksucker
And give yourself lockjaw.

But there was no one to confront with these jottings, and Lottie ripped all the papers into small pieces and feared she would remember the filthy poem forever.

Part Three

W hy'd you pick Michigan?" Charlie was asked by a short, curly-haired
reporter who wore rimless glasses and a yellow bow tie. "Why not
Notre Dame or Northwestern or Nebraska?" As he named each school, he
jabbed at the air with a pencil.

"Is it true you got over fifty offers?" another reporter asked, a lit cigarette
between his lips.

Charlie smiled and looked down at his shining shoes.

"You're his girl," the man said to Lottie, the cigarette rising and dipping
as he spoke. She wondered if his mustache would catch fire. "Did he really
get fifty offers, a hundred? Or is somebody pulling my leg?"

"I *am* his girl!" Lottie beamed. "But I can't speak for him."

It was a brisk February afternoon during their senior year of high school.
Snow crusted the ground and glazed the needles of evergreen trees, and ice
feathered out from the wooden mullions onto the windowpanes. In the
Hart family's small living room two photographers were hanging a bedsheet
over the bay window to soften the sunlight. Five reporters with pads and
pencils and a tape recorder were interviewing Charlie, who sat stiffly on the
couch in his winter suit. He was flanked by Lottie, who wore a new blue
wool dress buoyed up by a crinoline she kept trying to press down and navy
stockings secured with a garter belt; and his six-year-old brother, Ad, who
was home from school with the chicken pox. Tall for his age, Ad wore a

flannel bathrobe with small figures of Howdy Doody and Clarabelle and Princess Summerfall Winterspring printed on the material. Every few minutes he reached up under a pajama leg to scratch himself. When he began feeling his way down under the waistband of his pants toward his crotch, Charlie took Ad's hand and held it.

Gleaming trophies crowded each other on the mantel above the fire-place, and team photographs and several newspaper articles that Lottie had cut out and framed for Charlie hung on the walls. Above each headline, she'd typed in red the name of the newspaper and the school year:

> *The Ojibwa*, junior year, 1957:
> CHARLIE HART: MAGICIAN
> *The Wolverine*, junior year, 1957:
> HART RUNS 70 YARDS FOR TOUCHDOWN

In some articles Lottie had circled certain words in peacock-blue ink: "control," "fluidity," "glide." One article that was long and mentioned Charlie only in passing, she had summarized above the headline, adding her own editorial comment:

> A writer surveying high school football for the *Detroit Free Press* mentions Charles Hart as a "Michigander to watch" and calls his running style "subtle" and "aesthetically pleasing," words not often used in the context of football.

There was also a collage she'd made on stiff, gold-paper-covered cardboard out of newsprint epithets of different size type: Mountain Lion, White Panther, Fiery Fiend "a blend of Samson and David," "part Odysseus, part Achilles—but where's his heel?" arranged around news photos of Charlie in action.

A reporter with a fountain pen behind his ear said to Charlie, "How does it feel to have personally scored eighty-four points your senior year?" A small reporter stood up on his toes to ask, "And you made the All-Midwest team and the All-American high school team! What's it like for you, Charlie?"

Charlie smiled and bobbed his head several times.

"For Christ sake, no one's asking if you're a member of the Communist party!" The reporter with the bow tie yelled. "Give us a line! At least tell us why you picked Michigan!"

Charlie flushed. He pointed at the flock of trophies on the mantel and ran a hand over one. The sun glinted on his fingers. "Michigan's been good to me."

The reporters wrote this down.

"*You've* been good to Michigan!" Lottie cried out.

They wrote this down, too.

Charlie frowned.

Both photographers snapped pictures of Charlie frowning. They snapped the mantel from several angles, and a reporter picked up each trophy and copied the inscriptions.

"Why'd you choose football? You're All-County in baseball! You could go into anything! What do you need to get knocked around for?"

After a moment Charlie said shyly, "I've always felt that playing football was—was—what I was meant for."

"What's that?" asked the man with the tape recorder. "What'd he say?"

Lottie's father shot a roll of film on the occasion of Charlie's setting a high school record for the mile (4:24) at the state meet their senior year. A couple of photos taken from the twentieth row in the stadium showed blurred streaks of tiny runners sprinting at the end of the race. Most of the other pictures were posed ones of Charlie in his sweaty white racing shorts and T-shirt, one arm around Lottie, the other arm straight up, his trophy—a gold man in full stride—held above his head.

There was a shot of Lottie standing alone, her arms out at her shoulders, the trophy balanced on her head.

But the picture that pleased her the most was a mistake. It was a double exposure, a merging of an image of Charlie holding his shimmering trophy in front of his chest, with an image of Lottie holding the trophy out in front of her face. Charlie and Lottie look as if they have one body between them, a single white-clad torso with bands of different widths and densities, and one set of heavily muscled, deeply shadowed legs.

This botched photo embarrassed her as much as it thrilled her; although she couldn't say why, she had the sensation that she was naked in it, and splendid.

She graduated as salutatorian, an honor given her, in her opinion, as much for her father's being mayor as for her grade point average; her heart was not in her studies. And Nathaniel Burden, whom she still suspected of having written that "poem," was valedictorian. Tall and dark and stooped, an aspiring writer, he read from "Invictus" at graduation

> *It matters not how strait the gate,*
> *How charged with punishments the scroll,*
> *I am the master of my fate:*
> *I am the captain of my soul.*

and then he read from Kipling—

> *Yours is the Earth and everything that's in it,*
> *And—which is more—you'll be a Man, my son.*

And this all struck her as fake-thrilling and rah-rah; so maybe he hadn't written that takedown of her after all.

Although her grandmother offered to help send her anyplace she wanted to go, she wanted to go with Charlie, who had a good chance at becoming the best running back the University of Michigan had ever had. And so she accepted a scholarship to the university. (Burden had also been given a full ride there, somebody told her.)

Mostly, Lottie was relieved to get out of high school. She felt whipped and frightened, her belief that she was invincible gone forever. She thought about her dead son (she felt sure her baby had been a boy). And the shadow of that long-ago, maybe given-up, brother lay on her. Had she not wanted another sibling? Had she felt a boy would have been too much competition? The summer was hot and she sat listlessly on the grass watching Charlie run laps and leap hurdles as if he were from another world.

She tried out for the cheerleading squad and made substitute, not bad for a college freshman; grateful to be rushed by three sororities—new people really liked her?—she wore the Tri Delt gold and pearl pin with pride but also with a troubled sense of being an imposter.

Charlie *was* from another world. As a freshman running back, he broke the NCAA freshman rushing record, totaling nearly twelve hundred yards in just over two hundred attempts, and he topped one hundred yards in each of his first nine games at the collegiate level. He ran for over fourteen hundred yards in both his sophomore and junior years, made All-American both years, and was expected to be a major contender for the Heisman Trophy his senior year.

Lottie partook of his aura when she was around him: wasn't she applauded, too, when they showed up in the school cafeteria for dinner after the Saturday afternoon game? More often people grew quiet and awkward when Charlie entered a room and she found herself thinking the hush had something to do with her as well. Although she knew it was only her good old Charlie with his reliably stiff dick; when making love to him she was entered by Zeus the swan or Zeus the bull or Zeus the serpent or Zeus the cuckoo-bird. That he didn't stray amazed her; he could have had any goddess.

Alone, though, she had to talk to herself constantly. She sat in classes wondering what she was doing at the university anyhow. But she wouldn't feel better anywhere else. In science labs and lectures she felt least estranged and so she attended many, hoping they would turn her on to the world again. And as she daily traced the development of the chick through a small window she had cut in the shell of a fertilized egg and covered with transparent tape; and learned to calculate the pressure needed to open the lungs of different newborn mammals at birth ("The first breath is hard; the second is easier."—she hoped that was true); and examined rainwater and the white slough she scraped off her teeth, repeating Antonie van Leeuwenhoek's observations from the early 1700s, her old wonder at life began to peep out, like feeling returning to a sleeping foot, painfully, fitfully, unevenly, but it spread into every digit.

Just before Christmas break Lottie's junior year, her comparative anatomy professor gave the students cats to dissect. Hers was a pitch-black alley cat with green eyes, its mangy fur matted down with fixative, its starved body flattened from the weight of others that had been stored stacked above it in vats. She decided to take the cat with her to her parents' home for Christmas vacation and work on it there. It stank of formaldehyde, but the rubberized canvas bag she carried it in muted the odor enough so she didn't offend the other passengers on the long bus ride home.

Her grandmother embraced her and Charlie at the bus station, and her mother smiled and sniffed, and her father nodded at her and shook Charlie's hand. (Would her father go on like this forever? And would she go on stiffly nodding back?) Charlie laid his and Lottie's suitcases in the trunk, but Lottie held on to the canvas bag.

It was a cold December day, the pale sky darkening although it was only four in the afternoon. Fifteen inches of snow had fallen two nights earlier, and the plows had piled it high on the sides of the road, like massive glittering barricades, gray in the beginning darkness.

She sat in the front seat of the car between her father, who was driving, and Charlie.

Jeanie opened the window an inch and lit a cigarette, then leaned forward and tousled Lottie's hair. Lottie reached back and squeezed her mother's hand.

"You look wonderful!" Lottie's grandmother said. "Not sorry you didn't go to Radcliffe?"

Lottie shook her head and pressed her leg and thigh harder against Charlie's.

"You don't smell so good," her father said.

Lottie laughed.

"What kind of Christmas presents you got there?" He poked an elbow out at the black bag, but Lottie, prescient, blocked the jab with her forearm.

She explained.

By the time they dropped Charlie off, everyone's eyes were tearing. Lottie sat wondering, How had this not happened on the bus? Jeanie put out her cigarette and they opened all the windows.

"You can't bring that thing into the house," her father said as he pulled into the driveway.

"I'm going to dissect it."

"Not in my house."

"I'll do it in my room."

"Do it at school."

Lottie moved a hand gently over the small body in the bag. "I don't want to wait three weeks."

Her father whistled. "What's the emergency? Are you behind? Is that thing overdue?"

"No," she said proudly. "I'm not behind. As it happens, I'm ahead."

Her father nodded a few times. "Then it can wait."

Lottie took a deep breath of formaldehyde fumes. "It can't wait. It's my Christmas present—to myself. I want to spend the vacation dissecting and drawing."

"Drawing what, dear?" Jeanie asked. "I didn't know you could draw."

"The cat. I'm drawing the cat. I'm supposed to draw pictures of what I see, layer by layer, as I do the dissection." Lottie took a stained brown-paper-bag-covered book from her pocketbook and opened it to a U of Michigan bookmark. "First you cut through the skin and you reflect that and scrape away the fat—there won't be much fat—and you see the abdominal muscles. I already did this in the fetal pig. There're three layers covering the stomach and intestines: they keep the abdominal contents from falling out. You see, gravity is pulling everything down so these muscles have to be reasonably firm, because that's all there is in the cat between the viscera and the outside world. That's all there is in anybody, just this thin layer . . ."

"That's a lab book," her father said. "You're supposed to do this in a lab, not in a house."

"Henry," her grandmother began. "The girl is very taken with this."

"A few years ago she was very taken with sex. Not in my house!"

There it was. After a minute Lottie said bitterly, "Then I'll just go back to the bus station, please."

Her father tightened his shoulders. He shifted into reverse and began easing the car out of the snowy driveway. The left rear tire caught and began to spin. He drove the car forward and backward, forward and backward. He jammed the gear shift into neutral and, muttering something, went out into the garage and came back with a board (Lottie felt momentarily frightened), which he placed behind the mired rear tire. After several silent tries, the tire jumped out of the rut and he slowly backed out.

"I can't find my cigarettes," Jeanie said. "Stop the car!"

"When are you going to quit smoking?" Lottie asked her.

"Henry, you stop the car this minute!" her grandmother said.

"Why didn't you stop me before, when I was stuck?"

Her grandmother ignored him. "Get out of the car, Lottie, and go into the house."

"She's not taking that animal into the house!"

"What's the big deal?" her grandmother said.

"It's the holidays," her father said. "People are coming over for a glass of Christmas cheer. There's probably a chapter of the Anti-Vivisectionist Society coming."

Jeanie shook her head. "They came at Thanksgiving."

"Are you an anti-vivisectionist?" Lottie asked.

"I don't want the whole house stinking of formaldehyde. Why don't you just *piss* all over the place?"

"Watch your language!" her grandmother said. "Leave it in the car, Lottie."

Lottie held the bag stiffly in her arms.

"Nothing's going to happen to it," her grandmother said.

Lottie didn't move.

"The National Rifle Association is coming," Jeanie said. "The cat hasn't been shot, has it? That might actually be a plus."

"Take it with you then!" Her grandmother's voice grew thick and hoarse. "Just get out of the car and wait outside the house!"

Her father pulled up to the curb and Lottie got out. She stood on the cleared sidewalk holding the bag to her body. The wind blew loose snow off the shoulder-high shrubs between the sidewalk and their property and off the blue spruce trees that stood on the white lawn. It blew snow up and off the roof of the big white house, which was set back from the road. Snow stung her face. She could hear her father yelling in the car, the sounds muffled by the wind. She walked back and forth curling and uncurling her cold toes in her boots. She watched her breaths, like small clouds or ghosts, disappear in the dark.

After a while her father turned on the headlights. As her mother began to roll down a rear window, Lottie heard her father roar, "I don't care if she freezes her ass off!" Her mother rolled the window back up immediately.

Lottie would not cry. In the dark she stamped her blocks of feet. She walked back and forth rocking the dead cat in her arms.

Finally her father got out of the car, leaving the motor running. He opened the trunk and dropped Lottie's suitcase onto the sidewalk. "You can go sleep in your bedroom but leave that stinking cat on the porch. Do that dirty business on the porch!" Then he drove the car with his mother and wife back up the driveway and into the garage.

The next morning Lottie, awkward as a spaceman in red earmuffs, a red woolen face mask, and an old fleece-lined coat of Charlie's, as well as fleece-lined gloves, appeared on the porch to sweep out the fine snow and dirt that had sifted in through the floor-to-ceiling screens; and she dusted the plastic slipcovers of the faded couch and chairs. Her grandmother shoveled a new thin layer of snow off the shoveled and re-shoveled porch steps, then went out to the garage for an electric heater.

"Are you all right?" Lottie took the ice-cold heater from her grandmother, who was breathing heavily.

"I was better fifty years ago."

In the good morning sunlight, with the wind blowing at the pages of her lab book and the heater making a steady rattling noise like hail pinging on metal, Lottie eased the stiff cat out of the bag. She laid it, cradled in her arms, on an old wooden breadboard on the bridge table.

It was a female. From the elongated teats, Lottie judged the cat had borne a litter not long before she was "euthanized." Lottie counted the teats. She measured a dark-red mulberry of a skin tag dorsal to the second teat. She lifted the rubbery lips of the animal and counted the yellowed teeth. She wrote these observations in her lab book although they weren't required: she had read that Madame Curie had always taken extensive notes. She closed her eyes and felt over the animal with her cold numb hands (she'd had to take her gloves off; she couldn't feel anything with them on), two fingers stinging as the formaldehyde entered small cuts and scrapes. The fur was bristly. The cat seemed all hard, dark hills and depressions. *Yea, though I walk through the valley of the shadow of death.*

She held her hands before the heater for a few minutes, then turned the cat gently over onto its back and with the scalpel made a small incision into the abdomen. She inserted the tip of a scissors and cut straight up and straight down.

It was the largest animal she had ever opened. With eager careful hands she pulled the skin back. There were the dull grayish-brown abdominal muscles arranged as the book described, the fibers of the external oblique going one way, the internal oblique perpendicular to it. There were the few thin yellowish-tan streaks of fat shining among the muscles. She touched the oily striations.

For a moment it seemed to her as if the entire animal were anointed and shining.

She wiped at her eyes with her arm.

Then she cleaned her hands on a rag and sketched the muscles slowly in pencil, her fingers awkward again with cold.

Now and then as Lottie worked, she warmed her fingers on a mugful of tea.

When it cooled down, she threw the tea out through one of the screens and poured herself some more. Jeanie brought her soup in a cup and refilled the thermos with tea twice during the afternoon. Her grandmother came out with a ham and cheese sandwich and held it up to Lottie's mouth and fed her. Lottie kissed her grandmother's fingers. Evelyn touched Lottie's cheek.

"Grandma, you're short of breath. What's up with you?"

"I'm seventy-six."

"Is that normal for seventy-six? To wheeze like that?"

Her grandmother shrugged her shoulders. "I used to have asthma, but not for a while."

"Go to the doctor, Grandma."

"I'm a healthy woman." She hesitated. "Maybe you'll become a doctor?"

Lottie laughed. "Don't wait for that."

"Well, think about it."

"I'm thinking about this cat."

The next morning, although it wasn't part of the assignment, Lottie slit open the small bowel with a scalpel. Inside was a thick mush of green and brown food and mucus. She washed it out with tap water, then ran the muck and liquid through a large strainer. At the bottom of the strainer she found flat white worms, translucent, a few of them several inches long. There were also shorter round yellowish worms, coiled, and tapered at both ends. She counted them and put them into separate envelopes to look at under the microscope at school. Inside the washed-out gut were little folds that ran round and round, puckered like her fingers from the formaldehyde. She drew a picture of them.

She opened up the thorax and found the two blobby lungs, mottled black. A city cat! She felt like Sherlock Holmes. Nancy Drew. After she cut the trachea, she pushed on the lungs with her fingers, and bubbly air and mucous came out.

The heart was dark brown, grayish brown, like a tiny fist.

"Have you really been ... peeing ... out there all week?" Jeanie exclaimed, when she came out late one afternoon with the last thermos of the day.

"What?"

"Suppose somebody saw you? Don't you think it's small of you to get back at your father like that?"

"What are you talking about?"

In the growing dark her mother pointed at the large lacy islands of yellowed snow where Lottie had been tossing her tea.

Lottie set all the parts of the cat back in place at the end of the vacation, as if she were putting a puzzle together, and took it to school.

Senior year, in the course of a not especially important Sunday afternoon game, Charlie, who'd had only forgettable injuries his whole career, got piled on by an opposing guard, two tackles, and an end; his leg angled oddly, he was carried off the field screaming. They operated until three in the morning.

When he came to in the recovery room, he took his hand out of Lottie's and sat up groggily to feel for his legs. He moved his hands over them down to his feet. Then he managed to lift the injured leg a little. "What did they do, do you know? What shape am I in? What? Did anybody tell you anything? What?" His voice was thick and slurred and anxious.

She shook her head. She grabbed his hand and kissed it, but he moved his hand away. She went for the nurse, who was leaning over another patient. Lottie waited. Lottie explained. After what seemed a long time, three surgeons in green OR scrubs and cloth caps appeared at Charlie's gurney, along with the nurse. The men looked grim and tired; one doctor's eyes were bloodshot. The senior person, a six-footer with bushy steel-gray eyebrows—Lottie recognized him as the team doctor—spoke crisply and not unkindly, explaining about major nerve damage and a torn popliteal artery and diagrammed for Charlie all of his injuries on a yellow lined pad.

"What's it mean?" Charlie pushed, almost swatted away the pad. "What am I up against here?"

The team doctor held on to the pad. He nodded a few times. "You'll be able to walk. I'm sure of that. You'll have to do a lot of physical therapy, but you'll be able to walk."

"Walk?"

"Yes. Definitely. Almost definitely. We were worried you'd need a wheel-chair, or a walker, but I think that leg will hold up. You might not even have a limp. No limp. It'll take a lot of work on your part, but probably no limp."

Charlie grabbed the man by the front of his scrub top. Even seated on the gurney with his legs stretched out in front of him, Charlie was much bigger and taller than anyone else in the room. "When can I play? That's what I want to know. When?" His voice was harsh and blurred.

Except on the football field, she'd never seen Charlie menace anyone and she felt frightened.

"Let go of me," the doctor said, barely audibly. "I can't talk to you if you have me by the throat."

Charlie didn't have the fellow by the throat, but he held on to the man by his shirt for several minutes. The doctor stood pale and off-balance and, as he remained silent, his lips pursing and un-pursing, Charlie let him go.

The doctor rubbed his neck, as though Charlie'd tried to choke him.

For a while, no one spoke. Then the team doctor said, "This is a hard one." The other two doctors looked away. Charlie and Lottie watched the team doctor. Somewhere an EKG machine emitted jarring beeps.

"We tried everything we could, Charlie. But you've suffered—this is—there's no other way to put it—this is a career-ending injury."

After a while, the doctor with the bloodshot eyes muttered, "Sorry. I'm sorry."

The third doctor said nothing.

"How can you be so sure?" Lottie cried out. "You don't know what a hard worker Charlie is! He's a hundred percent disciplined. He's got more grit than anyone I know."

None of the doctors looked at Lottie.

"Why can't he try? I mean, if physical therapy can help him walk, why can't it help him play? It doesn't make sense."

"No coach could let you go out there again," the team doctor said to Charlie. "It would be—assisted suicide."

Nobody said anything for a moment. Charlie squinted as though he wanted to see better.

"Do you have any questions, Charlie? You must have a lot of questions." The team doctor swung the yellow pad back and forth. The pages fanned out despondently. "Do you want to take a look at my diagrams again?"

Charlie shook his head.

"I'll stop by in the afternoon, Charlie. You'll have questions later. Try to get some sleep." He held out his hand. Charlie made no move to take it. At last the team doctor let his hand drop and the three men turned away.

Lottie said, "It's not the last word, Charlie. It's the first word. We'll see other doctors." Lottie grabbed for Charlie's hand but again he pulled it away from her. She said to the doctors' retreating backs, "I want to look at those diagrams. I want to see exactly what the trouble is."

The three men did not turn back to look at her.

"Can I have those diagrams?" She ran after them. "I want those diagrams."

Outside of the recovery room, in the hallway, the team doctor yelled at her, "Why are you leading him on? Why aren't you helping him face what he has to face?"

"The diagrams. Please, would you give me the diagrams?"

"You're wasting our time. You won't be able to understand them. You don't know anything about anatomy."

She wanted to yell "I do!" but really what did she know? The anatomy of the cat, of the fetal pig.

Lottie wondered if the man with the bloodshot eyes had something contagious.

But she got the diagrams. Back in the room, Lottie looked at them. She had only a vague idea of what the doctor had drawn but she kept on looking as if there were a solution to the problem in those pages. Charlie seemed to be asleep although she wasn't sure. If he was asleep, she didn't want to wake him. If he wasn't, she didn't know what to say to him.

She went into a bathroom, taking the diagrams with her, and washed her face one-handedly; then she walked aimlessly around the hospital for a while, past rooms where families were chatting and eating, rooms where patients were moaning—was no one paying attention?—a whole floor of rooms where the nurses' station was full of pale pink and blue balloons and displays of fruit and arranged flowers in baskets decorated with pennants that read CONGRATULATIONS! NEW MOMMY! WHAT A BABY! She started tearing up and bit her lip to shut the tears down as if they were coming out her mouth.

In the family waiting area, Charlie's parents sat with his brother, Ad, and the twin girls, and Lottie went in and hugged each of them and no one said anything. Finally Charlie's mother said the doctors had stopped in and told them; she began to cry. Lottie squeezed her hand and said loudly, "They don't know everything. They're just three surgeons. Michigan isn't the world." Lottie held the yellow diagrams rolled up like a truncheon.

By this time they'd moved Charlie out of recovery, and everyone dragged chairs quietly into his room to sit and watch him sleep. Lottie waited, although she didn't know for what. His mother whispered to his father that they really couldn't afford a new tractor, no matter what model or make, and his father said he thought they could; then they both fell silent. Ad was working his way through a stack of comic books in his lap and the twins were sitting on the floor playing jacks, and when they had had enough of that, they got out a deck of cards and Ad joined them on the floor and they played War and then Go Fish.

When Charlie woke in the late afternoon grimacing in pain, Lottie went to the nursing station and managed after a while to get the nurse's attention. The nurse said she had to wait for a resident. Lottie returned to the room and watched Charlie's face contort and finally after a long time a resident showed up and Lottie asked for pain medication for Charlie. The resident said he had written for Tylenol and when Lottie said it was obviously not doing the job, the resident spoke about turning a healthy young person into an addict. She explained with some exasperation that Charlie didn't drink or smoke, never missed a practice sick or healthy, he'd played a crucial game with the flu and 103 temperature; and after a while, she followed the resident to the nurse's station where he made a few phone calls she didn't know to whom and after a long, long while a pump was set up for Charlie that he could push to release some morphine-like fluid into his IV. He seemed afraid to push it but with some reassurance from the nurse, he tried it once or twice, and then a little more often but still abstemiously; ultimately he grimaced less and went back to sleep.

No one knew how Charlie felt about what had happened to him, but Lottie figured, with the pump installed and Charlie asleep, at least she'd done something for him: she could leave.

It was Monday evening. Carrying her cheerleader's outfit and the yellow pages of diagrams in a paper bag, wearing jeans and a sweatshirt somebody'd brought her, she walked out of the hospital for the first time since Charlie'd been admitted thirty hours before. She skirted the parking lot, trying to move quickly although she felt unsteady, hugging her arms across her chest in the chilly night. Streetlights faintly illuminated the large bare trees. Dry leaves whirled in the gutters.

After a while, she entered a familiar Italian restaurant, a friendly place with a pizza parlor where students hung out, a dining area with candlelit tables, and a large back room for private parties or meetings. She'd been in the back room several times—the cheerleaders had thrown a party there and once the botany department had taken it over for a dinner. She sat down at the counter of the pizza parlor and asked for a slice and a Coke. When had she last eaten? There were a few other students, no one she recognized, and no one seemed to recognize her.

In a moment, she asked again for a slice and a Coke, unsure if she had asked already or only thought to ask. She felt strained and uneasy and very tired, and she held on to the stool as if she might fall off.

While she waited, she looked at the colored pictures on the wall. Most of them were reproductions of photographs of ruins—she recognized the

Roman Forum. There was also a picture of a black gondola, and a picture of
a mural of Saint Francis preaching to the birds. In the room to her left a few
couples were having dinner; most of the tables were empty, the red-checked
tablecloths cheerful but lonely, the cutlery shining, a bottle of wine in a
straw basket in the center of each table.

A man was speaking loudly in the back room over to her right. He
sounded as if he were praying or reciting an incantation.

She got up from the stool and walked down a short hall to an archway.
There was a sweet, harsh smell in the smoky air. Grass. A group of people
had arranged their tables and chairs in a semicircle, at the center of which
stood a tall dark-haired man in a black shirt and pants and a long open black
wool coat. It was Nathaniel Burden, from high school. She'd seen him a few
times on campus over the years; they'd nodded but never spoken. Now he
held a thin black book in one hand although he rarely looked at it. In the
other he held a dark pipe. Burden spoke in a deep booming voice:

> *What are the roots that clutch, what branches grow*
> *Out of this stony rubbish? Son of man,*
> *You cannot say, or guess, for you know only*
> *A heap of broken images, where the sun beats*
> *And the dead tree gives no shelter, the cricket no relief,*
> *And the dry stone no sound of water.*

Perhaps she fell asleep for a moment. The next words she heard were

> *I will show you fear in a handful of dust.*

She thought of her grandmother and the dusty, pebbly sound of her
breathing and she felt frightened.

Then Burden switched to falsetto:

> *"My nerves are bad tonight. Yes, bad. Stay with me.*
> *"Speak to me. Why do you never speak. Speak.*
> *"What are you thinking of? What thinking? What?*
> *"I never know what you are thinking. Think."*

Burden stage-whispered:

> *I think we are in rats' alley*
> *Where the dead men lost their bones.*

As he went on reciting, his mournful eyes glowed and burned like his pipe when he dragged on it. He raised and lowered his arms, the long loose black sleeves flapping.

She wrung her hands.

Although she couldn't make out his meaning, Burden's rising and falling cadences, his ever-changing voice as he mimicked the different speakers—he seemed in the falsetto to be taking the point of view of a distraught, broken woman—fascinated and repelled her. In the thick-aired room, her lungs felt tight and she was aware of her heart beating unsteadily and she felt frightened for Charlie, and unsteady, unrooted, near panic herself.

> *What is the city over the mountains*
> *Cracks and reforms and bursts in the violet air*
> *Falling towers*
> . . .
> *Unreal*

At Lottie's insistence, Charlie got the doctors at University of Michigan Hospital to recommend places to go for a second opinion and so his records and X-rays were sent to the Hospital for Special Surgery in New York City and also to Mass General in Cambridge. No hope arrived from the northeast although Mass General offered an appointment with a knee specialist to review the findings, but Charlie said it was a waste of time and money.

A sporting goods store in Grand Rapids wanted to hire Charlie as a sales clerk and a Detroit-based company wanted him to promote their motorcycle helmets. Lottie thought the helmet letter was a sick joke, but the company sent a follow-up letter and then a telegram.

Charlie was too stunned to make any plans. The only thing he knew for sure was that he wanted to get out of Michigan.

Part Four

1963

They flew low over a flat land covered with brown grass. From the plane all the roads in Texas were straight and grid-like. Smoky rivers looked like S-curves and there weren't many of them. Lottie cried.

In the small university town in southwestern Texas where Charlie was beginning graduate work in economics—the Michigan coach and an administrator had together pulled some few poor threads—they rented a modestly furnished shingle-and-stone bungalow on a street of shingle-and-stone bungalows. Lottie set out in the kitchen some of the wedding presents that kept arriving by mail—the Mixmaster and pressure cooker and toaster and waffle iron and the Betty Crocker cookbook. She laid treasures from her grandmother over the nondescript furniture—crocheted doilies, and appliquéd tablecloths, and brightly knit afghans—and hung on the walls an enigmatic sampler Jeanie had picked up at a rummage sale (the black embroidered inscription read "Every hair casts its shadow"—Goethe) and also a few posters from her dorm room. Her favorite was a picture of a tall masked Venetian woman in deep décolletage, sitting in the midst of a dazzling array of gaily colored costumes.

Lottie's mourning was peculiar. The death of her grandmother she thought about with a kind of disbelief, even bewilderment. Her parents had come up with bullshit reasons why no one had told her about her grandmother's cancer—Lottie'd had a bad enough year, what with Charlie's "accident"; everyone wanted her to be able to concentrate on her studies; and why should the upcoming graduation be tarnished? No one had expected the disease to advance "so rapidly." Adele was away at school and didn't know anything either but Gerry and Bridge had been at home; they were just kids, though, and they'd followed their grandmother's wishes and their father's. When the family appeared at graduation without Evelyn, Lottie found out what was happening. But her grandmother was already unrecognizable: Evelyn had lost most of her rich hair and some of her height (incredibly, she seemed wizened) and was moving in and out of consciousness. Lottie pulled together a wedding within a few days so her grandmother could be there; Evelyn lay in her bed, moved to the living room for the occasion. In the hush of the ceremony, Charlie and Lottie took their vows to the harsh counterpoint of her grandmother's sucking air. Afterward, Lottie leaned over the head of the bed and her grandmother reached up and took Lottie's face in her shaking hands and kissed her.

Charlie and Lottie went for a three-day honeymoon to Niagara Falls, during which time her grandmother died.

Charlie was mourning himself. He'd been left with a slight, almost imperceptible limp, some pain on walking, and a certain diffuse grayness of mood that, if you didn't know him, you could almost chalk up to his quietness. Lottie knew him. Some part of Charlie that had been gentle and curious despite the insular family he'd come out of, some door, some window, had turned into a wall; he had grown harder, he had become, understandably, angry.

In spite of their gloom, Lottie took pleasure in the company of a loved person in the house with his peculiar habits: Charlie always brushed his cookie crumbs into his empty milk glass, then placed it absentmindedly under the bed or next to the toilet. He left his bath towels hanging neatly over the doors to dry, and if she didn't take them down, you couldn't shut a door in the house by the end of the week. These unique signs of him gave her a rush of irritable affection, like an animal spotting the muddy paw prints of her mate. She was tickled by the train noises he made coming; and she liked to inhale the smell he left on the sheets. She was proud to be part of their uneasy, off-kilter twosome.

One evening while Charlie was eating dessert, Lottie handed him a page torn from a pamphlet. "Look at this ad, dear."

He held up a forkful of banana cake. "There's an odd texture to this . . ."

"It's made with coarsely milled cornmeal. I saw Pelé on television the other day and I was inspired to try a Brazilian *sobremesa*."

"Don't be putting on the dog with me." Then he softened his tone: "I like your regular cooking just fine."

"Well, I have to try new recipes so I don't get bored."

"How about *pfeffernüsse*? My mom'll tell you how to make 'em." He read the lines she'd circled:

> Med lab tech needed, Billingsville, Texas . . . where the skies are bluer and the people fewer! f/t: to work in an active rural hospital laboratory, generalist duties. Exper pref Refs nec. Apply Dr. A. A. Mihiner, TE3-7000 ext. 761.

"Where'd you get this?"

"The librarian gave me some throwaways . . ."

"Well, throw 'em away," Charlie grinned.

"They need somebody at *our* hospital!"

"They need somebody at *our* bowling alley." His grin contracted a bit. "I start Monday."

"You took another job? Doing what?"

"Sweeping. Washing windows. Setting up pins."

"You—sweeping?! Washing windows?!"

"*You* sweep. *You* wash windows." He looked at her hard. "You still think I'm some kind of prince, don't you?"

She felt heavy. "You shouldn't take on any more work."

"I have to."

"You don't—"

"As long as you're eating breakfast out a bunch of mornings a week and buying crap we don't need, this cornmeal junk, at the supermarket, I have to."

"Charlie!" She was still taken aback by his new, gruff self. "Do you begrudge me a few dollars?"

"That's all we're short is a few dollars."

She picked up the percolator to pour him more coffee, but he shook his head. She stood holding the percolator. "It gets to me, staying in the house all day. I don't feel part of the world."

"Eating at the diner makes you feel part of the world?"

What could she say to a man who'd lost his world forever? That eating pancakes and bacon next to Indian and colored and white workingmen meant something to her, made her feel more vital, sprung somehow. But it wasn't enough. She put the coffeepot down on the burner. "No, it doesn't. Charlie, I moon about things I used to do. Remember the cat dissection? The shark I opened that had the fetuses inside?" She had her arms around her chest and stood rocking back and forth.

"Why don't you clean out the attic? Maybe you'll find something valuable up there."

"I want a job."

"Keeping house is a big job."

"You said that already. I mean a job up my alley."

"You have a good eye: you put this mirror here, and those flowers there. You make the house look nice."

"Oh Charlie! I think sometimes about this teacher I had, Thalia Cheek, my micro professor. She was the divorced one, with three sons. I ran into her once on campus late at night a few days after you—after you got hit." She always dropped her voice when mentioning his injury, as though it were a shameful defect. "I was out walking, worrying, and she was on her way to the lab to finish an experiment. Everyone was asking after you but she just said did I want to come help her. I washed a few flasks, measured things, boiled water, but afterward I felt lighter. Maybe if I could do something like that every day . . . I can always quit if it gets in the way. This job sounds made for me—*generalist duties*. I could learn a lot."

"How is it made for you? You don't have any experience."

"Experience is *preferred*! I'm a quick study!"

"What about children? I thought you wanted children. Are you going to have children and work in some germy lab?"

Lottie narrowed her eyes. "I'll cross that bridge if I'm lucky enough to come to it." She cleared the table, clattering Charlie's coffee cup against his saucer.

She threw out the rest of the banana cake.

"Somebody could have eaten that," Charlie said.

"I made it for *you*."

"Sorry," he snarled back.

His roughness. His thuggishness. She wouldn't accept it. "Anyway, I have an interview tomorrow."

"Why didn't you tell me?"

"I'm *telling* you! Do you think I'd have a fight with you over a hypothetical?"

Charlie got up from the table.

"For God's sake, Charlie, I feel shadowy and birdbrained and cranky. I can't go on like this!"

He walked out of the house, and Lottie ran out after him, down the dark gravel road. She was sad that he had become so easy to catch up with; and she tried to take his hand. "Please," she said. "Please."

After a while he let her take his hand and they walked together for a few blocks, then turned around and went home.

She would go to the interview. If she got the job, he'd get used to it.

Lottie washed the dishes distractedly, without heart, but also angrily and she got water and soap bubbles on the wall and on her slacks and on the floor.

On a bright Monday in March, a well-scrubbed, nervous Lottie showed up at the hospital lab early for her first day of work. She was dressed in a dark suit set off by a gold and garnet pin she'd inherited from her grandmother and a small red cloche hat under which she wore her hair in a high bun.

"You the new girl?" The young woman who greeted her in the hallway wore blue-framed harlequin glasses and a long white coat on the breast pocket of which was embroidered LuAnne Lucas, Laboratory Technician. Her hair lay long in a smooth dark pageboy. She had large shoulders and a large torso and her feet were shod in black, polished penny loafers, complete with bright pennies.

Lottie said, "I hope I'm the new girl. I'm on trial for two weeks."

LuAnne cracked the pink bubble gum she was chewing. "Well, I'll show you the ropes. But those shoes—" she looked down at Lottie's black pumps. "You don't want heels, even small ones, your feet will be killing you. And that outfit! You look dressed for a tea party."

Lottie blushed in the hall.

"Get comfortable, girl! It's a lab! So let me tell you a thing or two right off the top." She dropped her voice almost to a whisper. "You have to stay on the good side of Mihiner, which is tough because sometimes he yells and other times he's trying to get a hand up your dress—" LuAnne looked around uneasily.

"Really?"

"But if you do good work, he might buy you a present. You have to make him look solid, and you never want to cross him."

"He sounds like a dragon."

She laughed. "We actually call him 'Snapdragon.'" She looked around carefully. "But he's real trouble." She opened the door to a large green-walled room across which ran black counters with recessed chrome sinks. Specimen containers filled with exuberantly colored fluids stood in wooden racks on the counters. Like a color chart, one series was composed of jars of liquid ranging from pale cloudy yellow to daffodil to bright orange. Bunsen burners and microscopes and boxes of pipettes and petri dishes were placed in orderly sequence on the counters. A centrifuge whirred in a far corner. Printed signs on the walls read:

SAFETY PAYS

SAFETY SHOWER FOR ACID BURNS

EMERGENCY EYEWASH STATION: PUSH CENTER BUTTON TOWARD YOU
    FOR EYEWASH.

FIRE BLANKET IN CASE OF NEED: PULL WIRE HANDLE SHARPLY.
    BLANKET WILL FALL OUT.

A window at the far end of the room looked out onto the garden of the hospital's small stucco chapel.

"That's the only bench with a view, and Angela's got it. When she goes, it's mine!" LuAnne raised her hand in a fist and grinned.

Angela's counter was scrupulously clean. The words *faith* and *charity* were calligraphed in black pen on white paper and taped to the front of a large electric typewriter that stood to one side of the counter. Next to the typewriter were color photographs of three small children.

"Hey, are those tears in your eyes?" LuAnne asked.

Lottie took a quick swipe at her eyes with the back of her hand.

"What's with you? You really can't have that bench. Angela's got seniority."

"No, no!" Lottie laughed. "I'm just moved to be in a lab again."

"What?"

"I feel"—Lottie fished in the air for a word—"at home."

"You are a fruitcake," LuAnne said good-naturedly, handing her a box of tissues. Lottie wiped her eyes. "I'll bet you're the type that can't get enough to do and is eager to read everybody's bloods, and butters up the boss. Got your number?" LuAnne grinned.

"I don't butter up the boss."

"No offense meant. Just remember, like I said, it's a lab, huh? The girl before you ate her breakfast and lunch at her bench and came down with hepatitis."

"Really?"

"You say that a lot! Look, it's easy enough to put your sandwich on the counter and then put it in your mouth. I wash my hands a million times a day." She held them out, red and meaty, for Lottie to see.

"All the manuals and protocols are back there on that shelf, and in this closet you'll find supplies." LuAnne unlocked a dark green metal cabinet; inside were stacks of beige cartons variously labeled FRAGILE, HAZARDOUS, POISON. Dark brown bottles of reagents with yellowed, gummed, hand-written labels stood on a high shelf.

"That's my bench over there." On the countertop LuAnne had taped a sign that read DON'T LEND MONEY TO YOUR FRIENDS. IT GIVES THEM AMNESIA. Next to it was a cartoon, cut from a magazine, that showed two happy parent bugs seated on a living room couch while their baby bugs watched TV on the rug: "We provide Neisseria with all the comforts of home."

"What's in there?" Lottie pointed at a wooden door with a glass window covered on the inside by a green shade.

"Oh, that's a little closet of a room where Mihiner does research."

"Really? What's he working on?"

"He's got volunteers in there with water dripping onto their foreheads. How many drops per minute does it take to drive a man mad."

"Is he working for the government?"

"Are you a Communist?" LuAnne cracked up. "I'm pulling your leg. I don't know what he's doing: he hasn't told a one of us."

That night she told Charlie, "The girls in the lab are washing their hands all day long with Phisohex. Everybody's got dermatitis. I didn't want to shake Angela's hand. She said, 'Don't worry—you can't catch it. You earn it.'" Lottie laughed as she chewed on the fried chicken. Then she got serious. "And Charlie, the whole place is color-coded. The doctors are all white men, and they wear white and they eat in a separate cafeteria. And then in the other cafeteria we lab techs wear white, and also the X-ray technicians and the inhalation therapists. And there's one colored technician and he wears white and you have the feeling something's wrong here. The people who stand behind the counter dishing out food are all colored, and the women who work the cash register, and they all wear light green uniforms. And then the Tiguas and the Kickapoo, they do janitorial work and they wear navy blue. Charlie, I'm talking to you—"

Lottie had never put a needle in a human being before. None of her colleagues ever seemed to need to learn anything, they were all super-women; she watched LuAnne carefully the mornings when she drew bloods. Still, on Lottie's first patient, a forty-year-old colored man with an amputation below the right knee secondary to diabetes, she missed the vein twice. Blood dripped onto his blue hospital gown.

"Three strikes and you're out," he said tightly. He wore thick eyeglasses. On the large ward five other patients watched sourly from their beds.

Her lips were dry. "How about fouls?"

He shook his close-cropped head.

Sitting on a stool four beds from them, a white man in a three-quarter-length white coat beckoned her over. LuAnne's Laws came to mind: *Short coat, short you-know-what, think "trainee."* Too old to be a medical student. Maybe a resident?

What did he want from her? She needed to concentrate. But there was something appealing about him: in his late twenties, he wore his thick black hair in a ponytail and he had clear hazel eyes. The young man was unwinding a large blood pressure cuff from the thigh of a patient who she suddenly realized had no arms.

She began to feel she was losing her balance.

Now with both long, slender hands, the fellow in the three-quarter coat called her over again.

"You look like you're guiding an airplane into a hangar," she yelled at him irritably, as though her irritability might anchor her. "What do you want?" She glued her eyes to her own patient's veins and shifted her weight on the stool.

"Come on over here," he called to her.

"You better go back to the bullpen," her patient said.

She could not help but give her patient a dark, hurt look. He said, "Why don't you pay attention to the coach? He knows his stuff."

"Bring the blood tray over here," the fellow in the white coat called.

"What do you want with me?" she half-sighed, half-hissed as she followed him out of the ward into a small supply room where folded sheets and pairs of green sponge slippers stood in orderly stacks on the metal shelves. He closed the door behind them.

"Who are you?" she demanded. "Why did you embarrass me?"

"*I* embarrass *you*? You think all the patients didn't know you were in deep shit?" Except for his generous eyes, he had a meager face—long, thin, hardscrabble, his skin dented and pitted. But there was something authoritative in the way he carried himself.

She looked away from him. The one small window faced an extensive fruit and vegetable garden; even from the fifth floor you could see the pale green watermelons and bright yellow pumpkins. A patient in a blue-striped bathrobe was watering the plants with a sprinkler can.

"Here, tie the tubing." He took off his white coat, beneath which he wore a short-sleeved pale green shirt and a thick silver expansion bracelet with an engraving of Saint George jousting with the dragon. He made a long wiry muscle stand up on his arm.

"Are you kidding?" Lottie said.

He tied the tubing himself with his right hand. "Now slap the vein till it comes up. You see? Get the needle, take off the clothes"—he grinned— "you know: the cellophane and that tight little plastic cover. Now sweet and easy does it."

With shaky fingers, she pushed the needle close to his protruding vein. He put his fingers over hers and steadied them.

"Atta girl! Go!"

And she got in: the dark red blood flowed into the lavender-topped tube.

Elated, she grinned at him.

"Okay. Now pull the needle slowly out." He took his fingers away from hers and she pulled back on the needle; he pointed to the gauze pads; after she opened the wrapping, he held the pad to his left inner elbow. "Now a Band-Aid."

"Who are you?" she asked. "Some angel?"

"Just a humble community servant." He laughed and pointed at the chair where his coat lay. The pin on the pocket read GEORGE KENADJIAN MD "My sword at your service. I'm a peds resident."

"What are you doing here? I don't know how to thank you."

"Try my left arm so you're sure you've got the hang of it."

"Really?"

"You bet. Tie the tubing. Okay, slap that vein up. New needle."

"I can't believe you're letting me do this." They watched the dark blood spurt into the tube. "Boy, do you have some veins!"

"You're not making a pass at me, are you?"

She flushed.

"In all conscience I have to tell you I have ordinary veins. You're on a vascular service where everybody's blood vessels are for shit."

"Did I look scared? Was it obvious I didn't know what I was doing?"

"Yes." He had a slow, wide smile that spanned his thin face. "Also I know your patient. He's a quiet, tense man and he has his limits."

"You were so sure I was going to miss?"

"Don't make a big deal out of it."

"How did that fellow you were working on lose his arms?"

"Friendly fire. He's half-blind, too."

"Oh," she said. "Oh."

He nodded. "I think it was the Korean War, although I didn't ask him."

"How do you stand it?"

He grimaced. "It's harder for him than for me."

She nodded. "How would you take blood from him?"

"You find a superficial vein." He took a shoe and sock off and moved his finger from one vein to another and another. "You want to try to get into that blood vessel at my ankle? Here. Use a butterfly. Don't mind the smell." He pointed at his bare foot and grinned again.

"You're too much!" She bent down eagerly over his foot. Then she looked up at him. He had dimples.

"Pay attention to what you're doing."

She looked back at his foot, then swabbed the skin over the vein with alcohol, got the butterfly in, and squeezed the wings. Some blood went into the tube. She opened the wings and when she got a quarter of a tube, took the needle out and put a gauze pad on his foot.

"You're not going to get this chance every day—great veins like mine." He laughed.

They washed their hands in the metal sink.

She said, "What's a peds resident doing on a vascular ward?"

"A lot of those blood vessels are hard to get into. Pediatricians learn to enter the smallest veins. So one or the other of us is called up here most days." Then he said, "Let me ask *you* a question, and forgive me if I'm out of line: Why are you a lab tech? You seem intelligent. Don't women nowadays have a chance at becoming doctors or scientists?"

"I'm not becoming anything," she shot back. "I'm just earning some money." But the question perturbed her.

As they went back to the floor, she thanked him with feeling.

He said, "You've got not-bad fingers."

That evening when she recounted her day to Charlie she didn't mention George Kenadjian. Was she entitled to feel attracted to a man who wasn't her husband? He wasn't as good-looking as Charlie, but he had a spark, or as LuAnne would have put it, he had a pulse.

For a few days, she hoped she would run into him again and she took special care with what she wore and whether she had lipstick on.

But she didn't see him.

Lottie rapidly developed a routine. First thing in the morning she would go to the floors and draw bloods, do throat cultures, and collect urines. In the lab she spun down the blood into a clear layer of serum, a yellow band of white cells, a dark, heavy band of red cells, then aspirated the serum with a pipette. She deposited the specimen on a slide, incubated it with reagent, then added the substrate and colorized it or read it in a tube in the spectro-photometer. She plated out the cultures with an inoculating loop and incubated them. After lunch she would read the previous day's cultures and the gram stains. If a pathogen was present, she'd identify it and do sensitivities. She took stat calls whenever they came in, and before she went home she made a check of all the floors and the emergency room.

Looking like a smallish rugby player, Dr. Mihiner charged in wherever Lottie was at different times during the day. She might be in a hospital room swabbing a patient's throat when he bulled his way over, thick-lipped. Or she was picking a colony from a plate and inoculating tubes of sugars in the lab when suddenly he was peering over her shoulder. Was he looking at her boobs? One afternoon she found him examining the lab book just after she had transcribed her results. Mostly, she saw him in the cafeteria, not surprising given how solid his body was, and how beefy his face. He had shaggy brown eyebrows and deep-set dark eyes and he shaved his head (occasionally she saw some gray fuzz behind an ear); in his long lab coat he seemed to stride or march rather than walk.

Most lunches and coffee breaks were the times she got to know the other lab techs. LuAnne was engaged to marry a round inhalation tech named Oliver who was as easygoing as she was. When she wasn't eating lunch with him, she would show the girls catalogs of silver patterns and china and glassware. "My head's not in the clouds," she would say. "It's in the catalogs."

"I'd keep my eye on Oliver if I were you," Trixie said.

"How far could he get with that belly?"

Trixie was divorced, with a freckled four-year-old son whom Lottie'd met at the hospital a couple of times. He was timid and red-eyed. A competitive swimmer, Trixie had married a long-distance runner she met at a statewide sports event and on their third anniversary he ran off with a discus thrower and left no forwarding address.

Trixie's parents were well heeled and she didn't have to work but she had taken the job as a way to find a man. LuAnne's Oliver had fixed Trixie up a few times and they had double-dated, but Trixie had her sights fixed through the doorway to the doctors' cafeteria. She came to work with large gold hoop earrings and festive dresses and high heels. In the halls and at lunch she always left her lab coat open so that her nice clothes and the outlines of her hopeful breasts showed.

Angela had never married; she lived with her aged mother and widowed sister in a small bungalow. She was a devout Catholic and when Dr. Mihiner teased her one day about the rash on her hands being stigmata, she called him a filthy Protestant and almost lost her job. Although she actually had less experience of the wide world than her younger colleagues, she saw herself as an older sister or chaperone who could advise them on household goods and clothes and how to keep their "beaus" in line.

Lottie felt well disposed toward these women, and so she was disappointed that their conversation did not interest her and that once she had mastered the lab routines, the other techs seemed unwilling to teach her anything.

"Why do the sugars turn different colors depending on the pathogen?"

"So you can tell them apart."

"Yes, but how does it happen?"

"It's a complicated chemical reaction," Trixie said. "How does 'periwinkle' look on me?" She shimmied her shoulders. "Would you believe a name like that? It's the 'in' shade."

LuAnne admitted to not knowing much more than she needed to, and not caring. "You're a rare bird," she told Lottie. "You'll fly away."

"I'm not going anywhere," Lottie said.

One time the centrifuge broke down and Lottie got a screwdriver and began taking it apart.

"Don't touch that!" Angela said. "It's not in your job description."

She took it apart anyway although it cost her an hour to figure what was wrong and half an hour to get the thing working. Dr. Mihiner came in while she was finishing up. "You fixed that?!" He put a tube in the centrifuge and when it spun down fine, he seemed baffled. And the other lab techs were a little more distant from her than they had been, it seemed to Lottie—except for LuAnne, who smiled and flapped her arms up and down.

After a while Lottie took to bolting her food and spending most of her lunch hour in the library. She sometimes found Dr. Mihiner there, round and sighing, reading. She realized that as she grew more sure of herself, she saw less of Mihiner.

One day when she came in, he got up from his seat and handed her a review article titled "Recent Advances in the Microbiology Lab." She was surprised and pleased and thanked him several times. A few weeks later he told her about a tissue culture experiment he was working on and he volunteered to show her the setup.

Lottie went into his small closet-room, where he explained his work with considerable excitement.

One day he appeared in the cafeteria and waved peremptorily to her to walk with him; she left her full tray on the table, and despite her greater height—she had a couple of inches on him, but was thinner and lighter, and felt less substantial—she found herself taking two or three small steps to each of his as if her feet were bound.

Mihiner said in the hallway, "Aren't you the one who does the blood gases?"

Lottie shook her head emphatically no. And as if she were saluting a sergeant, she said: "Lottie Hart here, sir."

"I know who you are," Mihiner said. "I hired you. What are you reading?"

Lottie showed him a microbiology text.

"A little knowledge is a dangerous thing . . ." Mihiner said as he strode out.

When the lunch hour was over, she returned to the lab. As she passed Mihiner's office, she heard through the closed door his big orotund voice raised in anger. He was answered by a smaller panicked voice; Lottie imagined a grasshopper rubbing its legs against each other frantically as winter closed in. She could not make out the words.

A few minutes later Trixie, who did the blood gases, slunk red-faced into the lab and sat down at her bench looking out the window. After Mihiner left, she began banging flasks and books around.

Lottie wanted to ask what had happened. Should she put an arm around distressed Trixie? But Lottie didn't know how to get close to a woman flailing away, who saw Lottie was there but ignored her. No one had ever yelled like that at Lottie, no one except her father. But her father knew she had a mind. What did Mihiner think about *her*? Would her turn come to get eviscerated? She hoped not to louse up, if Trixie had loused up. But it was entirely possible that Trixie hadn't done anything wrong—she was competent if unimaginative—and had merely crossed Mihiner in some way. Not sure she wanted to find out, Lottie left to go about her business on the different hospital floors. And she never did discover what had happened between Mihiner and Trixie; over the next few days, she imagined the other lab techs knew, although she had no proof, and she ended up uncertain where she stood with anyone.

Lottie was sitting on the side of their bed retching into the gray plastic wastebasket Charlie'd grabbed from under his desk. He sat beside her, holding her hair out of her eyes. "Do you have a barrette? Will a rubber band do? Let me get you a glass of water."

"I don't want any of that stinking water. There's oil in it." She retched again. "Maybe there's nuclear waste in it."

"Don't be silly," he said. "I drink that same water. You probably caught a bug at the hospital. You gotta quit that job."

It was the first spontaneous mention he had ever made of her job.

"I don't mind being a tech, Charlie, honest. If you earned more money, I'd be entombed in the house." She put an arm around his shoulder.

"You think of our house as a tomb?" He looked hurt as he wiped her lips and chin with tissues.

"Well, not our house in particular."

The next morning the doorbell rang early. A cup of coffee in her hand, the across-the-street neighbor, a tall, big-busted woman in a cardigan over a dress printed with sunflowers, invited them to a party at her house in the evening. Behind her, a black Labrador retriever paced back and forth on the stoop.

The odor of Ladja Kowiezca's hot coffee hit Lottie all at once and she managed to open the screen door and vomit off the side of the stoop. The Labrador looked on with concern.

"She needs a doctor," Charlie said.

"I need a shovel, is what I need," Lottie said.

That night the Kowiezca living room was decorated with pink and blue streamers and helium-filled balloons and the neighbors congratulated Lottie and Charlie and said it would be the first baby born on the block in seven years.

Afterward, Charlie sat up in bed with a pillow behind his head and watched her undress.

"Cut it out," she said. "I can't even unhook my bra."

"I'll do it, you fumbler," he grinned.

"You're looking at me the way I look at blood smears." She turned off the overhead light and the lamp on her side of the bed.

He reached over and turned it back on.

"For God's sake, Charlie, you can't see anything yet!"

He undid her bra and turned her toward him and looked at her breasts.

"Do you want a ruler? A tape measure?"

He cupped them from underneath with his large hands.

"A scale?" She grinned. "Hey, I remind you of Ladja Kowiezca?"

Charlie said, "Do you think it's true?"

She shrugged her shoulders, and her breasts rose a little and fell back into his hands.

"Did you feel—this way—the other time?"

"I felt scared. I don't know what I felt."

He pulled her gently down with him onto the bed, raised the half-slip up over her head, and snuggled his nose into her armpit.

"What are you doing?" She ran her fingers through his blond hair.

Gently, carefully, like a large buck with complicated, branching antlers, he nuzzled his way over her breasts and her belly. He began easing down her panty hose.

She lifted her backside to help him and wriggled out of the stockings. He turned her onto her belly and closed his eyes and slowly ran his nose down over her spine.

She giggled. "What are you up to, Charlie?"

"You mean, what am I *down* to."

"What're you *doing*, wiseass?"

"Honestly?"

"Mhm."

"I'm using all my senses to try to find him."

She was moved, and also upset remembering pulling his head down between her legs in the cold fall leaves so long ago. She aimed for a lighthearted tone: "Well, you're sniffing at the wrong oven." But the line plunked. She imagined she sounded like LuAnne. Lottie turned onto her back and put her arms around Charlie's head, and pulled his face up to her face and kissed him hard on the mouth. "Forget about him," she said. She reached for his penis, which opened out like a telescope into her hand.

Charlie shook his head. "I'm not banging around in there."

"He's a big maybe, Charlie. Maybe he's there. Maybe he'll stay there." She sucked at his nipples.

"Are you crying?" he asked her.

"Let's make love."

"Why are you crying?"

"Make love to me, Charlie."

He shook his head.

"What's the idea here? Let life bang him around, not his father?"

Charlie grinned. "I didn't know I was so clever."

"Just the prospect of fatherhood has turned you into a philosopher. You mean we're not going to make love until he's born?"

"Do you think there's really a baby in there?"

"I don't know," she said.

"We could go to the emergency room."

Never again. "Anyway, we have a nine a.m. appointment." After a moment she asked, "Why do you keep saying 'him,' 'he'? Do you want a boy?"

"I don't hear you saying 'she.'"

"I've thought maybe—that other baby—was a boy. Boys are fragile."

"Do you think so?"

"Premature birth, stillbirth—much more common in boys. All kinds of neural tube defects—spina bifida, anencephaly—"

"You really looked into this," he said gravely.

They talked all night. From their bed, their arms around each other, they watched the sun come up splayed out orange and pink and gold across the huge horizon. Slowly it drew in its bright bands to form a rising ball of fire.

Although Charlie felt she ought to phone in her resignation rather than chance catching a cold or worse, Lottie gave two weeks' notice at the hospital.

On her last day the other techs treated her to lunch at the Hounddog, where they toasted her with milkshakes. Dessert was a seven-layer cake with HERE'S TO LOTTIE'S FIRST! written in white script on the chocolate icing. Lottie thought she detected a tear in Angela's eye but it might have been the tear in her own. It annoyed her how leaky she'd become. They had chipped in on a present for the baby, a clown jack-in-the-box with a red polka-dot shirt and a mournful face. Lottie was tickled but also vaguely worried. Wasn't it overconfident to accept presents for him or her as if a live birth were a reasonable expectation, almost a sturdy fact? As soon as she got home, Lottie took the jack-in-the-box up to the attic. Why clutter up the house?

A week later the mailman brought a book wrapped in brown paper. It was *Microbe Hunters*, by Paul de Kruif, and on the title page, in small tight black letters, Dr. Arlow A. Mihiner had written GOOD LUCK, MRS. HART, and signed his name.

From being a slender young woman, Lottie rapidly grew bulky, someone you made way for, solid—oh, that the baby would prove as solid! She was relieved and proud to have a public pregnancy, to be entitled to a seat on the bus or a place at the head of the checkout line. When a child asked to touch her belly, Lottie beamed. She bought herself a thick cardboard-covered, black-and-white marble-patterned composition book, with lined pages, on which she wrote in expansive cursive: "dark patches on face," "linea nigra (line from navel to pubic bone) due to chloasma, melasma . . . ," "spider veins, varicose veins . . ." She reveled in every discomfort and disfiguration. And she enrolled herself and Charlie in the first Lamaze class in town.

Amid her mounting fear and excitement—He kicks! He kicks!—she felt a vague sense of loss. Unaccustomed to the balmy weather, she thought it might be the northern fall she missed, and so she looked through pamphlets from the chamber of commerce for the few places in Texas where you could see leaves changing color. They had names like the Lost Maples State Natural Area, Winnsboro Autumn Trails . . . But they were hundreds of miles away and you needed reservations because of the crowds.

Was it being so far from her parents that had her a little down? She had heard of women who wanted their mothers in the delivery room. Someone had even told her about a first-time mother who put *her* mother's name unwittingly on the birth certificate. But there were times Jeanie didn't even seem to be Lottie's real mother, seemed more like a character in one of the books Jeanie was always reading—Did her mother never read a biography, a history book, something true? And Lottie didn't want her mother around with all that smoke and certainly not her father with his edginess, his carping.

There was a Sears in town but although they went to look, she was too superstitious to buy even a bassinet before the baby arrived. And the materials the different onesies were made of felt coarse or plastic-spongy and the seams stuck out. At the Bump, the maternity–baby clothes shop in town, nothing met her standards either, not even the onesies she couldn't afford—although she couldn't figure what was wrong with them.

Lottie dreamed of her grandmother at her old Singer spinning a pure gold receiving blanket for the baby. She woke happy to the hilt.

And then she wept.

Lottie was sitting at the kitchen table in her bathrobe drinking a cup of tea and tensely watching a fictionalized television show about the Mercury 7 astronauts. Scott Carpenter ditched his space capsule, its mission completed, in the Atlantic Ocean. The spacecraft quickly began to sink: "Get me out of here! Get me out of here!" Carpenter begged.

Suddenly her lap and legs were wet. She looked down at her feet in their pink terry cloth slippers. She moved another chair toward her and lifted her feet onto it and opened her bathrobe and looked carefully at her wet thighs and legs. No clots, no blood. She touched her fingers to her thighs, held her wet fingers up to the sunny window. "Clear! Clear! Clear!" She kissed her wet fingers.

At the hospital Charlie waited in the hall as they shaved her pubic hair and gave her an enema. After she washed and dried herself, Lottie dotted her thighs and buttocks and ears with a freesia-scented perfume her grandmother used to wear.

"Let him in, please," she said.

The nurse wriggled her nose and shook her head.

"I need him!"

The nurse said, "You need a good baby. You don't want any distractions."

"He hardly talks!"

The anesthesiologist left the room carrying Lottie's chart. "I took a chance you were you when I saw the name," he said to Charlie. "I'm a Michigan alum, class of fifty—"

"Charlie! Charlie!" Lottie yelled out the open door.

He came running.

So did the obstetrician, a man almost as large as Charlie with red hair and beard, who wore a red bandanna around his neck.

Lottie clutched Charlie's hand.

The obstetrician said, "I've had husbands pass out on me in the waiting room."

"Please," Lottie said.

"Have you ever fainted?" he asked Charlie.

"When I got my leg injured."

"I'll vouch for him," the anesthesiologist said. "This guy was the greatest running back—"

"You play pro?" The obstetrician looked at him with new interest.

Charlie shook his head grimly.

The obstetrician shrugged his shoulders.

"He was unbelievable," the anesthesiologist jumped in. "Fans cried in the stands when he was downed. I got drunk—"

"Gentlemen, gentlemen!" The nurse stamped her foot.

The obstetrician positioned himself between Lottie's legs. "Okay, pardner, put on a pair of gloves pronto, and a gown," he said to Charlie.

Lottie felt a tearing pain as if her insides were being ripped out. She longed to bear down and push every damn thing out of her, push all these people out of her room. Even Charlie.

"Hold on, hold on!" The obstetrician yelled calmly.

As she had been taught in Lamaze class, she began panting, keeping her eyes on Charlie, who stood in the corner, one attendant tying the strings of a green hospital gown behind him at his neck and waist, another helping him put on gloves.

Lottie shuddered in great waves.

"Okay, girl, just give us three good pushes. That's all we need." The obstetrician positioned Charlie next to him.

She held on to the sides of the gurney and bore down with all her strength.

"It's the head!" Charlie shouted. "He's looking at me! He's got bright blue eyes."

"All babies have blue eyes," the nurse said.

"Here comes the right shoulder," the doctor said. "Catch him like a football, Charlie!"

"Is he alive?" Lottie demanded.

Charlie caught the baby between his gloved hands, and in one smooth movement tucked him to his chest, his shoulders hunched.

"Let me see! Let me see!" Lottie rose up on her elbows.

As the doctor clamped the umbilical cord, the bloody, bald, round baby girl squirmed and cried out in Charlie's arms.

Lottie cried out, too. She opened her arms and Charlie handed the living child over; and Lottie held her high above her head and levitated with her up, up out of bed, through the unopened window and way out toward the sun.

A strange little shadow or undertow: she found herself confused and mildly annoyed, even a bit ashamed—of what? That the baby wasn't a boy? Lottie was too embarrassed by her reaction to discuss it with anyone—not with Ladja Kowiezca, who came to the hospital with a present of a pink plastic cup and plate and spoon. Nor with Trixie McKloskey, whose lab coat was opened wide over a lush red sweater, her nipples winking. Nor with LuAnne, who sat on Lottie's bed cracking bubble gum and jokes—*"Did you hear that Marlene Dietrich's had so many face lifts she's got a beard?"*—her arm around the shoulders of happy, chunky Oliver. For sure, she wouldn't talk to her father about her disappointment. He had said on the phone, "A grand-daughter," then added, "How nice." Not even with Charlie. Where was her grandmother? Would *The Feminine Mystique* or *The Second Sex* have anything to say about her feelings of mortification? These books, mentioned on television, weren't at the gift shop or on the library cart that the hospital volunteer wheeled around mornings. And the urgent physical needs of the baby rapidly took Lottie's attention away from self-scrutiny; soon the only book she could concentrate on was Spock.

At home Evelyn wailed bitterly in the middle of the night—did she know she wasn't a boy?—and the only thing that helped was motion. Lottie would struggle to strap her screaming baby into the infant car seat and then back out of the black driveway as quickly as she could. As soon as the car began to move, Ev quieted, and after a few moments she slept. But when Lottie stopped at a corner or at one of the two traffic lights in town, Evelyn began to moan. So Lottie kept to the highways, empty at that hour. Their gasoline bills mounted, and Lottie was afraid she'd fall asleep at the wheel and kill them both. She woke Charlie, and he started riding with Evelyn during the night, since Lottie was breast-feeding and needed her sleep.

During the day, Ev seemed sunny and sturdy and placid. She was big like Charlie, blonde and blue-eyed like both her parents, and quietly sweet-natured.

Sturdy, sturdy, Lottie told herself, but it didn't stop her hovering over Evelyn. When she would reach with a smile for a shadow, for a dragonfly, for Charlie's trophies, Lottie would reach, too, as if there might be some danger she could avert. When the mailman took to timing his arrival for after Evelyn's nap, Lottie found herself worrying about letter bombs, and when the neighbor ladies on the block stopped in to hold "our Crocus," "our Buttercup," "Our Yellow Rose of Texas," Lottie made them wash their hands up to the elbows for sixty seconds and she stood close to them while they held the baby, holding her arms tight against her sides so she wouldn't stretch them out to form a safety net.

It wasn't until Evelyn doubled her weight, then tripled it and slept through the night that Lottie was convinced the child was real, was hers, would live.

She found herself annoyed that, as soon as Ev could crawl, she would make a beeline for Charlie—did everyone prefer boys? She told herself that after all she was there all the time, like the sun or the moon, while Charlie made brief appearances, a dazzling comet in the night sky. Surely it was a good thing for a child to have more than one attachment? It was important for a girl to love her father, wasn't it?

During Evelyn's naps Lottie took up the book Dr. Mihiner had given her about famous "microbe hunters." It was written in a gushy style full of exclamation points, but the work these men had done, much of which she knew about from college courses—grinding the first microscopes, uncovering the mystery of fermentation, conquering syphilis—was thrilling.

There were no women in the book unless you counted the references to Madame Pasteur:

> That night Pasteur turned over and over in his bed.
> He whispered his hopes and fears to Madame Pasteur—she couldn't advise him but she comforted him. She understood everything but couldn't explain away his worries.
> She was his perfect assistant . . .

or to Mrs. Metchnikoff:

> With Olga and the children flapping along and keeping up as best they could, Metchnikoff hurried to Vienna to proclaim his theory that we are immune to germs because our bodies have wandering cells to gobble germs up.

She identified with the scientists. But then she would remember she wasn't a man, and she felt small and ashamed. Maybe one day she'd write a book about women scientists—were there any besides the two Curies, Marie and her daughter Irène? She imagined a children's story in which she'd be carried to the lab in a coach drawn by rats, winged rats, and driven by her grandmother. She'd read it to her daughter—she had a daughter, she, Lottie!

In the meantime, she found a babysitter a few blocks from the hospital and went back to work as a technician. They were sorely in need of money, and Charlie didn't argue.

Mornings she would leave his cornflakes on the table and draw a heart on a napkin with an orange felt-tip pen. When she let herself out the front door, Evelyn strapped to her chest chortling in a baby carrier, and then walked a block to catch the bus to the babysitter's, and then another two blocks by herself to the hospital, she would often find herself humming, "Oh, what a beautiful morning!"

*   *   *

One winter evening Lottie came home from a double shift at work—both Angela and Trixie were out with flu—and found the house dark and cold. Upstairs the TV was on.

"Charlie?"

She switched on a lamp, unzipped Evelyn's snuggly, and lifted the child out. She unbuttoned Evelyn's red coat and laid her in the playpen in the living room with her coat and leggings still on.

"Cold," Ev pulled herself up to standing, holding on to the slats.

Lottie turned on each of the lamps in the living room and the overhead light in the kitchen. The thermostat in the hall read fifty degrees.

She walked down the basement steps to feel the boiler. *Colder than a polar bear's cock.*

On the second floor in their bedroom the only light came from the television. An interviewer wearing an Astrakhan hat and sheepskin coat and gloves held up the microphone to a football player one and a half times his size. It was snowing heavily. The player kept his hands under his thin number 11 jersey, opening and closing them into fists. He rubbed his fingers across his wide chest. His hands looked like panicked animals scurrying for cover.

"The football feels like a rock," the player answered in a Southern accent. "You can't throw it. My receivers can't catch it. And you can't get any traction in these fool sneakers."

She switched the light on and turned the television off.

Charlie lay asleep in his coat under a quilt her grandmother had sewn. It was deep blue with large red and white hibiscus flowers in the center.

"Charlie." She shook him.

He turned away from her onto his side.

She rocked him back and forth. He turned over onto his stomach.

"For God's sake, Charlie, it's freezing in here! Are you sick?" She felt his forehead, and with the other hand felt her own. There was no difference and for a crazy instant, she was relieved. "What's the matter with you? Did you call the oil company?"

He shook his head no.

She walked downstairs to the kitchen and dialed the emergency oil number.

She carried Evelyn upstairs and put her in bed under the covers next to Charlie.

Lottie looked at the dead television screen.

Ev crawled over her father's chest to the far edge of the bed.

"She's going to fall!" Lottie cried.

Charlie swung an arm out like a clamp and missed. Evelyn hit the floor headfirst, screaming.

Lottie ran around the foot of the bed and picked her up in her arms. Evelyn continued to scream, and struggled out of Lottie's grip toward Charlie.

He sat up slowly and reached for her. Evelyn's red coat and blonde hair shone bright against his gray face.

Lottie felt over Evelyn's head and then her arms and legs, and went down to the kitchen for ice, which she wrapped in a dish towel. But whenever she applied it to Ev's forehead, the child squirmed and screamed in Charlie's arms.

Lottie gave up and sat down on the bed.

When Evelyn quieted, Charlie handed her over. Lottie hugged her, then put her on the floor.

"What's wrong, Charlie? Did you go on a bender?" He hardly ever drank but she couldn't think of anything else.

Charlie's face looked as if it were carved out of weathered wood.

"Oh God, Charlie, what's wrong with you?"

Trying to attract her father, Evelyn tugged at the quilt. Lottie reached into her pocket and handed her a ring of keys. Evelyn jiggled the keys.

"You didn't pay the oil bill for three months."

He nodded.

Jingle-jingle.

"Did you go to school?"

"Yes."

"Did you go to the gym?"

"Not today."

Evelyn threw the keys across the room. They slid under the TV table.

"Why not?"

"I go Mondays, Wednesdays, and Fridays."

"Keys, keys," Evelyn called mirthfully, jumping alongside the bed and pointing.

"You don't go every day? I thought you went every day."

"I'm not in training." He laughed hoarsely.

"Well, train. Train for something. Swim. You're supposed to swim. For your leg."

"I'm a team man."

"Keys, keys," Evelyn hollered.

"There's a swimming team," Lottie yelled over Evelyn's yelling. "There's probably a goddamn walking team."

"Stop cursing," Charlie said, but she could barely hear him over Evelyn's bawling. "When did you start cursing?" Then he said, "A walking team? What are you talking about? I can hardly walk." Lottie went down on all fours and retrieved the keys from under the TV table and put them in Evelyn's outstretched hand. Charlie watched the black set.

"Are you going to the bowling alley tonight? Are you working too much? Maybe you're working too much."

Jingle-jingle.

"Don't worry about me," Charlie smiled.

Idiotically, she smiled back.

In the kitchen with her coat on she warmed a bottle and heated up a can of turkey noodle soup. The previous night, before she left for work, she had defrosted a rock Cornish hen. With some fancy stuffing, it might hit the spot, raise his spirits. If his spirits were down. She found a box of rice pilaf in the cabinet and started the water boiling.

When the doorbell rang, she gave the oil man a check for two hundred dollars and watched him back the truck into the driveway.

Charlie leaned over the kitchen sink and patted handfuls of cold water on his face.

"I have to be at the bowling alley in twenty minutes."

"Eat a little soup. It's hot."

"Save it for me. I'll eat it when I come home."

Charlie returned at eleven with snow in his hair and on his coat. She thought for a moment that he had been at the football game on the television set but that game had taken place in Nebraska. She looked out the living room window: a wet snow was falling. She shook her head, trying to shake off a feeling of unreality.

"Who would think, snow in Texas." She ladled out the turkey soup she'd heated for the second time this evening and sat down. "How was work?"

"Fine."

She chewed on a cracker.

He asked, "How's Evelyn?"

"Asleep. She practically has an egg on her forehead, an Easter egg, all red and black and blue. From where she fell."

"I can't even catch a kid anymore. My own kid."

Lottie winced. "Otherwise, she's all right."

He sighed.

She took up a spoonful of soup and waited for it to cool. "Were there many bowlers?"

"Just four."

"Do you want some crackers?" She held the plate out to him.

"No. Thanks."

She nodded.

"Well, I read five positive beta-hemolytic strep cultures today at the lab. They're calling me the Strep Queen." She smiled. "Do you want me to ladle in some more? Keep it hot?"

Charlie shook his head.

"Where are you, Charlie? Don't you like the soup? It's just Campbell's. From a can."

"Yes," he said. "I like it fine."

"Then eat it."

"I ate some," he yawned. "I'm not very hungry."

"Let me serve you the hen. You'll like the hen. I made a gravy for it." She went over to the oven and took out the black roasting pan. She lifted off the lid and fragrant steam gusted up into the kitchen. She pierced the bird with a large fork and lifted it up onto the carving board.

"Black or white?" she asked.

Charlie was asleep in his chair.

"Shit, Charlie," she said, loud.

She cleaned up the kitchen and checked Evelyn, who was breathing gently and evenly in her crib upstairs. She looked at the newspaper. On the front page was a story about a woman who had shot her husband and two small children. There was an article about snowstorms in Texas. There was a paragraph listing Vietcong and South Vietnamese and American body counts. She could not concentrate.

She woke Charlie, who lumbered upstairs.

She showered and brushed her teeth and got into bed beside him. He was asleep on his back, breathing heavily. She unbuttoned his striped pajama top and rubbed her breasts against his chest. She unbuttoned his fly and took his penis in her mouth. She sucked and sucked. He touched her hair. She sucked. She watched the clock on the windowsill. It had a fluorescent face and hands. After five minutes she felt him grow erect. She took her mouth off his penis and straddled him, then reached for his penis. It was gone. She kneeled between his legs and went down on him again. After five more minutes, he put his hands on her face and lifted her mouth off him. He turned over onto his stomach. Jaws aching, she sat looking past the clock out the window at the thickly falling snow.

Because she had mastitis shortly after Evelyn's birth and was applying ice packs to her breasts, she remembered the tingling and stinging of her nipples more sharply than she remembered Indira Gandhi's becoming prime minister of India. Lottie knew vaguely that Gandhi was the first woman anywhere in the world to hold such an important position. Was Indira related to Mahatma? She didn't think about it much.

Evelyn had had a fever of 104 the day the Texas Tower Sniper shot fourteen people to become the first of an endless line of mass school shooters. The baby bit Lottie's nipple, hard, three feedings in a row. Lottie started weaning her off the breast there and then, although Evelyn cried inconsolably and threw her bottles on the floor and tried to suck on Lottie's shoulder through her blouse and her neck and her hair.

Riots and looting and the calling out of the National Guard occurred across the country in a faraway corner of Lottie's consciousness while she was at the supermarket comparing the vitamin content of different Gerber baby cereals, and humming along with the Muzak arrangement of "I Want to Hold Your Hand." Lottie didn't have a clue whether the Beatles were more influential than Jesus. But she could tell almost exactly what Evelyn had eaten by the different stinks of her feces: she had never before realized how sweet breast-fed babies smelled.

A week after the snowfall Lottie woke and asked Charlie, "Is it Evelyn?"

Charlie was sitting up in bed looking out the window.

"Charlie, is it—is it my body?"

"What?" He did not turn to her.

"Well—" Her voice was low but she forced herself to go on. "Do you know we haven't made love for, for—a while . . ." She whispered to his back and his bowed head. "I tell myself we're both so busy but still . . . I get undressed in the bathroom." Did she need to speak about the white jagged lines across her hips and belly, the vague looseness in her breasts and buttocks, although her legs were still good?

She got out of bed, went to the dresser, and shimmied a pair of underpants up under her nightgown, then sat down on the bed next to him, stretching out one leg and pulling up her panty hose in a leisurely way. "Does it bother you?"

"What?"

"My body. Since I had Evelyn."

"I don't see any difference," Charlie smiled.

She touched his cheek and forehead lightly, then cupped his chin in her hand. "Have you stopped looking at me, Charlie?"

He extricated himself. "Of course not." He patted her shoulder.

It crossed her mind that he had another woman, but she dismissed the thought as a sign of panic.

The next morning, before she left for work, she asked Charlie how his thesis was going. He was lying in bed, the shades still drawn.

"What thesis?"

"What do you mean, what thesis? 'The Economics of College Football'!" She pulled the shades down hard so that they snapped all the way back up. A gray morning light entered the room.

"They didn't approve the topic." His eyes remained closed as he spoke.

"They didn't approve it! Why not?"

"It was too inclusive."

"So what did you narrow it down to?" His dungarees and gray sweatshirt and briefs were on the floor on his side of the bed and she bent and picked them up. They gave off a stale, musty odor.

"I'm not interested in writing about college football anymore."

"What are you talking about? When did they turn the topic down? Sit up, Charlie, for God's sake."

He straightened out the white and blue hibiscus cover so it came smoothly to his chin. "Three months ago."

"Why didn't you tell me?"

"I told you."

"You couldn't have! Come on."

"I did."

"What was I doing when you told me?"

After a while he said, "I think you were reading . . . some book about laboratory techniques."

She sat down next to him on the bed. "Was I paying attention? Did you have my attention?" She apologized several times, then took his hand and put it to her lips. It was limp as if the fiber had been pressure-cooked out of it. "Did you come up with another topic?"

"I'm doing research."

She nodded. "Are you *sure* you told me they rejected your topic?"

"I believe I did."

"But you're not *sure*."

"I remember telling you." He edged the cover up higher until it covered his chin and lower lip. Would he pull it up completely and disappear?

She nodded again. "And what's your new topic?"

"I told you, I'm still thinking."

"Is this"—she patted the bed—"your think tank?"

And then she started apologizing again.

*   *   *

When she came home from work that evening, she went straight upstairs without taking off her coat or Evelyn's. She switched on the overhead light in the black bedroom. "Charlie, you have to get used to people not wanting your autograph—"

He rose slowly, squinting, and, in his faded striped pajamas, moved heavily, clumsily, out of the room. Was his bulk greater, his flesh slack? Once in a nature movie about hibernation she had seen a giant brown mountain bear slouching through snowy underbrush into a dark cave.

Still carrying Evelyn, who was calling "Cha-Cha-Pa! Cha-Cha-Pa!" as if it were a rhumba tune, Lottie followed him downstairs, turning on the lights behind him. "I wish we knew a famous person who isn't famous anymore . . ."

"What are you talking about?"

"Anyone would feel sick to go from being Mr. Somebody to being Mr. Nobody." She followed him into the living room.

Charlie laughed. "That's your problem, not mine." He reached out his heavy arm and swatted the trophies, one by one, nonchalantly, almost playfully, off the mantelpiece. They bumped and clattered onto the wooden floor.

In Lottie's arms, Evelyn chortled with delight.

Lottie put her in the playpen, then squatted down and picked the trophies up and carried them carefully to the couch. She got a rag and cleaned some dust off the mantel, then turned to the trophies, easing the rag gently over the dents and scratches as if they were wounds.

"You should have married one of them and cut out the middleman."

"I take care of them because they're *yours*! Don't you know that?"

He eased himself into the reclining chair and lay back, his head against a doily crocheted by her grandmother, his eyes closed. His whole body shook slightly as if he were an old man.

"Is it not playing football anymore? It must be very hard to give up something you always wanted to do. Maybe everything else feels beside the point, gratuitous." She wiped her wet eyes with the back of her hand. "You'll find something, Charlie. If not economics, something else will turn you on. And after a while it will feel natural, even beloved . . ."

Charlie farted.

He seemed as startled as she by the sound. He looked momentarily sheepish.

"Again! Again!" Evelyn made happy blowing noises with her mouth and jumped up and down in the playpen and held her arms out to her father.

The baby became the focus of Lottie's life. Although she wasn't a boy, Evelyn was a beauty of the "All-American" hue: fair and rosy and blue-eyed, she had at first looked like the baby in the Ivory soap ads, then like the toddler on the zwieback biscuit wrappers, and she seemed destined to become the Breck shampoo girl. Wherever they went, Evelyn was noticed and admired, and this lit up dark Lottie, ignored and unseen by Charlie. She sewed her daughter complicated dresses and baked cookies shaped like teddy bears and pigs and elephants, and talked to her as if she were an adult. Evelyn was seemingly docile during the day and precocious, catching on quickly to what Lottie wanted: she ate without fuss, allowed herself to be handled easily and bathed, and copied Lottie's words and intonations, to the delight of both of them. She loved numbers and letters and drew them quite successfully, holding the crayon in her fist.

But she was stubborn about her bowel habits, often refusing to go when she was set on the potty. Lottie tried offering her an M&M when she sat down, and another one if she made a doody. Ev would take the first M&M and then get off the potty, foregoing the second. Lottie let her write letters on a pad on the toilet and she liked that, but she defecated in the toilet maybe only once out of four times.

One Monday morning after both of these maneuvers had failed, fifteen minutes into the bus trip to work, Evelyn, sitting on her mother's lap facing her, got a concentrated, faraway look on her face. She grunted softly a few times. Then she grimaced, her face whitening. Slowly the odor spread. A woman in a raccoon coat sitting on their right and a man in a postman's uniform on their left stood up and wended their way to the back of the crowded bus. Three women standing facing Lottie and Evelyn moved toward the front, one of them excusing herself. Although the bus picked up more passengers and several people were sharing straps, the aisle in front of

Lottie and Evelyn had emptied and there were two vacant seats on either side of them.

This happened another time that week. The following week Evelyn was continent on the bus until Friday when, sitting in Lottie's lap, she again softly began to grunt. Lottie slapped her twice hard across the face. As she tried to soothe her screaming, stinking baby, she had an image of everyone getting off the bus and going to the police.

Lottie bought several books, but nothing worked. Finally in a fury one Friday night after she got back from work, Lottie took the diaper off her thirty-two-month-old (Weren't girls supposed to toilet train earlier and easier than boys?) and let her run naked around the house.

"What are you doing?" Charlie asked from the couch, where he was lying reading the newspaper.

"Do you care?" Lottie yelled in his direction.

Every time Evelyn urinated or had a bowel movement, Lottie shouted "Bad girl!," stuck Evelyn's nose in it, and put her on the potty. By Monday she was trained.

(Years and years later Lottie was so bothered by the recollection that she never told teenage Evelyn how she had toilet-trained her and she never attempted to train the two more babies she would go on to have, both sons; she wouldn't even housebreak dogs, and so they had to stay outside all the time.)

But in those days, those diminishing Charlie days, it seemed to Lottie she was doing what had to be done: her life stank and she couldn't have her child give her shit in the morning on her way to work.

Working at the lab at least cleared her mind, gave her a sense of purpose, although it was hardly a vocation. (Did women have vocations besides motherhood? She worried she was daily betraying her natural vocation.)

But nights . . .

Sleeping next to Charlie, who was dead to her, Lottie began feeling dead herself; she tried masturbating in their bed, but it didn't awaken him, let alone turn him on. Squeezing her nipples hard no longer gave her feelings in her uterus—her nipples just hurt. Rubbing her clitoris even with a fingerful of spit didn't take her anywhere, it was irritating; and she eventually gave herself a urinary tract infection with that shenanigan—she certainly wasn't having intercourse, so what else could have done it?—and had to go see her gynecologist and start a course of antibiotics. Often she lay hours in bed awake, restless, flummoxed. Or she read half the night but had trouble concentrating.

The childcare person called in sick on a Monday morning and Charlie had classes so Lottie took Evelyn to work with her, although she'd never seen anyone take a child to work. There was a coat closet the techs all used that opened onto the lab and like a doll, Evelyn sat quietly on the floor on Lottie's folded-up jacket doing puzzles Lottie'd brought for her, making creatures out of the play dough Lottie kept moist in a plastic bag. Fortunately, Mihiner didn't appear in the lab that day, the other techs stayed mum, and LuAnne kept an eye on Ev when Lottie had to leave to go up to a floor. At lunch Ev was understandably restless, and so she and Lottie explored parts of the hospital Lottie considered safe—the vegetable garden, the gift shop, the library, the cafeteria. In their roamings, Evelyn came upon a place Lottie hadn't known existed: the on-call room. It had six cots, a refrigerator, a small hot plate, a TV, two bathrooms. A man Lottie's age was asleep on one of the cots and Lottie and Ev got a kick out of tiptoeing around the room without waking him.

That night in bed it occurred to a wide-awake, overtired Lottie that maybe she could occasionally sleep with her daughter in the on-call room. It seemed improbable she'd get away with it but yet . . . The next week she packed a change of clothes for both of them, dropped Ev at Betty-Jo's in the morning, and after an eight-hour day at the lab, picked up her daughter and took her back to the hospital cafeteria for dinner. Ev now "knew" the hospital, so she felt at home, and yet it was an adventure. Lottie left a phone message for Charlie and heard nothing back. She and Evelyn bedded down in the back of the on-call room, the two of them on one cot. First-year residents (they were all men) doing overnight call were the only people who came and went, and as long as they were able to snatch their occasional ragged hour of sleep undisturbed, they didn't seem to notice the woman and small child who were asleep in the back of the room. And toilet-trained and a good sleeper, Ev made it quietly, quietly, uneventfully through the

night! For a bitter moment, Lottie worried she'd never again attract attention from anyone, anywhere, but she came to see that these young men,
zombies after thirty-six-hour shifts, would not have been aroused if, in the
middle of the night, the models who peopled *Playboy* centerfolds appeared
in the on-call room in all their naked splendor. And so Lottie calmed down.
And one or two nights a week they slept at the hospital.

Betty-Jo, who took care of Evelyn on weekdays, reported that she ate,
drank, seemed absorbed in play alone and also with other kids. This calmed
Lottie even more, cheered her—Lottie and Ev: with it during the day,
adventuresome the occasional night. Mother and daughter. For sure, they
spent most nights a week and every weekend at home with Charlie, but
Charlie often took off, who knew where? She couldn't get an answer out of
him. She tried not to know how sad she was.

She was assigned regularly now to draw bloods in the vascular ward; she
had become, hard to believe, a crackerjack phlebotomist. (And it was good
to be a crackerjack somewhere, at something!) And one afternoon, like a
white rabbit out of a long-empty magician's hat, there was that George
Kenadjian fellow—taking blood again. Kenadjian wore a black-and-white
bandanna around his ponytail, and his muscled arms stretched his white
jacket sleeves. She remembered the terrain of the skin of his arms as she felt
for his veins. Kenadjian didn't notice her, seemed to be concentrating
intensely: he was taking blood out of an earlobe and she saw that his patient
was a quadruple amputee. She focused on the foot of the man she was trying
to get a butterfly into. After a while she looked again in Kenadjian's direction. He was bending over and she saw the taut cloth of the back of his
jacket.

She was lubricating!

How long . . .

Afterward, as she walked past the nurse's station, she waved, surprising
herself, to Kenadjian. He looked at her quizzically for a moment through
the window, then waved back.

Frightened and emboldened, she entered.

He was writing notes.

"How's it going?" she asked, trying to sound nonchalant.

He looked up at her, focused on her, but he seemed confused, almost blank as if he couldn't place her.

She shifted her weight from one foot to the other. "I learned what you taught me."

"Yeah?" He smiled.

She pushed up the sleeve of her sweater and slapped her biceps.

"Ahh," he said. "Aha. Okay." And now she could tell he knew her. "That was long ago and far away," he said. "I was a first-year, maybe a second . . . How're you doing?"

She nodded.

A nurse with a voluminous afro looked their way. "She's the best phlebotomist on the floor."

Lottie flushed with pleasure. She said, pointing at Kenadjian, "There's my teacher."

Kenadjian said, "I was green myself. But drawing blood, that was my thing." He handed over his bloods to the nurse, then looked hard at Lottie and took them back. "You still work in the lab?"

She nodded, embarrassed, remembering he'd asked her way back then why she wasn't training to be a doctor or a scientist.

He said, "What say I walk you down there? You can tell me how it's been going."

Lottie stiffened but smiled.

"What's your name, I don't remember your name."

"Lottie Hart," she said.

"Funny name. Come on, let's go, Lotta Heart."

Lottie continued to smile but didn't move.

"What is it?" he laughed. "You have some secret route you don't want to divulge?"

"She's scared," the nurse said. "Give her a minute."

"I'm not scared," Lottie lied with great force.

"Then come on," Kenadjian said.

They walked beside each other in the thronged halls without speaking. She felt as if she were moving through an electrified field. A volunteer was rolling a patient on a gurney down the center of the hallway and Lottie and

George each moved in opposite directions to avoid a collision. To Lottie's relief, they met again behind the volunteer at the head of the gurney. They all laughed.

Just before they reached the lab, Kenadjian handed her the bloods and said, "Why don't you come to my house for dinner tonight?"

"We haven't said two words to each other."

He laughed. "But I remember you now, I really do."

She got out, "I remember *you*," and shifted the tubes of blood from one hand to the other. "But I can't—have dinner. I have a child."

"He doesn't eat?" Kenadjian grinned.

"She."

"Better yet."

"I mean, I'm married."

"Well, so am I, sort of. My wife left me."

Lottie felt her face flush with hope. "So you're alone. I'm not. Alone. Not really."

"Come over tonight. You can tell me about your marriage. Or not. You don't have to tell me. Just bring your kid. How old is she?"

"Three," she said breathlessly. "Three and a half."

"Six o'clock." He wrote his address on a piece of paper. "Any food restrictions? Allergies? Lactose intolerant? Celiac disease?"

She shook her head. "I need to think this over."

"No, you don't."

"Yes, I do."

"*You* came after *me*."

She blushed harder.

He touched one of the blood tubes in her hands. "Six o'clock." And walked away.

The rest of the afternoon Lottie worried what Ev would tell her father about the evening; she was a big babbler, and there was no way of predicting what she might say nor any way to shape the story. Lottie wouldn't tell a three-year-old to lie to her father; that would be to introduce a shadow into Ev's relationship with Charlie, and into Ev's relationship with Lottie; and besides, she didn't even know if a three-year-old could be trusted to lie. In the end Lottie decided she was entitled to a dinner, wasn't she? And maybe Evelyn's bearing tales would even create some movement in their paralyzed situation. Lottie managed to stop worrying, but barely.

Kenadjian lived in a brick and clapboard bungalow, not much bigger than the house Charlie and Lottie rented. Evelyn, reaching high, pushed the door-bell. Kenadjian greeted them, Evelyn hiding behind Lottie. Inside, the walls of the front foyer were hung with yellow gauzy silk on which were sewn small round mirrors; the living room walls were lined with loosely woven burlap; large posters—Gandhi in a white dhoti, Martin Luther King Jr. holding aloft a Bible, an anonymous black man having his head clubbed as he walked off a Greyhound bus—covered the kitchen walls. Books and journals were everywhere. They lined the staircase; they fanned out around the legs of chairs, and lay on top of the old ebony baby grand piano; they covered the dining room table.

"Where are the trophies?" Ev asked, looking around the living room.

Lottie pointed at the burlap. "The walls are lovely."

"My wife did them."

"She wove the material?"

"And she did the stenciling upstairs."

"Trophies! Trophies!"

"Most people don't have trophies," Lottie said to her daughter.

"What trophies? What's this about trophies?"

"My husband is a—was a football player."

"Trophies," Evelyn said.

"Ah," he said. "Well, I have a Phi Beta Kappa key!"

"You do?!" Lottie said.

"It's not exactly a trophy."

Ev looked confused.

Lottie said, "He doesn't play anymore, my husband. He was injured."

"Shame," George said politely. Then he added, "I'm embarrassed I said I have a Phi Beta Kappa key."

"It isn't true?" Lottie was disappointed.

"It's true but it's gauche."

"I want to see the trophies." Evelyn said again.

"I want to see the Phi Beta Kappa key," Lottie said.

"I'm not sure where it is. Maybe it's in the bedroom. Like I said, it's not really a trophy."

"It is," Lottie said. "It's a real trophy."

"Anyway, let me show you the upstairs." He gestured to them to go ahead of him. Lottie did not want to see more of his wife's fine wall work, but she wanted to see that key. Was it a real key? Did it open anything? Evelyn half-walked, half-climbed up the steps, Lottie behind her, a hand outstretched to break a possible backward fall. Beside the unmade king-size bed in the master bedroom, Ev looked unsure. "Up? Up?"

George gave her a boost.

Two feet down from the ceiling a repeating pattern of pineapples was stenciled in a border on the cream-colored walls.

"Pineapples are an old symbol of hospitality," George said. "I know—you usually find them in the dining room."

Evelyn pulled two journals out from between the covers. "Read to me!" She waved a journal at her mother.

"My wife's living in a commune now. It's a religious commune. Her parents are from India." He said to Evelyn, "These magazines are for grown-ups. Bor-ing!" He closed his eyes and snored a few times.

"Read! Read!" she cried to her mother.

"They're not children's books," Lottie said.

Kenadjian took the *Journal of the American Medical Association* that Evelyn was holding, Chagall's *Green Violinist* on the cover, and sat down on the bed. He opened it to an article entitled "Intra-uterine Morbidity and Mortality."

"You're not going to read *that* to her?" Lottie looked over his shoulder.

He shook his head as he held up the magazine, its pages dense with print. "No pictures," he said to Evelyn. "Only on the cover."

"Read the cover," Ev said.

"It's not a children's book. He doesn't have any children's books."

"Downstairs?" Ev asked. "Are the children's books downstairs?"

He shook his head.

"In the girl's room?" Ev was bouncing on the bed.

"Do you need to pee?" Lottie asked.

Kenadjian said, "There isn't any girl's room. I don't have any girls. I don't have any children."

Ev looked confused. "You're a child doctor?"

"Mothers ask me that all the time."

"Read!"

"That's enough now, Evelyn," Lottie said.

Ev found another book under the covers and pulled it out. Large, leather-covered with gilt-edged pages, it was open to a richly colored stylized drawing of an Indian man with an enormous erect phallus entering the buttocks of a full-breasted Indian woman on all fours, a red jewel teardrop on her forehead. She was facing the reader and smiling. Evelyn pointed at the man in the picture and then at George.

"No!" Kenadjian lunged for the book and yanked it away from her. "No, that's not me! That's for sure not me!" He smiled in embarrassment, holding the book behind him. "I'm so sorry about this," he said to Lottie.

Evelyn reached for the book, screaming.

"What is it?" Lottie asked angrily.

George held it high above his head. "The Kama Sutra. I apologize. Really. It's an ancient book. It's practically a religious book."

"Gimme back the bat-man!"

Lottie took the book from George. "I never heard of it," she said, turning the pages.

"It was written by a celibate monk," George said.

"Gimme the tushy book!" Evelyn was screaming.

"It's not a children's book, dear," Lottie said.

Kenadjian was blushing under his dark skin. He took the book from Lottie and put it on a high shelf in his closet.

"Gimme the vagina-face!" Evelyn screamed.

"How do you know about this?" Lottie yelled at her daughter. "That's enough now, I said it's enough!" Lottie bent over to lift Evelyn off the bed, Evelyn who was flailing her arms and kicking. She caught Lottie's chin with her foot. Lottie cried out and grabbed Evelyn's legs.

"Look!" Kenadjian said and withdrew a pen-size white flashlight from his pants pocket and—"Abracadabra!"—lit it.

Evelyn went on squirming and screaming.

He grabbed his black medical bag from the bookcase and got a silver tuning fork out of it. "Look! Look! Look here!" He whacked it against his palm to make it vibrate. He showed them a hammer with an orange rubber head; and still hollering, Evelyn watched as he threw the flashlight, the fork, and then the hammer up, up, up in the air, and began to juggle them.

Slowly, mouth open, Evelyn quieted.

Lottie said, "Well, I'm impressed."

"I'm glad," Kenadjian continued juggling. "I worried I lost you over the Kama Sutra."

"The whole thing caught me off guard," she said irritably.

How did one talk to a man who wasn't Charlie?

He took them downstairs to the kitchen, where the table had been set for three, and while he grilled four skewers of meat, he filled what looked like a miniature glass tower with carrots, pressed a button, and voilà, juice. Evelyn was fascinated with the *grrrroooosh*-ing sound the carrots made as they disintegrated (although she wouldn't taste the juice), and Kenadjian made three batches for her until he was out of carrots. Lottie had not seen such an apparatus before, and she itched to dismantle it. After dinner Kenadjian served mint tea with fresh mint leaves and sugar in it, and parallelogram-shaped pastries sticky with honey. He had a small Dixie cup of vanilla ice cream for Evelyn. They both attended to Evelyn throughout the dinner, and Lottie was appreciative although Kenadjian waved away her thanks. "She's a lovely child," he said.

"Well, she's also a conversation killer." Lottie did catch that he was from an Armenian American family, that he was a Quaker, and that he was trying to get conscientious objector status. An Armenian Quaker. She didn't know anything about Armenians and she didn't know anything about Quakers. He was about her height, she figured, or maybe a couple of inches taller. He had olive skin—pitted olive skin—and a dark mustache and those bright hazel eyes.

"What will you do if they draft you?" she asked.

His dark face darkened. "I don't know. There's always jail. Or Canada. What's your husband going to do?"

"He's Four-F."

"How'd he swing that?"

"His leg. He was injured, I told you that. He tried to enlist," Lottie said defensively.

"Are you kidding?"

"Is that strange to you?"

"It isn't to you? Where do you stand on the war, anyway?"

"I don't know." She lowered her voice. "I always stood with Charlie."

"Come to a 'counterculture' meeting with me next Thursday. It's at the home of one of the pediatric attendings, Sam Appelfeld. He's a New Yorker. A doc who's been to Vietnam will speak, show a movie . . . Evelyn could come: there'll be other kids—"

Evelyn clapped her hands.

Lottie touched Evelyn's hair. "I try to keep her away from the war."

"They have a sitter who takes the kids down to the finished basement where they draw and play games while the movie's on. These evenings are very well organized. The guests give money before they leave for medical supplies for the Vietcong."

"That's strange . . ."

"Why is it strange?"

"Supporting the Vietcong."

"Who's supporting the Vietcong? We're helping injured people. Why is that strange? We're doctors."

She said, "How do you know the money goes for medical supplies?"

"We package the stuff and ship it over there. They can't shoot us with sutures."

"Sure they can! They patch the soldiers up and send them out to fight again!"

"You think we should let their soldiers bleed to death?"

She remembered his blood flowing into the glass tubes beneath her fingers. "I don't know."

His face stiffened. "I'm supposed to save lives, no matter whose."

She shrugged her shoulders. "I have to think about this Vietcong business."

"You should. Come to the meeting with me. It'll be an education. And we'll get to see each other again."

Lottie said nothing. Her eagerness made her uneasy.

"Yes! Yes!" Evelyn bounced on the couch.

George said to Lottie, "What do *you* say? I'm the kind of man who needs reciprocity."

She looked at the rug beneath her feet. Her answer felt half-wrenched out of her. "You've got it."

On a sunny weekday afternoon Lottie and Evelyn waited for Kenadjian at the front entrance to the hospital. Mother and daughter wore white cotton scoop-neck dresses and pearl necklaces and each carried a white sweater against the cool that would come with evening. Lottie stood fanning herself with the morning's *Longhorn Herald* while Evelyn, her face moist, rose up and down on the toes of her new saddle shoes, as if they were dance slippers.

"You don't want to scuff them." Lottie kissed her daughter's bobbing head without disturbing the thin white ribbon in her hair.

Kenadjian, in silver-plated sunglasses and a casual navy-blue long-sleeved shirt and jeans, stepped out of his bright green Volkswagen. On the back of the car someone (Lottie didn't ask if it was his wife) had painted almost life-size figures of an olive-skinned, bare-chested man in cut-off dungarees kissing a slender woman in a fuchsia muumuu, gardenias in her long dark hair. Their sandaled feet seemed to rest on a long bumper sticker that read MAKE LOVE, NOT WAR.

Kenadjian smiled broadly, nodded a few times at Lottie, and ruffled Evelyn's hair, which Evelyn seemed to take as a matter of course. This surprised Lottie, who checked to make sure Evelyn's ribbon was still on straight. Kenadjian opened the back door. He bent to lift Evelyn—and she let him—into a child seat in the back.

"You have a child seat?" Lottie said.

He laughed.

"I mean, is that standard pediatrician gear?"

He shook his head.

"You bought that for her?" Lottie asked. "You bought the seat for Evelyn?"

He nodded.

She felt herself go warm.

"Do you think that's presumptuous?" Kenadjian asked.

"I think it's swell."

But after a moment, she turned over her open hands questioningly.

"Oh, come on," he said. "Do you feel two ways about everything?"

She said quietly, "What do you expect? I'm a married woman, out with a man not my husband. How do you expect me to feel?" Suddenly she was very sad.

They left the hospital grounds, George drove on the highway for a while, and Evelyn yelled herself to sleep. George drove down a dusty main street with a gas station, a general store, a pizza shop, and a bar. A dozen black motorcycles were parked in the lot next to the bar, most flying American or Confederate flags and one flying a skull and bones.

A few blocks away the neighborhood changed. There were ranches and split-level houses, each on a few acres of sandy land. They drove past a green park watered by turning sprinklers. A granite statue of a buffalo grazed the land watched over by a granite Indian with granite feathered headdress. Yellow and purple bougainvillea grew around the bases of the statues.

Two blocks away, Kenadjian parked the car between a Volvo and another Volkswagen, both with MD plates.

He unstrapped the child seat from the car and lifted it out, Evelyn's head wobbling in sleep, her ribbon undone. Lottie made a neat bow and double-knotted it. Carrying their sweaters and his denim jacket, Lottie followed Kenadjian up the slate path lined with cacti in red flower, and ascended the stoop. A brown and green lizard darted across the grizzled wood of the house and down over the gray doorbell button. It slithered carefully down the steps and disappeared into the gravel of the front lawn. The door was open. In the smoky living room a Vivaldi concerto played on a stereo. Their host, a stocky, bald, white-bearded man with curly white hair on his arms and legs, came over to greet them. Appelfeld wore Bermuda shorts and a turquoise shirt with an orange sun beating down on palm trees. Evelyn was waking now and George put the car seat on the floor. Lottie unstrapped her daughter. Appelfeld clasped George's hands in both of his.

George introduced them.

"Very pleased to meet you both." Appelfeld shook Lottie's hand heartily and stooped to greet Evelyn, who was rubbing her eyes and getting up out of the car seat.

Appelfeld put an arm around Kenadjian's shoulder. "I have him do *every-thing* for me. If George reads the spinal fluid or looks over the slides, I know it's done right."

Hearing Kenadjian praised gave Lottie goosebumps. She tugged at her pearls to hide her pleasure and looked away.

Lottie and Kenadjian took Evelyn down to the finished basement, where a babysitter was dishing out taco chips and hot dogs and watermelon to a small group of children.

In the living room, someone lowered the Venetian blinds and a white man in his twenties with a port-wine birthmark on his cheek carefully pulled down a movie screen. People looked for chairs. Lottie spotted a young woman wearing a SYLVIA PLATH FOR PRESIDENT button. Most people there were Lottie's age, in couples, and a few of the couples were interracial. She spotted a Caucasian and a black, a Caucasian and a Mexican, a Caucasian and an American Indian. There was a black and Asian couple. Seeing these pairings, she tried not to stare. Were there laws against this kind of thing? The air was somehow charged. Were these people in danger? She felt protective of them. She felt somehow endangered herself. How white her world was! What *she* was doing was wrong. What she was contemplating. Adultery. She hadn't done anything yet, she reminded herself. She'd told Charlie she was staying overnight at the hospital. And she planned to stay overnight at the hospital, so it was the truth. Sort of. But suddenly she felt endangered as if it were the antiwar meeting that was endangering her, these couples, and she had an impulse to tell Kenadjian they had to leave.

At the same time, she was intensely curious and kept looking. Many of the women wore brightly colored beads or flowers; Lottie felt uneasy about her pearls. George and Lottie sat together on a needlepoint-covered piano bench, Lottie careful to leave a few inches between them although it meant sitting at the edge of the bench.

Dr. Appelfeld shook hands with the man with the birthmark, whom he introduced as Dr. J. Austin Penforth, a psychiatrist from Yale. Dr. Penforth spoke earnestly about his recent fact-finding trip to North Vietnam, where he had seen fervor and determination along with great physical suffering. The North Vietnamese and the Vietcong were extremely short of medical supplies. He asked them to excuse the crudeness of the technology of the film and its propagandistic overtones. Unfortunately, this was the only film in existence that showed actual footage of Vietcong treatment units.

The lights were turned off and the movie projector whirred on; there followed several minutes of blurred images and then the camera focused on a man and woman in blood-spattered fatigues and off-white masks bent over what appeared to be an open abdomen from which blood spurted up and fanned out. The projector whirred for a long while before the pumping blood slowed, then stopped.

Someone in the film said something in a language Lottie assumed was Vietnamese.

In the next scene a dark-skinned Vietnamese boy, around twelve years old, wearing a green-and-brown camouflage uniform, sat on a metal table while a kneeling man with a whitish cloth tied over his mouth and nose cut away the boy's left pant leg and the dirty caked bandage beneath to reveal a large, weeping, clotted wound. The doctor rolled up the boy's right pant leg; the boy's left leg was swollen to one and a half times the size of the right. After hosing down the wound, the doctor dipped an army knife into a bucket of solution and quickly cut at the raw wet wound on the boy's dark leg. The boy squinched his eyes shut and covered his mouth with his hand and sat absolutely still.

The camera shifted to a toothless woman in a filthy white ao dai holding a bundle wrapped in sky-blue silk in the crook of her arm. A man in khaki fatigues gestured that he wished to examine the bundle. Her head remained bowed but she held the bundle closer. A tussle ensued between the man and the woman and finally the man got the bundle away and opened it to reveal . . . a dead dog? A dead baby? Lottie couldn't see clearly.

The movie was over. A few people applauded hesitantly. Dr. Penforth stood up and asked for donations to buy scalpels, clamps, sutures, hypodermics, anesthetics, subclavian and nasogastric tubes, Vitamin K and heparin, and antibiotics in particular, any kind of medicine, as well as blood and plasma. They were especially in need of advanced burns treatment units to counteract the effects of napalm.

While Drs. Penforth and Appelfeld rolled away the screen and projector, Lottie told Kenadjian she had to go home.

"You ought to *stay*. There's a brief question-and-answer period. These are well-informed folk, a little humorless, but decent."

"I have to get Evelyn to bed."

Kenadjian went downstairs after Evelyn. When he brought her up, there were watermelon stains down the front of her dress and Lottie felt embarrassed, although she also felt ashamed to feel embarrassed. In the bathroom she tried to wash the stains off Evelyn's dress but Evelyn screamed "Wet! Wet! You're colding me!" and Lottie turned off the water and tried to dry the front of her daughter's dress with a towel.

Kenadjian placed a check in a brown wicker basket on the coffee table. "It's from both of us," he said to Lottie. There were several other folded checks in the basket and two sealed white envelopes.

"You didn't put my name on that check?" Lottie asked.

He shook his head.

When they were outside, she said, "Aren't you afraid of the FBI?"

"Yes."

It was dusk now and cool. Kenadjian carried the car seat, and Lottie carried Evelyn facing forward because the front of the child's dress was wet with water and watermelon juice. "Cold," Evelyn said.

"Do you think that film was authentic?" Lottie asked as Kenadjian hooked the child seat into the car.

"I'm sure they're short medical supplies . . ."

"Do you think the patients were real? That woman with the dead bundle . . . Where was it taking place?"

"Mama, stop!"

"What?" Then she realized she had Evelyn clamped tight against her chest. Lottie loosened her hold. "Advertisers use models all the time in drug ads . . . I don't mean these people are from Madison Avenue, but they could have been commandeered by the Vietcong."

"The wounds are real: look, it's a war. Could there be some hocus-pocus going on? Possibly. I don't believe any government."

She handed Evelyn over to him. "Why go to this kind of thing then?"

"I like to hear the little guy's lies as well as the big guy's."

He strapped Evelyn in. There was a breeze and a full moon.

As they drove past the park, two wooden sawhorses were blocking off the road ahead. Kenadjian slowed and stopped, and Evelyn began to scream.

"She's ready to go to sleep again." Lottie turned to hush her. In the park in the dusk there seemed to be a man in a black leather jacket and pants with a white stocking over his head sitting astride the statue of the buffalo. She pointed him out to Kenadjian.

Suddenly engines roared and tires screeched and dust rose up in the beams of their headlights. Men in feather headdress, war paint obscuring their faces, spread out on their idling motorcycles in front of the sawhorses.

"What's going on?" Lottie said.

"Get down!" Kenadjian whispered.

Lottie didn't move. "It's probably a football team, or a fraternity hazing."

"Get down, I'm telling you—"

"Don't get all upset . . ."

"God damn it," he fumbled with her seat belt.

"Maybe it's some kind of demonstration." But she helped him undo the belt and went down on her knees holding the skirt of her white dress off the floor. She cocked her head on the seat so she could look out the side window.

In the back Evelyn continued to scream.

"Shhhhh, my dear, shush, shush . . ." Lottie could not reach her daughter.

Kenadjian shifted the car into reverse, but there were motorcycles now behind them, too. A few men held flaming torches.

Somebody jumped onto the hood of the Volkswagen and began bouncing up and down. Another jumped onto the roof.

"Stop it! You're going to collapse the car!" George yelled out the window.

A man lifted himself onto the running board on Kenadjian's side.

It occurred to Lottie that she should feel afraid but the scene had an unreal air, what with the Indian garb, as if it were taking place in a Western.

Kenadjian said, "Come on, guys. This isn't Halloween. What's the story?"

"Are you an Indian? Are you Vietnamese?"

The metal roof boomed and boomed as the man above continued jumping.

"Do I look Vietnamese?" he said to the guy whose face was half a foot away from his, and then yelled out the window at the guy above: "Get off there! You're breaking my car!"

"Answer me."

"I'm an American. I'm an Armenian American."

"What were you doing at that Commie party?"

"What *Commie* party? That was no *Commie* Party! That was a party of doctors and nurses . . . Hey, you know what you guys look like? You look like the Boston Tea Party."

"You there, on your knees. Are you Looney Tunes' wife? Are you a nurse?"

Lottie shook her head. She tried for a dignified, indeed stern voice. "I'm a lab technician."

"You look ready for a crash landing." The man laughed.

"We have to go home," Kenadjian said. "She has to put her daughter to bed."

The man on the running board looked over at the man on the hood, who looked up at the man bouncing on the roof. In a moment the first man said, "*She* can drive home with the kid. *You* get out of the car."

Kenadjian hesitated.

"Don't go!" Lottie whispered. She caught his arm. "They could hurt you."

"You'll be all right. Evelyn'll be all right. Just drive the hell out of here."

"How do you know? You don't know—"

"What are you two whispering about? Shut up, both of you." The man moved his face closer to Kenadjian's face.

"What's this about?" George asked. "What do you want?"

"You escort us to that tea party . . . We want to meet your friends."

"Those people are all hospital workers. They take care of you and your families!"

The man grabbed George's hair.

"Let go of me!" George yelled as he tried to pull his head away.

Lottie screamed.

"Now we're going to take care of *them*." The man began pulling Kenadjian through the window by his hair.

George pushed at the man's chest with his left hand and tried to shift into first with his right. He had one foot engaging the clutch, the other the gas. Lottie pushed the gear shift forward for him. She prayed the engine wouldn't stall. As the car lurched ahead, the man yanked out a fistful of George's hair before he fell off the running board.

Kenadjian screamed. Lottie grabbed the wheel. Kenadjian pressed on the gas pedal. The booming on the roof stopped as the man fell over the side of the car, yelling. The man on the hood held on to the windshield wipers. The car rammed into a parked motorcycle and a wooden sawhorse, which flew up in the dark. Kenadjian took the wheel from her and she found the windshield wiper knob and turned it on. The man held onto the blade, which came off in his hand. He held on to the other blade as George accelerated. Lottie grabbed Evelyn's thermos out of her pocketbook; she pulled off the metal cup and threw it at the guy and unscrewed the cap and tried to hurl the water at him, and then the thermos itself, but she was at a bad angle and didn't connect. Still, he was sliding down backward over the hood and then he rolled under the car and she didn't feel anything—so maybe they hadn't hit him.

Sweat was running down the sides of her face, and when she moved her hands to brush the sweat away she saw that her fingers were shaking.

A few miles from where they'd been surrounded, Kenadjian pulled into a gas station and drove into the dark parking area behind it; he leaned against the steering wheel. Lottie pressed the hem of her white dress up against his scalp. As the material grew wet and dark, she inched it along carefully, gently—her grandmother feeding fine silk under the moving sewing machine needle. Finally the bleeding stopped.

"Why don't I hear Evelyn?" he whispered thickly. "Where's Evelyn?"

Lottie turned around so quickly she thought she'd sheared a blood vessel in her neck. "She's asleep. Evelyn's asleep." She began to giggle.

"We've got to warn Appelfeld," he whispered. "I have to call the police."

She was still giggling. "Do you think we killed that guy?"

"I hope so." He shook his head and started bleeding again. Lottie shimmied her half-slip down and handed it to him. George went over to the phone booth with her white slip around his head. Lottie continued to chuckle quietly. Through the car window she could see him hunched over in the dimly lit phone both. She hoped no one else was watching him. Behind him the sky blazed white with stars that seemed to be dazzling or winking or in motion somehow; she realized sweat was running into her eyes. She continued giggling, she couldn't stop it; she was half-giggling, half-whimpering.

She watched him put coins in the phone. He was dialing. He was waiting. He hung up. Then he was putting in coins and dialing again. This time she could see him speaking. After a few minutes he hung up, got quickly out of the booth—the light went off—and, looking nervously around him, came back hurriedly to the car. He opened the driver's-side door and slid in behind the steering wheel fast and shut and locked the door.

"Did you get Appelfeld?" She whispered.

"No answer. I called the police."

She nodded. She had to call Charlie. She'd told him she and Evelyn were staying at the hospital. But now she wanted to go home. Lottie looked carefully around—What was this shadow? What was that one? But no shadow moved.

"I've got to call my husband."

He nodded in the dark. "I'll go out with you."

"No. Stay with Evelyn."

Only her own shadow moved as she left the car and went to the phone booth and dialed. What would she say? She'd put him off, improvise when she got home. But there was no answer.

Was no one reachable anywhere?

He'd be furious, and rightfully so. She'd make up something.

Yet she couldn't stop quietly, hysterically laughing.

At one in the morning Kenadjian pulled the car into Lottie's driveway and turned off the lights. She had the hiccups.

"Do you want me to come in and explain?"

"That's crazy. With my slip around your head, you're going in to explain to my husband—exactly what . . ."

He took off the slip and handed it to her. The bleeding had stopped. "God, I'm sorry. I'm so sorry about all of this."

"He's not my father. I don't even know if he's home. Does your head hurt?" She couldn't stop hiccupping.

"No. No, it's numb." He moved a hand toward her and she pulled away, looking around uneasily at the dark houses.

"I better go in," Lottie said.

He opened the door to get out of the car.

"Don't," she said. "I can manage myself."

"How're you going to get the front door open with Evelyn in your arms? You'll have to carry her up the steps, then what are you going to do? Lay her on the stone stoop while you fish out your keys?"

"I'll go open the door first." But as she stepped out of the car she could feel how wobbly she was. She was afraid to carry Evelyn on wobbly legs.

Soup legs.

She quickly closed the door so the car light went off. How frightened she was. It was ridiculous to feel guilty. She'd gone out with a colleague to a meeting and things had gone wrong. She wasn't hurt. Her daughter wasn't hurt. Period.

She let Kenadjian unstrap and carry Evelyn up the steps and through the door, into the dark foyer, and up to the second floor. Charlie wasn't lying in wait for her, wasn't even waiting for her. Lottie pointed George toward Evelyn's bedroom and he laid Evelyn down carefully on her bed in her watermelon-stained dress. Lottie hurried him down the stairs.

"Good night," he whispered in the dark foyer at the same time that she hissed, "Shhh." As he left, his face brushed Lottie's and she smelled the blood on him and the strong smoky odor of his dried sweat. She closed the door carefully behind him.

Lottie smelled him on the slip she held in her hands and on the dress she was wearing.

Upstairs in the hall she heard Charlie's thick, even breathing. She did not want to go into their bedroom smelling of George. She took a light blanket from the linen closet and covered Evelyn with it.

Lottie ran cold water in the sink, then stood in her white bra and pants scrubbing at the stiff spots and streaks of dried blood on her dress and on her slip. The bar of soap kept slipping out of her hands into the sink. She had trouble picking it up. She tried to blow-dry the wet parts of the dress with a hair dryer. She missed a few spots, and in one place there remained the outline of a blood splotch although she had scrubbed the center clean. She rolled the dress and the slip into a ball and stuffed it between some boxes on a high shelf in Evelyn's closet.

Lottie sat down on her daughter's bed and watched her breathe, her chest moving slightly beneath the stained dress, her pale eyelashes casting shadows on her cheeks. In the moonlight Lottie counted eight freckles on her cheeks.

Evelyn could have been hurt.

Lottie got a white bath towel from the hall closet and wrapped it around her bare shoulders. Her legs were still shaking and she felt light-headed. She sat down on the floor in the hallway, her knees up, her head down between her knees.

Perhaps if she ate something with sugar in it . . . Holding on to the bannister, she felt her way unsteadily downstairs. Why hadn't Charlie left a light on for her? She could have fallen carrying Evelyn. Didn't she deserve a light? Then she remembered she wasn't supposed to be coming home. She turned on a lamp in the living room and the overhead light in the dining room. The bread box contained a few hard slices of rye bread and in the refrigerator there was a quart of milk that smelled sour, a pot of cauliflower soup she'd made a few nights earlier, an unopened jar of mango chutney, and a can of Maxwell House coffee. She had an image of the mother in *I Remember Mama* with her long blonde Norwegian braid pouring coffee into white cups in her television kitchen with the backyard set painted in the window. *Good to the last drop.*

Where was her grandmother?

Lottie had a sudden impulse to yell, "Is anybody home?"

She had been home three nights this week and one time Charlie wasn't there and another time he left when he saw them. The third time he talked to Evelyn, but not to her.

He had deserted her. She had deserted him. She had placed their child in peril.

As she walked back through the lit dining room and living room, she imagined the furniture shorn of her grandmother's doilies and pillows and quilts. With the tarnished trophies and old newspaper clippings on the walls, the rooms would look like the lobby rooms of a seedy hotel.

Passing the foyer, she caught a whiff again of blood, and the harsh, pungent odor of Kenadjian's dried sweat. She made herself open the hall window and the three living room windows.

Now she got into bed without touching Charlie, and he didn't wake, and it seemed to her that the smell of him had vanished and the blanket, the sheets, her pillowcase, and her whole body were permeated by this strange new odor. She got out of bed and went into Evelyn's room, and as she leaned over to kiss her sleeping child, even from her daughter's hair she breathed in Kenadjian's smell.

The next morning when Kenadjian came into the lab, Lottie whispered, "I can't see you anymore."

"I don't blame you. I know how you must feel." He wore a small bandage on his scalp. "Your husband must have been beside himself."

She did not say that Charlie was probably still beside himself, in dreamland. "You don't know how I feel," she whispered. "You don't have a child!"

He bowed his head. "I didn't think there was any danger, Lottie, so help me." The words sounded like "so hump me" and she didn't understand him at first.

"How is she doing?"

"What? All right."

"I'm very fond of her. I wouldn't want any harm to come to her—"

"Shh! Someone'll hear us!" Lottie looked around. Nobody was there. Then she walked to the back of the lab and looked sideways out the window, in the direction of Evelyn's babysitter's house, although it could not be seen from the lab. She opened the door to the hall. A candy striper was pushing a cart of books down the hall. Lottie closed the door carefully.

"Did anything happen to Appelfeld?" she asked him. "Did anything happen to anybody at the meeting?"

"Nobody got killed, but there was a melee and a few people ended up in the ER. No one from the peds department." George shook his head, then winced.

She had an impulse to touch his pained face. To caress it. Lottie felt her own face heat up. "If anything had happened to her," she said hotly. "My husband's a sick man!"

"What about me? I almost got scalped!" He pulled the bandage away from his head. Underneath, his skin was pale and hairless, and there were bright red marks where the sutures bit in.

"You needed sutures?"

He nodded. "I lied to you. There *was* somebody in the ER from the peds department. *Me.* The bleeding started up again after I left you."

"Oh, I'm so sorry. Oh, oh. Does it hurt?"

"Not much," he admitted.

She touched his chin. She turned to look around again, then kissed him passionately. He kissed her back and held her close.

She breathed in that dark smoky smell of him again. She felt herself pushing against him, her breasts, her thighs, her tongue. She felt as if she wanted to get into him, get him into her; she felt dazed, almost dizzy. She made herself back away. "You don't know how miserable I am," she whispered, trying to steady herself. "My husband barely speaks to me. Half the time he's not home. I don't know where he is. I don't know what's going on in his head."

"Oh Lottie. Dear Lottie."

She was whispering and crying at once, "I don't know if he's depressed, if he has another woman, or he's just completely fallen out of love with me."

"How long has this been going on?"

"Months."

He said, "Move in and take care of me."

She shook her head. "You've forgotten about Evelyn."

"It's no deal without Evelyn."

Lottie laughed.

"You need a man with a few jokes in his doctor's bag."

As he waved good-bye, Lottie whispered, "Don't even joke about our moving in."

Although no one said anything to Lottie, she daily worried that Charlie had somehow gotten a whiff of her attendance at the meeting, or of her "connection" to George Kenadjian, and so she avoided the house even more than usual. The one time that week she did see him, he was starting a fire in the living room fireplace with the week's newspapers, but all he said to her was, "I wish this frigging war was over." She was not sure which war he meant.

She also tried to steer clear of Kenadjian. Yet, when Lottie drew bloods in the morning, George would happen to be teaching medical students on the floor. If she was checking out a lab technique in the hospital library, he was in the reserve room reading a journal.

One afternoon she had a late order to do a throat culture in the private wing of the hospital. There was a single patient, his face and arms heavily bandaged, in a room reserved for burns trauma.

"Are you able to open your mouth?" She tried despite her fright and pity for a tone of gentle straightforwardness.

The mummy shook his head no.

"Can you move your lips at all?"

The patient took her hand and slowly drew it to the part of his bandaged face where his lips must have been.

She felt awkward and terribly sad. "I don't know how to get a throat culture on you," she said softly. "I'll call somebody to help me." She thought she'd call Kenadjian.

He took the cotton-tipped stick from her with his bandaged hand, opened his mouth wide, and swabbed the back of his throat deftly himself.

"You—you little weasel!" she blurted with surprise and rage.

That afternoon on the bus home with Evelyn next to her, Lottie began to laugh. A couple of people stared at her, but she went on laughing.

Whenever she succeeded in not thinking about Kenadjian, she could sense coming down on her like a shroud that colorless anesthetized feeling she'd had for months; and she couldn't bear it. Was she in love with him?

One night three weeks after the Appelfeld meeting, she woke winded from a nightmare that she and Evelyn were struggling to get out from under an enormous white whale that was beached upon them, surging, flailing its tail. A small wooden Pinocchio figure ran around shrieking.

Sitting up in bed in the dark, she tried to calm herself. She had always disliked *Moby-Dick*. Charlie breathed heavily beside her. All those men and murder and mayhem. But she was a Pinocchio fan and liked that he lied to avoid school, although she had always loved school. She had read the original Pinocchio to Evelyn not long ago.

She needed somebody to crack a joke. She got up unsteadily and, as her eyes adjusted, began to pack, opening each drawer noiselessly, taking her dresses off their hangers and folding them, and laying them flat in the case.

She went into Evelyn's room and packed up her daughter's things as she lay sleeping. Lottie was thinking of Little Red Riding Hood's mother—or was it her grandmother?—packing the basket of goodies. Lottie had had three hours of sleep and she felt old and stale and numb.

As if she had been planning this for a long time, she was able to fit everything essential into the luggage she had on hand. She did not forget Thrower, Evelyn's monkey; her bear, Downey; nor her own two cartons of science notes and projects. She had a separate case into which she folded the quilts and doilies and samplers her grandmother had made. Lottie left the three scrapbooks she'd assembled for Charlie, although it pained her as if she were leaving a young, hopeful, loving part of herself. Those scrapbooks should go to Evelyn. But there was no room. Would Charlie destroy them? SAVE FOR EVELYN! she wrote in large grim letters on three slips of paper, and inserted one slip, like a bookmark, in each.

She washed her face with cold water in the bathroom. In her mind she had a cartoon image of Little Red Riding Hood skipping through the woods. She taped Kenadjian's address and phone number on the inside of the front door and then carried Evelyn asleep in her pajamas into the waiting taxi.

A gray sky was lightening. As the driver arranged her luggage in the trunk, then lifted her cartons onto the front seat, the first streaks of pink appeared on the horizon. Her daughter mumbled in her arms. Lottie was only a few blocks away from the house she'd lived in with Charlie when the sun came up, large and red in the vast gray-blue sky.

Part Five

L ife with Kenadjian proved unlike anything she'd ever known before; she could not believe her luck.

Growing up as the daughter of a small-town part-time mayor, she occasionally saw people coming and going, this farmer in trouble or that businessman on the outs with the chamber of commerce, but they came in the front door in the evening, sat in the living room where the family never went, and were quickly ushered into her father's office. The next morning at breakfast, her father would be silent, as though keeping everything secret was a condition of being mayor. Her grandmother said her son had always wanted to be a doctor and was behaving now as though he'd taken the Hippocratic oath. Gerry joked that Dad really worked for the CIA. Her father grimaced and grinned but did not open up. At dinner he would talk a bit about science if he was in a good mood, or Jeanie might tell about a book she was reading or her grandmother would discuss some local or state project or town official gone awry or astray. Otherwise, conversations were about homework or clothes and usually just the extended family was around.

But Kenadjian's house was *peopled*, overrun with meetings and readings. There were gatherings of would-be and recognized Conscientious Objectors at which young men read from the Constitution or from Tom Paine's *Common Sense* and many talked about Martin Luther King Jr.'s stand on the Vietnam War or the Brothers Berrigan or Ben Spock ("our own Ben," Sam Appelfeld called him) or the Fort Hood Three.

One night, people stood up and recited poetry. George's favorite poet was William Carlos Williams: "He's a physician, you know, from New Jersey, my home state." And that had made her fond of New Jersey. A psychiatric social worker declaimed sections of T. S. Eliot's *The Waste Land* and Lottie recognized a few of the lines Nathaniel Burden had chanted that night in the smoky pizza parlor when Charlie was in the hospital; but the difference was that listening to the woman hold forth at George's house, Lottie didn't feel frightened, she felt curious, excited, braced.

The first weekend she was there the place was taken over by a new organization tentatively called NOW, and young women and a few men, especially George, talked their heads off about women's rights.

Although she was the youngest and least credentialed, and sometimes she felt intimidated, even awed, these gatherings recharged Lottie after her draining months of worrying over Charlie; they lit her busy, lonely life.

At George's urging, she even sent away for some applications to graduate school. Anatomy had interested her as an undergraduate, and also physiology, and she applied to a few universities, although she wasn't sure she was serious; perhaps she did it to please Kenadjian, or to convince herself that she might one day become a person to reckon with, at least in fantasy. A person like one of these men—they were mostly men—or one of the women who spoke up at the NOW meeting in Kenadjian's living room.

But it was impossible, really, to go to graduate school. How could she take Evelyn away from her father? And Lottie still secretly hoped for a reconciliation with Charlie.

The physical thrill that she'd felt watching Kenadjian draw blood deftly, the sensual feeling on seeing him bent over, his white jacket stretched and taut over his back, that had gone, she didn't know where. Lottie slept on the living room couch and Evelyn stayed in the guest room on the second floor. Kenadjian was irritated at Lottie's insistence on paying room and board; she explained that her grandmother had done that, which didn't make much sense to him, but Lottie refused to stay otherwise. He had emptied out a bureau for her in his bedroom and one in the guest room for Evelyn, and they stood that way day after day, bare cupboards. She lived out of suitcases, springing for the phone. She picked up Kenadjian's emergency calls in the middle of the night. But she refused to make love with him.

He said, "I feel like a way station."

"I can't, I won't—sleep in your room—until I—until I can. Evelyn's not ready for it either. For me—to do that."

"For God's sake, I'm only asking you to unpack."

She couldn't unpack. Not even a token suitcase. She, who always unpacked everywhere, when she and Charlie visited their folks in Michigan, even when they stayed one time, the three of them, in a motel room for a weekend at the beach, she had laid everything into drawers, emptied their dopp kit in the medicine chest, called the porter to take the suitcases and store them out of sight. The illusion of permanence.

The illusion of impermanence. If she didn't unpack, maybe Charlie would call her, undo her desertion, undo his depression, if that's what it was, his dead-dom. "Again! Again!" Evelyn would insist when Lottie told her a good story. And she'd be Charlie's childhood sweetheart, his best friend, lover; she'd undo Charlie's injury, she'd get their son back whole alive . . .

After the first week her worry and guilt about Charlie were so intense that she called—no answer, although it was ten thirty at night. She phoned the bowling alley—he'd quit. She phoned the house again at eleven thirty, and at midnight. When George turned off his reading light upstairs and after a few minutes began to snore, Lottie anxiously dialed the taxi company.

The night was warm and black, moonless with a few stars spaced far apart in the long, low-slung sky. There were no other cars, and she had the odd thought as the taxi moved quickly through the quiet, familiar streets that she was riding in a cemetery. She asked the driver to return for her in half an hour. "Don't forget, you hear?"

Alone she stood still as a stone before the totally dark house. Why should she feel uneasy? She'd lived here, they'd conceived their child here. Afraid she'd fall in the dark, she moved slowly up the walk as if she were an old person, fishing in her pocketbook for the small flashlight she always carried. At the front door she rang several times—her husband was a heavy sleeper—and although she heard the double bell chime unmistakably, she knocked anyhow. After a while, she went down the steps and picked her way over the unmown front lawn around to the back of the house, where she pushed in the kitchen buzzer and held it down—it made that grating noise—until it hurt her finger.

Lottie walked up the gravel driveway, pebbles scattering and crunching under her feet in the still night. She shined her flashlight at the garage window, then cleaned a pane with a tissue: a lawn mower and a shovel were inside, or maybe it was a pitchfork, and also their two old bicycles.

No car.

At least he wasn't stubbornly pretending not to hear her.

Nor was he dead in the garage, slumped over the steering wheel, the engine running.

Where was the fucker? As she walked back across the front lawn and up the stoop, she bet he wasn't sleeping on anybody's living room couch, his crap in suitcases.

She unlocked the front door, smelled the dark dank air. As she felt for the hall light, something moved in the shadows near the slipcovered chair. "Charlie! Charlie!"

The house had developed a panicked echo.

Whatever had scuttled away was small, maybe a mouse. Turning on the lamps in the living room, she kicked a few times at the skirt of the uphol-stered chair, then returned to the front hall and padded up the carpeted stairs to the silent second floor, the unmade, empty beds. She opened her husband's bureau drawers—empty, too. Was this an abandoned house? In the bottom drawer she found large knots of unsorted clean socks, and several undershirts and shorts mixed in with unfolded pillowcases and towels.

She went into her daughter's room and made the bed.

There was old stinking piss in the toilet bowl. She turned on the faucet in the bathtub and the water spasmed out brown.

To warn off any more small, toothed creatures—if what had scuttled away had been a small, toothed creature—she made a racket opening and closing the attic door, snapping the light on and off, booming up the stairs: Why was she going up there anyway? Some obsessional need to force her way into every cranny? Or did she expect to find him hanging from the rafters? There was a filthy red-glass hurricane lamp, a carton of mildewed law books, the pair of petrified work pants—legacy of the house. In a corner a dusty wooden jack-in-the-box lay on its side; she pushed a button and out jumped the clown with a faded polka-dot shirt and a mournful face. Nearby were some tiny desiccated droppings. She looked around fearfully but nothing was flying, nothing was hanging.

In a far corner was a heap of dusty white plaster molds, body casts Charlie'd made of her pregnant. He'd smeared olive oil on her proud naked self, wrapped the plaster of paris bandages around her. Now when she lifted a cast, the edges crumbled to powder.

She walked down the attic stairs, down the second-floor stairs to the first floor, through the living room and dining room into the kitchen, where she opened the refrigerator. A gust of something evil rose up, and although she immediately shut the door, she couldn't trap the odor. The putrid stench must have come from a brown-paper-wrapped package that lay alone on the second shelf, hamburger meat she'd purchased a few days before she left.

She turned off the kitchen light and walked into the dining room, hesitated, went back to the kitchen. She opened the refrigerator quickly, took the unopened jar of mango chutney from the shelf in the door, slammed the refrigerator shut. Making sure first that the jar had really not been opened—the lid wouldn't give—she washed and dried the jar and put it in her pocketbook. Then she turned off the kitchen light, the dining room light, the living room light. In the dark house she opened the front door and was face to shoulder with a large, solidly built man, his arm raised. She screamed.

"Hey, I'm just checking up on you, making sure nothing's happened." It was the taxi driver, his hands clasped now as if in prayer. "You don't want to wake up the neighborhood."

Only when he dropped her off at Kenadjian's sleeping house and she tiptoed hurriedly upstairs to see Evelyn in her bed, her thumb in her mouth, did Lottie's heart slow down.

In the morning she called the university.

Yes, of course Mr. Hart was still teaching, in fact he was teaching right this minute. Was it an emergency?

Well, then would she like to leave a message?

No, he hadn't returned from anywhere, he hadn't been away. This was his wife, wasn't it? Well, then who was it, please?

Lottie imagined strangling him with the telephone cord because, she told herself, he didn't even care about his own daughter.

That evening after Evelyn was in bed, and before George came home from the hospital, Lottie sat down stiffly on the living room couch, her bare feet crossed Buddha-like in front of her, and dialed her parents.

Her mother picked up. "Yes? Hello? Who is it?"

Lottie's mouth was full of ashes. "Would—would you tell Dad to get on, too?"

"Lottie?" An anxious flurry in her airy voice, Jeanie asked, "Are you all right? You're all all right?"

"Nothing's wrong with anybody, Mom. We're all healthy."

"Oh, I'm so glad." Jeanie stepped away from the phone and called out, "Hank, get on, it's Charlotte. Nothing's wrong, don't worry."

"I didn't say nothing's wrong."

"You didn't? Is something wrong?"

Lottie dug her fingernails into the flowery material of the couch. "Mom, have you heard anything from Charlie?"

"We only talk to him if he picks up when we call you, dear."

"The Harts say anything?"

"What do you mean? They're not exactly raconteurs, your in-laws." Lottie imagined her mother smiling. "I saw Alberta yesterday at the supermarket: she had Ad with her, and she said, 'He eats a lot.' He's sixteen, you know, and six feet three or four or five. She looked proud enough to burst." Jeanie stopped herself. "What is it, dear? Was she supposed to tell me something?" Her voice had a high trill in it. "Let me go see what's keeping your father."

Lottie wondered yet again if there was any way to put this that was better than any other way.

Her father picked up. "Sorry. What can I do for you, Lottie?"

"Are you there, Mom?"

"Yes, dear. I'm in my study. Your dad's in the kitchen."

"She's not asking for landing instructions."

Lottie had to laugh.

"This is costing money," her father said.

"You're the one who held things up, Hank. Do you and Charlie need money, dear? Do you want to hang up and call us back collect? Hank, does she need money?"

"How do I know? Will you let her speak?"

"I'm paying for the call, Dad." Lottie couldn't stop laughing. "Please leave Mom alone."

"Don't get sassy, my young friend. I'm still your father."

"I know, Dad. I guess I'm under a lot of strain." She bit her cheeks and her lips until she got hold of her laughter. "I have some—painful news. Charlie and I are breaking up. I mean, maybe we're breaking up. It looks that way. I moved out last week."

She thought her father said, "What a family," at the same time as her mother asked, "Where's Evelyn? Who's got Evelyn?"

"Don't worry, Mom. She's with me."

"Do you want to come home, dear, you and Evelyn? We have plenty of room. Where are you staying?"

"Thanks, Mom. But I'm living with a friend." She pushed against the far side of the couch with her bare feet as if she were trying to gain leverage for a takeoff. "He's a doctor, actually. A pediatrician. It isn't what it sounds like. I sleep on the living room couch. He sleeps in the bedroom."

Her father made a noise like a roar.

"I didn't catch what you said, Dad."

"I didn't either," Jeanie spoke in a shrill voice. "Try to enunciate more clearly, Hank, if it's something you want us to understand." She said hurriedly to Lottie, "It's lucky you have a place to stay, although sleeping on a couch sounds uncomfortable."

"Talk about not understanding—" Her father's voice was coiled tight. "First"—he must have tapped once near the mouthpiece of the phone for emphasis—"first, you were knocked up by Charlie and you lost the baby but you stuck it out with him. Now"—he tapped twice—"now you have a baby, and you go live with another man."

"Hank—"

"If you're calling for money, forget it. I won't finance any more of your monkey business."

"I don't need your money—I can take care of myself and Evelyn—"

"—with the help of this doctor-boyfriend—"

Lottie could see her father sneering. She made herself speak slowly and calmly. "He's not helping me, at least not financially. Don't you believe me when I say there's nothing sexual going on?" She felt a strong desire to rip off her clothes and call Kenadjian at the hospital and tell him to race home and hop into bed with her right here right now.

"You forget you lied for months to all of us about your pregnancy," her father said. "Even to your grandmother."

"That was years ago. She was sixteen, Hank. She was frightened," Jeanie said.

"She's probably frightened now."

"Hank, it's no sin to be frightened, we ought to help her if she's frightened, shouldn't we, Hank? Dear, what was going on that you had to leave Charlie? Did he want to get rid of Evelyn?"

"Get rid of Evelyn?! What are you talking about?"

"Did he hit you?"

"Charlie hit me?" Lottie was grateful and exasperated at the same time. "The truth is, I don't know what's going on with Charlie. He's in bed a lot of the time. Not that we're doing anything, I mean, we weren't doing anything." Hearing these last words, Lottie felt so humiliated she thought she might have to strangle her father and herself. "I mean, he wouldn't talk to me. He still won't talk to me."

Her father said, "You talk too much; you talk your way right into a filthy mess."

Lottie shouted, "I called with good intentions, not for a bawling out. I called as a courtesy, so you wouldn't find out from the Harts. In case they know."

"Please don't yell at your father," Jeanie said.

"You move back in with Charlie, you hear me? You're a married woman, you have a child—"

"Don't you tell me what to do! I don't even know if Charlie wants me back"—her voice caught and broke and she stopped speaking for a moment—"*if* I wanted to go back. Look, Dad, are you with me, or against me? Are you my father or are you my enemy?"

"Hank, please don't answer right away—"

"Why shouldn't Charlie want you back? Evelyn's Charlie's, isn't she? What's the story with this doctor fellow anyway?"

"You think Evelyn's not Charlie's? You think I could sleep with someone—you think I could have a child with someone who isn't Charlie?" Lottie kicked at the arm of the couch.

"Oh, will the two of you stop this please." Her mother sounded on the edge of tears. "It isn't helping Lottie, and it can't be good for you either, Hank. Lottie, dear, please give us your phone number and we'll call you back when he—when we calm down."

Lottie screamed, "The man—whose house this is—his name is—" She lowered her voice, remembering Evelyn asleep upstairs, remembering herself. "George Kenadjian, Dr. Kenadjian, you can call him that, no, you can call him George if he answers—"

"Jeanie, we don't want that phone number. I won't speak to her paramour. You have her work number, that's enough."

"Hank, please—"

"Your mother and I are hanging up now. Hang up, Jeanie."

"Let me say good-bye to her, please, dear." Jeanie's voice quavered.

The sound of her father banging down the receiver was like the wind crashing shut a door.

When the aftershock had passed, Jeanie said, "You have to excuse him. He's upset. He's not used to the way you all live. I mean, the younger generation."

"You think I'm not upset? You think I'm used to leaving my husband?"

Jeanie said, "He was born at the turn of the century. His resilience is gone, he can't accommodate. Try to see it from his point of view. You have the larger responsibility now."

Lottie wanted to ask, when had he been resilient? When did he ever accommodate? But she didn't want to load any more on her mother.

"Give me your phone number, dear. I don't mind speaking to—to your boyfriend."

"He's not my boyfriend, Mom." Lottie gave her mother the phone number.

Despite her phone calls to Charlie and her visit, she had never left a single message, nor written him a note. She wanted *him* to call *her*, to call of his own volition; she needed a sign he still loved her. Was he playing some kind of game? But Charlie never played games, not that kind of game. In the end it was Evelyn's "cold" that got through to Lottie, that broke down her waiting for Charlie to call. It became crucial that the man show he loved his daughter. Evelyn walked around making frequent low sniffling or sighing sounds, tears dripping constantly as if there were a leak behind her blinking eyes or irritated nose. George wondered if she was allergic to something in the house. The prospect of injecting Evelyn under the skin with a series of possible allergens got Lottie to eat whatever she had to eat—face, rage, disbelief, sorrow—and leave Charlie a message to call his daughter. Evelyn was doing badly, Lottie said.

When he called first thing the next morning, Lottie, who had intended to try to find out what was going on with him, maybe come to some under- standing, even perhaps a rapprochement, exploded. "What's the matter with you? Where've you been? I called you in the middle of the night— I went to the house—"

"You went to *my* house?"

"I went to *our* house!"

"Do you know that's breaking and entering?"

"I can't believe you saw a lawyer, or are you just watching a lot of TV? Who else have you seen? Or maybe you went to the lawyer in the middle of the night?" Lottie laughed bitterly alone.

"Put my daughter on."

"What about me? Don't you think you owe me an explanation?"

"For what? For leaving me?"

"You were an absentee husband, an absentee lover, an absentee father—" she shouted until she became aware of Evelyn standing in the kitchen, her eyes full of tears, her nose running. "I thought you were upstairs," Lottie whispered. She passed the receiver over to her daughter, who wiped her face with her skirt, sniffled into the telephone, and said something too soft for Lottie to hear.

Charlie must have said the right thing back because Evelyn smiled. In a few minutes she was giggling. "You did? You will?" She clapped her hands in delight and dropped the phone. Lottie picked it up and moved to hand it to her daughter, who snatched it away—"Daddy? Daddy?" she said worriedly—and smooched several loud kisses into the mouthpiece.

Lottie walked out of the house and sat down on the front steps, where she could not make out her daughter's words but could hear the animated lilt of her voice.

It must be a record-length conversation for Charlie.

It occurred to Lottie that her daughter was flirting.

After a while Lottie didn't hear anything, and then a flushed Evelyn was at the door beckoning her mother to make the meager arrangements.

"Would you let me know when you tell your parents?" Lottie asked Charlie in a robotic voice.

"What's it to you?"

She shook her head. "I know them most of my life."

As he hung up the phone he said, "Your father beat me to the punch."

She felt bereft, as if everyone she knew from childhood were leaving her, were all moving away from her together, or she was falling alone through dark outer space, tethered to nothing, the warm green and blue earth far, far away, the size of a pinprick. She lifted up smiling Evelyn and hugged her to her breasts so tightly that the little girl cried out.

Lottie unpacked.

In the days and weeks after that phone call Lottie felt dazed, as though she had walked out of Plato's dark cave into bright light and couldn't focus her eyes. She couldn't see George at all; and when she saw Charlie at the baby-sitter's, neutral territory where they effected the transfer of Evelyn, he seemed blurred to her—sometimes gigantic, mostly shadowy, unreal.

In the beginning Charlie took Evelyn for a day or two a week, then after a while, only for a morning a week or an afternoon. Lottie didn't ask for money. Evelyn once mentioned something about a lady cleaning at Cha-Cha-Pa's, but Lottie didn't know if it was a lady friend or a cleaning lady. She didn't ask about anything for fear Charlie would try to take Evelyn away. Living at George's house, she'd likely be seen by a judge as an unfit mother.

Whenever Lottie met Charlie, she searched his sullen face for the dreaded signs of disintegration. But always he was carefully shaven, his khaki trousers and bright sports shirt clean and sometimes freshly pressed.

On the other hand, there was a hole in the canvas of his right sneaker through which his big toe stuck out in a dirty white sock. The sock changed, but the hole didn't.

One afternoon at Betty-Jo's, Evelyn was upstairs in the bathroom and Lottie and Charlie were alone together in the living room waiting. He stood examining Betty-Jo's few books in the cinderblock-and-white-board bookcase.

"She napped," Lottie said.

Charlie was fingering the binding of a book.

"She ate," Lottie said.

He did not wear his wedding ring. She fingered hers.

"I'm sending a lightweight jacket with her."

Charlie nodded slightly. A stranger might have thought Charlie was a bibliophile, or that they were both spies communicating in code, that there was a message passed in the taut silence through the slight hunching and straightening movements of his back, the stiff set of her head.

Evelyn ran down the stairs from the second floor and burst into Charlie's opening arms. Grinning, he swung her around once, her arms around his neck, and boosted her up to sit on his shoulders.

Watching them, Lottie remembered herself swinging from Charlie's bull neck the night of her fifteenth birthday. He had given her small gold hoop earrings and she had worn them happily to the local fair. In the evening they undressed behind a farmer's dark barn, listening to the horses shifting and snorting inside, one nervous animal whinnying and kicking at the stall. It was a warm spring night, with a light breeze that carried the green smell of trees and the full, dusky odor of newly turned earth. Charlie, wearing only socks and sneakers, had lifted her up, his hands under her bare buttocks, and carried her, her arms around his neck, up and down a moonlit field, biting at her shoulders, kneading her buttocks, plowing her. The earth was black, and as he gained momentum it looked to Lottie to be at a tilt, in motion: she felt imperiled and ecstatic. He ran them both, wet, into the soft, pungent ground. When she undressed for bed, she had lost one of her earrings, and although she retraced her steps first thing in the morning, she never found it.

"I'll bring her back at six."

She had mourned the earring a long time.

"Wait, Charlie . . ."

He turned, his face closed to her. She felt a sudden dark envy of her daughter.

"Where . . . where are you going?" Lottie asked.

Evelyn bouncing on his shoulders, Charlie hardly looked at Lottie. "What's it to you?"

"Don't talk that way in front of her . . ."

"Don't teach me how to talk. Tell me what you want because I'm out of here."

"It's no big deal, I just wondered are you going to the movies, or hanging around, or—or what?"

"What are you getting at?"

"When did you get so suspicious? It's me, Lottie!"

Charlie looked away from her, whether in grief or impatience she couldn't tell.

She went on, more softly, "I want to know, as her mother, is there someone with you . . ."

"You're asking, am I living with anyone?" he shot out.

Lottie flinched. "I—I sleep in the living room!"

He shrugged his shoulders.

Her face went hot. "Frankly, I worry you're in bed asleep alone and Evelyn's on her own."

He turned his head now to the right, now to the left as he kissed the calves of Evelyn's legs. "What do you take me for?"

When Charlie brought her back to the sitter's, Evelyn would clutch tearfully at his pant leg or belt. Sometimes Lottie had to strap her still crying child into the car seat in the back of George's Volkswagen, where she would fall asleep on the ride home.

When Lottie's luck was really bad, Evelyn would still be wailing as they pulled into George's driveway, and then Lottie could figure on half an hour of carrying her back and forth around the living room crooning, "That's a girl. Yes. Yes. It's all right. Shh . . . You'll see him again next week." Lottie worried that George would not tolerate his small times of peace being swept away in their grief.

One evening Lottie, exhausted from having been on at the lab the night before, stumbled carrying her crying daughter. Lottie managed to fall into the couch.

"Give her to me," George said.

With relief Lottie handed her over. But Evelyn's cries changed to screams and then stopped abruptly as she clamped her teeth into George's cheek. He cried out and tried to push her head away but she snarled at him, holding fast to his cheek. Tears in his eyes, he put his fingers inside his own mouth and was pushing at her teeth from inside his cheek when Lottie slapped Evelyn twice hard across her face.

Squealing, Evelyn pulled out of George's arms and scrambled under the piano.

"You don't bite, you hear me!" Lottie yelled, seeing herself and her daughter camped out on the street. A small oval of tiny pinkish slots indented the flesh of George's cheek.

Evelyn kicked the piano leg.

"You're going to scratch the finish!"

"It's all scratched as it is," George said, a fine line of blood meandering toward his chin. "The piano's old. Don't worry about it."

"Stop this tantrum and come out of there!" Lottie squatted down and reached for Evelyn, who backed away farther and began to howl.

"Let her cool down." George touched his wet cheek.

Evelyn continued to howl.

"If you're so sad at leaving your father, you can just stay there next time, you can go live with him for all I care!"

"Are you crazy, Lottie? Shut up! What are you saying?!"

Evelyn was screaming and gasping for air.

"I'm sorry, sweetheart. I didn't mean it, God knows. But you can't bite George! You can't bite anybody!"

Evelyn's chest was heaving.

Miserable, Lottie watched George tissue away the blood from his face. His hand with the tissue appeared to be shadowed by an overlapping, less substantial hand holding a tissue and she realized she was seeing double from exhaustion.

George knelt down on the floor next to Lottie. "You lost your temper," he said to Evelyn. "Grown-ups lose their tempers, too. When your mother loses it, she slaps you and she screams out things she regrets. When you lose your temper, you cry and wail and, well, you bit me." He tried to grin.

"I take back what I said." Lottie pretended to pluck words from the air and toss them back into her open mouth, then swallow them, bobbing her head. "I wouldn't let you go live with anyone else for all the world. Not Cha-Cha-Pa, not anybody. Not until you're all grown and you have your own husband and babies . . ."

Evelyn was lying on her back kicking both feet into the carpet.

And then suddenly she was asleep, a finger in her mouth, another in her ear. Lottie got a blanket and crawled under the piano to cover her, then lay down on the floor beside her and went to sleep herself.

After a while, George carried sleeping Evelyn up to her bed, and Lottie stumbled onto the couch.

The next day Evelyn crawled under the piano again, rocked back and forth, and made low bleating sounds, a distant look in her eyes. Lottie knelt beside the piano bench and urged her out, then ordered her out.

George sat down on the floor beside Lottie. He had a square gauze pad attached to his face with flesh-colored adhesive tape. "Ev, honey, listen, maybe you're upset now that you bit me." He pointed at the bandage on his face. "Kids bite sometimes. I'm a child doctor, a pediatrician, and once in a while, some kid will bite me. It hurt, yes. It still hurts.

"But you won't do it again. I'm the only person in your whole life you're going to bite."

She looked in his direction but said nothing.

George didn't speak anymore either, just sat there on the floor. After a while he said, "How do I know that, that you won't bite anyone else?" He said, "I know you." George uncrossed his legs and stretched them out. "You get sad and you get mad. But you won't bite again." And then he said, "I'm a child doctor. I know."

After a while she crawled out from under the piano into his lap.

And right there and then Lottie got turned on to George.

Oh, his talkativeness and sociability and cultivation, that the house was always intellectually alive, had meant a lot to her. And still meant a lot. But she enjoyed that the way she would a beautiful, even glorious, tamed animal, a fanning-out, puffed-up peacock, tied to a long handsome chain.

Now all at once her earlier desire for him reappeared, a different, barely related beast, connected somehow to when he lay bare his arms for her to push needles into, took the sock off his foot for her butterfly penetration. Now she went wet to a little-known but deep law of nature: that a man's loving kindness toward a woman's child was an aphrodisiac. Stronger than a rhino's horn. A bandage on his face, especially if the wound was caused by the child and willingly endured by the man, that bandage wrapped itself around the rhino's horn and enhanced its potency, turned the wound and the horn hard and thick and honey-gold. It elicited some kind of female melting, of insistent swelling, of yearning . . . The sound of George's voice when he talked to Evelyn under the piano was sweet, even a little sorrowful; it had a sureness to it. He sounded like a man singing a sad lullaby, guaranteed to settle a child to sleep. He sounded like her father at his rare best, when he was slowly, patiently describing the electrons moving excitedly around the nucleus of the atom, or what caused lightning and thunder while there was a terrifying storm overhead. She only dimly remembered that father. George with his bitten face sitting humbly, trying intelligently to gather his wits, to take kind control of a wild scene so that her life and her child's would be bearable: that George turned her on.

That night after he carried Evelyn to sleep upstairs, Lottie started licking his ear as he studied at the kitchen table, then moved her fingers caressingly over the crotch of his pants until she felt him grow hard.

"What is this?" he asked.

"An erection."

"Don't be funny. What are you doing, is what I'm asking? What are you up to? I'm not asking what I'm up to."

"Upstairs," she said. "Come upstairs."

Unsure, he followed her. "I just got Evelyn to sleep," he whispered. Inside his bedroom, she locked the door and turned the handle to check. She stood listening for a while but heard nothing. Then she began to undress him—he moved to undress her, too, but she shook her head. "I want to do everything, let me do it all."

After she undressed him, she took off her own clothes.

"Lottie, dear batty Lottie, what's going on? You've never done anything like this before. Not that I'm complaining. Do you know I've never seen you naked?" He stepped back and looked hard at her. "You're gorgeous."

Lottie had never seen any man naked other than Charlie. George was smaller than Charlie, his penis was darker, shooting out of his black pubic hair like a wrapped tube. And his balls were hairy. She couldn't stop staring. Finally, she said, to say something, "You like the stretch marks?"

"I don't need virginal—you're marvelous."

He got down on his knees and started kissing the insides of her thighs.

She stepped away and signaled him to be quiet. She pointed at the door. They both listened.

"Lottie dear, I don't want to look a gift horse in the mouth," he whispered. "But this isn't the way to do it. This is nerve-racking. We have to get out of the house or get Evelyn out of the house or both. If you're serious. Are you serious?"

In response, she got down on *her* knees and lapped his balls and finally when she got her mouth over his penis he groaned and came.

Apologizing.

"For what?" she whispered. "What are you apologizing for?" She was on her knees still.

"I didn't do anything for you. I didn't do what I wanted to do for you."

Both of them on their knees, she took his hands in hers. She didn't know the answer to his question—was she serious? A bizarre thought kept coming to mind: *He doesn't look anything like Charlie.*

"I don't have problems," he said. "Honestly. But it's been a long time, just me and my right hand."

"Shhh." She stuck her ear to the door again. They didn't move for several minutes.

"Get your clothes on," he hissed. "This is not the way I want this to go."

They got dressed. They went downstairs and sat next to each other holding hands on the couch in the dimly lit living room.

"How come?" he whispered to her. "Why didn't you want me to touch you?"

"I don't know."

"What is this all about?"

"You've done so much for me, you've done so much for both of us."

"Is this payback?" he asked.

"Nope."

"I don't want sexual payback."

"George, you're only the second man I've slept with in my whole life."

"And you haven't even slept with me . . ." he said.

"You're the only man other than Charlie I've ever . . . sucked off."

He nodded, paused, seemed not to know how to take in what she was saying. "Still, I'm worried this has something to do with gratitude."

"Well, I *am* grateful—but that's not all I am." And she lifted up her skirt and flashed him her underpants, pointing at the wet white strip of cotton over her crotch.

"A rain forest!" He grinned. "Or else you peed on yourself."

"It doesn't rain from gratitude."

"I want to get into that rain forest," he said. He put his hand on the wet material over her crotch and pushed up hard while keeping his eyes on the stairs. "I want *you* to come. How do you come, anyway? Do you come? You had a husband—"

"I have a husband," she said grimly.

He pushed and pushed at her crotch. "Do you suck him off and not come yourself?"

"Don't talk that way about Charlie! You've got him all wrong. I almost always came."

While he pushed around her crotch with one hand, he pulled at her nipples through her dress and bra with the other while somehow keeping his eyes on the stairs. He stopped and said, "This is juvenile. I want to do something for you. But not like this."

He put his arms around her and kissed her hair. "This is like high school," he whispered. "I mean I really didn't expect anything from my WASP from the Upper Peninsula," he said to her. "But not high school."

They sat holding each other, their eyes on the stairs. "I'm not a Protestant," she said.

"What are you?"

"I'm not any religion. I was brought up to think God was like Santa Claus. Only children believed in him."

"I hardly know anything about you. I'm lonely," he sighed. "I'm truly lonely. I used to miss my wife after she left. Now I miss *you*, Lottie. I want you close to me. I care about you deeply, and about Evelyn."

They got a few hours of sleep, George in his bedroom, Lottie on the couch, before George had to leave for work, and then Evelyn was up and Lottie took her to day care and went to the hospital.

George was on the next night and they had whispered phone conversations. "Are you worried you'll get pregnant? Is that why you didn't want me to touch you? I'm glad to use a condom if you don't want to go on the pill. Or are you on the pill? Or you could get a diaphragm. I don't even know what kind of birth control you use."

"I'm not going on the pill. Why should I mess with my hormones? Why don't they develop something that messes with *your* hormones?"

"Whoa! Whoa!" he said. "I'm not asking you to! I'm just trying to get prepared. To understand. You've never even slept in the same bed with me."

"Unless we're serious, unless we're going to get married, I don't want to expose Evelyn to anything."

"Do you know what's going on at Charlie's house?"

"No." She didn't like to think about it. "But I don't want to add to Evelyn's problems."

"All right, so don't move into my room yet. But let's spend a night together somewhere," he whispered. "A whole night together. We owe it to ourselves."

Lottie didn't answer.

George said bitterly, "You're not really unpacking, are you."

A week later Lottie offered, "Okay, you're right, maybe a change of venue would help." She added, "It's for sure Evelyn's presence, maybe it's even being in your house—your wife's house—that gets in the way."

"My wife's house?"

"Well, she was the interior decorator—the burlap, the pineapples."

Lottie called the babysitter, and after dinner Lottie and George each packed a small bag and Lottie packed a bag for Evelyn, and they dropped her off along with her stuffed animals.

While George got the keys to the motel room, Lottie sat slumped down in the Volkswagen, its motor running.

In the room there was a bed, two night tables with Bibles, a television set, a desk with a faded blue blotter, and a chair. A squat pearly-pink vase with red plastic roses in it sat on the dresser, and above the bed hung a gilt-framed print of a white boy showing a black boy his sore toe in front of a picket fence. Norman Rockwell.

Lottie stretched apart two slats of the Venetian blinds to scan the darkening parking lot for Charlie's baby-blue Chevy. A large black car moved past the window and for a moment Lottie thought it was her father's old Lincoln.

As Lottie spoke to her daughter on the telephone, George unpacked the picnic box. On the desk he placed a bottle of red wine, a bowl of fruit, and a round sourdough loaf and a log of goat cheese on a wooden board.

"Get Betty-Jo to read to you, sweetie," Lottie said into the telephone.

From his pants pocket George took out a white envelope and some cigarette papers and put them beside the ashtray on the night table.

"Hold on a minute, dear." Her hand over the mouthpiece, Lottie whispered to George, "Listen to this, would you? Do you hear a noise? A clicking noise?"

George listened. He put the receiver against his chest. "What are you worried about?"

"I don't know."

"Are you thinking the phone is tapped?"

"That's too crazy, isn't it, George?"

"Yes."

"You don't think Charlie could be looking for evidence to take her away?"

"He hardly wants to take Evelyn at all, let alone take her away."

Lottie nodded grimly. "Maybe someone's tapping the phone because you're trying for CO status . . ."

He groaned. "Lottie. We're alone. Not even the FBI could tap a phone that fast." He said into the receiver, "Evelyn, are you knocking against the phone? You know—clack clack, bang bang?" He nodded a few times. "With what? With a fork?" He handed the phone to a chagrined Lottie, who yelled into it, "Why would you hit the phone with a fork?!" Then she said, "I can't right now. I'll tell you two stories tomorrow. Put that fork down this minute!"

George said, "For God's sake, tell her a story!"

Lottie put her hand over the mouthpiece: "You don't mind?"

"No, no," he growled. "She's a child, don't you know that? I'll take a shower."

When George came out of the bathroom, Lottie was dabbing her breasts and buttocks and inner thighs with White Shoulders.

"How'd the bedtime story go?" His black hair was long and wet and shiny.

"I told her about Louis Pasteur."

"As a bedtime story?"

"I told her about pasteurization."

"And that put her to sleep?"

"Milk is calming. Anyway, the story calmed me."

He laughed and screwed the corkscrew down into the cork of the bottle. "How're those applications coming? To school?"

The sound of the cork whooshing out startled her and she looked fearfully at the closed, chain-locked door.

He shook his head at her jumpiness. "Are you doing anything with those applications?"

"I had a few transcripts sent. And I asked old professors to write letters of recommendation."

"Good. You can always put an acceptance on hold. There's nothing shameful in that."

She felt vague. "You think I can do it, graduate school?"

He nodded.

"I need a drink," she said.

He poured two glasses. "Well, here's to us!" Sitting on the sagging bed, the air conditioner rattling along, they touched dark glasses. "Here's to pasteurization!" he grinned.

"To fermentation! To vaccination!" She noticed suddenly how slender his hands were, one cupping the wineglass. They seemed almost feminine.

He put down the glass. "I'm worried about us." He put his head on her shoulder. "Tell me what you want me to do."

"Just try something and I'll let you know how it feels."

"Give me a hint . . ."

"Oh, George . . ." She kissed his wet head, aware that she had to bend her head down.

"Do you find me—am I—" He looked up anxiously. "Am I—attractive to you?"

"Is that chewing tobacco in the envelope?"

He laughed. "You're a real rube! It's grass. Want to try some?"

"I am not a rube. What's a rube?"

"An innocent, sort of. I say it with affection. A country bumpkin. In some ways, you're wild. In others, you're completely naïve." He picked up the envelope from the night table.

She'd never even smoked a cigarette; her mother's example had turned her off completely and Charlie had always been in training. She did not want to appear stupid and she had to assume that a physician would not give her something bad for her. She stuck out her tongue mock-suggestively and said in what she hoped was a sophisticated tone: "Will it drive me to unimaginable heights and depths?"

"It might relax you."

"I'll try it."

He rolled a joint on a piece of aluminum foil, then folded the foil into a V and tapped the leftover flakes and seeds back into the white envelope. He lit the joint, inhaled deeply, and, holding in the smoke, passed the joint to Lottie. "You didn't answer my question," he said.

She took a deep puff and choked. She coughed a few times, her throat burning. "I *am* a rube!" she sputtered and hurried to the bathroom. She gargled, trying to ease her sore throat.

In a few minutes she came out carrying a glass of water and sat down on the edge of the bed.

"You didn't answer me," he said to her. "I guess that's a kind of answer."

"What didn't I answer?"

"Am I attractive to you?" He said this loudly.

"What do you mean? Am *I*—attractive—to *you*?"

"You? Are you attractive to me? Of course you are! Your body's generous. Your dark blue eyes . . . I love your thick hair." He ran his hand through it. "You're not beautiful, your mouth's too large. But hey, I'm in praise of imperfection." His eyes filled up. "What about me? I'm asking about me!"

"Well, you're attractive to me, too. I'm just not used to you."

"We've known each other for months! Look, either somebody's attractive or they're not. I never heard of anybody having to get used to somebody."

"If your husband died recently, you'd have to get used to somebody."

"Is that how you feel?"

"I know Charlie almost my whole life!"

He nodded a few times.

"Let me have another drag of that," she said.

"Maybe you want to call it a night?"

"What do you mean?"

"Maybe we should call it a night on the dope."

"If you think it would ease things . . . I'd certainly like to . . . ease things." She sighed.

"I want to ease things, too. I don't want to stick it in, Lottie. I want to fly you on me like a flag! I want to be your pole!" He sat back against the headboard and grinned and inhaled again. He had a brave erection. She put her fingers out for the joint and hoisted her legs onto the bed and sat back next to him.

They smoked for a while. "Close your eyes," he said.

"Why?"

"A surprise."

She heard him get up and walk toward the closet.

"Can I open my eyes to take a drag?" She liked the way "drag" sounded. She said it again. She wanted to open her eyes to get a take on the room because she was starting to feel unmoored, unsettled; but when she opened her eyes, the room seemed to be rocking. And everything was slowing down.

"Be careful with that stuff," he called out to her.

"What could happen? What could happen?"

"You could repeat yourself."

"My thoughts are getting . . . thick, gelatinous. I have this terrible feeling you know what I'm thinking. Like I have no privacy." And she wasn't thinking loving thoughts about him.

"Don't smoke any more," he called to her. He was at the other end of the room, bent over his suitcase.

"Why not?"

"You could get sick."

"You mean, throw up? Throw up?"

"Stop it! You sound like the goose in *Charlotte's Web*."

"I'm the spider."

"Just close your eyes and keep quiet. And stop smoking!" Then he said, "Okay. You can look now." George stood before her smiling. His smile seemed crooked although she figured it was the grass.

He held out a light blue-and-white checked stuffed porpoise with rolling eyes and a navy-blue stitched smile. It was the size of a chihuahua.

"He's very sweet." Lottie wondered whether her own eyes were rolling.

"Take a good look at him."

"Why? Will he turn into a frog?"

On his front flipper the animal wore an open spiral gold ring with the head of a porpoise on one end and the tail, overlapping the head, at the other. The gold porpoise's beaky mouth was slightly open and he had a raised gold collar around his neck.

She eased the ring off the stuffed animal. "It's beautiful. Beautiful."

"Read the note."

A small envelope was taped to the animal's tail. Inside was a cream-colored card on which George had written, "You give my life porpoise."

She guffawed. Her laughter sounded too loud and she tried to lower her voice. She tried to put the ring on the ring finger of her left hand but her wedding ring was there. And she couldn't pull it off: it was on like a vise. She put her finger in her mouth, then tried wriggling the ring off; it wouldn't budge. Finally she placed the porpoise ring on the ring finger of her right hand.

Her eyes began to run and then she felt wet between her legs. She put a hand under her on the sheet. She began to rock with laughter. "Would you believe it, I peed!?" She laughed and laughed, and kept on peeing.

"Go to the toilet!" George roared.

She ran, peeing as she went.

In a few minutes she returned with a towel, laid it over the wet splotch on the bed, and sat down on it. "I'm sorry."

He waved away her apology.

She held her hand out in front of her, looking at the gold porpoise as she laughed and wept. "I love it! I do!" She lifted her glass high.

He clinked his glass against hers and they drank.

"You don't mind if I tell you you're a real pisser?" He sat next to her on the side of the bed and put his arm around her. "You make me feel a bit like I'm on a busman's holiday, what with your peeing in bed."

She started laughing again and poured more wine. "I've never peed on a man before. Have you ever had a woman pee on you? Has your wife ever peed on you? How long do you know your wife?—Okay, wait, wait, I remember now: Only since you were both sixteen. You met her kayaking through the Grand Canal—Grand Canyon . . ." She giggled. "She's your Western love. Could I be your Midwestern love?" She continued giggling. "Put your drink down for a minute. I'll give you something better." She got up on her knees beside him and eased her nipple into his mouth. He sucked on it until it stood out. She moved his head to her other nipple. "Do you think I could hang a strand of pearls off this bugger?"

"What do you mean?"

She ran her hand through his hair. "What kind of hair is this that stays curly even when it's wet?"

"That's Armenian hair. I'm not really a descendent of Sitting Bull."

"Keep sucking," she said. "Oh God, that was the scariest night of my life. You know Charlie was asleep when I got home and I never told him what happened. Did you tell your wife?"

"What night? The Indian night? When that guy pulled my hair out?" He snatched a breath and went on sucking.

"Mmmm . . ."

"I told her."

"You look like you're swimming," Lottie said. "You know how a person turns his head up for air every few strokes?" His head seemed narrow. She had never noticed that before. He looked like a hairy eel. She closed her eyes. "Did you say you told her? Why?"

"It seemed natural to tell her—Hey, is this doing anything for you? My sucking?"

"I don't know. Hang in there a bit. I'll bet that cheese board was a wedding present, huh? Huh?"

"I don't remember."

"Yeah, you don't remember. Say, what do you think the chances are that your wife is with some guy on that commune, doing with him exactly what we're doing, you and I, right this minute?"

"I don't want to talk about my wife with some other guy."

"Are you still carrying a torch for her?"

"Do you want me to lose my erection?"

"I thought you said it was utterly reliable. All right, all right, what was your honeymoon like?"

"I don't want to talk about my honeymoon."

"Oh come on."

"No! It's about as important as how many other people slept in this room . . . Look, are you trying to pick a fight?" He gestured at his erection. "Because I really want to get in, I badly want to get into you."

She pointed to some darkened areas on his penis. "What's that?"

"That's my dick! You've seen it before. Didn't Charlie have one something like this, or was his like a Greek god's? Excuse me, like Wotan's."

"The spots. I'm talking about the spots."

"I think that's a lubricant rash from all the jerking off I've been doing."

"Are you sure? Have you been with your—have you been with—with anybody else?"

"Do you think I'm having an affair with my wife? She's in Idaho. My prick is long, but—"

"Are these the kinds of sarcastic remarks you make when you lose your temper?"

"It's my patience I've lost. Did you think I'd never tire of whacking off?"

They were eye to eye, and he had a leg hooked over her leg. Suddenly he looked like a ferret, and then she was not sure if she had said that or thought it.

She needed some privacy. She was accustomed to burying her head in Charlie's chest for a moment or two to catch her breath, but George was too slim.

She pulled him over her. Little lizard. Had she blurted something out? There was barely enough of him to cover her, let alone shield her from his eyes. Her shoulders were up against his shoulders, her breasts against his chest.

She felt his erection touching her pubic hair. He snuggled it up against her groin. She felt dizzy. His penis with its mottled foreskin had looked like a blistered fireman's helmet. She hoped she hadn't said that. His body hair suddenly made her itch.

He pushed himself down and flicked his tongue over her genitals for a few minutes. A garden snake.

"Is this all right, Lottie?" He paused.

"Don't ask me, just go ahead!" She shut her eyes and grimaced.

After a moment he said, "Are you in pain?"

"No—no, just go on!"

He touched her labia with his fingers. "You're dry dry dry . . ."

"Stop talking, for God's sakes! I can't build up any momentum!" She began to cry although she could equally have begun to laugh.

You little leech, you runt.

"Easy does it," he said. "There's no rush." He was licking, licking.

You make a vice out of patience, Lottie thought.

He handed her some tissues to dry her eyes, then turned her onto her stomach. He ran his hands over her back. "You're all tensed up." He moved the heels of his hands over her shoulder blades and pounded his fists down the length of her spinal cord. He pressed his fingers into the small of her back.

Bug off, she thought, as she fell asleep.

George woke her at six in the morning so they could get Evelyn before they went to work. Lottie's throat and tongue were sore.

"Sorry." She didn't look at him and she aimed the one word down toward the floor so he wouldn't smell her morning breath.

"The truth's the truth. You don't want me."

"Why is the truth how I act when I'm full of dope?"

He took her head in his hands. The whites of his soft hazel eyes were bloodshot, as if he hadn't been to sleep.

She turned away. "I have to brush my teeth." She extricated herself and went into the bathroom.

In the car in the gray dawning light she feared she would cleave to Charlie all of her life.

A few months later Lottie was beeped out of lunch to draw routine bloods on a VIP in the emergency room. Irritated, and always uneasy about emergency rooms, she organized her blood tray hurriedly and went over to look for the patient.

"Where's eight-oh-three-six-seven?" she asked the head nurse, a thick-legged woman in her sixties. "It's supposed to be some celebrity."

The head nurse pointed to a cubicle crowded with adults. A slender eight-year-old boy lay whimpering and coughing as an orthopedist cast his right leg up to the thigh. The child was exceptionally handsome, with very white skin and almost blue-black hair and eyebrows, and large black frightened eyes. He had bruise marks on his forehead and around his pale mouth. He clung to the hand of a plump middle-aged black woman who wore a bulging orange apron and a bright green coat that was too small for her.

"He'll be all right, Doctor, won't he?" The fear in the boy's eyes was echoed in the woman's voice. She ceaselessly massaged the back of the boy's head and neck and shoulders with her free hand.

The others—a gray-haired man in a three-piece suit and a meaty man in black gym shorts and shirt—looked anxiously at the doctor, whose auburn hair and rimless eyeglasses were flecked with wet plaster. He nodded and grunted.

"Is the child a movie star?" Lottie asked, out of earshot of the web of people in which the boy looked caught, as she readied her syringe and tubes.

The nurse shook her head. "The father's a councilman, a big lawyer who donates a lot of moolah to the school every year, and to the hospital, too. That's the principal and the other guy's the gym teacher. I think the woman's the housekeeper. Kid fractured his leg in three places."

"Jesus," Lottie said. "How'd that happen?"

"On a seesaw. He fell off and some kid slammed the board down on his leg. Playground accident."

Lottie felt her chest contract. Did Betty-Jo keep a hand on Evelyn at all times? After a moment she asked, "Why is he coughing?"

The nurse shrugged her shoulders. "He's afebrile. Lungs are clear. Maybe it's nerves."

Lottie spoke gently to the child as she tied her tubing around his arm. "It'll only hurt for a second. Taking out a splinter is much worse." The boy didn't seem to be paying attention. He let her handle his arm as if it were a thing.

But when it came to doing a throat culture—since the child was coughing, why not?—he suddenly clamped his mouth shut and looked more frightened of her than of the orthopedist.

"What's your favorite song?" Lottie asked. "We could sing it together. My little girl and I sing our hearts out at the doctor's: La! La! La! La!"

He looked at the floor.

"If it's more your thing"—Lottie looked doubtful—"a sports cheer will do the trick just as well. Get your mouth open so I can see down to your toes: Hit 'em high! Hit 'em low! Come on, Michigan, go go go! What's the name of your school?"

The gym teacher said, "Saybrook."

"Hit 'em high, hit 'em low, come on, Saybrook, go go go!"

The boy backed away from her inch by inch on the gurney as Lottie advanced with the swab.

"Hold still!" the orthopedist yelled at the child.

"Do you really need to do this?" The plump black woman in the uniform looked plaintively at Lottie. "He's upset."

"Well, he's coughing," Lottie said. "Did anybody get a look at his throat?"

The boy put his hand over his mouth.

The woman caressed his cheeks: "Let the girl doctor take a look, honey. She's a nice girl."

Suddenly Lottie screamed. The boy's mouth gaped in surprise and she got her swab in, and out.

The nurse whistled. "Where'd you pick up that technique?"

The orthopedist shook his head in grudging admiration. "Give me some warning next time."

The boy kicked her in the belly hard with his good leg.

Hunched over and holding her abdomen, she didn't hide her grin.

In the lab she took an inoculating loop and plated out the throat swab specimen on a blood agar plate and, for good measure, on a chocolate plate. She placed them in the incubator.

She spun down the blood and measured the sed rate. She placed a drop of blood on a grid under a cover slip and began counting white blood cells per high power field. She counted stabs, eos, monos, lymphos, basos. She used to love the way they looked, the way they sounded.

But lately she figured maybe she had counted all the blood cells she was meant to count in this life. Whatever that meant. As if there were a grand plan out there for her, and she had finished the first part of the plan and now had to move on to part two. No, she could stay counting blood cells forever, but the thrill was gone. She wasn't learning anymore. Sometimes she even likened it to working for a laundry service. She rode the truck around, picking up the dirty stuff. She sorted it into machines, threw suds in here, bleach there, that pile she dry cleaned. There were a few mystery stains to which she applied a few known solvents; either they worked or they didn't. Then she dried everything and pressed it all and folded it up and sent it on out. And the next day it all came back in again.

She didn't want to be always following orders, applying somebody else's ideas. Not that she was sure things would be very different at graduate school, but at least she'd be working toward an advanced degree.

What would she do with Evelyn? How would she support herself and her daughter?

There were fellowships. Maybe she could be an adjunct professor.

Was she thinking about graduate school because it was over with George?

She was thinking about graduate school because she was thinking about graduate school.

That night she put together polite inquiries to see if two undergrad professors had in fact sent in letters of recommendation for her. She framed a note for Mihiner's secretary asking the boss to write an evaluation of her performance as a tech: dare she put it into words? *She was hoping to go to graduate school.* She lay awake imagining herself among her fellow students (and they were all fellows) surrounded by flasks and Bunsen burners, heating this and pipetting that: "Is it mice day or rabbit day or monkey day?" Lottie went in to work in the morning on no sleep at all, elated.

By lunchtime Mihiner had scribbled her back via interhospital mail a simple "Good luck!" and asked for the names and addresses of the schools. Delighted, she immediately shot him a THANK YOU in large letters. She would send the details the next day.

Humming to herself in the lab, she took the plates out of the incubator. Two of them were the cultures from the boy with the leg fractures and she looked at those first to be rid of the case. The blood agar plate had grown out normal flora and she set it aside after noting the growth in the book. When she picked up the chocolate plate, for growing out *Haemophilus*, she saw that in her haste she had mistakenly inoculated a Thayer-Martin plate, which was the same color but supported Neisseria organisms almost never found in children's throats. More surprising, she found something growing in the medium-gray glistening slightly mucoid colonies. If she could inoculate the wrong plate in her haste, couldn't she have brushed in some contaminant as well?

With a loop, she picked a colony from the plate and emulsified it in a drop of distilled water that she pipetted onto the slide. She let it air dry and then heated it in the flame of a Bunsen burner. Holding the slide with a forceps, she dipped it into a little jar of crystal violet dye and then rinsed it with distilled water. She dipped and rinsed, dipped and rinsed, and then counterstained with safranin, a red dye, rinsed a third time, and blotted it with blotting paper.

After she Gram-stained the slide, she placed it under the microscope and focused down, expecting to see red rods of different lengths. But what swam up through layers into focus were blue diplococci: the coffee beans of *Neisseria*.

The only pathogens that looked like that were *meningitidis* or gonorrhea. Could the child have meningitis? Except for the cough, he hadn't been sick at all. She ran down to the ER but the boy had of course been discharged. A doctor there who'd seen him briefly assured her that he had shown no signs of any illness and that meningococcus was often a normal inhabitant of the nasopharynx of healthy individuals; it had frequently been noted in military recruit camps. She was impressed and calmed and went back to the lab, where she picked another colony from the plate and inoculated tubes of sugars: glucose, maltose, and sucrose in a rack. She put these tubes into the incubator for twenty-four hours. Maybe a good night's sleep would straighten them out.

When she removed the tubes the next afternoon, she expected the glucose and maltose to have changed color from red to yellow, indicating *meningitidis* in a healthy boy.

But only the glucose had turned color: she checked her lab manual in the expectation that she was mistaken. She was not. Glucose alone turned yellow only in the case of *Neisseria gonorrhoeae*.

The boy had gonorrhea?! In his throat! It couldn't be! How could she have picked up such a contaminant?

Wearing plastic gloves, she shook her wastebasket to see if the previous day's garbage was still there, as if it would have been of any use.

Maybe the contaminant had been in the swab all along then? Had she pushed a dirty swab into the child's throat? Preposterous! She had only twice seen positive throat cultures for gonorrhea, and the last one had been a month earlier.

As she picked up the day's specimens from the different floors and ran them through, she mulled over the problem of the positive culture. When she took her lunch break, she sat on a bench in the hospital's gardens spooning her yogurt mechanically into her mouth, reading the same sentence again and again in her tissue culture book.

Could she herself be a carrier, a typhoid Lottie? A gonorrhea Lottie?

Perhaps she had been the source of the other two positive cultures as well?

Oh, come on.

She would have to go back to the child and get another throat culture. Then she remembered the ruckus he had made about opening his mouth. Had he been hiding gonorrhea?

Where was he now? He must be at school. Or at home. She called Records and gave the clerk the chart number.

The chart was out.

George came home late after Evelyn was asleep. Lottie dished out spaghetti for the two of them: she was trying to pay some attention to his needs. He entered the kitchen and kissed the back of her head in an almost paternal way.

As quickly as she could, she told him what was going on.

George chewed thoughtfully. "It doesn't necessarily mean anything that the kid wouldn't open his mouth. Half the kids won't open their mouths. Pediatricians have had to take throat cultures under anesthesia. Do you want my opinion?"

"Of course I do."

He finished the last strand of spaghetti and mopped at the sauce on his plate with a piece of bread. "Get another culture and put the kid on penicillin. Why didn't you put him on penicillin right away?"

She laughed. "I'm honored you accord me prescribing privileges. I figured I was a hero for taking a throat culture without an order."

"Who's the peds resident who missed it?" He stood up to clear the table.

"I didn't look for his name."

"At the same time there's something to be said for the fact that anybody else sticks his dick in that throat, he'll get what's coming to him."

"Oh God, George . . ." She tried to stop imagining a large penis going into that child's delicate mouth and got up to wash the dishes. "What about sensitizing a kid to an antibiotic? That's a clinical issue, isn't it? And we don't know for sure he's got anything."

"Stop thinking like a scientist! You don't leave a kid with a mouthful while you futz around."

"Am I thinking like a scientist?!" She was delighted.

"You better talk to the other lab techs about this. It's either some weird accident or else it's a public health issue and a child abuse case—I mean, the bright news is that often oral gonorrhea clears up by itself."

The next morning she told her story to Trixie and Angela and LuAnne and showed them her plates and slides and sugars. "Maybe it was something in the air? I waved that stick around for a good couple of minutes before I got it in."

Angela said, "I know you. You're very careful. You wouldn't contaminate anything." The others nodded agreement.

She bowed her head as if she'd been knighted.

What to do about that boy?

She stopped by Mihiner's office but the secretary said he was out of town the rest of the week. And that he'd signed off on her letters and they'd gone out. Lottie beamed at the secretary, then took the first available opening on Monday.

After work Lottie bought a map of the United States and taped it up on Evelyn's bedroom wall. She stuck white tacks in the map where the five graduate schools she had written to were located. She sorely hoped five applications would be enough to yield one acceptance.

Lottie lost herself in hopes of a new life—in science. She did wonder from time to time whether an advanced degree would mean the end of her chances for marriage. Thalia Cheek, her undergraduate biology professor, had been divorced. At the hospital there were three female attendings: a pediatrician and a psychiatrist—both unmarried—and one radiologist, divorced. Lottie had heard that the only woman resident, a gynecologist, told prospective dates she "worked in a hospital."

When she thought how fond Evelyn had grown of George, and how Lottie would have to uproot her yet again whether or not graduate school was in the offing, Lottie vowed never to move in with another man unless it was for life.

And what about taking Evelyn far away from Cha-Cha-Pa? She looked forward to seeing him the one morning or afternoon a week—at least it *was* every week—and she no longer wailed when he took her back to the baby-sitter's. She seemed to have adjusted to their life. Suppose Lottie ended up in some other part of the country. Could she put an unaccompanied five-year-old on an airplane? The airlines assigned stewardesses to children, she'd read somewhere. But how would they afford airplane trips with any regularity? Maybe Charlie would take Evelyn summers.

There was no point worrying about Evelyn when Lottie didn't even know if she'd be accepted anywhere.

On Monday at noon she went to Mihiner's office. His secretary said he would be back at one, but he had an appointment. What had happened to *her* appointment? Some snafu. She decided to hang out and catch him.

In the hall Lottie stood reading the department bulletin board. People sought tutoring positions, microscopes, roommates. Someone offered to sell horse serum. Someone else claimed he could write poems on scientific subjects for all occasions. What could she do to pick up some extra cash?

Dr. Mihiner strode past her.

"Sir—Sir—"

"What is it?" He frowned. She suddenly imagined that his long white lab coat ended in a train borne aloft by creatures who were half lab techs, half mice.

"Thank you very much for writing those letters for me."

He waved his hand. "You've done good work here."

She smiled and bobbed her head repeatedly. "Sir, I was wondering what happened to that boy I cultured. The one with . . . perhaps with . . . you know . . ."

He gave no sign of recognition.

"That young boy with the problem—"

He looked at his watch.

"The one with the venereal disease!" she fairly screamed out. "You know, in his mouth."

Mihiner's face purpled and he hissed: "We don't discuss patients in the hall! It's a breach of ethics as well as decorum."

She looked around. "There's no one here."

He had already walked past her through his secretary's office. Lottie hurried after him.

His office was spacious with several large clean windows that overlooked fields and flat blue sky. She'd never been in it before, which was strange; where had he interviewed her? In the center of the room was a massive walnut desk on which stood a gold-colored astrolabe and a compass. Three cocoa-colored leather swivel seats with brass studs were arranged at a great distance from each other and the desk; in back of them were built-in walnut bookshelves that held thick dark books and bound journals. The wall behind the desk was covered with diplomas and citations. In the center was a framed blown-up color photograph of Dr. Mihiner shaking hands with Dwight D. Eisenhower, both of them in khaki army uniforms; Dr. Mihiner had a full head of dark hair and was the same height as the general. Lottie stared baffled at the photo.

"Sit down," the current Mihiner said. The chair behind the desk was raised higher than the other chairs.

She did not feel invited so much as ordered. Dr. Mihiner himself remained standing next to his chair.

As she sat down in the Texas-size chair, the leather yielded to her body with a long sigh, which embarrassed her. She resettled herself and the chair expired again. She leaned forward. "I don't know the boy's name but he was in the emergency room ten days ago. You must have seen my cultures. All the results get passed by you."

He was sorting through some papers on his desk but stopped to look at her: "It's the one infraction you've incurred at the hospital."

"What do you mean, sir?"

"Where do you come off doing a throat culture without an order?"

"He was coughing . . ."

"How about sputum cultures? X-rays? Do you operate?"

"A throat culture is an inexpensive, noninvasive procedure . . ." Her voice quavered.

"Next time you play doctor, you better have an MD. Otherwise, you'll be looking for a job."

"But it was crucial—"

"Says who?" He slapped the desk with his open hand. "The whole thing was a fluke! A monkey might have ordered some tests, one of which could have turned out to be positive . . ."

She stood up and leaned toward him over the desk. "Just tell me, did the child get treated or not? Did they find out who—who might have done it to him?" She couldn't believe she was interrogating him.

"I'm not at liberty to discuss that with you."

"What do you mean?" He had grown a slight bit taller than she, and she wondered if he was standing on his toes.

"I consider myself bound by patient confidentiality . . ."

"But I work for the hospital! I did the throat culture!"

Dr. Mihiner looked attentively at her face and neck from the other side of the desk: "It happens the orthopedist put him on penicillin prophylactically as soon as he saw him."

"Prophylactically? What do you mean?" Lottie asked, alarmed.

Mihiner chortled: "Against wound infection, young lady! The boy had a complex fracture. I re-cultured him myself as soon as I saw your results, but I couldn't repeat them."

"Before you went away?"

"Yes."

"But he'd been on antibiotics three or four days by then."

"You should have informed me immediately."

"I wanted to be sure . . ."

"This isn't a research lab! This isn't a theoretical problem!"

Lottie sat slowly down. "I didn't think I should make such a serious accusation without being sure."

"It's not your job to be sure. That's my job. And you aren't the one who ends up making accusations. That's also my job. You really don't know your place, do you? It's good you're getting out of here. Let's hope you're getting out of here. Frankly you've created something of a problem."

"Do you think I'll get into graduate school?"

He shrugged his shoulders. "I wrote a good letter." He smiled at her.

She smiled back happily. Then she shook her head. "You wouldn't have gotten anything anyway even if I'd told you right off the bat. You said the boy was put immediately on antibiotics."

"Usually you can still get something twenty-four, even forty-eight hours later," Mihiner said.

She'd been overly cautious. Woman that she was. She felt as if she were descending too quickly in an airplane.

Dr. Mihiner took a handful of pencils with perfect points from his desk drawer and began sharpening them, one after another, in his electric pencil sharpener. It made a grinding noise. "His father and mother are in a rage at the hospital for bumbling. They've hired a private detective. The boy claims he's never had sex with anyone.

"And you have to stop yelling about this in public places. This family—any family—is entitled to privacy."

She thought about it. "But this is a crime. Shouldn't it be reported? At least to Social Welfare?"

His forehead wrinkled in annoyance, his entire scalp moving as if it were a rubber mask. "As I told you, the parents would prefer to let the private detective do his work unencumbered by the board of health, the Department of Social Welfare—"

"I want to enter my results in the patient's chart."

"We owe this family quite a lot . . ." He looked across at her now, his eyes gleaming dangerously.

She thought of Yul Brynner playing a pirate.

"You're a stubborn little thing," he glowered.

On the other side of his desk, she leaned back away from him: "I'm the same height as you are," she whispered. "Maybe I'm an inch taller. Or shorter. We're very close in height." Listening to herself discuss their relative heights, she feared her thoughts were becoming disorganized.

He stood up. "If you report this, you'll humiliate one of our first families. You'll make it harder for ordinary people to come to the hospital for help if they think they've got a venereal disease . . ."

"Sir, with all due respect, I think there's some kind of cover-up going on here."

Mihiner's face turned purple. "I'm trying to cover up your ass, young lady, which is hanging out! You don't seem to understand that in all likelihood you've made a mistake. Lab errors are a dime a dozen. Why would you want to compound yours by spreading it all over town? Where's your sensitivity to other human beings?"

"I'd like the chart, please."

"Arrogance is out of place in the sciences, and it's especially unbecoming in a young woman. You're in for a fall, miss. And if you report anything, I will see that you take that fall."

"Just give me the chart."

"You find it."

The next day Dr. Mihiner phoned her at the lab. "You don't fit in here, Mrs. Hart. You don't know how to be part of a team. If I were you, I'd start thinking about some other line of work. You'll get a pink slip if you report this and I guarantee you, you won't be able to get a job washing floors in any hospital, let alone in a lab"—he paused—"and forget graduate school." He hung up.

But he had already written his evaluation of her. Might he call the schools and rescind it?

Moving on autopilot about the hospital, she spewed forth rejoinders at him the rest of the day: "I don't know how to be a member of a chain gang!" "I'm fed up with marching bands!" "Go take your baton and shove it up your ass!"

She wrote to the five schools she'd applied to, and asked if she might be considered for acceptance at midterm.

Suppose she bypassed Mihiner and sent her results directly to the board of health. Would Mihiner blackball her?

Maybe she had made an error.

Two weeks later Lottie received notice that the University of Wisconsin was willing to take her into the department of physiology at midyear. George brought home a split of champagne.

She typed up a brief note about the boy's culture for the board of health but days passed and she still hadn't sent it.

Because she was up for a graduate assistant teaching post, which was how she'd afford school, they wanted another letter from her place of work, a job reference.

She kept thinking about Evelyn: If this had happened to her, wouldn't Lottie want a police investigation? She'd want a knife, a gun.

But these parents, according to Mihiner, were going a different way, their own way. Didn't the parents have the child's best interests at heart?

By accepting a place at Wisconsin, she was not acting in Evelyn's best interests. She was putting herself before her daughter.

Maybe her results were wrong.

She asked Mihiner for the job reference. She shoved her results aside. He obliged her.

They drove across a dry, dusty Texas that grew gentler and greener and then flowered as they approached Louisiana. Lottie zigzagged, she roamed and rambled, looped and lazed her way on up to Wisconsin. Having lakes of time, she wanted to see this land is my land, this land that was easy and rolling and fragrant. Evelyn suffered the carsickness of young children and so they drove with the windows wide open, their hair blowing and the underwear and socks Lottie had washed the night before flapping on the makeshift clothesline strung across the back of the used VW bus she'd bought for the journey. It was an old hippie van that had cost her practically nothing; the body had been painted bright blue some years earlier with a tentacular orange sun and a lemon-lime moon and sprays of flamingo-red shooting stars, all out at once and faded. No longer the psychedelic in-your-face druggy bus it must have been in the mid-sixties, it was more like a hungover, sleepy old circus car, which was okay with Lottie. She kept every window open but in spite of all that air, they still had to make frequent stops, usually for the dry heaves, but occasionally for the real thing, and then Lottie drove her reeking child to a gas station or a diner—"What is throwing up, Mommy? Why am I throwing up?"—where Lottie washed Evvie and changed her clothes and got her a Coke or some Life Savers and once in a while a plastic ring or bracelet or necklace out of a machine. The girl delighted in the jewelry; as her mother attached each new piece to her small body, Evvie cooed and wouldn't take any of it off, not even at night, not even for a bath. Feeling over the plastic beads at her neck or her wrist, she would often, mercifully, nap in the van, freeing Lottie to see the countryside while riding high, high, high, mostly on her own high hopes.

The inhabitants' accents grew lush and dense like trees choked with Spanish hanging moss from which occasionally a local word or turn of phrase stuck out like a great exotic flower: beignets or lagniappe or even boutonniere. Lottie rolled the words around on her tongue, feeling their strange smoothness. She chanted them in a happy nonsense mantra. Evelyn joined in giddily.

At roadside picnic tables Lottie cut casaba and watermelons with a meat knife and lay them out on paper towels and ate the large curved wedges with her hands, the juices coloring her nostrils and running down her mouth. She speared a few pink squares with toothpicks for Evelyn; but the child wanted to roll her face in the fruit like Mommy and so they got wet together and messy—sweet-smelling creatures cozying up to each other, nosing each other, grunting together.

In the car while marveling at the passing scene, Lottie ate boxes of movie candy: Good & Plenty, and Jujyfruits and Necco wafers. "Ev dear, I bought your favorite: chocolate-covered cherries."

Evelyn smeared syrup and chocolate all over her face and the car and Lottie let her, let her be.

But as the days wore on, the child's high spirits ebbed. "When are we there?" Like a cranky jack-in-the-box, Evelyn began punctuating the trip with this question.

"In four days. Count the sunsets."

If Ev counted, she didn't count aloud.

Once Lottie thought she heard her daughter mumble "Cha-Cha-Pa," but she wasn't sure.

They drove on small roads along the borders of states because Lottie wanted to see not only Arkansas and Oklahoma but also Dorothy's Kansas, and Missouri. Although she had imagined the thrill of putting her toe into Huck and Jim's river, the Mississippi in reality looked so brown and polluted she never even took her shoe off. Lottie drove slowly past a shantytown or squatters' community where the unpainted wooden shacks seemed both rudimentary and ancient, as if they were made of eroded bone. There were no adults in evidence, only barefoot children in outsize faded hand-me-downs, mostly of denim and coarse cotton materials, sitting on front porches looking out at the road beyond the broken wooden slats of bowing fences. One white-haired boy, around Evelyn's age, wore only a short shirt so that as he walked down the porch steps, his genitals bobbled. Evelyn stared at him. The boy stared back at Lottie and Evelyn going by in their formerly vivid circus car.

"Is that boy having a divorce?" Evelyn asked Lottie. "Are those kids divorced?"

Stretching beyond the shacks and outhouses were lush large-leafed tobacco plants growing in the yellow thin-looking earth, acres and acres of them broken only by a single handwritten sign: NITCRAWLRS FR SALE.

Later that day they had to make a belly-like detour through dusty fields to avoid a straggly line of sweating black men who looked to be working in pajamas. With picks and shovels, the men were mending a broken piece of road. At either end of the line a white man in olive uniform stood watching with gun drawn. If she drove closer, would she spot a chain on the ground?

When Lottie halfheartedly began to read *The Wonderful Wizard of Oz* to Evelyn at the motel the third night, Evelyn would not let her get past the fact that Dorothy wasn't living with her parents. Had they "spear-rated"? Had the father died? Did the mother kill the father?

In a rainstorm where the day went black and the rain battered the metal top of the van and came at the windshield in swells so that it seemed as if they would surely be drowned in some strange Midwestern sea, Ev suddenly screamed and grabbed Lottie's arm and did not stop screaming.

"Let go, Evvie! It's just water. Don't be afraid. You have to let go of my arm!" Driving so slowly that the speedometer needle barely bounced off zero, Lottie was hunched over the steering wheel trying to peer into the streaming dark, windshield wipers flailing.

But Lottie couldn't shake off her screaming child, who kept pointing at the black gushing windshield.

Something was flailing there besides the flailing wipers.

Unfamiliar with the car, Lottie fumbled with the dials and got the wipers slowed, then speeded up, and finally off. In the deluge she pulled over onto what she hoped was the bank of the road and ran out and around to the passenger side, where a dark bird was caught by the throat, its wings still beating. In the blinding rain she managed to retract the wiper blade but the bird, released, did not fly away, only slid down onto the ground. In the car she held the drenched broken trembling bird in the warm nest of her hands where, struggling feebly to get away, it died.

They waited out the rest of the storm parked on the side of the road, Evelyn crying fitfully, Lottie, soaked, rummaging dispiritedly through the luggage and cartons for their towels. The wet bird carcass lay on the floor in an empty popcorn box Lottie had saved for garbage.

When the rain stopped, Lottie found her small gardener's trowel—the bird weighed so little Lottie looked in the box twice to make sure the bird was still in there—and buried it on the side of the road.

Ev sat down on the mud of the grave. Lottie thought how dirty Evelyn's legs were and then how dirty the car would be, but it was already dirty and she said nothing.

"What is 'dead'?" Evelyn asked.

"The bird is dead, honey."

"What is dead?" Evelyn didn't look at her.

"Well, I suppose it means you don't move your legs or your wings anymore, your blood doesn't circulate—it doesn't move around; you don't breathe . . ."

"Will you die, Mommy?"

"Yes, but not for a long time."

"And Cha-Cha-Pa?"

Lottie waited. "Yes, Daddy, too. But not for a long time."

Evelyn cried a little. Suddenly she said, "I'm not going to die?"

"All living things die."

"Am I a living thing?"

Lottie nodded.

Full of mud, Evelyn stood up and stamped on the grave. "How could you?"

"How could I what? What did I do?"

"You died the bird."

"I didn't 'die' the bird. I didn't kill anything. It got caught there in the moving windshield wiper. Come on, let's get going."

But Evelyn wouldn't move; she dug her feet into the wet earth and stood there disconsolately, her eyes shut, arms limp at her sides; and finally Lottie had to pick up her stiff, muddy child and carry her back kicking into the bus.

Part Six

I t snowed even in her dreams during the six years she spent in Wisconsin. From the second-floor apartment they rented, Lottie would watch the landlady's chunky brown dachshund trot down the shoveled steps. Dwarfed by the snow banked high on both sides of the front walk, he looked in his orange knit sweater like a courageous arctic explorer as he sniffed and scratched and circled and reversed before finally lifting his leg to squirt yellow wavering lines in the snow.

Every weekday morning Lottie watched Evelyn, bundled up in a navy face mask and jacket and leggings and bright red rubber boots, run across the same frozen front walk to the idling school bus. Just before boarding, Evelyn would turn at the bus door to look up at her mother and give her a determined, serious wave.

Lottie learned under these subzero conditions to anesthetize her rats and blunt-dissect out their salivary glands and align the skin and hold it together with little metal clips. After Lottie lost one rat because her temperature dropped post-op, Lottie took a pair of warm bedroom slippers Evelyn had outgrown and lined them with old cotton underpants and sewed on snaps so the slippers could be partly closed—if her grandmother could see her now!—and strapped these small body baby carriers to her belly. Then if an anesthetized animal looked to be in trouble, Lottie picked it up and put it in one of her pouches—not exactly standard technique. She supposed she looked like a kangaroo with twin joeys.

The times that really froze her heart were when she had to leave Evelyn in the middle of the night: Lottie would tiptoe out of the house, opening the door between the upstairs and downstairs apartments so the landlady would hear Ev if she cried out. Lottie would walk uneasily to the university through stinging snow-filled wind that sounded like Evelyn calling, Lottie's lips protected by a quarter of an inch of Chapstick, wearing a white parka and a white wool scarf around her head to make her visible to the occasional passing car. Visible as a shifting snow drift. Every eight hours around the clock for four and a half days she let herself into the lab to do vaginal smears on her rats. Her dissertation question: Do the salivary glands have an endocrine function? She learned to hold the animals by the nape of the neck, between her index finger and middle finger and thumb, the way the mother carries the babies in her mouth when they're young. The rats would grow quiet, then Lottie would draw normal saline up into a blunt-tipped medicine dropper, turn the animal over onto its back, insert the dropper into the vagina, squeeze out a little and then draw it back, fluid and cells, and smear it onto a slide.

After a while the rats purred when they saw Lottie coming. They walked up her arms and lay still in her hands waiting to be turned onto their backs.

Although the other students teased her, and even Lottie, in her later years, jokingly called herself Dr. Rat Westheimer, her technique was actually the way all the work on oral contraceptives was done; and it looked like she was on to something. Because without the salivary glands, the rats' estrus cycle was prolonged. So rat salivary glands must be producing something that affected the reproductive cycle. Salivary glands, known only to produce spit—could they have something to do with sex? In the end, after numerous replications, she didn't come up with anything definitive.

One day there was a notice on a campus bulletin board that Nathaniel Burden would give an evening talk to the drama and film students. Billed as a screenwriter and assistant professor of English at Berkeley, he had a PhD from Iowa, according to the short bio, and had published a book of poems called *The Cheetah's Teeth* and a novel called *Powerhouse*; he also had two screenplays to his credit. Lottie was impressed. Burden was called "an antiestablishment writer, a maverick, and under thirty."

He couldn't be more than two minutes under thirty.

Had he written that high school poem and dropped it down her blouse? That old stale question.

Wasn't a man—no, wasn't a boy—innocent until proven guilty?

And Burden was certainly intelligent, and vaguely familiar, a sort of weird dark link to Charlie. An anti-Charlie. Of course, she had hardly noticed Burden, dark scrawny kid talking stilted, walking stilted. She'd seen him once on a playing field in high school: he'd been a dark wet newborn calf whose legs splayed out, and down he went.

Curious (what harm?), she sent her dreary-white winter parka to the cleaner's for brightening and engaged a babysitter. On the evening of the talk she wore the coat over a green skirt and a matching sweater and cardigan set—*fern green*, according to the tag, a description that brought to mind Trixie McKloskey the lab tech and her quest to snag a giant fish. A pair of jade filigree earrings that had belonged to her grandmother swaying lightly from her ears, Lottie walked the few blocks to the drama building. It was beginning to snow again.

A smattering of students had shown up and spread thinly throughout the auditorium: boys with bleached hair and leather jackets, girls without lipstick, with white eye shadow and sequins on their faces. One black girl with a fiery Afro wore long crystal triangular earrings with SNCC stamped on them in black. A busty straight-haired blonde in a low-cut T-shirt had painted OUT OF NAM in violet nail polish across the dunes of her breasts.

Lottie didn't think she had seen any of these students before. She took care of her daughter, did experiments on her rats, went to classes, and taught her science sections; to whatever else was going on in the huge campus she was snow-blind.

A slight young man with a full black beard and rimless glasses stepped up to the podium and identified himself as president of the Drama Students' Organization. He introduced Nathaniel Burden, read a few lines from Burden's books, and added that Burden was a vigorous participant in many teach-ins against the war. The scattered students applauded and Nathaniel gathered his long self up onto the stage, raising his index and middle finger in a V for peace.

He wore a black turtleneck sweater and loose black slacks and black leather boots. He had more mass or muscle than she remembered, although he was still on the lean side, looming larger and darker and more self-assured as he thanked the audience for coming. "Every day there are more of us oddballs and freaks—we're making converts at a prodigious rate—and we are going to stampede that warmongering bastard out of office!"

The audience applauded wildly and began chanting "Out of Nam! Out of Nam!"

The black girl with the red Afro stood up and raised her fist and yelled: "All power to the people!"

Nathaniel lifted his fist back to her. "It's good to be in a friendly part of the Heartland," he roared into the microphone over the shouting and cheering.

Lottie felt repelled by all the noise, and relieved that Evelyn was safe at home.

As the students screamed and stamped, Lottie had a vision of the building exploding around her, and all of them standing, bleeding and dazed and forlorn, in the falling snow.

People quieted in response to Burden's raised arms and repeated requests. A sour-faced janitor pushed a blackboard on wheels over to Nathaniel, who at once drew a large circle with a V in it. "General Westmoreland calls our sign 'chicken tracks!'"

The students jeered and booed. A few chanted "Down with Westy! Down with Westy!" and others yelled, "We won't go! We won't go!"

The janitor, who did not look at the speaker or the crowd, yanked down the rolled-up movie screen that hung from the ceiling and slunk off the stage.

The house lights dimmed and even before everyone settled down, Nathaniel began showing a film he had written the screenplay for: A young couple walks through the woods; birds fly overhead in V formation; pheasants are startled out from behind bushes; an intelligent-looking fox watches the couple from a grassy plain.

> Margaret, are you grieving
> Over Goldengrove unleaving?

recites a female narrator.

A male narrator says,

The world is charged with the grandeur of God.
It will flame out, like shining from shook foil.

Lottie was pleased to recognize Gerard Manley Hopkins as the poet, but surprised that Burden would have chosen to quote a mystical priest. She was also perplexed that the movie had so much to do with nature. As she watched the leaves of the trees change color in the film, she realized with embarrassment that she had half-expected Burden to have written something about *her*. But the couple was generic and the film ended, unexpectedly, in a murder. Lottie felt disappointed and confused.

The president of the drama organization announced that Nathaniel Burden had graciously agreed to take part in a Q and A.

Lottie, who had a fifteen-year-old babysitter to relieve, rose reluctantly (she had hoped to exchange a word with Burden, but, who knew? maybe it was for the best) and walked up the center aisle toward the back of the auditorium. Burden was answering a student's question when he called out: "Lottie? Lottie Kristin? Is that you?" He waved and beckoned her forward.

She turned, flushing.

"Yes? It's you? It's Lottie Kristin? I can't hear you back there."

"Yes!" she said loudly. "It's me!"

"Don't leave! Please wait!"

The other students looked at Lottie with curiosity and, she imagined, envy. She sat down in the back of the room, embarrassed and flattered, and pleased she'd worn the matching fern outfit. And gotten the parka cleaned. Nathaniel took one more question and ended the evening. Ignoring a waiting group that included the president of the Drama Students' Organization who'd introduced him, Burden strode past them down the center aisle.

"I'm delighted you came! I had no idea you were here! What are you doing here? Can we go out for a drink?" He took her hands in his.

"I can't. I promised the babysitter's mother I'd be home by ten thirty."

"You have a child?" He looked disappointed. "I heard you were separated."

"I am."

"Of course, why shouldn't you have a child? How stupid of me!"

"I have a nine-year-old daughter."

"A daughter! A girl! Could I meet her?"

Lottie laughed. He seemed so glad to see her that she became more wholehearted herself. "Evelyn's asleep, I hope. Would you like to come over for a drink?"

"You bet!"

"Sorry, folks, I'm off duty." Burden smiled at the students who had followed him down the aisle—several were thrusting books at him for his autograph—and helped Lottie on with her coat. Lottie had an impulse to sign the books herself as Nathaniel steered her out the door.

Snow was falling fast and thick. A gibbous moon lit up the flying snow and made the old heaped-up snow glint as if it were studded with mica. Lone students moved across the campus along a maze of narrow shoveled paths. Lottie and Nathaniel walked down the middle of the plowed streets. He held her arm at the elbow, their breaths white smoke that appeared and merged and dissolved as they talked.

After she paid and dismissed the babysitter, she returned to Nathaniel, who was looking at a large poster in the hall. It showed a masked woman whose breasts were pushed up high in a low-cut black dress.

"I remember that. Didn't you have that poster at college? I like it!"

Lottie felt complimented, although she could not recall a single time he had been in her room.

"I went out with a girl on your floor," he said as if reading her thoughts. "Your door was open and I looked in."

"Who? Who was the girl?"

"Who remembers? I probably only went out with her once." Nathaniel added, "Things about *you* I remember."

Lottie remembered that poem. Had he written it? Perhaps he'd had a crush on her all the way back in high school. Some boys who were sweet on girls would pull their braids or reach behind their backs and snap their bra bands through their sweaters. Juvenile stuff, but then Burden had never been one of the popular, sophisticated guys. Although that was one sophisticated poem. If he'd had a crush on her, did that make it not so bad if he'd written that poem? Awkward and stupid, yes, but not necessarily malicious?

He'd called her name from the stage, almost begged her to wait. It had given her a feeling of importance. Lottie blushed. "Do you really want to see my daughter?"

"Second only to you."

Before this evening, when was the last time she'd blushed?

She led Nathaniel down the hallway past the small kitchen where the dirty dishes were stacked in gray water in the sink, past the living room with its worn couch and easy chairs, and into the dark bedroom. She took the flashlight from Evelyn's night table and shined it on her sleeping daughter, whose hair was spilled out over the pillow.

Nathaniel whispered, "It's Eppie when Silas Marner first sees her asleep on his hearth."

Lottie smiled happily, and resisted saying, *"It's Evvie, not Eppie."* Because it would have been showing off. She remembered a lot of the book, which had been a ninth-grade reading assignment.

"It's Rumpelstiltskin's room full of gold."

"Don't overdo it," Lottie laughed.

She led him to the kitchen where she opened a bottle of cheap white wine.

"Excuse the disarray." She put her hands in the cold soapy water and came up with two glasses.

"You should see my place," Nathaniel chortled.

She washed and dried the glasses, surprised at how relaxed she felt. She put a two-day-old loaf of rye bread and a large block of extra-sharp Wisconsin Cheddar cheese on a bread board, which he carried in. She followed with bread plates and paper napkins.

He swept his arm in an arc that took in the tweed couch he was sitting on, as well as the two big upholstered chairs and several hassocks from which grew unruly bushes of newspapers and scientific journals and children's books. "Nice living room."

"You like the Salvation Army originals?"

"Well, it's comfortable, pulls you in." He pointed at a sampler that hung on the wall. "Now *that's* beautiful." It was an embroidered picture of a

Norwegian village, consisting of a small silver church, a redbrick school, a few brown and gray and pink houses, different shades of green fields, a gray-blue fjord.

"My grandmother made it. You're saying all the right things tonight." She laughed. "You didn't say if *you* were married."

"Come sit next to me."

"First answer my question."

He laughed. "I'm thinking about getting unmarried. I married a student of mine two years ago. Not a very good student, I'm afraid." He frowned and hunched his shoulders, managing to look both mournful and clownish.

"Oh. Sorry." She couldn't imagine Nathaniel married to a mediocre student.

"Nothing to be sorry about. We'll each remarry. I doubt she or I will remember the whole thing for long. Anyway, keep it under your hat. I haven't told her yet." He smiled widely. "Now will you sit next to me? I've been honest with you."

She sat down a couch cushion away from him.

He held up the wine bottle to the lamplight and examined the label. He poured a small amount and sipped slowly, then ran his tongue over his lips. "It's quite good."

"What are you talking about? It's terrible."

He grinned. "Well, I'm just happy to see you."

"You don't even sound like yourself. You used to be reserved, even arrogant. You're practically effusive!"

"Talk about change. You never spoke much either, at least not to me. I remember you as aloof in high school—and I hardly saw you at Michigan. Truth is, I'm delighted you won't be spending the rest of your life with that jock."

Lottie blushed again. She was glad he'd criticized Charlie, who hadn't sent her a penny for Evelyn for months now despite Lottie's writing him several times.

"How did you two come to cut the knot?"

It took her a moment to realize what he meant. "I'd rather not talk about Charlie," she said.

"Yeah, okay, he was an asshole."

She suddenly felt uneasy sitting next to him on the couch, not happy with Nathaniel's characterization of Charlie. Not unhappy either.

"No offense meant."

"You *did* mean offense."

"Well, I've always been interested in you."

Nathaniel poured himself more wine; her glass was still full. He took a suede pouch and an elaborately carved black wood pipe from his pants pocket.

"Would you smoke some hash with me?"

She shook her head. "The one time I had"—she paused and decided to sound easy, familiar rather than technical—"the one time I had pot, I went to sleep."

"Do you mind if I do?"

She hesitated. "This isn't an opium den. Is my daughter going to be able to pick up the smell in the morning?"

"Only if she's smoked it herself." He packed the pipe and tamped down the hash with his fingers. "And we can always open the windows." He grinned.

She made a face. "I pay for the heat." Then she said, "My, that's a handsome pipe."

He handed it to her. The wood felt smooth, sleek. She held it up to the lamp. Two entwined snakes made up the stem. On the bowl were two heads of vultures, and between them, composing the circumference of the bowl, were two lizards, one astride the other, and two monkeys who were licking each other's genitals. (Perhaps the carver would be interested in Lottie's research?)

She handed the pipe back. "How come the vultures aren't doing anything?"

"They're watching like vultures."

She laughed.

He drained his glass—she filled it again for him—and lit up. She smelled phosphorus and then the harsh acrid odor of hashish.

"Do you smoke much?" she asked.

"I do drugs like a screenwriter, and I drink like a poet." He moved closer to her on the couch. "I mean the American kind—Berryman, Lowell, Delmore Schwartz. Is it all right if I put an arm around you?"

"I don't know. I don't really know what kind of man you are."

"You don't?"

She resisted saying "Why don't you come clean about yourself?" and said instead, "Maybe you ought to tell me about yourself."

"Well, one critic, in reviewing my novel, *Powerhouse*, said, 'When you write a book, it tells on you, it tells about your character, and you are the only one who doesn't know what it tells."

"What did the critic say the book told about you?"

"That I write a mean sentence and am a nasty, unfeeling son of a bitch." Nathaniel grinned or grimaced, Lottie couldn't tell which.

"Is it true?"

"That I write a mean sentence? Yes. At least I try to write tight, condensed sentences that whiplash the reader."

"I mean, is what he said about your character true? About you as a person? Are you a 'nasty, unfeeling son of a bitch'?"

"The guy doesn't know me at all. He's never met me. What right does a critic have to take down a man's character? I wouldn't say it to you if I thought it was true. It's calumny. But interesting calumny."

She looked at him straight on and said: "Did you write that poem?"

"What poem? The ones in the movie? I wish I had."

She shook her head. "I know those were by Hopkins."

"You always *were* a smarty-pants. Well, what poem do you mean?"

"There was a poem in high school, an obscene version of a Keats poem. Were you thinking of Keats when you mentioned American poets?"

"He's not an American poet." He turned his palms up and raised his shoulders.

"I know that," she said, annoyed.

Was he being defensive? Lottie wished the light were brighter so she could see his face better. "The poem I was talking about—it was about me and Charlie. Somebody typed it up and folded it and dropped it down my blouse."

"Lucky poem." He shook his head. "It must have been a doozy for you to remember it all these years."

"It was about fucking and sucking. You were the only one smart enough to write it."

"I'm honored. But while I'm not above handing a girl a line, I'm no pornographer."

She imagined herself getting the flashlight from her daughter's room and shining it full in his face. Would he hunker down his neck, throw his jacket over his head as if his photo were being taken on the courthouse steps?

"Lottie, I don't know a thing about it. I'm truly sorry you had such a vile experience." He put his hand on her shoulder.

"It was a nasty business and it hurt me because I was so young. I always thought it was you who wrote it." Tears came, she didn't know why, and she wiped them away with a napkin.

"That poem must have been a killer."

The tears kept coming. "The whole thing just seems dumb and crummy to me now. I was so wide open then."

Nathaniel put his arms around her. He was about Charlie's size although leaner, less muscular. He swept up her hair and kissed the back of her neck above the collar of her sweater. She nestled her face into his shirt. She wept, she wasn't sure why. He kissed her gently and took her face in his hands.

"I'm sorry you had to go through that." He touched the tears on her face. He moved his wet fingers over her chin, down her throat, to the neck of her sweater.

He kissed her again.

She kissed him back.

"Sweet Lottie," he said. He licked his fingers.

His sadness for her young self moved her. She had a deep longing to be held by someone she knew. She overrode some lurking distrust and leaned into him.

"You dear woman." He held her tightly to himself, then moved her face back and kissed her deeply.

She responded with sadness and fervor.

He kissed her neck and then he kissed her breasts through her sweater. "Is it all right?" he asked. He moved his hands up under the back of her sweater and fumbled with the catch of her bra.

"I don't know," she said again. He managed to unhook her bra and she lay back on the couch and closed her eyes, although the tears kept coming. "I don't know." He lifted her sweater over her head.

Had we but world enough, and time,
This coyness, Lady, were no crime.

Nathaniel whispered the lines hoarsely in her ear as he helped her out of her bra, then shimmied down her skirt and tried simultaneously to unzip his pants.

My vegetable love should grow
Vaster than empires, and more slow;
An hundred years should go to praise
Thine eyes and on thy forehead gaze . . .

"I'm not being coy," she said. "I'm not coy. You're coming on too fast." Were those lines by Keats? Were they by Burden? She breathed in his hot burnt breath. She had her eyes open now and saw the bony slope of his shoulders and his dark hair and the beginnings of a bald spot about the size of a quarter on the crown of his head;

Two hundred to adore each breast;
But thirty thousand to the rest;
An age at least to every part . . .

"I've already spent that long fantasizing about you," he said, panting. He got his long fingers in between her legs. She had three simultaneous sharp impressions: that his hands were cold; that despite having been around him since the beginning of high school, he was an unknown to her, a black box. She also saw a sudden shimmer of light in the archway to the living room—was it Evelyn with her bright hair and white nightgown?—and then it was gone.

She sat up abruptly and grabbed for her sweater. She pulled it on over her bare chest.

"What's the matter?" he whispered, unhooking the belt of his pants.

She hissed, "It's my daughter! Get your clothes on!"

He looked around. "There's no one here."

Lottie pulled up her skirt and grabbed the bra off the floor and hid it under a couch pillow. She hurried down the hall to Evelyn's room, her nipples erect beneath the sweater.

Her daughter was in bed, on her back now, breathing rapidly and shallowly, her eyes shut tight.

Lottie shone the flashlight on the bed, on the headboard, then on the pillow beside her daughter's face. "Evelyn?" she whispered.

The child did not move, only seemed to close her eyes tighter as the circle of light came near.

"Come on, Ev, are you asleep? Don't lie to me." Lottie spoke low, in worried exasperation.

What had Lottie seen, if not Evelyn? What had Evelyn seen? She thought to shake her daughter awake.

In the living room, Nathaniel was sitting on the couch in dark shorts, with an erection. "Let's go to the bedroom. You have a lock on your bedroom door, don't you?"

Lottie was trembling. "You have to leave!" she whispered. "Get your clothes on fast. I made a big mistake having you up here with my daughter in the house."

"What are you talking about, 'I have to leave, Get my clothes on.'? Who do you think you're talking to?"

"Shhh! I'm sure my daughter saw us."

"I didn't see anybody." He did not lower his voice.

"You had your back to the door."

"Well, that's a shame if she saw us, but what's done can't be undone." He pointed down at his erection. "*This* isn't done."

"It's no time for jokes. Just get dressed and go."

"Who's joking? I've been waiting thousands of years." He leapt at her and they went down on the floor with a thud, Nathaniel on top.

"For God's sakes, you hurt my back!" she half-yelled, half-whispered. What was he doing? She was suddenly frightened. "Nathaniel, stop this right now! Cut the crap!"

He pulled at her underpants and got his fingers up between her legs and was trying to hold her open and jam his penis in.

"Get off me! What's gotten into you? My daughter could walk in any minute!" She tried to slap at his face without making any noise.

He slammed her head back against the floor. She felt a sharp hot pain in her neck as if a blood vessel had burst. This couldn't be happening. She bit his arm and he slammed her head down again and the room began to darken and she lay still. She could feel her heart rocking in her chest. What would he do to her? Would he bang her head against the floor again? Would she lose consciousness?

As his penis slid in, he groaned something that sounded like "At last!" or "In at last!" She thought she heard him say, "My princess," but she might have heard wrong. He pumped back and forth, back and forth, holding her shoulders down with one arm while she squirmed under him and tried to break his hold.

He lifted her sweater up so it was over her face and bit at her breasts and moaned.

Was this really happening to her?

"You're hurting me, for Christ's sakes! Get off! My daughter—"

"How could I be hurting you, you wet thing . . ." he crooned at her in time to his rhythm. "You moist, brimming . . ."

"Don't *come* in me, you hear?"

"You cock-tease you, you hot Lottie!" He got his whole mouth over her breast and seemed to be trying to swallow it.

"Please, please don't *come* in me—" She saw him through the weave of her sweater.

His breathing slowed, his pumping slowed. He pulled the sweater up over her head, off her, and threw it across the room, then came slowly out of her, straddling her, his dark erect penis dripping, his balls sitting on her breasts.

"Did you come?" she whispered. "Oh my God, did you come?" She was afraid she would scream.

"That's *your* juice, not mine."

"You're sure?"

"Don't you see my cock?" He moved on his knees so his penis was close to her face.

"Well, people don't always lose their erection right away."

"What 'people'? You mean Superschmuck?"

Why don't you go fuck *him*, she wanted to cry out. "Well, detumescence can take a few minutes." She felt ridiculous, as if she were reciting in class. She *wanted* to be in class, reciting. How could she get rid of him? She couldn't scream because that would bring in Evelyn and what could Evelyn do? Maybe he'd hurt Evelyn. This thought terrified her. Maybe he'd fuck Evelyn after he was finished with her. She wanted to say, *Do anything you want to me, but leave my daughter alone.* No, no. She mustn't say anything, mustn't mention her daughter. She tried to sound stern, commanding, in control. "Come on, get out of my face." She could barely move her head, he held her forehead down immobile.

"Why don't you detumesce me?"

"What are you talking about?"

He grabbed both her hands, pinned them down on the floor above her head, then played his penis along her forehead and nose and lips.

"Get that thing away from me! Are you out of your mind?"

"I'm considerate: you don't want me to come in you."

"There's a child in the house!"

"She's asleep. And if she did see us making love? It beats the body bags on TV."

"Making love? You call this making love!"

He tried to push his penis into her mouth but she closed her teeth and moved her face away. "Milk me, milk me," he whispered. "You're my milk and honey, honey." He smiled sweetly at her.

"Get off me, you son of a bitch!" She kneed him in the buttocks.

He slapped her hard across the face. "Just open up, you hear me?" He pulled one of her arms down and yanked it up behind her back.

"Stop it! You're going to break my arm!

He pulled her arm up harder. The room dipped for a moment. Perhaps she would really black out. Then what would happen to her? What would happen to Evelyn?

"Get up on my stick."

"Are you serious?"

He pulled her arm up even harder.

"I can't suck you off if I faint," she whispered. She struggled onto her knees and took his penis in her mouth. He shoved it back into her throat and she gagged.

"Sorry," he said. "Is that better?" He thrust a few times more gently. "You know, I want to watch this closely. I mean, I used to think about you so much."

He loosened his grip on her arm slightly—"There"—and sat down on the couch, pulling her up by her head, holding her head between his thighs.

"Get on it, little Lottie. Little brainy Lottie. Get your mouth open. Get it wide open for old Nathaniel. I'm going to shoot my load right up into your brain! Your gorgeous brain!" He thrust his dick into the back of her throat, making her cough. She felt nauseated and feared throwing up and choking, although her worries were not enough to distract her from the pain in her arm. He moaned rhythmically and fondled her nipples with his free hand. "Aaah, Lottie! Ah, you precious cunt, you!" As the hot liquid shot into her mouth and throat, he let go of her arm. Backing off him, she grabbed the bread knife from the coffee table, then turned and spat his semen full in his face.

He opened his eyes in surprise.

"I swear to God I'll cut you if you come near me!" Shuddering and coughing, she held the knife in front of her.

He touched a finger to his wet cheek. Then he pulled up his shorts and lunged for her. She sliced at his arm, then at his throat. He jerked his head back, then cocked it, trying to see his neck. Blood began to trickle down his white elbow.

Lottie's teeth chattered. She tried to see his neck under the shadow of his chin.

He looked at her as if she had betrayed him.

"I missed. I hardly nicked you. Hold still and it'll stop." She stooped, keeping her eye on him, and retrieved some napkins from the floor—the plates and napkins had gotten knocked over during their struggle—and threw them at him.

She could see the knife shaking in her hand.

"You're crazy. You're a lunatic!" He pressed the napkins at his elbow and his neck but the bleeding at his elbow didn't stop.

"Get out of here! You're not going to bleed to death. Get the hell out of here before I kill you!"

He took off his undershirt and tried to tie it around his arm. He couldn't tie a knot with one hand.

"I'll kill you, you uncoordinated bastard," she bit out between shudders.

He raised his chin—she thought she saw a dark bead there—and felt his throat, then looked at his fingers. "My neck, my neck!" A frightened child, he held his neck out toward her, the undershirt hanging over his outstretched hands like an offering.

He said soothingly, "Listen, why don't we start the evening over again? Maybe I drank too much, smoked too much—"

"You pig, get your sweater and your pants and go back to your hole!" Still holding the knife, she lifted his sweater off the floor and threw it at him.

"Easy does it. Hey, it's old Nathaniel! I lost my wits. Spitting my own come in my face isn't exactly nice either. Maybe we both got carried away." He started to reach for the knife and she sliced at the air in front of him. He jumped back.

As he pulled the turtleneck down over his head, she thought he said, "The quality of mercy is not strained." But that just couldn't be.

"Are you quoting bullshit at me?" Lottie came toward him slowly, the knife a foot in front of her. Slicing the air between them, she backed him out of the living room, down the hall, through the kitchen.

When she had him up against the door that led outside, he said: "It's cold out there. Can't I sleep over, for past services rendered? I'll freeze my balls off—"

"Don't talk to me about your balls . . ." She lowered the knife from heart level and touched it to his pants. *At the end of the fight didn't the matador slice off the bull's balls and throw them to the crowd?*

Slowly and carefully Burden turned his back on her and unlocked the door and opened it. A frigid wind blew snow into the hallway. He shivered. He turned and looked back at her with half-mocking, half-beseeching eyes. "How do I get a cab? What do I do? I don't know this town at all!"

"Get out of here, and put your shoes on!" She threw his heavy coat and fancy boots out in front of him.

He stepped one foot onto the snowy landing in his socks and snatched up his pants and sweater, shaking the snow off. He got them on, then hurriedly thrust his arms into his coat and buttoned a few buttons, then struggled to get on a boot. As he moved his other foot out the door and reached for the other boot—would he throw it at her?—she slammed the door shut and locked and bolted it and leaned against it, heaving.

"You bitch!" His voice was muffled by the wind. "You crazy bitch!" Hopping on one foot, he banged with the other boot at the two heavy panes of glass on the door. Would he break them?

Downstairs her landlady flickered the porch lights on and off.

"You keep that noise up, I'm calling the police!" the woman yelled.

Nathaniel stopped banging. He lowered his voice, but she heard him loud and clear:

Ah, what can ail thee, wretched Lot?
So haggard and so woe-begone?
Is Charlie's dick all red and hot
Up your ass again?

Does he set you on his pacing steed,
And nothing else do all day long;
But suck your tits and bang your cunt
With his great big dong?

"I knew it!" she hissed, though he couldn't hear her.

After a moment she heard him crunching down the stairs. He screamed something else at her—long, convoluted. Was it more of his poem? And then she couldn't hear anything.

As she got the flashlight from the living room and shined the light onto Evelyn's bed, all the stanzas of that miserable poem came to her, word for word. Was nothing dreadful ever lost?

Her daughter was sitting up in the dark.

"Are you all right?" Lottie whispered.

Evelyn said nothing.

"What did you hear?"

The wind-up clock in the girl's room ticked loudly.

Was Evelyn asleep sitting up with her eyes open? Keeping the blanket between her hands and her child, Lottie tried to ease Evelyn down to a lying position. Evelyn resisted at first, but finally let herself be moved. Lottie longed to lie next to her, to hold her, but she did not want any part of her filthy body to touch her child.

When Evelyn's breathing evened out, Lottie left her bedside and went to the bathroom and washed her mouth out with hot water, then gargled with what was left of the mint mouthwash. She sat on the toilet seat and continuously flushed the toilet so Evelyn wouldn't hear her crying. She took her clothes off and got into a steaming shower and soaped herself from head to foot and shampooed her hair. She washed her mouth out with shampoo and spat it at the tiled wall, then cleaned the wall with a washcloth, then scrubbed the washcloth. She dried herself and got on warm pajamas and got into bed and pulled the covers up over her wet head.

In the dark she told herself Evelyn hadn't seen anything, but then what was the flash of light in the living room? A guardian angel? Lottie didn't have one.

Maybe Evelyn hadn't seen much.

Suppose Lottie had hit an artery when she sliced at Burden's neck!

She hurried out of bed and emptied the pouch of hashish down the toilet and threw the pouch and his pipe out the living room window. In the dark she imagined it sinking into the old crusted snow, to be covered with new snow. Gone.

Would it show up black and fetid in the morning?

She prayed to the cold night air coming in the window that her child had not seen much.

The next morning she woke with her arm aching, the back of her head exquisitely tender to the touch. Should she get an X-ray? She had the crazy thought that the radiologist would see the sperm. The landlady asked what had been going on and she said she supposed some frat guys had gotten drunk and come banging down the street and up her stairs.

She had a sore throat.

That little boy in the ER . . . Had it happened to him?

Lottie, cut it out. That way lies madness.

In the following days whenever Lottie saw one of the posters announcing Burden's lecture, she ripped it down. A week later, waiting for a light to change so she could cross the street, she saw Burden's face in the window of a passing bus. She cried out, and an elderly woman put an arm around her. At the post office she saw his photograph among the "ten most wanted" but the man looked Hispanic and was described as five foot seven.

Evelyn never said anything about the evening. Fearing to worsen matters, Lottie didn't either. She told herself she'd saved Evelyn's life. She'd done that, she, Lottie. But there was no evidence Burden would have hurt Evelyn. The real danger was that Evelyn had seen something, that Lottie had exposed her to something so damaging that it would become a part of her child in some deforming, destructive, ineradicable way.

She buried herself in her thesis, in her experiments, in teaching, but an undergraduate would ask a question, and she'd find herself focusing on his mouth; memories of Burden's teeth biting into her breast would come to her and she'd have to ask the student to repeat himself.

She couldn't look at the limp, shriveled penises of the cadavers without feeling his dark erection playing over her forehead, her eyes, her nose.

The graduate students (all male except for Lottie and a married Nigerian woman who wore colorful caftans and head scarves to class and shook her head when Lottie tried to sit beside her—Lottie's face flushed hot in shame and rage) had their benches alongside each other in large basement labs called "the dungeons." Students joked and chatted with Lottie, but no one offered to be her partner in physiology and so she operated on her dog by herself; and in Gross Anatomy, all the graduate students teamed up, four to a cadaver, and left her out. She ended up assigned to a table with three medical students who dissected so poorly that she had to visit other tables to see intact structures.

Before Burden, Lottie had been so excited to be a student again that she paid little attention to how distant her male colleagues were. But now, although she couldn't imagine ever "making love" again, she wanted to make friends. At least acquaintances, people to talk to so she wouldn't be besieged with images of Burden's hands, his long hanging balls. It was true that she rushed home every day to be with Evelyn, in large part because she was worried about Evelyn's state of mind: Was Evelyn more inward? More secretive? But even if Lottie had wanted to hang around school, no one seemed interested in her. She invited Christianne, the Nigerian woman, for lunch, but Christianne said softly that she always ate with her husband; at least she didn't simply shake her head. Did she know something about Lottie? Lottie asked Jack Richter, the cell biology grad student at the next bench who was looking at peroxisomes, to eat with her, but he said he worked out lunchtimes at the gym. Max Perlbaum, a biochemist who was analyzing crayfish eyes, said he was in a daily lunchtime journal group.

"Could I join?"

"Well," he said. "We've all been buddies since undergraduate days—we were A-E-Pi. You know, Alpha Epsilon?"

Why didn't the married students and especially those with children invite her to their homes? Did the wives see a woman on her own as a potential poacher?

She planned a cocktail party and wrote on the invitations: "Spouses and children welcome." To her mortification, only ten people out of twenty responded, and only four of those positively; she canceled the party.

Occasionally she found tubing and crucibles missing from her lab equipment. One day the doors to her cages were open (her animals were kept in a closet of a room adjacent to the dungeons) and two rats were gone. A janitor found them hours later running frantically around the men's restroom. When she snapped at another student for cutting a piece of liver so close to her fingers that she was almost nicked by the scalpel, he yelled at her, "What's the matter? You on the rag?"

One guy actually said, "You know, when you first got here, we all hated you, Lottie, because you were a girl. Now we've gotten to know you and you're not so bad."

Her eyes teared up—in gratitude!—and she rushed off to the bathroom furious with herself.

Misogyny was a problem for every woman in science, to put it mildly, and she tried not to take it personally, but any feelings of righteous indignation dissipated: Whom could she speak to about them? Maybe everyone hated her because they knew about her. What kind of mother was she anyway? Who dragged her daughter a thousand miles away from the girl's father? She'd put her own needs first, her daughter's second. True, Evelyn was doing well in school and had friends, but the babbling buoyant child who had moved in with her to live in George Kenadjian's house had disappeared. Or was that normal, that an unguarded, bouncing three-and-a-half-year-old might metamorphose into a reserved, even cautious eight-year-old? The boy who had tested positive for gonorrhea drifted through her mind like a ghost. She'd taken the throat culture on him four years earlier. She'd done nothing about it. Nothing. Well, how much bravery did she expect of herself? Was she a heroine in a child's storybook? Medical students talked about unspeakable mistakes, inexcusable fatalities they'd witnessed in the ER, in the OR, in hospital rooms. It was rare that anyone reported anything. In fact, she couldn't remember a single instance.

Trying to keep her mind together, she read *The Double Helix*, about how James Watson, the author, and Francis Crick came up with a cardboard model for the structure of DNA, for which they won the Nobel Prize. It was one of the biggest discoveries of the twentieth century, but they figured it out in part because, without her permission or knowledge, they sneaked looks at Rosalind Franklin's X-ray photographs of crystalline DNA, which gave them important clues. So this is what the practice of science comes to: dismissing the one female scientist, "Rosy," as ill-dressed and "un-chummy" (read "not docile"), and then shamelessly pirating her work. Lottie was glad she hadn't known about the book years earlier, or it might have turned her off science altogether.

The ultramicrotome broke down and none of the guys in the department could fix it. Joe Baxter, an assistant professor, said, laughing, "Somebody go call Lottie." She came and looked the machine over and fiddled around for an hour—and fixed it. "Ball buster!" Joe Baxter yelled at Lottie. Except for the secretary, no one in the department spoke to her for a couple of days.

Slowly, gradually, she felt a flu-like feeling come down on her, or maybe it was pneumonia. She got herself checked in the infirmary: no fever, her lungs were clear. Still, her head felt foggy, water-logged; she wanted to shake it so she could concentrate: her mind kept wandering off—to Burden's cock making her cough, to Charlie's limp dick in her mouth. Her body felt like macerated meat. She lost her appetite and began losing weight, as much as a pound a day. And she was waking at four A.M., ruminating about suicide: every window beckoned to her. But she lived on the second floor and worked on the third: at most, she'd break her legs. There were higher floors she could go to.

But she mustn't . . . leave her daughter . . . Irreparable.

In the early mornings after lying sleepless, her mind whirring for an hour, Lottie would shuffle into Evelyn's room, crawl into her bed, and lie there to breathe in the sweet sleep smell of her, to feel the warmth of her body in the sheets. She longed to hold Evelyn but felt contaminated, as if Burden's saliva were still all over her nipples, her mind coated with his jizm. It was eight months now since he'd raped her. Would the feelings never go away?

This time when she dragged herself into the college infirmary she was diagnosed with a depression. Dr. Constanz kept asking, had anything happened? She told him nothing, nothing had happened—and he started her on amitriptyline. It made her dizzy and nauseated but she hung in and visited the gentle Dr. Constanz weekly. He was concerned, he even made a house call, but she told him nothing. At each visit he listened to her heart and lungs. One time he lifted her breasts as if to hear without these impediments. She thought it strange, but she was so dizzy from the medication that she might have misunderstood. Or she was so traumatized from Burden. After six hopeless appointments, Evelyn shook her awake at seven o'clock in the morning to hurry up and help her get downstairs to the bus—and Lottie realized with astonishment that she'd slept through the night! And then she was hugging Evelyn and, as her daughter waved from the bus, Lottie was crying (yes, tears!). And Dr. Constanz was very pleased and called her one night at three A.M., his speech drink-slurred, and asked could he come again, this time just to visit her. No way, she said. Damn you.

But the depression was gone!

Evelyn turned nine, and then ten. Lottie finished her PhD. She invited only her daughter to watch her walk across the stage to get her degree.

Hoping some good would come from a new setting, Lottie accepted a research postdoc at the University of Pennsylvania. Getting a job anywhere was hopeless. But she was not hopeless—not happy-go-lucky, certainly, but not altogether grim.

Evelyn talked about moving in with her father. She had visited him for at least a few weeks every summer, and she liked his new wife and didn't mind his sons—there were three of them now, all under the age of six. Lottie believed she'd sink back into a depression if she lost Evelyn, and said, although she knew she shouldn't, "I'll start crying and never stop." Evelyn looked frightened. She put her arms around her mother and Ev and Lottie held each other tight. The following night Lottie apologized for her unmotherly behavior and told her daughter it just wasn't true about the crying, Lottie would manage, Evelyn needn't worry: she should try to work something out with Charlie and they'd see. Evelyn never mentioned it again, so either she'd been unable to work something out with Charlie or she never tried. As time went on, Lottie felt relieved and guilty, sure she really was a cruddy mother. Who said things like that to her daughter?

In order to refresh her memory and also to see someone else's technique, Lottie signed up as an auditor for the basic Gross Anatomy course at Penn. On the first day in mid-August, the class was addressed by Chloe Olivia, PhD, her name engraved on a badge she wore on the pocket of her lab coat. In Lottie's entire career as a graduate student, except for Dr. Helen Caldicott—the pediatrician and activist, who had appeared on campus once to speak out against nuclear war—the first woman Lottie had seen in a position of authority was Chloe Olivia. Lottie watched her uneasily, as if a poor showing would finish them both.

Dr. Olivia, who looked to be not much older than Lottie, was short and busty, with long brown hair—some of it in a braid, the rest held back by a tortoiseshell barrette—and radiant large brown eyes. To address the class, Dr. Olivia climbed up on top of a lab bench, stumbling over her white coat.

"Can you hear me?" she called out. There were two hundred students, four to a table; Lottie counted seven women, including herself. On the top of each table lay a body covered by a black tarpaulin.

"I want to welcome you to Gross Anatomy. Come here, come gather around me. Leave your tables." The students moved to the front of the room. "For many of you, this will be the first time you will see a dead body. It is a fearsome experience. You needn't be squeamish or self-righteous—or full of jokes, either, for these are just different manifestations of fear.

"Know that unless the person has died, there is no way to fully appreciate the marvelous structure that is the human body. We can't even visualize the abalone shell unless the mollusk is dead." She held up a pearly white and bluish shell the size of her head. The shell was so beautiful that Lottie reached out to touch it, and the teacher put it in her hands. "Pass it around.

"These bodies"—Dr. Olivia swept an arm wide to indicate the entire large room, taking in the students as well as the shrouded shapes—"are more gorgeous than any abalone shell. In my opinion, and no one need agree with me, if anyone had made us, we would never die: no one could bear to see such handiwork go to waste.

"Most of you don't need to be told to show respect. A certain number are the bodies of fellow scientists or physicians who have donated their remains so we can learn. Others are people who died without anybody to claim them. Still others the university has had to purchase at a thousand dollars a cadaver, which covers the cost of transportation and the 'diener'— look it up."

"Can you catch anything from them?" a tall, pale young man with thin blond hair blurted out.

Someone yelled, "A necrophiliac could get a slow burn!"

Titters and gagging sounds.

"Which reminds me," Dr. Olivia said. "Some years ago a few med students were playing Monkey in the Middle with a testicle."

Forced guffaws.

"They were suspended for a year." In the quiet that followed, Dr. Olivia said to the light-haired man: "No, you can't catch anything."

"Does this course help you with plastic surgery?" a burly black student yelled out to the good-natured laughter of several students standing near him.

"Of course! And we don't laugh at each other's questions. What's so funny, anyway?"

"He's already trying to make a buck!" said a rangy light-skinned black student with rimless glasses, his arm hanging over the would-be surgeon's shoulder.

"Well, may you prosper, everyone! And I hope some of you come to love Gross Anatomy, because next to Embryology, it's my favorite thing in the world." There were widespread *yick*s, hearty applause, and laughter. As the teacher leapt off the table, Lottie, standing nearby, watched her hair fly and caught a whiff of her decisive perfume.

During the next weeks Lottie became aware of the scent of the teacher before she heard her, and the fragrance would set off an anticipatory pleasure as Dr. Olivia jumped up onto a central bench to address the class.

"When you rest on your elbow while you're studying and your arm 'falls asleep,' what gives you that pins-and-needles feeling?

"What's a muscle whose point of origin is distal to the soleus on the fibula? What muscles arise laterally on the fibula? Where's the tailor's muscle and why is it called that?"

Another day Dr. Olivia stood up on the bench with a piece of paper in her hand.

"A colleague of yours who evidently prefers to remain anonymous writes: 'In your opening remarks you described death as "a waste." I take issue with that. It is the final part of this life: it is God's calling His Treasure home.'" Dr. Olivia folded the paper and put it in her lab coat pocket.

"I respect the First Amendment, and I hope you will all feel free to differ with me, as this student did, on matters of opinion—in person, in signed notes, or in unsigned notes. I happen to see us not as God's Own, but as a part of Nature. We become individualized for a while and then we return—as ash, as compost, as whatever. So I was wrong to speak of death as a waste. Certainly these deaths"—she once again made a sweeping motion with her arm to take in all the now-opened cadavers around the room "are not wasted at all. They are donations to Life, which I consider the highest good."

With a greasy hand, a young white man who wore a powder-blue yarmulke raised a hacksaw and shouted *"L'chaim!"* The class broke into laughter and applause, and Dr. Olivia got down off the bench blushing.

Lottie went back to work wondering if the students' laughter obscured for the professor the respect they all felt for her. Did she know that Lottie often jotted down her sayings for future use? That day Lottie wrote: *Remember to teach the body as more than the sum of its parts.*

Chloe Olivia's lectures were the high point of Lottie's life in Philadelphia, but she was able to attend them only by serious sneaking around. The work Lottie was *expected* to do, the lab research, required her spending twelve to eighteen hours a day trying to prove her boss's ideas about how cells replicate according to the model he had developed. She was injecting radioactive uridine, specific for RNA, into the peritoneal cavities of rats and then at regular intervals, sacrificing the rats and harvesting the salivary glands, homogenizing them in different buffers, and separating out the different fractions. She had become a highly skilled, glorified, and grossly underpaid lab technician. In graduate school she had at least been able to follow out her own ideas. Could she make it through two years of this? And then what?

Meantime, her work was so demanding that days went by when she hardly saw Evelyn—her daughter was now eleven, and in sixth grade at Martin Luther King Jr. Middle School. In late March, eight months into that Philadelphia postdoc, Lottie came home early one afternoon to find Evelyn in the kitchen humming along with Madame Butterfly to "Un Bel Dì" on the radio as she washed a week's worth of tights and pantyhose and hung them out the window on a small clothesline.

"You dear!" Lottie kissed her daughter.

"Long time no see."

"Sorry." Lottie kissed and hugged Evelyn again, then turned the radio down. "I didn't know you were into opera," Lottie said admiringly.

"There's a lot about me you don't know."

"Ouch." Lottie nodded a few times, then moved Evelyn away from the sink and rinsed out the fogged chrome percolator, filled it with water, spooned ground coffee into the metal basket, and plugged it in. "Just let me sit down a minute and get my bearings. How've you been?" Lottie pulled over a second kitchen chair and lifted her feet onto it and sighed. "Don't answer. Let me proofread this grant application first, and then I'm all yours."

"Couldn't you be all mine first and *then* proofread the application?"

"Work before pleasure." Lottie looked through her stuffed pocketbook for a pencil. Evelyn took a pair of dingy white tights from the sink water and wrung them out as if she would wrest the gray from them.

"Your work *is* your pleasure."

They both listened to the coffeepot begin to clear its throat.

"Well, thank God *some* of it is a pleasure—because that's how you eat. I can tell you, writing this"—Lottie waved in front of her face the many pages of the grant application she had filled out for her boss—"writing this has been a pure pain in sextuplicate." Lottie looked around for a more mollifying tone. "Honey, if I leave this until later, I'll just be too edgy to listen to you. Don't let's fight. Haven't you got any homework?"

Evelyn clamped the tights to the line with two clothespins, then dried her hands and applied pink liquid lotion to them. "Yeah, sure, I have homework." She sniffed her fingers pensively.

"Do you want me to make you some hot chocolate?"

Evelyn shook her head.

"With marshmallows?"

Evelyn shook her head again and left the kitchen.

Lottie spread out the grant papers on the kitchen table, then read the first two paragraphs without attending to them. She got several pillows from the living room couch and set two under her feet and sat down again. She got up and set one behind her back. From the cupboard she took out a mug that said John Dean for President and stood poised waiting for the coffeepot to stop chugging.

Evelyn came in with a library copy of *The Autobiography of Benjamin Franklin*.

"You know, I read that book right after you were born, maybe a year after," Lottie said.

"Did you like it?"

"It took my mind off things." Lottie closed her eyes, remembering the time when it seemed like Charlie was dying, and she was dying, too, and she'd read one biography after another, alternate lives; but now she got her eyes open quickly, afraid she'd fall asleep standing up. "I was impressed he started the first lending library and volunteer fire department."

"Is it true that Franklin fucked around a lot and had a bastard?"

"What kind of language is that?" Lottie would have put her hands on her waist, but she felt like a caricature. Would she have asked a boy the same rhetorical question?

"Is 'bastard' a curse word? I even read it in a book."

Lottie looked for a glint of mischief in her daughter's eyes but, seeing none, poured herself coffee and sat down. "Well, it's all right in books. You can find everything in books." Lottie got an off-centered feeling, a bit of nausea as she realized the implications of what her daughter was saying.

"Many of the kids at MLK say 'bastard' and 'fuck' this and 'fuck' that."

"Well, if all the kids commit hari-kari, are you going to do it, too?"

"What's hari-kari?"

"It's fancy suicide. I just don't want you to be such a sheep."

"If I don't talk that talk, I'll be made fun of. They're already calling me Miss Priss and Miss Piss."

"What?"

"Also 'Shit White.' One guy calls me 'Miss Puss 'n' Tits.'"

"Who? What's his name?" *Ah, what can ail thee, wretched Lot?* Lottie saw herself slicing at a tall boy's windpipe. "I'll go to school tomorrow and talk to the teacher. She'll give those kids a piece of my mind."

"Don't you dare!"

"Well, somebody has to know about this."

"It's enough *you* know. I'll get by. I always do."

"What do you mean, 'always'? You mean at every new school they yell obscenities at you?"

"No. But fitting in again and again is hard. This is my third new school."

Lottie nodded. She also wanted to blend in. But her daughter was eleven and one of the only white kids in her class. And she seemed to be getting picked on. Lottie was willing to have her white kid attend a predominantly black school, but if Evelyn was routinely bullied and ostracized . . . The neighborhood wasn't exactly one hundred percent safe: a counter guy at the deli two blocks away had been killed a few months earlier in a holdup. No one had claimed the body; and it was rumored he'd be a cadaver next year in the Gross Anatomy lab. How could Lottie afford to move to a white area on what she was earning as a postdoc? And how could she think about such an undemocratic thing? How could she not think about it? And who said Ev wouldn't be picked on in an all-white school? Kids picked on kids. It was the fucking human condition.

She needed to know what her daughter's life was really like. The girl's grades the first semester had been good. Two twelve-year-old girls, one black, one white, hung out now and again with Evelyn and studied with her or watched TV. She ate, smiled. She'd started studying violin. And Lottie didn't have time to investigate anything other than the whereabouts of tritium-labeled RNA.

She again felt a tide of nausea. "We're both having a rough time."

Evelyn said glumly, "But it's because of you. You keep dragging me to new places."

Lottie had to agree.

"Just tell me, is it true about Benjamin Franklin?"

"Is what true?"

"That he fucked around."

"I don't know. He doesn't talk about it in *The Autobiography*."

"Well, is it true that a man does it to a woman—"

"A man doesn't *do* it to a woman. The man and the woman *do it* to each *other*. I mean, it's a loving act." What did she know about it anymore, anyway? She felt sad. "Well, at least it's a friendly act. It ought to be. I mean, it's not a hostile act. Not usually. Not necessarily."

"Mommy, my question is, if a woman has a baby and the man takes off, he's still the father, right? Because a lot of kids in school say they don't have fathers. They say Thomas Jefferson had bastards, and John F. Kennedy probably had some, and LBJ and Nixon too, because all the big white guys fuck around."

Despite her growing queasiness, Lottie poured herself a second cup of coffee and sat down at the kitchen table peering into the steam rising from her mug as if she might find some answers there. "Are you talking about yourself?"

"What? No. I don't fuck around."

"No. No. I didn't mean that." Lottie feared she would throw up or cry out. "Are girls your age at school fucking around?"

"No." Then she said, "Just two or three." She added, "Mom, I'm going to be twelve. I'm not gonna do that."

Lottie kept nodding.

"Mommy, do all the big guys fuck around and have bastards? Am I a bastard?"

"No, no, you're *not* a bastard. Your father and I were married when we had you. That's the crucial distinction."

Evelyn nodded tentatively.

"You are not a bastard, you were not a bastard, and you'll never be a bastard." And she wanted to say, *and don't mention that bastard Nixon in this house again*, but she knew it made no sense, she was off on a tangent, evading a situation she had to face. Tired.

Evelyn smiled, although she looked confused. "Maybe I better just write what I'm sure about."

"You weren't going to write about Benjamin Franklin having bastards, were you?"

"Mom, are you going to have more children?"

Lottie fought to get out an answer. "I doubt it."

"Mom, listen just a minute—"

"Yes?"

"You know I like Sapphira and the kids, but the truth is I don't get much homework done there." Sapphira was a woman who ran a day-care program in her apartment down the street; Evelyn spent evenings and nights there when Lottie needed to stay at the lab. Evelyn was the oldest of the kids Sapphira was taking care of, but Evelyn was also a "big sister" and got fifty cents an hour for helping out.

"Because there's so much lights, camera, action?" Lottie scanned the first page of the grant application, trying to distract herself from the feeling that her daughter was in trouble.

Evelyn shook her head. "I'm the lights, camera, action. I play violin pieces for the kids. I make up stories. I'm left in charge. If I'm there during the day, she does her shopping or just steps out for an hour to have one of her black cigarillos. If I'm staying overnight she dresses up and goes to a movie, or she meets some of her husband's buddies for a drink. She gave me this." Evelyn took a calling card from her pocket and handed it to Lottie.

THE BROTHERLY LOVE COCKTAIL LOUNGE
2046 SPRUCE STREET
PHILADELPHIA
374-8923

Lottie nodded a few times. "You get almost all As anyway."

"But I'm tired the next day at school."

Lottie kept nodding. She feared she would nod off, and not get the grant application in. But there was no missing that her daughter was calling out to her. Would Evelyn grow up crooked, broken? Lottie didn't think so, but, for sure, Evelyn was growing up behind Lottie's back. And she was asking her mother to turn around, take a look.

Should she get Evelyn away from Sapphira? Let her daughter stay home alone?

Was that good for an eleven-year-old?

For a moment, the old foggy depressed feeling invaded Lottie, the Wisconsin miasma returned.

Lottie told herself the girl had friends, that was a good sign—and they didn't seem like girls who would be fucking around. Michelle Witten was the white girl, Susie Lacks or Lux or Leeks was the black girl, she couldn't remember the black girl's last name. What did it mean that Lottie didn't know the other girl's last name?

Lottie was sitting with her rear end on one chair, her legs on another, her eyes shut. She tried to pry them open with her fingers but they wouldn't stay open. Finally she leaned her head down on the kitchen table and fell asleep.

At the end of June, Gross Anatomy was over; and Lottie felt emboldened to ask her teacher to have coffee. Still, at the restaurant Olivia chose (and she didn't like to be called Chloe, she preferred Olivia) a sleek, blond-wood-and-mirrored place far from the university, Lottie was reserved at first; but Olivia was lively and curious and they ended up talking their heads off. Olivia had always wanted to be an anatomist, she had done well at school and was already the first author on half a dozen published papers. Her career path, aided by a physicist husband, had been straightforward: he was accomplished, older than she, and he never accepted a job unless a suitable position was offered to his wife. Lottie was envious.

Olivia was envious of Lottie; Olivia had always wanted children—she and her husband had been trying unsuccessfully for years and were now seriously investigating adoption. It pained Olivia that she might not have a child—"For a developmental biologist to miss out on that experience!" Olivia shook her head.

A week later she invited Lottie and Evelyn to dinner at her roomy brownstone. When Olivia found out about Evelyn's unhappy arrangement at Sapphira's, she immediately offered to put the girl up whenever Lottie needed to work nights. Evelyn was willing.

And she wrote letters of recommendation for Lottie, letters in which she described Dr. Hart as a superb scientist and clear teacher and, by the by, an excellent mother. Excellent mother! Lottie was embarrassed to be praised where she knew she fell short and, without going into the real reasons, convinced her friend to leave that detail out: it wasn't relevant, Lottie said, and it might even hurt her chances. What male scientist was ever described as an excellent father?

Lottie was thrilled to have a friend. She'd never been as close to a woman in her life as she was with Olivia. Well, there had been her grandmother; but a grandmother wasn't a friend. Lottie'd had cheerleader friends and sorority sister friends, but no one had been able to squeeze into the no-space between her and Charlie. Certainly there weren't strong bonds between her and the other lab techs. The strongest ties she had were with Evelyn. And your child could not be your friend.

And then finally Lottie dug herself and Evelyn out. A real job in New York City opened up, an assistant professorship in a medical school. Despite considerable competition, Lottie made the cut; there were seventy-five people she'd triumphed over, most of them men. Tenure-track positions were rare altogether and New York City was a plum location although not to Lottie, who disliked cities.

With this rise in her fortunes, her sleep improved; for the first time in a long while Lottie wasn't at war with the world; a future might be possible.

It was true that Lottie mourned Olivia; they had become bulwarks of each other's lives. And she knew a whole lot more biochemistry because of that ridiculous postdoc, and she was proud of herself.

Evelyn was furious. "We're moving? Right after I got things figured out? You want *me* to help you look for an apartment? Are you crazy?"

"I'm so sorry, sweetheart." Lottie put an arm around her. "I hope it will be our last move."

Evelyn shook off her mother's arm.

Lottie forayed for apartments alone.

An hour upstate from the job, in Orange County where the local schools were pretty good—she checked that out carefully—Lottie discovered a few semirural areas where she thought she could live. And she didn't do her usual—look for just enough space, the monastic apartment; rather, she wanted an extra bedroom or two with the dim idea, which she hardly let herself think and which she certainly didn't mention to Evelyn, that perhaps she'd meet someone who wanted children and they'd fill up the house. Was it possible? She settled on a place with three bedrooms and a skylight in the master bedroom. She'd never had a skylight before and once they moved in, she spent some time every day trying to describe the exact color of the sky; and she took to photographing it and dating the photographs and posting them on a wall of her bedroom. She tried to figure the sources of strange colors—milky white, sometimes a dull orange or brown, much of it from pollution, some of it dust that came all the way from East Africa! At night she enjoyed identifying the constellations and she thought of buying a special camera to snap the night sky.

Meanwhile, for the first time in her adult life since she'd left Charlie, she had a guest room. Her parents visited for a weekend; her sister Bridge came with her husband; Gerry stayed over with a spiffy guy—Lottie assumed they were lovers. Olivia came up twice, very pregnant—Lottie embraced her with fervor, but Evelyn hung back, upset—and then with a handsome nearly newborn baby boy named Shiloh, an alert little fellow, with shining obsidian eyes, and Lottie felt spring was in the air and why not for her, too?

Didn't she deserve it?

Evelyn continued complaining for a while and then stopped. Lottie met with the eighth-grade homeroom teacher, who thought the girl was fitting in well and doing fine scholastically. She was also taking violin lessons one afternoon a week at Orange High with a teacher who had organized an award-winning orchestra; he accepted very few students from the middle school. Ev auditioned and made it. Lottie paid for Evelyn's lessons but left her daughter to her own inclinations about practicing, especially after Evelyn came upon her humming through her scores and told her to butt out. The only subject Lottie was ever consulted on was science; this year it was biology. It hurt Lottie, made her feel left out (after all, her French was pretty good and she knew a thing or two about history), but when she thought of how she'd left Evelyn out over the years, left her alone, maybe the girl *was* entitled to leave *her* out. And maybe it was just being a teenager. Doing her own homework, what was wrong with that? Lottie found it hard to forgive her father for the way he'd interfered in her young life and shamed her. Of course, having a pregnant daughter was much more trying than having a daughter doing her own homework.

In January Lottie went to hear the final orchestra performance of the semester. It was an unusual program: Bartók's *Concerto for Orchestra* Lottie knew, but then there was Piazzolla's *Fuga y Misterio* (Who was Piazzolla? And what kind of instrument was a bandoneon?) followed by Louise Farrenc's Symphony No. 3. Lottie had never heard of Louise Farrenc and she suspected no one else had heard of her either: *name one female composer.* It was harder than *name one female scientist.* It amazed Lottie how much it continued to amaze her that social strictures had crushed women throughout the centuries; some dark part of her assumed that women were inferior, that she was inferior, so her grandmother must have been inferior! And Evelyn! Evelyn inferior! Consciously Lottie never felt inferior, but now and again she wanted to punch the nearest man.

In the auditorium, Lottie scanned the female musicians as they walked onto the stage, all in black skirts and sweaters with white pearls; she was looking of course for Evelyn, who'd bought her own sweater out of babysitting money and wore Lottie's grandmother's pearls. There she was, walking sapling-straight with her high, strong breasts and her good neck and of course she was taller than most of the girls and some of the boys. Lottie sat up straighter in her seat and had to tell herself not to start whooping it up or, worse, file up on stage herself—although here and there parents stood up and broke out in cheers. One mother yelled out, "Way to go, Hacooby-dooby!" and Lottie saw a flush-faced boy on stage smile shyly and look down at his feet. The conductor came on and the musicians screamed and stomped on the floor and waved their instruments in the air. His students must love him, she thought, this conductor, this Jake Levinson, who smiled shyly in his tall black tuxedo, bowing briskly a few times, quieting down the musicians with his large hands. Then with a huge sweeping gesture Levinson quieted the whole auditorium. He raised both his long arms, waited while everyone got her or his music open and settled down, instrument at the ready, and then on the downbeat the musicians began: first the dark ominous violas and cellos, then in came the trembling violins, then the flutes! Lottie closed her eyes for a moment and just listened. But she wanted to watch this Levinson guy, always on the move, beckoning the different sections of the orchestra, leaning this way and that and bending his knees and stooping and making his thumbs and index fingers into closing pincers when he wanted quiet sounds, opening his arms out wide to elicit a crescendo. The man was in vigorous, nonstop motion. And she was in the second row and could see how clean and short the nails were on his evocative fingers. Half the time she was watching him, the other half she focused on her daughter, whose curly blonde hair was held back with a black grosgrain ribbon and who played tremulously but with total concentration, watching the score and the conductor and not once looking around. The piece was long and solid and vibrant and after the first half hour, Lottie thought, *This is going to be okay, really okay*, and she relaxed, as if she were off some hook, and she could love the rising horns and then in a while the sudden surprise ending. And the audience applauded mightily and Lottie thought deservedly, not that she was a connoisseur; but she had always liked music. And only while everyone was clapping and the musicians were bowing before the intermission did Evelyn look at Lottie and nod, and Lottie raised both arms above her head in a victory sign and Evvie grinned and then she looked away and when it was the turn of those in her row, walked off the stage very seriously, very decorously.

Lottie felt pleased and a little exhausted, as if she had done the conducting herself or at least played the violin; she wanted to stay put in her chair and rub her neck or her feet. But she thought she should mingle. As a newcomer she knew no one, so she told herself go, girl, go—it would be good for her and Evelyn if Lottie became part of the community. She made her way over to the hospitality table and talked to a friendly, self-assured woman elegant in a navy sequined long-sleeved dress, dark hair teased up into a beehive, who headed the high school PTA. Of course, Lottie couldn't join the PTA because it wasn't for middle-school parents, but she was welcome to attend the after-concert party for the musicians; they had a few parents as chaperones and one more wouldn't hurt. Lottie wasn't sure if Evelyn would like having her mother at the party, especially with no warning. But Evelyn was thirteen, barely out of childhood, for God's sake (although Lottie'd seen the outlines of blood in underpants her daughter had scrubbed and left to dry on a rack in the downstairs bathroom). Lottie made her way to the women's restroom and reapplied some lipstick and mascara while taking notice in the mirror of the other women who were talking together in groups of twos and threes, many with long dyed hair crimped and blown out. And she thought again about her own hair neat and clean in one long braid down her back, Middle Ages style, she feared, or farm style, which was worse. Everyone seemed to be wearing wedding rings. One or two women introduced themselves and asked who her kid was although it turned out they didn't know Evelyn, which was just as well. They each seemed to have sons three or four years older than her daughter, and Lottie didn't know how she was going to negotiate Evelyn's starting to connect with boys.

During the rest of the concert she again alternated between watching her daughter, who was concentrating fiercely, even ferociously, her arm slicing with the bow—she was a strong player, Ev, but she could also be delicate; and watching Jake Levinson, who jumped and swooped but was also very quiet. He kept his hands at his sides while the first violinist played a few plangent solo lines, and later Levinson pressed down on the air with both big hands in small, firm gestures to quiet the rumbling drums. He wore a watch but no other jewelry.

When it was over, the orchestra received a five-minute standing ovation and the applause for the conductor went on every bit as long and he beamed at his students and smiled and bowed to the audience, and Lottie's arms were so tired.

Lottie found Evelyn and hugged her and told her what a bang-up job she'd done. Evelyn looked pleased and handed over her violin in its case and her music in a black loose-leaf folder. "I'm going to the after-concert party. Would you mind taking my stuff home?"

Lottie said, "Fine, yes, I'll take it but I'm going to the party, too. I was asked to chaperone." Lottie explained about the invitation from the PTA lady.

Evelyn frowned. "I don't want you to come to the party. Why did you accept without checking with me?"

"I'm your mom. We're new here. I'm being friendly."

"It's *my* concert."

Lottie repeated, "I'm your mother."

"It's my first concert. I'm thirteen. Just go home!"

"I want to meet some people, too. I could use a social life."

"Get it at the medical school. This is my turf!" But then perhaps seeing the upset on her mother's face, she muttered, "Okay, okay. All right. Just don't stay more than ten minutes. Fifteen at most. And keep away from me."

Lottie nodded, irritated—she felt like she was the child, and her daughter the mother—and also pleased. Was Evelyn going to turn out to be a normal teenager? Would Lottie really have that good luck? "I'll just stay a little while. I promise. Ten minutes. Maybe twenty." But her daughter had turned her back and left.

Taped across the ceiling of the gymnasium in the basement were royal-blue crepe paper streamers crisscrossed with white streamers and bright yellow ones. And there were red balloons with SAMMY'S SHOES printed on them gassed up to the ceiling and a large handwritten sign hanging down that read CONGRATS TO OUR ALL-STATE ORCHESTRA CHAMPS! Michael Jackson records were blaring from speakers and a big poster of Michael Jackson dancing in a white glittering suit hung on a wall. A few couples danced. Girls stood talking. Six boys still wearing their dark jackets but with their ties loosened threw a basketball around.

A parent was in conversation with Jake Levinson, who was bending over to hear her. Lottie stood nearby and waited for them to finish. She thought Levinson looked a little like someone she knew. Then she realized that, with his considerable height and boniness and dark hair and warm thoughtful eyes, he reminded her of Abraham Lincoln. But he didn't look sad. He was speaking in an animated way. When the woman finished, Lottie went over and thrust out her arm. "Fine concert, Mr. Levinson."

He shook hands formally. How could those loose, limber arms be so stiff? "Yes," he said, smiling. "Weren't they first-class, those kids."

"That was an extraordinary program you put together. You have a lot of confidence in your students."

"I do. Have a lot of confidence in them. Thank you. You sound like you know about music."

"A little. My sister is a pianist, an amateur." Lottie nodded apologetically a few times.

"Who are you? I mean, whose mother are you?"

"Evelyn. I'm Evelyn's mother. Evelyn Hart. Plays the violin. Middle-school student."

"Oh sure, Evelyn. Good girl. Hardworking. Careful. Glad to meet you. Evelyn's mother—your name is—"

"Lottie. Lottie Hart."

Jake nodded. "Her father here? I'd like to meet him, too. I want to congratulate him on his daughter's performance. She's very conscientious, Evelyn is. And respectful."

Lottie was terribly pleased and she burst out, "I did it myself. That is, she did it herself. Her father's in Texas. We're divorced. She sees him summers. I can hardly believe she's coming through okay. *If* she's coming through okay."

"I'm sorry," Jake said. "About the divorce."

And, to her surprise, Lottie's eyes flooded up.

He looked intently at her. "I'm sorry. It isn't recent, is it, the divorce? You said she goes to him summers. But these things can be hurtful. I know. From experience."

"No, no. It was long ago. I'm crying because it looks like maybe she's coming through, maybe she's pulling through all right. I'm crying because I'm happy."

Jake pulled a handkerchief out of his jacket pocket. "It's a little sweaty. I used it after the concert."

Lottie shook her head that she didn't need it but she could not stop crying.

Jake put a kind, awkward hand on her shoulder.

She was embarrassed—To cry! In public! She, Lottie! And in front of this stranger! She looked around but didn't see Evelyn. At least that was good, that Evelyn didn't see her cry. And somehow as Lottie cried, she felt relieved. She cried more and more.

"Do you want to go out to talk somewhere? We could go someplace and have a drink," Jake Levinson said.

"No! No! I don't want you to take me out out of pity!" She could not stop crying. It was as though a valve had broken.

"Don't be silly." He shook his head. "I have a daughter, I have an endangered daughter, too." After a moment he added, "And you seem an unusual woman."

"How do you know?" Lottie gasped.

He laughed.

"How?" she insisted. "Tell me how."

"Well, look at you. Crying in the gym and at the same time insisting I tell you how you're unusual!"

Lottie continued crying but she nodded emphatically. "Sure, I'll go out with you. Just let me go tell Evelyn."

She went to the bathroom and washed her face, angry with herself for crying but excited at the prospect of going out with him. Evelyn was talking to another girl and Lottie took her aside and explained that she was going out for a drink with Jake Levinson.

"Shit!" Evelyn said.

"Don't use that language."

"I don't want you going out with him!"

Lottie suddenly had a vision of Jake Levinson romancing all the mothers. What about the music students? Had he made a move on her daughter? She stiffened. "Is he a rat or something?"

"He's my violin teacher!"

"But what kind of person is he?"

"He's a good guy. A really good guy. Leave him alone."

"That's an odd recommendation."

Evelyn turned her back on her mother, who walked around to face her. Lottie asked, "Wait a minute. Do you have a crush on him?"

"No!" Evelyn yelled and walked off.

Somewhat relieved, Lottie followed her. "You have a key? Can you get a lift from another parent? I don't want you to take a ride with one of the seniors, not the girls and not the boys. I don't trust their driving. Do you understand?"

"If you're going out with my teacher and I've asked you not to and you're doing it anyway, I don't see how you can tell me who I should go home with."

"*Whom*," Lottie said stupidly. And then she said, "Because I'm your mother. I tell you what to do because I'm your mother."

"You never do what I ask you to!"

"Do you mean that?"

"Yes."

Lottie knew this wasn't the time to open a big discussion. Instead she said, "You wait for me here. I'm going out with your teacher and I'll be back in an hour, an hour and a half at the latest, to take you home."

"Oh, great," Evelyn said. "Mom, I don't need you to take me home. I don't need you hanging out in the house with me. I'll go home when I want to go home."

"Can I trust you to get a ride home with a parent?"

"I don't know any of the parents."

"You must know some of the kids. You've been practicing with this orchestra for months. You have to be able to negotiate yourself a ride with a kid who has parents. Do you want me to arrange a ride for you?"

"Get out of here. Just go away. Leave me alone."

Lottie wanted to say, "You're being rude," but what she said instead was, "Promise me you won't go anywhere without a parent, without a parent being present."

Evelyn made a face, but she said, "Okay. Of course. I'm no fool."

Jake and Lottie drove two cars to the only nearby bar-restaurant that was open at ten thirty on a Thursday evening. Jake opened Lottie's car door to help her get out and then they went through the door of the restaurant and entered a fog of smoke. Lottie started coughing at once and tried to say her lungs might be hypersensitive because of the experiments she'd been doing. She could see he didn't understand, but when she couldn't stop coughing he gave her his keys and told her to wait in his car and he would bring out their drinks in plastic cups.

It was biting cold but the air was clear and Lottie stopped coughing almost at once, although her chest continued to hurt. There was thick snow everywhere except on the pathway from the restaurant; the parking lot had also been cleared and there were six or seven cars there besides Jake's and Lottie's. His was a van. She moved a dark brown leather briefcase off the passenger seat and onto the floor so she could sit down; then she picked up the briefcase and opened it—sheet music—and hurriedly closed it, looking out uneasily for him through the window. In the backseats were several instruments in black cases—one small thin one looked like it housed a piccolo or flute; another was the size and shape of a violin and a third might have been holding an upright bass or cello or something else big. He had the two small cases wedged in with books and towels and fluorescent yellow tennis balls on the third backseat, and the bass bag was standing on the third back floor with its straps tied to the window cranks of each door. All the instruments were fixed and immobilized. She turned the ignition on and the heat came up quickly—he'd only just turned it off—and almost immediately the windshield began fogging up. She locked her door and the driver's door and after a few moments of fiddling, figured out how to turn on Jake's cassette player; a pianist came on playing Bach, she was almost sure, and she closed her eyes and told herself that nothing bad would happen to her, she was waiting for him in his safe, civilized car. Was it really the first time she'd been out with a man alone since Burden?

Still, she was startled by his knocking on the passenger's-side window. When she cranked it down, he handed her a very cold plastic cup. He went around the car and she leaned over to open the driver's-side door for him. He put his drink in an open-out metal cup holder and took hers from her and opened up another cup holder, and he blew on his hands for a while and blew on hers, too, then recommended they both wear their gloves because the icy plastic cups would freeze their fingers. He'd gotten her the virgin Mary she'd asked for: even though she'd had only a few sips of wine that night with Burden, she was jumpy about drinking alcohol with a man. She sipped at the tomato juice—it was very cold going down, and her chest still hurt—and she felt excited but also uneasy.

They sat silently in the dark for a while drinking, the red and white neon lights of the restaurant sign and the light from inside the restaurant the only illumination. She suddenly realized she expected him to lunge at her. She looked closely at him. He was sitting behind the steering wheel holding his drink with his gloves on, his long legs stretched out in front of him. He was looking back at her and smiling. And then it came to her: this man would share his last piece of bread with her, if not give it to her outright. Her eyes flooded up. She wanted to sleep with him.

"Feeling better?" he said at the same time as she said, "You have a daughter?"

They both nodded.

He said that Ruth was nine years old, and she lived with her mother in California, in L.A. "It's a worry, the distance. But that's where her mother wanted to go and I didn't have much say. Fathers generally don't. Have much say."

Lottie said, "That's why I was able to get a PhD."

They were silent. Finally he said, "Okay, tell me about it. What's it in, your degree? How'd you do it? Not many women earn PhDs." Then he added, "Of course, you're right. Men have too much say. About most things."

In the dark Lottie felt encouraged. She explained the bare bones of getting her PhD. There were many bones.

"Wow," he said. "That's an adventure story."

"You think so?"

"Oh, yes." Then they were quiet. They listened to the piano playing. "Glenn Gould," he said. "I have to turn that off. I can't talk while it's playing."

"You don't like background music?"

He shook his head. "Music for me is foreground. There's nothing more foreground."

She nodded although she didn't think music was foreground. She didn't think about music at all.

"I don't have a PhD," he said. "I've got a master's. Not too many musicians who make a living playing get advanced degrees. I make a kind of living, an uneven kind"—he laughed—"but I love to play."

They sat silently a while longer. He said, "Are you feeling better now about Evelyn?"

Lottie remembered crying in the gym. Her eyes were still hot and now they were moist. "Honestly, I was crying from happiness."

"You worry about her. Look, do you want to go home?"

"What do you mean?"

"Go home and check her out."

Lottie shook her head. "We just got here, didn't we?"

"Well, half an hour ago. Frankly, I can't just sit in the car anymore. I'm all charged up from the concert—it went well, don't you think?"

She nodded vigorously in the dark. Did he really want to leave her? Had she lost him somehow—said something, done something? Or had she misread him all along and he was never really interested in her, he was just a kind man? Thoughtful. She felt empty in her chest and belly, bereft.

He said, "What I really want to do is dance. If you're all right with that."

She was momentarily relieved: he didn't want to leave her. "But where can we dance?"

"Well, we can't dance in there because you can't breathe. I could invite you to my house—"

Again, the image of him tackling her came to mind. She could almost feel the back of her head thwack against the icy window.

"—I have the second floor of a house; the downstairs is rented out to a family . . . It's only a couple of miles away, but you might be wary—I wouldn't blame you, not that I'm anybody to be wary of. But why should you believe me? You probably ought to go home to Evelyn, so maybe after we finish our drink I'll just follow you and then I'll go home and dance by myself!" He gave a hearty laugh.

She relaxed for a moment and let herself think about going home with him and then she had a gagging feeling in her throat and began coughing again. She reached into her pocketbook after tissues and felt the Swiss army knife she'd bought the day after that night with Burden. In her pocketbook, she opened the scissors and the nail file and the corkscrew.

Jake got a box of tissues from under his seat and handed it to her. "Maybe you want to look into that cough? It could be serious." Then he added, "What do you say? I'll follow you to your place and we'll call it a night?"

"Why do you want to follow me?"

He looked surprised at her question. "To make sure you get home okay."

He was who she thought he was? She let go of the knife, and took her hand out of her pocketbook and reached for his box of tissues. "No," she said. "I don't want to go home. I don't."

"You sure?"

She was still coughing. But she said, "I'm sure. One dance. Just one."

He grinned happily and said, "I'll drive your car to my place so you don't have to get into a cold car." Then he added, "But many people don't want a stranger driving their car. Up to you."

She didn't want a stranger driving her car. But she thought, *Listen, Jake Levinson, I'm going to do everything in my power to make you not a stranger.*

But there was a balled-up pair of (clean) underpants on the backseat of her car, a couple of pairs of socks, three science journals. There was even a thermos with some leftover, probably dried-out coffee in it.

Fuck it.

"Drive," she said. "Drive my car. I'll drive yours."

She hadn't driven anything that big since she and Evvie had meandered up the middle of the country in their hungover hippie van. His car was big enough to transport a chamber music group in, instruments and all— and she drove slowly. The roads were barely plowed and she didn't want to get into an accident; but she had no trouble. The car stuck to the road, *It must have four-wheel drive,* she thought; she liked the way it handled. After a few minutes, he signaled for her to pull into a driveway. The walk to his house was shoveled and had rock salt on it as did the steps and the porch. Except for a light on over the porch, the downstairs lights were off; she felt frightened for a moment that no downstairs family existed, but it was possible they were asleep. She walked up the inside steps ahead of him to the second floor and he let her into a room that was cold as all get-out. He turned on the lights—it was a spacious living room—and he upped the thermostat immediately and went to the fireplace with a box of matches. The logs and kindling and newspapers were already in place and he started a fire in a few minutes. The big room was nearly empty of furniture; there were two chairs, a couch, a piano, a drum set, and several music stands. He left her alone as he went down to bring the instruments up from his car— "The cold won't do them any good." And he carried them carefully, as if they were sleeping children, into a back room.

Then he reached for a cassette. "Do you know Leonard Cohen?"

"Of course. Nuclear physicist. Professor, University of Pittsburgh."

Jake looked startled. "No, no, I mean the musician: the songwriter. He writes sad, strange, lyrical songs."

"What do you mean 'no, no'? Your Leonard Cohen is a songwriter. Mine's a physicist. There are probably sixty other Leonard Cohens."

Jake laughed. "You have a point. You probably have sixty points." Then he said, "You want to hear a song by my Leonard Cohen? One song. One dance. Then I follow you home."

"You're really going to follow me home."

"Of course."

Did she deserve this man? "Okay. Yes, I'll listen to your guy."

And he turned on the cassette and took her respectfully, gently in his arms. She heard what sounded like a very sweet, persistent violin. Then a guitar? Maybe another guitar? La la, la la la la la la. The violin again and again? She made out some of the words:

Dance me to your beauty with a burning violin
Dance me through the panic till I'm gathered safely in

How did Leonard Cohen/Jake know she was in a panic? Was she moving stiltedly? Was she hyperventilating? She was waiting for a certain pressure, for him to get forceful, but he was holding her loose and easy. Although very tall (as tall as Charlie?), he was slender and light on his feet, as though he were a smaller man. His hand at her waist was spread open and held half her back.

Dance me to the children who are asking to be born . . .
Raise a tent of shelter now though every thread is torn . . .

There was some warm comfort spreading from his big open hand through her sweater to the skin of her back. She danced, heated by his hand; it was as if not only heat but also a current were running through his fingers into her back. The pulse spread into her waist, down her buttocks, her legs. It was almost painful to keep moving.

She looked up at him. He was half a foot taller than she. Was he feeling what she felt? His brown eyes were bright, seemed to her to be swimming. He was looking at her intently.

Touch me with your naked hand or touch me with your glove

She touched his neck.

His forehead was creased and there were smile lines near his eyes and around his mouth. They weren't youngsters, either of them; and they kept looking at each other, taking each other in. She closed her wet eyes, wanting him, half-expecting him to kiss her.

He did not kiss her. After a moment, she felt him tug on her braid and when she opened her eyes, he winked at her. "Home, girl. Let's go."

"Play it again," she said. "I like your Leonard Cohen."

He said, "He's good, isn't he? That song is like a Strauss violin waltz, and it's also like gypsy klezmer music. Or Jewish klezmer music."

She said, "I don't know klezmer music. Play it again, please."

"No," he said. "You have to go home. Come on." He got her coat, that old white goose-down parka that was who-knew-how-many-years-old now, and helped her into it. "La la, la la la la la la." He had a low, breathy, almost cracked voice that she found dangerous and dear. He stopped humming going down the inside steps, and she picked up, softly singing, "la la, la la la la la la," but he shushed her. And she remembered the family who lived downstairs. He whispered, "I'll play it again for you next time."

So there would be a next time, she thought, and felt oh so happy.

"Alto," he whispered to her. "You're an alto, almost a contralto. You have a good, low voice. Rich. Do you sing?"

She shook her head. "But I will now."

They got into their separate cars and he followed her to within a block of her house.

Evelyn was studying at the kitchen table. She didn't look up when Lottie entered.

"Wonderful concert," Lottie said.

Evelyn continued writing in her notebook.

"Really, it was glorious. You must be so proud. *I'm* so proud."

Evelyn wrote more quickly and darkly.

Lottie let her be. Lottie went up the stairs to her bedroom singing *la la, la la la la la la.* She sang *la la, la la la la la la* for a long time before she fell asleep.

The next evening when she got home from work, Evelyn told her that she had a message "from my violin teacher."

"Me? It was for me?" Excited, Lottie reached over to press the button on the answering machine but Evelyn said, "I erased it."

"You *what*? You did *what*?!"

"It wasn't a real message. Mr. Levinson just said, 'Call me.' And he left his number."

"That's what he said? Exactly what did he say?"

"Well, maybe he said 'please call me.' I mean, it was two or three or four words."

After a long time, Lottie said, "Don't ever do that to me again, you hear? I never erase your messages."

"So you've got the hots for him . . ."

Lottie thought to say, "You're talking to your *mother*," but said instead, "What's his phone number? Did you erase that, too?" Looking at the yellow pad next to the phone, Lottie saw that Evelyn had written down Jake's name and phone number.

"You know, it's not true that we never erase each other's messages. That's why we keep that pad there," Evelyn said.

"But personal messages. Why would you erase a personal message?"

"You're expecting a personal message *from my violin teacher*? How come? Did you fuck him? Did you suck him off?"

Lottie slapped her across the face.

Evelyn cried out. And in the next minute she stood up and slapped her mother back.

They stood facing each other, the same size.

Lottie howled, "Did you see anything? Did you hear anything?"

"What? What? What are you talking about?" Evelyn's voice was dazed and angry and unsteady. Half of her face was reddened from where Lottie'd slapped her.

Lottie felt her own face hot and smarting. "You don't know?"

"What don't I know?"

"Forget about it."

"Forget about what? Did you do something with my teacher? With Mr. Levinson?"

"No! No! I'm talking about something that happened way back. When you were a little girl. In Wisconsin. Maybe you were four, five?"

"What are you talking about?"

"You didn't see—what he did to me. What happened . . . What I did to him."

"What, Mommy?! Who are you talking about? Tell me!" Evelyn grabbed her mother's hands.

They stood holding hands in the kitchen.

"Mom, you can't leave it like that!"

Lottie thought she could, that her parents had done that to her, had never given her a clear answer about her baby brother. Not getting a straight answer made it hard to think straight, to know what was what. Finally Lottie sat down at the kitchen table. Evelyn sat down, too.

Lottie put her head down and cried. Her daughter put her hand on her mother's head and massaged it. Finally, Lottie told Evelyn in general terms what had happened that night in their living room long ago with Nathaniel Burden while Evelyn was asleep.

Her daughter asked questions, which Lottie answered briefly, with as little graphic language as possible. She didn't pull punches. She used the words *rape* and *fellatio*. But she was shaking. "You're the first person I ever told." She kissed her daughter's hand that had slapped her in the face, that had massaged her head.

Evelyn wiped at her mother's tears with her fingers. "Is that why you never go out with anybody, Mom? You must be so scared!" Evelyn soaked two washcloths with cold water, then wrung them out and applied one to her mother's face where she'd hit her. Lottie held it there. Evelyn applied the other to her own face.

They began laughing.

Lottie said, "I got a few good cuts in myself. And I chased him out of the house; I threw his boots after him, I said I'd call the police." She began crying again.

"Did you? Did you call the police?"

Lottie shook her head. "I felt ashamed." She touched her daughter's bright hair. "But it's why I don't want you ever to go to a boy's house alone. Why I want to make sure there's always a parent there. You understand? And if anything happens to you, don't you feel ashamed to tell me. And don't wait six years."

They stood up and held on to each other.

On Saturday night after she dropped off Evelyn for a sleepover at her best friend's—Evelyn had a best friend!—Lottie drove carefully but joyously along the icy streets to Jake's house. Over and over in her mind were her daughter's words when she got out of the car with her backpack: "Have a fine time, Mommy. Mr. Levinson's the best!"

That Evelyn should give Lottie her blessing! Unimaginable that hitting her daughter and telling about that unspeakable night should end in a blessing!

Her daughter was all right, Evelyn was all right, Lottie felt sure now in her whole being.

So she drove with wings. (Well, she had her period, a downer in that it restricted what was going to happen, but maybe that had a positive side, nothing horrendous was going to happen. What horrendous thing could happen? Would Burden never leave her mind? Anyway, it was a first night, maybe a second night. Nothing need happen so soon.) Although she'd written down Jake's instructions, she never looked at them and didn't make a single wrong turn. She prided herself on being able to practically smell her way anywhere, but given that she'd driven home from there only once, and in the dark, there was something preternatural about her sense of where he was: she was part-woman, part-bat. She felt as if she were echolocating. And he must have been watching for her at the living room window because as she cut the ignition in his driveway, he was coming down the porch steps in a big red barbecue apron, his shirtsleeves rolled up. (Coatless, he must be freezing.) She handed him a begonia plant with pale orange flowers and he thanked her vehemently as they hurried up the steps. He had a good fire going in the fireplace, and the stands had music on them and there was music on the piano and the place had a warmer feel—a more thick, fully-featured feel to it than when she had been there two nights earlier. He turned off the music.

"Beethoven?" She asked.

"Yup."

She showed off: "Piano Sonata No. 23."

"Right-o. How'd you know that?"

"I told you, my sister is a pianist. She was practicing all the time."

"Well, good for you, that you paid attention."

"There was no way to avoid it."

He laughed. "Don't you like music?"

"I think I do. I don't know much about it."

"I'll teach you. You'll love it." He looked inexpressibly happy as he helped her take off her parka and hung it on an empty hook next to a dress coat of his, a dark nylon hooded raincoat, several thick flannel shirts.

"Oh, I'd like that." She smiled back at him, very happy herself.

She inhaled the fragrance of warm garlic and olive oil and the astringent, almost hurting smell of lemon. She followed him into the kitchen.

And he poured her a glass of white Bordeaux, then dropped pounded floured veal cutlets gingerly into a hot frying pan; he lowered some angel hair pasta into a pot of boiling water. On the counter there was a large salad with a layer of red leaf lettuce, a layer of arugula, then layers of other vegetables.

"You did all this?"

"Not the bread," he laughed. "What's the big deal? I cook. You cook, no?"

"Do you cook often?"

"I used to. When I was married. Now I cook on special occasions."

"Well, I'm honored to be a special occasion."

"You are. A special occasion." He smiled.

But he was also looking seriously at her.

He took her plate and served her food, passed her the bread. Then he said, "Eat, my child. It'll get cold. Eat. It's something my grandmother used to say to me—in Yiddish."

"Say it in Yiddish. I've never heard any Yiddish."

"*Es, mein kind, mein balibte kind.* Eat, my child, my beloved child. Do you mind my calling you 'my child'?"

"I don't mind it in Yiddish. How old are you, anyway?"

"Thirty-five," he said.

"I'm thirty-six. Were you close to your grandmother?"

"My mother said that on her way to work she would hand me out the bus window into my grandmother's arms. My grandmother would take care of me all day and then hand me back through the bus window as my mother came home. She couldn't read or write in any language, my grandmother. She never learned to speak English so she practically couldn't walk to the corner without my aunt or uncle. It was an act of bravery standing on the street alone waiting for me.

"She was always busy but kind of depressed—who wouldn't be with such a circumscribed life, a life without mastery over a single language—but she loved me. And she cooked wonderful food. *Es, mein kind.* While it's hot."

Lottie cut into the veal piccata on her plate. "Do you speak that language? What is it, Yiddish? Look, I don't know that much about Jews." She wasn't sure if it was all right for her to use the word "Jews," but he didn't seem to object. "I thought they're supposed to be very educated."

"Well, my grandmother wasn't. And there were many old women like her."

"You know," she said, "this veal is wonderful."

"It's not a family recipe. I know one or two family recipes—a noodle kugel, potato latkes."

She wasn't sure what was happening to her, but she was feeling wet. She feared she was bleeding through. "Where's the bathroom?" She took her pocketbook with her to the bathroom, where she got down her underpants and pulled out the tampon and saw that she was hardly bleeding at all but she was lubricating thickly. She stuck her finger in it. Viscous. Well, good for her!

"Are you all right?" he asked when she returned.

"I'm fine," she laughed tensely.

She was actually a bit dazed and on the edge of explaining to him what was going on—that would be like her, Lottie—but what would she tell him? That his talking about his grandmother had turned her on—no, it was he who was turning her on; or was she looking for her grandmother? For a mother-man? She began to worry that her excitement would disappear as it had with George Kenadjian. She couldn't bear that. Was she incapable of love? But she knew she'd loved Charlie; even if it was a different kind of love, a young love, there was no doubting that it had been love. And that counted.

He poured them each a second glass of wine and asked after Evelyn.

"She's fine, too. I don't know why I was so worried the other night." Then she thought she was being dishonest. "It had to do with concerns I've had about myself as a mother. I remember thinking after she was born and I left the hospital with her, they're just going to let me out with her? No one's going to keep an eye on me? They're not going to give me a test?"

He laughed. Then he said quietly, "Every child is imperiled," and he bowed his head.

"Tell me about *your* daughter," Lottie said.

In answer, he brought her a framed photo. The wind was blowing Ruth's hair around her face, and she was smiling. She was handsome. Lottie felt jealous, as if the girl were a threat to her. She actually shook her head to shake the jealousy out. Jealous of a nine-year-old? But if she was jealous, then this man meant something to her.

In her whole body she felt that he meant something to her.

He said a few things about his daughter—she was temperamental, very smart—that Lottie had trouble paying attention to, although she thought she should pay attention. From the refrigerator he took out iced zabaglione. She tried a few spoonfuls. Ate her plate clean. "Ooosh," she let the air out of her mouth. "What a meal! The cooking musician. What else do you do?"

He stood up and took her hand. "Let's get something on and dance."

"I already know you're a fine dancer." She rose immediately. They walked hand in hand to the living room, Lottie holding on to her glass of wine.

"Here, let me play you this one." And he put in a cassette.

It was the same voice of the other night. "That physicist." She grinned. "Cohen. You know, the physicist's name is actually Bernard Leonard Cohen."

Now, I've heard there was a secret chord
That David played, and it pleased the Lord
But you don't really care for music, do you?

She had the top of her head at the level of his shoulder and was inhaling along with the sweet odor of his sweat the smell of strawberries from the zabaglione. No, his sweat couldn't smell sweet; it had to be the zabaglione. She was drunk from two glasses of wine, and she was thrilled and maybe she was falling in love, and perhaps *she* was imperiled. "I want the other one. The one you played me last time."

He let go of her to change the track and she felt momentarily lonely.

Dance me to your beauty with a burning violin.

He came back. He held her close but not oppressively so. And then he kissed her and she kissed him back. His black hair smelled fresh and clean. They kissed and kissed and kept dancing. She feared she might pass out, but that seemed impossible. She could feel his erection at her belly. As he danced, he began undoing her hair, which she'd worn this night braided and swept around her head like a high crown, her grandmother's style. He put the hair pins on the lip of a music stand, then began undoing the one long braid. And he kept kissing her and she was kissing him back.

Oh, let me see your beauty when the witnesses are gone
Let me feel you moving like they do in Babylon
Show me slowly what I only know the limits of

She put her hand on his erection. She knew it was oddly forward to have her hand on his erection, but she felt her hand belonged there, she was at home, and he didn't object, he even put his hand caressingly over her hand for a moment and continued moving to the music. And now he was running his fingers through her long hair, straightening the kinks where the hair had been twisted into a braid. It was as if he were undressing her as he undid her hair.

"I can't sleep with you," she whispered.

"Why not?" His voice was thick. He continued working his way gently through and down her hair.

"I have my period."

"Is that the reason?" he said slowly. "Is that the only reason?"

She paused and then realized, happily, "Yes."

"You've never made love with your period?"

She shook her head.

"Is it that you can't stand the mess? You can't bear blood?"

She laughed. "I slice up rats all the time. I work in blood and feces . . ."

He kept dancing.

"And I'm a messy person, except when I'm doing experiments. I'm very careful then." She kept her hand lightly but firmly on his erection.

"So what are you worried about? You're worried about me?" he breathed into her ear. "What I'll think of your mess, your fertile mess?"

"Yes." She nodded.

"Well, first I'm going to eat you out," he whispered.

"No, no!" she said. "I told you, I've got my period."

"Nobody's ever done that for you before? It's a very macho thing. Bikers—you know, motorcyclists—they brag about it. I don't think of myself as macho. So I'll tell you who else does it, not that they brag, they keep it very quiet so few people know this, but here's a pearl: horn players. To eat a woman out with her period, it improves your control, your control of your lips and your tongue, maybe even your lungs—"

"Really?"

He nodded.

"Why is it better if the woman has her period?" she asked. "How does that improve a horn player's control?"

"You have to move your tongue harder. Blood is thicker than water." He laughed at himself for a moment. "And you gag more easily with blood so you have to perfect your breathing techniques."

"Are you serious?"

"Dizzy Gillespie. Bird. Satchmo. That's what they do, what they did to augment their practicing, to gain real control."

She felt him talking, talking and carefully, kindly straightening her hair; and her pants were wet and wetter.

"How do you know all this? Are you a horn player? You're not a horn player."

"I play woodwinds—flute, piccolo."

"Those are much more delicate instruments! What have they got in common with horns?"

He grinned. "Lottie, honey, I'm putting you on. I'm pulling your leg. I'm going to get some towels and open up both your legs and turn off the music and get that tampon out of there and eat you out. I don't care at all about horn players just now and not bikers, certainly not bikers."

She was reluctant to let go of his neck. "Why are you fooling me?"

"Because you're too serious. Do you mind my teasing you a little?"

She shook her head, although she thought maybe she did mind.

"I want to do everything for you. Everything nobody's done, everything everybody's done, I want to do it all, I want to do it better, I want to do everything better."

Was he talking about his past, or her past—but he didn't know anything about her past. Was he talking about everyone's past?

He left her to return with tissues and towels and pillows and he went down on his knees and shimmied off her skirt and she stepped out of it and she pulled down her tights herself and got her underpants off and stood there with a wet white string between her thighs . . .

And he tugged at it gently until it came out. Then he got his nose into her and sniffed and came out. "Very heady, that Lottie smell."

And she felt embarrassed and said, "You look like Rudolph the Red-Nosed Reindeer."

And he laughed and went back in and licked and licked. At first she had trouble relaxing but he worked so diligently and enthusiastically, so lustily and determinedly, with his nose and his tongue that she came standing, noisily, out gushed her fluid, rose-colored, and he lowered his face into it, his nose, and he caught some in his mouth and he got his pants off and his shirt and her white sweater and she sat down on the floor and unhooked her bra and he kissed her breasts again and again and he tore open a rubber and fitted it carefully on—

And he moved her gently down on the floor and came slowly into her and pushed and poked now this way and that and she had a swimming feeling as if everything that was in her was softening up and swooning or maybe preparing to ooze out of her over into him and would live there in him and she would never be able to leave this man . . .

"How are you doing?"

She said, "I'm going to die. It's lovely, it's lovely. You—you know what you're doing, don't you?"

He smiled a big smile. "I'm trying to get it right."

"You have a lot of experience." And she felt jealous.

"Shhh," he said.

"I don't have so much experience," she said. "Well, I have enough. Maybe more than enough."

"Shush, dear Lottie. Not now, sweetheart. Let it go, dear Lottie. Let everything go."

And he thrust and thrust and she held on to his neck, rising and falling with him, feeling the towels and pillows beneath her and then his breathing got harsh, almost harried, and he came, and after a moment began nuzzling her neck gently, licked it like he was a deer after salt, and then he pulled out of her slowly and got up on his knees between her legs over her. And seeing him above her with blood on his nose and cheeks and his eyelashes—his eyelashes!—and blood on the bloody condom you could see the spooge in, dangling down at the tip—and his pubic hair all matted with her blood, he looked so damaged, so wounded. She had the strange thought, strange thought for anyone, but especially for a gross anatomist: they die, too; with their penises and testicles, they die, too. And she thought, I will marry this man. Yes. I choose this one.

Part Seven

When the phone rang in the lab late in the afternoon, Lottie had a rat in the ether jar and she didn't want to pick up the call.

It was the day after the music-on-the-front-lawn episode with Ruth, so Lottie was especially grateful to be back at work alone in her air-conditioned lab, content to be far away from her whole rowdy family.

"I'll call you back," she told Jake. "Fifteen minutes." Then she lied, "I miss you," to soften her abruptness.

The rat ran around the jar double-time, frantically. For an instant it stood up on its hind legs, its front paws against the wall of the jar, and looked at Lottie with its weak pink eyes. It took in gulps of the etherized air, ran around, stood up, and then dropped. Its breathing grew fast and hoarse. She waited two minutes, then lifted the unconscious animal out of the jar and laid him on a paper towel beside the sink. Attached to the cage six inches above the rat was a feeding bottle that had been filled with fixative an hour earlier. Now it was two-thirds empty. A piece of clear plastic tubing was hooked to the neck of the bottle and clamped off there; the other end of the tube reached to the counter. She opened a sterile needle package, then cut through the rat's rib cage with a scissors and, holding his heart between her fingers, slipped the needle into the aorta. She hooked the needle to the plastic tube—a little blood backed up—and taped it in place. Then she cut through the auricle and, as the blood oozed out into the sink, opened up the clamp; the fixative, a clear liquid, gushed down the tube. The animal stirred and began to convulse violently, first its upper limbs, then the lower, and finally its tail. After a moment he was still.

Lottie had fixed him alive, arresting all his cells in motion as if she were filming a sports event, a football game perhaps, and had stopped the film at one particular frame where the players were all moving in different but coordinated directions: this one leaping into the air, that one starting to fall, another blocking for the passer as torn-loose clods of earth flew into their faces but never reached them. She had stopped the rat dead so that her results would be less artifactual in her critics' eyes. Poor creature, he was really all artifact. With his soft white fur and pink eyes he looked like a store-bought Easter bunny. Put him out there on his own with all those streetwise rats and he wouldn't last half an hour. Swiftly and cleanly, she slit the animal's throat, then dissected out the salivary glands. She lifted them gently with the forceps and placed them in the vial of buffer. She unhooked the rat, washed her hands, and called Jake.

"I've got a job for tonight," he said. "A choir concert up in Winango. The accompanist took a nap this afternoon and died. An old guy, in his nineties. I played with him once in a group."

"That's lovely. I mean, about the job."

"Well, he was very old. It's three hundred fifty bucks. They're desperate."

"That's okay money," Lottie said. Then she remembered. "What about Ruth? What about the dinner you two were making?"

"She told me to go fuck myself."

Lottie let out a sigh.

"I have to leave now. It's an hour-and-a-half drive."

"And Evelyn's got a date."

"I feel bad about it but I'm not going to turn down three hundred fifty dollars to eat the casserole at its peak."

"Ruth will have to babysit," Lottie said.

Mincing the glands, she had a moment's pleasure thinking about that snotty kid trying to feed their fancy dinner to a five-year-old and a two-year-old. Ruth had learned to cook from Jake, it was something they did together; her mother tried to join in or compete by taking an expensive course at the Cordon Bleu school in Los Angeles, paid for naturally by Jake. His ex-wife had not remarried and when after all these years, she cried to him (collect), Jake's heart still bled money. It angered Lottie that he was such a soft touch and they'd had terrible fights about it, but there was no budging him. Behind his stubbornness was his belief that leaving his daughter was the worst thing he'd done in life. She remembered how bitterly he'd laughed one day when he got a printed request to adopt a fatherless child for an afternoon a month: "I already *have* a fatherless child."

As Lottie washed the minced fixed tissue with buffer, she tried not to breathe in too deeply. The fixative, that lethal film, could fix her lungs as well as the rats'. Many of the chemicals she worked with routinely were carcinogens or poisons of other types. She was killing cells in order to have a look at them. At least when she was using osmium she tried to work under a hood, a high-domed chamber with an air vent that sucked off fumes. But the noise was annoying and she felt confined. Occasionally she wondered if she would die of her work. Madame Curie's precious radium had destroyed her blood cells. At least Lottie wasn't working with anything radioactive.

She thought again about Ruth. She wondered if it hurt Ruth, being surrounded by a family that she was part of but not part of; and if when she returned to her mother she missed them. Did she want her mother to remarry and have more children? Or was Ruth glad to be free of her father's brood, with all the dirt and noise and arguing, and be once more the only child, her mother's focus? Although Lottie knew the girl now for five years, it was as if Ruth put on a lead shield in her presence so that, except for what Lottie could infer, or Jake told her, Lottie was ignorant of her stepdaughter's inner life.

Lottie wondered if Ruth armored herself because she felt in danger of being drawn to Lottie. In family discussions Ruth was especially attentive to whatever Lottie had to say, although in the end, as though catching herself, she would make a derogatory remark. And Lottie was usually missing a scarf or handkerchief in September after Ruth had gone.

Great Women of Science, the first book Lottie'd written with Olivia, had come out the previous year to the authors' considerable pleasure and to respectable reviews. Sales were modest, but who knew? Barbara McClintock had won the Nobel Prize a few months after *Great Women* was published; Lottie'd get her into the next edition, if there was a next edition. One day if the world flew right, there might be greater interest in the subject. Lottie had sent Ruth a copy and inscribed it *To My Ruth, With Love from Lottie.* (Was it honest to call the girl *My Ruth*? Lottie didn't have any other Ruth, thank God.) Ruth never acknowledged receiving it and brought it to New York the following summer seemingly for the sole purpose of leaving it in Lottie's kitchen garbage can. When confronted with the stained, stinking book, Ruth looked truly stricken. "I swear I didn't put it there!" A few days later, laying clean underwear in Ruth's drawer, Lottie came upon a paper-back copy which had just been issued but was already dog-eared, high-lighted, many margins filled with Ruth's handwritten comments.

Now Lottie called home but hung up after one ring. She did another rat. Then she called again and asked Simon, who picked up the phone, to get Ruth.

"If you can wait until eight thirty to serve dinner, I'll come home and eat with you."

After a long pause Ruth said, "Suit yourself."

At seven o'clock Lottie tried to sort out what to take with her. Having planned to stay at the lab overnight and into late Monday afternoon, she had brought rations as if she were going camping, tuna fish sandwiches for dinner and peanut butter sandwiches for breakfast, a quart of milk, two thermoses of iced tea; Virginia Woolf's *A Room of One's Own* and the most recent issue of the *Journal of Histochemistry and Cytochemistry*; also a heavy-weight blue wool scarf she was knitting for Evelyn as part of a hat, scarf, and gloves set for college.

In the end she took everything home because, although she would prob-ably return to the lab Sunday morning, she might not, and then the sand-wiches would go stale. She set the vials containing the glands minced in buffer in a big bucket of ice, and one of the janitors took it down to the station wagon for her. She put several bottles of alcohol of different strengths and a large dump jar on the floor in the back of the car, then packed thick rags between them so that each was cushioned and wedged in tightly.

Although it was not yet dusk, the light was thinning. Lottie double-parked in front of a row of open stores. Would someone break into the car and steal her precious buckets? She laughed out loud but kept an eye out while she bought a bottle of cold Chablis and thought about getting a small bunch of deep-colored rose buds, tight dark ones that hadn't begun to open yet. She decided not to: it was nutty enough that she was on her way home.

"It's nice of you," Ruth said uneasily. She unwrapped the wine as if it would blow up. Lottie tried not to laugh.

Davy and Simon wanted to help unload the car. Lottie said that she had her lab work with her and they were to keep away from it. "You could get hurt."

"How come you brought it home?" Ruth asked.

Lottie explained that she was halfway through a tissue preparation and that there were a number of different procedures she had to do in a strictly timed sequence, otherwise the tissue would be ruined.

"What kind of tissue?"

"You know—the usual—rat salivary glands."

"Yich," Ruth said. "You kill the rats?"

"You know that, too."

After a moment Ruth said, "How can you?"

Lottie began explaining her procedures.

"How can you stand it, I mean."

"Oh." Lottie laughed. She thought for a moment. "It's really very complicated. If you want to come to the lab sometime, you're welcome."

There was a momentary sparkle, gone like a shooting star, in Ruth's dark eyes. "Thanks but no thanks."

"Where's Evelyn?"

"Showering upstairs." Ruth was sponging off the table. She looked at Lottie standing by the back door. "You need a hand?"

They carried in the ice bucket together.

After Lottie set up in the downstairs bathroom, she told the boys, "You have to pee or M, you go upstairs. I don't want you in here. Don't go near the spit glands."

She pushed her fingers up at the angles of Simon's lower jaw.

"I know where they are, Mom. You don't have to show me."

As she closed the door, she saw Simon push his fingers up under Davy's jaw.

Lottie worked in the bathroom with a stopwatch, pipetting the buffer out of the vials and into the dump jar, careful not to touch the tissue. She replaced the buffer with a thirty-percent alcohol solution. In the kitchen she could hear Ruth washing dishes. Ruth felt the dishwasher didn't get them clean enough; when she made her special dinners with her father, she didn't want any film on the plates detracting from the taste. Lottie had always assumed Ruth went through this to embarrass her, but if she was washing dishes even when Lottie was out of the room, then maybe there was something wrong with her, maybe she had some washing mania. Was Lottie responsible for this girl or not?

Evelyn called down, "Ma, can I use your blue eye shadow?"

"What's the matter with yours?" She put her finger on the vial she'd just filled so as not to lose her place.

"Davy put it in the toilet."

"Sure," Lottie said. "It's down here. And don't yell from upstairs."

Evelyn wore a cherry-red sleeveless blouse and a ruffled skirt that tied in back at the waist. Her skin was pink from the shower. She had on gold hoop earrings and Lottie's white sandals. She was fuller than Lottie had been at her age. She was coming into her own time, like a bright bloom of some promising new strain.

"Can I wear the sandals?"

"You're wearing them."

"Do you mind?"

"Not much. They look better on you than on me."

"Oh, Ma."

"Truth is truth. Even your feet are beautiful."

"Oh, Ma. Just tell me where the eye shadow is. Why don't you wear gloves? That stuff can't be good for your hands."

"They're clumsy, gloves."

"Surgeons wear them."

"You really look lovely."

"Oh, Ma."

While Evelyn put her pinkie into the pot of pale blue eye cream, traced a soft shadow over her lid and up toward the outer tip of her blonde eyebrow, Lottie watched her daughter as if she were doing something of extraordinary interest. Often Lottie found herself caught in this way, looking on with intense absorption as one of her children did a routine thing. Nowadays every move of Evelyn's had taken on a special poignancy, a heightening, as if Lottie might never see it again.

"Ma, what is this stuff? It stinks. And your eyes are tearing." They looked at each other in the mirror. "Don't touch yourself," Evelyn said. With a tissue she wiped her mother's eyes.

The doorbell rang.

"I get! I get!" Davy yelled.

"Go talk to him, Ma, would you? I'll be a minute."

Lottie pipetted alcohol into the last two vials and wrote down the time. Then she washed her hands and patted her eyes with cool water. In the kitchen she asked Ruth if it would be all right to offer Ted, Evelyn's boyfriend, a glass of the Chablis.

"Suit yourself," Ruth said.

It took Lottie a few minutes to find the corkscrew at the bottom of a drawer of utensils they rarely used, beneath a set of pastry brushes, a small pasta machine, a cork you could re-cork champagne with: most of these were presents from her first wedding. Lottie went into the living room to shake hands with Ted.

"Hi, Mrs. Hart. Nice to see you."

He always called her Mrs. Hart, although Lottie had explained to Ted that she was divorced from Evelyn's father and no longer used the name Hart. Simon had corrected him several times and finally Lottie took Simon aside and told him to let it be. Simon let it be but it cost him something. He would frown or cough or stamp his foot. This evening he threw his head back repeatedly as if he had hair in his eyes, then offered Ted his hand. Ted bent down and shook it.

Wearing only a diaper, Davy toddled over holding out his hand.

"You remember my daughter Ruth," Lottie said.

"Stepdaughter," Ruth said. "Would you like a glass of wine?" She had the bottle in her hand.

"Sure, thanks. Let me open it for you."

"Oh, that would be wonderful!" Ruth beamed, the sun suddenly out in the Arctic night.

"Yeah, sure," Ted reddened. He took the corkscrew from Lottie and pulled the cork out steadying the bottle on the floor between his feet.

Davy said, "Wonderful!" and toddled into the kitchen after Ruth for glasses.

"Well," Lottie said, embarrassed. "Thanks for the hand."

"Oh, it's nothing." He seemed about ten feet tall and he had his shirt open to the fourth button, two silver chains around his neck. His skin was red from the sun and there were a few blond, almost white hairs on his chest. He was a nice-looking boy, on the basketball team, in the honor society, and he had a good-natured, easy way with Davy and Simon.

Lottie wondered if Ted resembled Evelyn's father but she could no longer recall what Charlie had looked like in high school. The Charlie of her memory was in college running down an endless football field, or in bed watching TV as their marriage eroded. Even these few images of him that remained had worn smooth, lost their nuances, grown nearly two-dimensional.

Lottie and Ted stood sipping wine and making small talk while Ruth did ballet exercises, occasionally touching Ted's knee with a toe. After what seemed a long time Evelyn came out, radiant, apologizing. Ted reddened, both his face and his chest. Lottie resisted the impulse to look at his crotch. She waved from the door as he helped Evelyn into the front seat of his father's pickup truck.

Ruth had laid the table with a white cloth and napkins, a bouquet of wildflowers—jewelweed and honeysuckle and dog roses—in a crystal vase in the center. She had found two three-armed candelabra, heirlooms from Lottie-no-longer-remembered-which side of which family, and six long white tapering candles, which Ruth had lit despite the warmth of the night. The candles drew attention away from Simon's baseball glove on the floor under his chair and one of Evelyn's big lacey bras hanging over a basket of unfolded laundry and focused it instead on the fresh flowers, the wine bottle, which Ruth had set in a glass bowl filled with ice, the name cards she'd put at each setting (an unnecessary act since each of them sat in the accustomed place, although they seemed farther apart because of the absence of Jake and Evelyn). The silver candelabra shone in the soft candle-light, and Lottie wondered if maybe they were what Ruth had been scrubbing. This new idea cheered her. The glass of wine had gone to her head and she was feeling pleased with herself, after all, for having made the pain-in-the-ass trip home.

"Oh, it's so elegant," she said to Ruth. And that silly phrase went on booming through her brain for hours afterward, as if it had great import, as if it were the last sound anyone would hear and needed urgently to be decoded, emphasized properly, absorbed.

She remembered the scene as if they were fixed: Ruth coming toward them, a silver tureen (wedding gift from Charlie's mother, whose mother had brought it over from Dresden) of vichyssoise in her hands; Simon touching a jewelweed, asking Lottie the flower's *real* name; Lottie standing behind her chair surveying the table with a sense of well-being. "Oh, it's so elegant."

Immediately after she spoke, they all heard the sound of some substantial thing crashing and shattering, and at the same time loud, eerily high-pitched screams. She was at the bathroom door at once or else Davy was there and then she was there, Davy with his hair wet, alcohol dripping down the sides of his face. He screamed in spurts as he jammed his fingers into his right eye. Alcohol dripped down the temple, down his right cheek, down near the ear lobe. The dump jar was in shards on the floor.

Lottie grabbed a handful of napkins and mopped at his eye. She carried him howling into the bathroom and turned on the shower as if it were a fire hose. She had to exert great force to hold his hands away from his face as he wriggled and screamed under the cold water.

He was sobbing.

"Did you swallow it? Did you drink it?" She began to shake him. It was the dump jar he'd spilled on himself. *Everything* was in the dump jar: *everything* she didn't want to pour down the drain because it would contaminate the water supply! Not only alcohol but glutaraldehyde, xylene!

By now he was wet through to the skin and shivering despite the warmth of the evening. Coughing, gasping, Davy tried to turn his face out of the way of the oncoming water but Lottie held him tight. His brown curly hair lay long and straight over his forehead, on his cheeks, and she pushed it back so the water sprayed unimpeded, directly onto his face. Into his eyes. He kept screaming.

"Mama, you're drowning him!" Simon said in an anguished voice. "You're filling him up with water!"

Lottie yelled to Ruth, "Call the rescue squad! The number's on the wall, next to the telephone."

Davy kept his right eye tightly shut and when she tried to pry the lids apart with her fingers to let more water in—"Mama, you're killing him! You're making him blind!"—she thought she saw blood.

"Get out of here!" Lottie yelled at Simon. "There's no room! There's glass all over the floor!"

Sputtering, screaming hoarsely now—was she drowning him?—Davy wriggled free. She got a hold on him again and lifted him up, brought his face as close to the shower head as she dared.

Simon wailed.

"Shut up! For God's sake, shut up!" She could hardly hear herself over the boom in her brain.

They spent the night at the hospital, Lottie walking back and forth between the nearly empty emergency room where they were observing Davy, who whimpered in a curtained corner, gauze shading his right eye, and the fluorescent-lit waiting room where Ruth and Simon sat propped up against each other, asleep. One of the overhead lights was broken and flickered on and off repeatedly. The attendant discussed with the nurse whether the hot tube could be removed with a potholder.

The pediatrician, who looked to be six months pregnant, had been very crisp with Lottie although perhaps that was her way. When she took Davy into an examining room, she seemed reluctant to have Lottie follow her.

Half an hour later an administrator came out and asked Lottie a series of questions, writing the answers on a printed form. Had this child ever had an accident before? Had he ever been in the hospital for any other reason? Had the other children had accidents? He looked at Ruth and Simon.

"What do you take me for?" Lottie asked sharply.

The man seemed surprised. "I ask everybody the same questions. They're on the form."

Evelyn and Ted showed up at one, smelling faintly of beer. Lottie noticed that Evelyn's red blouse was misbuttoned.

At three in the morning Jake came in wearing his tuxedo, his face tight. He hurried past her into the emergency room.

Lottie sat down apart. The light flickered on and off in the harshly lit room and after a while she closed her eyes. She wished she could close her ears.

She kept hearing the phrase, "Oh, it's so elegant," with the emphasis now on this syllable, now on that, as if it were coming out of a megaphone, as if it were the only thing real. How long she sat she didn't know. She wasn't sleepy but she felt very odd and strained, as if she hadn't ever been to bed. She waited although she forgot for what.

When Jake came out of the emergency room, he took her hand roughly and half-dragged her through the waiting room, pulling her outside. She felt listless, could barely walk. They stood on the sidewalk a little away from the yellow-lit entrance, which swarmed with tiny bugs. The night was still hot.

"What kind of idiot, what kind of—" Jake clenched his fists.

"Go on, say it." Lottie couldn't look at him.

Jake opened one hand and punched his fist into it so loud that Lottie flinched.

"What kind of mother—wasn't that what you were going to say?" Her voice was dead.

Jake punched his palm again.

"Don't stop. I wouldn't stop. I'd hit you and hit you."

Jake looked at her with disgust, let his arms go limp at his sides. "Left eye's all right."

Lottie nodded numbly. "Are you sure? How can they be sure?" Tears trickled down.

"Right eye affected. No doubt. Lose some sight. Can't say how much. Neck burned, in the front, under the chin down to the collarbones, like someone put a hand there. Skin graft later on, down the road."

Lottie covered her face.

Jake said bitterly, "Why'd you take that shit home with you?"

An ambulance pulled in, siren sounding. Two attendants swung open the back doors and hoisted out a stretcher on which lay a delicate-looking young man whose bare chest heaved so rapidly it was almost fluttering, the strap muscles of his neck bowed out with the forcefulness of his effort to breathe. The attendants ran him past them into the emergency room.

After a long time Jake said, "You did the right thing to pour water on him."

"Having set him on fire."

"Cut it out," Jake yelled. "Just cut it out." Then he said, "He's sleeping. They gave him something." He turned away from her and started back toward the ER. But he didn't open the door. He stood outside in the yellow buggy light and bowed his head.

She stood immobile watching him, his long boney back in his tuxedo, his head bent, his big beloved hands covering his face.

She had caused this, too.

After a while, he straightened up. He walked slowly over to her and touched her hair distractedly. "You must be so wretched, Lottie."

She nodded.

He put his arms around her stiff back. She couldn't lean into him.

They stood like that sweating, he with his arms around her, she unmoving. "Come on," he said. "Come on in and let's watch him sleep."

The next few days she stayed home and stood guard over Davy. She put clear drops in his right eye every hour and she applied antibiotic ointment and fresh gauze pads to the large raw patch that tapered off between his clavicles. Were his steps slurred? Was he bumping into things? She watched him as he ate, looking for signs of gagging or vomiting. She asked him about double vision and black spots although she didn't know why and anyway couldn't make him understand. Maybe he couldn't hear her? She screamed at him and he crawled under his bed. Usually eager for her attention, Davy seemed uncomfortable with her worried shadowing of him. He avoided her. Lottie could not stop herself. She continued to be hounded by that vapid phrase, "It's so elegant," and occasionally she would see it as well as hear it—cut in granite, as on a gravestone.

Davy scratched at his neck despite the bandage and the large white mittens Lottie knitted him during one long night, remembering her grandmother.

Lottie sat home holding Davy's hands so they wouldn't have to be tied down. He tried to scratch himself with his toes. For some reason, thank God, he didn't pull the bandage off his eye. Tears ran down his cheek from time to time even when she wasn't administering the eye drops. She had never before seen tears run down one cheek. Sometimes he cocked his head like a dog at distant sounds or sights and seemed to position himself so that people stood on his left, spoke into his left ear, looked into his left eye. But the audiologist said his gross hearing was good enough so that it wouldn't interfere with ongoing speech development and they'd fine-test him later when he was old enough to cooperate. The ophthalmologist said Davy was seeing out his right eye but the image was blurry as if he were under water. The cornea might heal more. Or they might be able to transplant a cornea. If the surrounding tissue was healthy.

Davy fell running away from Lottie and skinned his right elbow and right knee.

Jake cleaned Davy's cuts, in part because Davy wouldn't let Lottie touch him. "You hear the joke about the grandmother who was walking with her grandson on the beach when a wave pulled him out to sea?"

"I don't want to hear it," Lottie said.

"'Please, God,' the grandmother begs, 'please, please, *please*, bring him back.' Another wave comes, washes him into her arms. She kisses him"—Jake kissed Davy's curly head—"then looks up at the heavens: 'He had a hat.'"

Lottie said, "You can't say he isn't damaged."

"Compared to the four-year-old at the plastic surgeon's office who got burned when the gas heater exploded?"

Lottie said, "The four-year-old wins the damage contest, hands down."

If only Lottie hadn't come home.

Jake said coming home was a gracious, if stupid, act.

Gracious! Crap. She'd *wanted* Ruth to feed her fancy dinner to a two-year-old and a five-year-old. And Lottie didn't like that she was spiteful, and so she'd come home. Goody Two-shoes.

If only she hadn't been a scientist, had been a home ec teacher, had never been.

He reminded her that she had gone a few months earlier to the ER with a neighbor who had been hanging out the wash while her two-year-old son ate the clear red berries of a deadly nightshade plant and had to have his stomach pumped.

And hadn't Lottie choked on something herself, Jake asked, and nearly drowned when she was a girl?

"You talk too much," Lottie told him, but she called home and had an uncharacteristically long conversation with her mother, although she never mentioned Davy except to say they were all fine.

Lottie went to work and re-ran her experiment and sent in the results but she got little pleasure from proving herself right and the journal's referees wrong, and her sleep was disturbed by nightmares. In a recurrent one she was exposed to radiation from a leak in her lab and had lost all her hair. She wore a purple afro wig and mirrored sunglasses. Behind them her eyes were gone, replaced by two of the boys' bright marbles, an agate one and a cat's-eye. She would wake shuddering and Jake would hold her until she quieted.

Just before Labor Day the editor phoned to tell her off the record that her revised paper would be accepted. She did feel vindicated—not a bad feeling.

She wondered if she would feel expansive when she received the referees' crow-eating reports. Jake said they should celebrate now as well as later and again when the paper was published, so the six of them piled into the car and went to Randy's Grill for cheeseburgers and milkshakes.

Afterward, Jake wanted to take a walk in the marshes. Evelyn had planned to sort out her books and wall hangings that evening—she was entering Swarthmore in a week—but she agreed to go along "for old time's sake." They put on their galoshes and rubbed their hands and faces with mosquito repellant. Jake got out his star constellation charts. The dogs couldn't stand still as they waited for Lottie to unlatch the gate to the backyard: they shivered ecstatically.

It had been a hot day but there was a slight breeze now and it was pleasant to be in the cool, dank marsh. The flashlights Jake had brought in the backpack were unnecessary because the sky was drenched with stars and there was a full moon. Ruth was walking on the far side of her father, a little apart. It occurred to Lottie that she would always be there, a little apart. Or perhaps not. Perhaps she would keep away, cut them dead, or just cut Lottie dead.

Perhaps Jake would disappear. No, he'd never leave her.

That any of her children would die was unthinkable.

Perhaps they each stood apart, one from the other, and it was only in Lottie's mind that they were grouped.

Jake and Evelyn were trying to explain something to Simon. Davy tugged at Lottie's hand because he wanted to hear, too, and for a moment she held him, then let him tug free. He cocked his head leftward toward his father.

Jake held a tube of rolled-up star charts, which he was waving for emphasis. Simon was pointing up at the milky sky and Jake was shaking his head.

"Nobody knows. By the time the light reaches us the star may have changed or disappeared or exploded even. Something may have happened."

It didn't make sense to Simon.

"It's like a photograph of someone taken years ago." Jake handed the star charts to Ruth and took his wallet out of his pocket. He got a flashlight from his backpack.

"There's you at six months. Would you recognize yourself? It's nothing like you now."

Simon said his hair was still the same color.

Jake sighed. He turned to another photo. "Here's my father, your grand-father. He's been dead for twenty years, may he rest in peace. Looks fine in the picture, doesn't he?"

Simon said querulously that he didn't understand.

Jake flipped to another picture. "Look, there's your mother, way back before any of us knew her." Lottie moved closer and took the wallet away from Jake and also his flashlight. With the children crowding around her, she shone the flashlight on the old photograph, which had been torn in several places and then repaired with tape that had yellowed and contracted so that the various parts of the picture were no longer exactly aligned. She never understood why he kept this photo in his wallet. It was indeed Lottie as a child, standing beneath the white apple tree in the backyard of her parents' house, a wooden swing barely visible off to her left. She wore a spring outfit and a hat; she never wore hats, so maybe it was one of her grandmother's hats, but the details of the hat had disappeared so that it looked like a hazy, lit-up cloud or halo.

Lottie's head was markedly cocked. Maybe she had taken this uncharacteristically awkward position deliberately, for some reason she could no longer remember, or perhaps she was simply self-conscious at the time about being photographed. It was also possible that the inclination of her head had resulted from the tape's having shrunk.

As she looked at the pale face and thin arms and legs, the still undeveloped and now slightly asymmetrical child's body, a dreadful feeling came over her in the bright marsh, of disconnectedness, as if she were herself some strange taped-together creature, the likes of which had never been seen before.

After a while Lottie handed the light and the wallet open to that photograph over to Simon, who remained upset—Simon, who was younger and smaller than the girl in the picture. Lottie had a fleeting thought about her work, that she wanted to find out much more about cells, and that she wanted to tell these truths, true for a while anyway, to Simon, who couldn't yet understand. To Evelyn, who wasn't interested, who was on her way. To Ruth? She longed to comfort all of her children, to explain the stars and herself to them, to be able to tell them that even when she eventually disappeared like the stars, she would still be their mother for all time.

ACKNOWLEDGMENTS

I am writing the final draft of these acknowledgments during the awful times of the coronavirus. In the light of so much suffering, bringing out a book seems a small thing. But expressing the gratitude I feel toward those who have so generously helped me can never be out of place.

Artifact wouldn't exist were it not for Jo Anne Valentine Simson, who tried to teach me the science I needed to know and also gave me introductions into tech labs and anatomy labs. Any blunders are of course my own. I particularly recommend her brave autobiography, *Saving My Life*, from which I stole a thing or two, with her permission. Generous and brilliantly accomplished, she is one of my dearest friends.

And *Artifact* wouldn't have been published were it not for Sandra Newman, who read it in an early 793-page monster form and said, "There's a novel in there," and made many crucial suggestions. She is the best editor I know. And a fine, fine writer.

Victoria Hobbs, my agent, sold this novel on her first try. She is a fierce fan and protector of her authors. And completely responsive. Twenty-four hours is the longest she's ever taken to get back to me. I don't know any other agent of her caliber.

I am grateful to Alexandra Pringle, Bloomsbury's editor in chief, who has championed my work on both sides of the Atlantic. A charming woman, she is openhearted and openminded and, at the same time, rigorous.

Callie Garnett, a young poet with a fine sense of language, edited the book once Bloomsbury bought it. Being a graduate of Stuyvesant High, she has a nose for numbers and dates. To construct a timeline, each of us did a lot of Googling and listening to videos on YouTube. I believe we got most things right in the end. However, we did decide to let Lottie and Jake dance to two Leonard Cohen songs that hadn't yet been recorded; those were the songs the couple needed to dance to; Lottie and Jake were ahead of their time. Callie has been a delight to work with.

There are many people at Bloomsbury New York I want to acknowledge: My final editor for *Scary Old Sex*, Nancy Miller, vigorously supported *Artifact*, as did Liese Mayer, editorial director for fiction. Laura Phillips, the extraordinary managing editor, helped me with head-breaking particulars raised by fine proofreader Nate Knaebel and copy editor Janet McDonald. Rosie Mahorter and Marie Coolman in publicity and Laura Keefe and Nicole Jarvis in marketing worked tenaciously in my behalf. Artist Rogan Brown made the wonderful paper sculptures of cells that Patti Ratchford, art director, turned into an unusually elegant cover. For the British *Artifact*, the lovely photograph on the book jacket was shot by Neil Libbert; and Greg Heinimann did the subtle, old-fashioned design.

Friend and colleague Judith Viorst has helped me persevere for many dry years in my career as a writer; she has set me straight a few times when I was bloviating; and she has always kept my sense of humor alive about writing as a profession.

Ruth Ahntholz Golian generously read and reread *Artifact* over decades and in different writing groups. I am grateful for her extensive comments and for the joy she shows when she thinks a passage is particularly good.

Walter J. Miller, who died in 2010, was a poet, playwright, translator, literary critic, Jules Verne scholar, NYU professor, and publisher. I had the good fortune to take a writing class with him at the 92nd Street Y in the early 1990s and then I continued taking writing classes with him at his apartment on Bleecker Street. His thoughtful criticism was helpful with early versions of *Artifact*.

Rosa Gonzalez, MD, guided me through Lottie's obstetrical history, in particular her disastrous early stillbirth.

I am deeply beholden to my patients and to Otto Kernberg, MD. They have taught me about the complexity and beauty and sneakiness of the human mind and the relief and pleasure to be found in understanding it.

And I am grateful, so grateful for the loving presence in my life of my husband, Len Rodberg, my two sons, my daughters-in-law, my grandsons, and also my *machatunim*. They keep things lively.

Finally, I want to acknowledge three people who are long dead but who are often with me and especially now as I bring this book out. One of the earliest permutations of *Artifact* was begun so long ago that I have in the house a typed manuscript from 1980 with handwritten notes by Bernard Malamud. Throughout our twenty-five-year friendship, he criticized my writing in the most serious way and always urged me on.

My first husband, Shepard Kantor, was a physician, a psychiatrist, psychopharmacologist, and psychoanalyst and excellent in all those capacities. He worked hard to support our family so that I could spend much of my time writing—not exactly a high-paying endeavor. I used to say that I had a writing fellowship and his name was Shepard.

And, last, I want to honor the memory of my father, Jerome Heyman, a man who lived by empathy and by his fists. I remember him saying, as we watched Newark on fire through our den window in a white suburb, "If I were black, I'd burn down Newark, too." If he saw a fight going on, he would stop the car to run to the side of whoever was outnumbered, overpowered. And he had three simple precepts that stayed with me: Never cross a picket line. If a cab driver cuts you off, don't curse him—he's trying to earn a living. And any man who had a mother ought to be a feminist.

A Loose Part

NANCY MULLOWNEY: This is WQPD Newburgh where your friends are. You're tuned in to *Ring Around Orange County*, New York State, Nancy Mullowney here. And my guest today is Dr. Lottie Kristin Hart Levinson. Cell biologist. Gross anatomist. Lottie Kristin Hart Levinson. Have I got all those names right, Lottie?

DR. CHARLOTTE KRISTIN HART LEVINSON: Yes.

NM: You don't mind if I call you Lottie?

CL: Well, I do mind. If I were a man, you'd call me Dr. Levinson now, wouldn't you.

NM: . . . Aha. You have a point. But we're two women, you know—

CL: Why shouldn't women treat each other with respect?

NM: . . . Okay. Dr. Levinson. Just from curiosity, why don't you use your maiden name, Kristin? Many professional women nowadays use their maiden names. Rather than all those names, all those other names.

CL: I like to have the same name as my children. Why should I use only my father's name? [Laughs.] Malcolm X would have called it my slave name.

NM: Aha. And Levinson, that's a German name, isn't it, Doctor? Are you—of German extraction? If you don't mind my asking.

CL: No. It's not German. It's Jewish. Russian Jewish. I'm not Jewish. My husband is. Look, don't you want to ask me about my work?

NM: Yes, of course. I'm just trying to get some background information—human interest. You're a woman and a scientist, a doctor, and we're going to be talking about men and women, science and scientists. For starters, can you tell us any differences you notice between male and female scientists?

CL: Their gender affects whether or not they get funded.

NM: Aha.

CL: You're a broadcaster, an anchor? Right? A man in your position makes how much more than you, do you think?

NM: Good point. Excellent point. How about the way they treat animals? Does gender affect the way scientists treat animals, gender of the scientist, of course, not of the animal. You probably know that some of our regular listeners are animal activists. What do you think of animal experimentation, Doctor?

CL: It's a necessary evil. Sometimes I don't even know if it's an evil. These animals wouldn't have been born otherwise, and most of us treat them better than we do our pets: they get not only food and shelter, but all the sex they want.

NM: This is *Ring Around Orange County*, your talk show hostess today is Nancy Mullowney chatting with Dr. Lottie Kristin Hart Levinson.

CL: Correction! I need to correct what I just said. It's the breeders who get all the sex they want, the animals selected for breeding.

Do you know that if a rat gets out of its cage—sometimes you are working on a rat, and a loud noise occurs and the animal bolts. Then you look all over and you can't find the animal. When you finish at night you leave that animal's cage open and the next day you find it back in its cage. That's where it wants to be.

Actually, I do think in some ways animal activists have done a lot of good. Years ago a few investigators didn't care if they were causing animals pain.

NM: And were they men or women, those few investigators?

CL: Probably men, because ninety-nine percent of scientists are men. More violent cruelty is of course perpetrated by men because of their testosterone loading, the jails are full of men.

There should be laws prohibiting men between the ages of sixteen and thirty from owning guns. Of course, most of the leaders of countries should be in jail—they're almost all old men so their testosterone levels really aren't very high—and, unfortunately, they're therefore even busier showing the world how macho they are. But are women kinder than men? I don't know what measure you'd use for that or how you'd test for it.

NM: Aha. Men. Has your own handling of animals changed at all because of the activists?

CL: I've changed, but not because of them; I've changed because I know myself better. During the last few years I purposely try to keep my experiments short, because otherwise I become very fond of the animals, and then when I have to sacrifice them—

NM: Yes. It's hard for you. You'll forgive my going back to the man-woman thing but this is an afternoon program and my audience is mostly women . . . Women are very fond of small creatures. Perhaps you could cite some instances of special sensitivity to animals on the part of women? That would interest my listeners.

CL: [long pause] I don't know that it shows special sensitivity, but no man would do exactly what I did.

NM: Please, Doctor, tell us.

CL: You know I'm not a medical doctor.

NM: Yes.

CL: I just wanted to make that clear.

NM: Yes, we want the audience to be aware of that.

CL: Okay, an instance of special sensitivity. It was in the middle of winter in Wisconsin. I was in graduate school. After that I did a postdoc—in Philadelphia, a ridiculous postdoc. But only one. Lucky me. Most women do postdoc after postdoc after postdoc. Because they can't get jobs. Do you know, women who won Nobel Prizes worked as assistants, or they had unpaid positions. Now we do postdocs. I'm off topic but it burns me up.

Okay. Grad school in the winter in Wisconsin. A thing you have to worry about with rats is their sensitivity to anesthesia.

Anesthesia causes hypothermia—lowered body temperature. When animals are cold and under anesthesia, they tend to die. People who worked on animals after the sixties—they had warming plates they'd put the animals on. But we didn't have that.

So after I'd operate on an animal and take out her salivary glands, I'd be working on the next animal, and if I saw that the first animal, the sialoadenectomized one, the animal without the salivary glands, was . . . getting cold—

NM: She was still asleep from the anesthesia—

CL: Yes. If she looked like she was getting into trouble, I'd pick her up and put her down under my blouse, inside my bra. My breasts got a little bloody, I have to admit.

I don't know what a man could do that would be the equivalent . . . put a rat in his jock strap, I imagine.

NM: Well, well. Yes. Interesting idea. Let's go to children for a moment. Last week I interviewed Sally Newbriar, a civic leader from Port Jervis, runs the homeless shelter on Mott and Pacific, and she is also the mother of a child with cystic fibrosis, a terrible disease. I understand your work on salivary glands may shed light on cystic fibrosis.

CL: It may. It might. But I doubt it. There's thick mucus in cystic fibrosis. The child coughs it up. So one might imagine salivary glands would be important in cystic fibrosis. They're certainly involved but I don't think the salivary gland is the main problem. Anyway, I don't study the salivary gland because of cystic fibrosis.

NM: No? Why do you study it?

CL: Because it interests me. Secretion interests me.

NM: Yes. Okay. Secretion interests you. And children, I'm sure they interest you, too. You have a daughter—and two sons, I believe. They're healthy, right?

CL: . . . And a stepdaughter. Yes, I'm fortunate, they're all healthy.

NM: What are their names? They might like to hear their mother say hello to them on the radio. Are they listening?

CL: I have no idea. Hello, Ruth. Evelyn. Simon. [Louder] Hello, Davy.

NM: Despite what you say, and I certainly don't mean to psychoanalyze you, I don't think it's purely accidental that you're working on something that may prove relevant to cystic fibrosis. Babies are born with cystic fibrosis. A woman's feelings for her babies run deep. We all know that female animals will kill to protect their offspring.

CL: Female rats eat their offspring.

NM: Well, we're not rats. Wouldn't you say your children come before everything else?

CL: [long pause] I—I don't care to comment on this.

NM: You wouldn't say your profession comes before your children, would you? [Pause.] I'm trying to push you on the differences between men and women in the sciences . . .

CL: Yes, I understand that. I'll tell you a joke that's on point. A transsexual goes to Johns Hopkins for a sex change operation and says he's worried about the pain.

"The procedure's painless," the surgeon tells him.

"What? You cut off my penis and testicles and there's no pain?"

"You're under anesthesia. There's no pain."

"And afterward, Doctor, when I come to, there's still no pain?"

"Nope, there's no pain."

"Now how can that be? You mean, there's no pain at all? None whatsoever?"

"I didn't say *that*. The pain comes later when you return to work and find your pay's been cut in half."

NM: [Long pause. Nervous laughter.] This is *Ring Around Orange County*, your talk show hostess today is Nancy Mullowney chatting with Dr. Lottie Kristin Hart Levinson.

A NOTE ON THE AUTHOR

ARLENE HEYMAN is the author of the short-story collection *Scary Old Sex*, and a recipient of Woodrow Wilson, Fulbright, Rockefeller, and Robert Wood Johnson fellowships. She has been published in the *New American Review* and other journals, won *Epoch* magazine's novella contest, and has been listed twice in the honor rolls of *The Best American Short Stories*. Heyman is a psychiatrist/psychoanalyst practicing in New York City. This is her first novel.